To: Penney

Thanks for the awesome [book?] Thanks for [?] you are. Truly Blessed being may God tremendously [?] — Cynthia

my secret place

Copyright © 2015 by Cynthia R. Johnson

All rights reserved, including the right to reproduce this book or portions thereof in any form whatsoever.

This is a work of fiction. Names, characters, businesses, places, events and incidents are either the products of the author's imagination or used in a fictitious manner. Any resemblance to actual persons, living or dead, or actual events is purely coincidental.

MY SECRET PLACE

Never Underestimate the Power of

A Secret Place

CYNTHIA R. JOHNSON

I dedicate MY SECRET PLACE to my sister Angela; to my family, friends and coworkers; the influential people in my life who by some form or fashion has supported me, encouraged me, prayed for me and most of all inspired me. It was indeed God's grace and mercy that guided me through life's difficult terrain but it was also the love of those surrounding me that allowed me to become the person that I am now today.

Contents

CHAPTER 1: God's Secret Place for You   1

CHAPTER 2: Search for Your Secret Place   98

CHAPTER 3: Not Just a Physical Place   112

CHAPTER 4: A Place of Beginnings   148

CHAPTER 5: Not Just a Safe Place   173

CHAPTER 6: A Place of Abundance   233

CHAPTER 7: A Place of Rest   244

CHAPTER 8: A Place of Revelations   269

CHAPTER 9: A Place of Second Chances   330

CHAPTER 10: A Sustaining Place   393

Never Underestimate The Power of A Secret Place

1
GOD'S SECRET PLACE FOR YOU

"I cannot imagine for the life of me why Cindy would leave a home of stability and safety then move away from the only family she knows. Atleast I finished college before I left home and I also had a plan for my future. Nathan and I were well balanced, educated young men who could care for one another. We made certain we had our parent's blessing before we left their abode. How could we ever return to our parents if we disregarded the sacrifices they made for us? It would have been considered of the utmost disrespect among our peers. We believed that our value of others directly correlates with the relationship we have with our parents."

Jonathan regains focus to prepare for a possible tornado. His wife Melba and the triplets Cidney, Lindsay, and Lacey are frantic.

"Granny where are you," asks Cidney.

"I am in here toots, open the door so that you can see me," answers Melba.

Cidney pulls the door to her while she peeks inside.

"Where are you granny?"

"Here I am!"

"There you are granny! Why are you in the closet?"

"For a lack of a better word she is in denial, interjects Jonathan."

Never Underestimate The Power of A Secret Place

"Oh shut up you old hoot. Do not listen to your grandfather he is senile. Senile did you hear me Jon," she yells.

"If you say so Mel but allow me to remind you that my hearing is fully intact."

"Well I wish your mind was; it is ridiculous that you will not get out of harm's way. You have never been in a tornado before in your life."

"Oh, I have seen worse. A hurricane has the strength of five tornadoes and if I remember correctly we have never hid in a closet from a hurricane."

"When in Rome do like the Romans Jon."

"I have never heard of anything so foolish in my life."

"Come on papa the tornado is coming," says Lacey.

"What does that have to do with the tea in China?"

Lacey and Lindsay position themselves behind Jonathan and push him inside the closet.

"Will you look at all of these shoes," says Jonathan when he enters the closet. "It does not make any sense to own that many shoes. I have two of them in my sight; there was three last I counted."

"Here I am grandpa!"

Cidney leaps from behind a rack of clothes.

"There is my angel, you know you are my favorite."

"Grandpa you said I was your favorite," Lacey admonishes.

"Me too papa," admonishes Lindsay.

"There you go with the foolishness again Jon. Do you ever get enough?"

"Oh stop getting yourself all worked up Mel the triplets know I love them all the same."

"No way papa, defends Lacey. For our birthday you bought Cidney a baby doll and me and sister got bikes."

"You both have asked for bicycles ever since you learned to ride the other children's bicycles at Nathan's Place."

Never Underestimate The Power of A Secret Place

"How did you know we didn't want a baby doll too?"

"Oh, I see what this is about. You girls think you are going to strong arm me for a doll too."

Jonathan looks around while the girls observe him for his next move. Lacey and Lindsay fold their arms while they wait for a response.

"Where is everyone," a voice sounds from the entrance of the home.

"Mommy!"

The girls race from the closet to greet their mother.

"Where is everyone?"

"Granny and papa are in the closet."

"How did you get daddy in the closet?"

"We pushed him inside," Lacey admits.

"Be careful you know your grandfather has gotten older now."

They proceed to the bedroom where Cindy Lou's parents exit the walk-in closet.

"Just do not get ahead of yourself and ruin the occasion," says Melba. "Sometimes you got to learn to be tactful."

"I am a business man. I have always been tactful."

"Well you almost shot a man's hand off and that was not considered tactful in the least."

"Daddy, did you almost shoot someone's hand off? Did you really?"

"He is fortunate that I spared his life."

"Jonathan, please not in front of the girls."

"He told us all about it," Lacey replies.

"That is not nice papa," whispers Cidney then wags her finger at him.

"Daddy what is going on with you? You have become so bitter."

"I have every right to be."

Never Underestimate The Power of A Secret Place

"Oh, no you do not mister! Vengeance is the Lord's and he will repay," quotes Melba.

"Why does he have to take so long?"

"Anyway mother how was your trip?"

"What do you mean how was her trip? I am the one that drove her here must I remind you."

"Yes daddy but you never ask for directions and always forget to bring a map."

"Not this time ladybug. You would be proud of your old man."

"Daddy, if I can recall Uncle Nate bought you that car three years ago for your birthday and you were too stubborn to drive it. I am surprised you knew how to operate it."

"He knows I have always been a truck man. He bought that contraption to get under my skin."

"Come with me daddy," Cindy Lou directs him to the front door.

Jonathan and Cindy Lou retreat to the front porch.

"Where is Uncle Nate daddy?"

"He is taking a tour of your University."

"Well there is not much to see."

"You sure are right about that. I cannot for the life of me comprehend why you would walk away from an institution like NYCU."

"Daddy I have nothing against NYCU. I just wanted to experience what a Colored University had to offer."

"There are plenty of Colored University's in Louisiana. Why did you come to Oklahoma? I felt like you did not appreciate anything your mother and I worked so hard to give you and your sister."

"It was not that at all. I was so accustomed of being raised around people of color that when I visited the campus here it felt like home."

Never Underestimate The Power of A Secret Place

"I never thought that you would attend a Colored University. I expect it from Angie but not from you."

"Why not daddy is it because I could pass for white?"

"Now do not start with me. You know your Grandmother did everything in her power to conceal her identity. Colored women were treated so harsh when we were your age. I imagine that is why I fell in love with your mother. I just could not understand for the life of me how someone so beautiful suffered in the manner in which she did. I did everything in my power to make up for the wrongs against her."

"You do not make any sense daddy. Why did you leave her behind?"

"I never imagined that my father would accept our relationship. It was taboo back then. When my father found that she was pregnant he said that he had a strong suspicion that I was the father. He brought her to Louisiana and Rev. Opio married us right away. I am surprised that the marriage is legal considering the falsifying of legal documents he committed to change my race to African. That was also the day he revealed to Nathan and I that we were fraternal twins. I will never forget that day. You know I was told that Nathan was a child that mother adopted from the orphanage. I soon found out that mother was too weak to care for either of us after birth. Linda and Raphael cared for us while mother regained her strength. Raphael is a remarkable woman; she has a distinctive smell that I remember to this day. I would describe Linda as a children's advocate. She cared for Nathan and taught him how to read. Raphael gave me the love for literature."

"How are they daddy?"

"They are doing quite well. They will leave Nathan's Place to live with their children when I return."

"Daddy please explain to me why you forced mother and I to move to New York after Angie was abducted? You allowed her abduction to control your every thought. You spent very little time with me."

"Listen baby girl there is not a chance on earth that I would allow this to happen again. I will never accept the loss of my baby girl. A father and daughter bond is very unique. Any father who does not take advantage of it is a downright fool. I will lay down my life for your mother, your sister and yourself. Without a doubt I will. When your sister was taken my whole life shattered. I remember the many accounts of the former slaves whose children were taken away. Often I prayed Lord please protect my children. I could not for the life of me understand how they could continue on with life the way they did. I imagined that they were apathetic to the human bond, but I now realize that it has become essential to survive life's tragedies. At first I could not accept the thought of your sister being dead. But I have come to realize it was out of my control. I decided to give up the search after I experienced my heart attack and it was then when we found her."

"What are you saying daddy?"

"A few months ago Sheriff Badeaux died. Before he died he asked his son to locate his brother Charles. Charles flew down from New York and went straight to his brother's bedside. He described his conditions to be deplorable."

Jonathan shakes his head then begins to recount Charles' encounter with his brother.

Charles enters the room remorseful that his mother could not join him on the trip.

"I should have told her that I have found him. No, she would only relive the memories of our past. How could someone sell his family into slavery? It is incomprehensible that anyone would do such a thing. But nevertheless I took the hand that I was dealt and did my best with it. Maybe we can mend differences this one last time."

Never Underestimate The Power of A Secret Place

"Thomas," he whispers then with care he shakes him. "My goodness I can feel his bones."

The room smells dank and musty. The wooden floors have not been swept for months. His sheets contained pale brown spots from the failed attempts to reach the washroom. Dishes some still contain food line the floor near his bed. It appears that he has begun to lose his appetite. His youngest son enters the room and stands beside him. Benjamin resembles the likeness of his father. He is a tall, thin, red head with freckles. Wearing overalls without a shirt he stands next to Charles.

"He ain't ate nothin for a few days now. I suspect it won't be too long."

"Why did you call me?"

"Cause he is ya brotha," says Benjamin.

"What does it matter?"

"It matters a hell ova lot. Family is all ya got."

"Who taught you that?"

"He did," Benjamin points to his father.

"Did he tell you that he sold his family into slavery?"

"Is that what ya think he did?"

"Hell that is what I know he did."

Charles anger begins to stir.

"My papa done tole me the whole story so don't ya think ya gonna brain wash me."

"What exactly did he tell you?"

"He exac'ly tole me that my grandpa was gonna lose this here farm on account of my grandma sneakin slaves off ta freedom. So my grandpa commenced ta beatin grandma an killed her dead. He says ya kicked up a fuss so he sent ya and Lily up north to a good home."

Charles looks at his brother while he lies listless in the bed.

"Let me tell you something boy," Charles snorts. "My mother is alive and well. She lives with me at Nathan's Place.

Never Underestimate The Power of A Secret Place

Lily lives in Georgia and earns a living for herself. Your devious brother and grandfather sold their family into slavery for money. He gave our rights to freedom away for something he will never see again."

"Well if ya ask me ya look like ya did fine fo yo'self."

"You are truly your father's son. If it had not been for the merciful grace of God I would not be the man I am today. Your father my brother threw his family away," Charles shouts while he gazes at his brother. "I cannot for the life of me figure out how we are all one family. I suffered many a nights."

Charles begins to choke.

"I kept watch over my mother and sister so that no one would harm them. I was just ten years old. I had to become a man and protect my mother because your heartless father was a coward. Just like his father he was also a coward."

"But ain't he yo father too?"

"No, God is my father. We did not deserve to live like slaves. No one deserves a life of slavery. We are all one in humanity. There is no difference from one to another."

"I beg ta diffa. Negras will never account to nothin. That's why they slaves."

"If there is any truth in that then why is the plantation in ruins? Can you answer that?"

Charles squares off with Benjamin.

"I will tell you why. Because you have abused the favor God had given you. God did not design us to reign over one another. You took this very opportunity to degrade rape, beat and kill the Africans. You taught them your wicked ways, fed them the slop from your table and never did you consider the works of your hands evil. Instead you stripped the Africans of their dignity and self worth and for that you now live like heathens."

Never Underestimate The Power of A Secret Place

"Yes I have done well for myself. It is because I chose to take the road less traveled. That road is lonely and difficult at times. Yes it has ups and downs. But I must tell you it is well worth it. I will never have to look over my life and be ashamed of what I have done. I pray that you will seek forgiveness for the deeds that you have committed and that you will have the guts to love someone other than yourself."

"I love my papa," says Benjamin.

"One day you will experience what love truly means."

"But I do love my papa."

"Who are you trying to convince?"

"Nobody, I woulda left wit Timmie if I ain't love my papa."

"What is it about your papa that makes you love him?"

"He took care of me up til now; an when he dies this house be mine."

"You are mistaken. My name is on that deed and I will fight to the death if anyone tries to take it from me," says Charles.

Benjamin becomes irritable.

"Let me rephrase that. In truth you do not love your father; you are just like your father."

Charles leans over the bed and grabs Thomas by the shirt.

"Where is she, he yells! You better not die until you tell me where she is. You have got to be the lowest form of existence."

Charles releases him and he falls back onto the bed. Benjamin looks on astonished.

"She buried wit tha rest of tha slaves."

"Who is buried with the rest of the slaves?"

"Angie Lou. She got a doll buried wit her. She in tha grave marked Nathan."

"Why Nathan?"

"That is tha grave papa had waitin fo him."

Never Underestimate The Power of A Secret Place

Charles leaves the room and stands out on the front veranda. While night begins to settle Benjamin continues to care for his father. The old slave hand comes to the entrance of the house.

"Mista Charles, suh."

"Yes, Ma'am what can I do for you?"

"It is time ta send fo tha docta. I think he dead."

Charles begins to gaze off into the night sky while he ponders what to do next.

"I will be back."

"Please be back befo tha body start ta rottin suh."

"What is your name ma'am?"

"My name is Miss Mercy."

"Miss Mercy can you please come with me?"

"Wheres ya takin me suh?"

"I am taking you home."

"I had curious thoughts about those two long before Angie was taken. But I never would have imagined they were related. Charles came to the farm the next day and handed me a piece of paper. On that paper was a map of the Badeaux's property that details the graves of all his slaves. Marked on a stone in the very last plot was the name Nathan."

Tears begin to roll from Cindy Lou's face and lands on the head of her daughter Cidney.

"Mommy, why are you crying?"

"Go inside with Granny until Papa and I finish our talk."

Cidney clings to her grandfather's legs.

"Go do what your mother says and we will see Uncle Nate in a minute."

Cidney begins her way into the house before she allows herself a glance back at the two.

"When did you find out?"

"I found out a couple of months ago."

"Why are you just telling me?"

Never Underestimate The Power of A Secret Place

"We did not want to interrupt your graduation ceremony."

"Daddy did you realize that the date of my graduation is scheduled the exact same day twenty years ago to the date that sister was abducted? I wished so much that she could be here."

Unable to control her emotions Cindy Lou begins to sob while Jonathan pulls her close and holds her tight.

"There is something else I have to tell you."

"What is it daddy?"

"You have a nephew that is at the motel with your Uncle Nate."

"My sister has a son? Oh daddy, when can I meet him?"

"You have I am afraid we just did not realize it at the time. Do you remember the small boy who would appear out of nowhere and throw rocks at us while we traveled along the trail a couple of summers ago?"

"Do you mean the dirty little boy with the filthy mouth?"

"Yes."

"We used to tease Uncle Nate that he resembled him so much. Are you saying that rotten little kid is related to us?"

"Yes baby girl."

"Oh do you have your work cut out for you. You do remember how he would yell through the barbwire fence, 'Y'all worthless negras," Cindy Lou mocks.

"Sweetheart he is a product of his environment."

"Most definitely he is, but we should not have to live with it."

"We have to he is family now. You will never believe what his name is."

"I am afraid to ask."

"His name is Nathan Badeaux. Of course I will have to make sure that is changed when I return."

"Are you saying that Sheriff Badeaux fathered a son by my sister?"

"I must say it is unfortunate but it looks like it."

Never Underestimate The Power of A Secret Place

"When can I see him?"

"Well here soon they are headed this way now. I hope the girls take to him or it is going to be a long hard life for the lad. If anyone should know it would be me."

"Daddy the girls love you."

"They would love to ruin me. I cannot for the life of me get any sleep until they have fallen to sleep first. Did you know they painted my toenails and fingernails while I slept one night? Cidney gave me a heads up so that I would not embarrass myself at service when I shook hands with the members. Now that is my little angel. Those other two rub my hide raw every chance they get. They are your uncle's favorite and together they are twice the trouble. All the shenanigans those three conspire when they are together is undignified. I tell you every summer they rub my hide raw."

"Oh daddy you have just gotten older that is all."

"You just watch the three of them and see if I have gotten older or they are trying to drive me to an early grave. Speak of the devil here comes your uncle."

"Now daddy don't you get started. You stay right here while I go meet Uncle Nate."

Cindy Lou walks to the paved drive and welcomes everyone to her home.

"Wow! Uncle Nate you have not changed a bit."

"Uncle," the girls scream while they run into his arms. They begin their private handshake only meant for the four of them."

"My baby girls have grown up. Do you get your pushups in every morning?"

"I do, answers Cidney. See my muscles?"

Nathan squeezes her arm; "You are almost there. What about you Lacey?"

"I am on the basketball team this year."

Never Underestimate The Power of A Secret Place

"Yeah uncle and you should see here skip down the basketball court," says Lindsay.

"So what are you doing my little genius?"

"She makes us play school with her every Saturday morning."

"That's my girls. Now tell me who are you?"

"We are Conquerors," the three of them shout in harmony.

"Where is your wife," asks Cindy Lou.

"She is back at the motel. The long drive was a bit too much for her."

"It is understandable. Now who is this young lad that you have with you?"

Cindy Lou rubs the young boy's head. Nathan is smaller than the girls although he is older than them. He is thin and but well nourished.

"Don't touch me," he yells.

"Oh, I am so sorry I did not mean to harm you."

"He is fine he just needs a minor attitude adjustment."

Nathan takes the little boy by the hand and leads him into the house then down the hall to the restroom while everyone follows. He closes the door and everyone becomes silent. They listen for that sound. All of the sudden they hear the scream of the little boy. They wait because Nathan gives the children two swats when they misbehave. The door opens and they both reappear without any sign of what transpired in the bathroom. With ease little Nathan approaches Cindy Lou and says, "Sorry for misbehavin." Cindy Lou bends down and looks him in the eye.

"Thank you for taking responsibility for your behavior. But for the record I will ask before I touch you next time. I am sorry that I invaded your space. Now would you like to meet my girls?"

Cindy Lou takes little Nathan's hand and guides him to the living room to meet her daughters.

"Now you are a little older than my girls but I am pretty sure you will find them good company while you are here."

Never Underestimate The Power of A Secret Place

Cindy Lou's girls begin to size him up. All three girls stand around him with their arms folded and a frown on their faces. Little Nathan smirks then he eyes them uneasily.

Lindsay announces, "You better wipe that smile off your face little boy."

"Little boy," little Nathan questions.

Cidney and Lacey chime in together, "That is what she said; you need to clean out your ears."

Cindy Lou sighs, "Oh boy. Girls little Nathan is family and we will treat him like family."

"He better act like family," Lindsay adds.

"What did you say Lindsay," asks Melba.

"Oh she said welcome to the family grandmother," Lacey answers.

"That is what I thought. You girls get ready we are going out for dinner."

The girls race to their room to change for dinner. Jonathan pulls little Nathan close.

"Allow me to help you make your life, let me say a little more bearable, Jonathan begins. You do not know anything when those girls are around you hear me? You can argue with them if you want, but you will never win and they will make sure you pay somehow. Believe me I know firsthand. Your great uncle has taught them every trick in the book to make my life miserable. They can tie you up somewhere and we will never find you," chuckles Jonathan.

"Stop Jon before you scare him."

"I can fight too," insists little Nathan.

Jonathan gets face to face with him and says with a tight lip, "You will never win. Those three together can make your life miserable. My wife thinks I got lost on the way here by mistake. I intentionally got lost on purpose because I knew when I got here it is going to be pure terror that I will have the pleasure to know."

Never Underestimate The Power of A Secret Place

The girls begin to approach their grandfather.

"Papa are you talking about us," they ask in harmony.

"I just said how beautiful and smart you girls are and I would have none other as my grandchildren."

"Really papa?"

"That is the truth. I look forward to the three of you at the farm for the summer."

"Will Uncle Nate be there?"

"I will not miss it for the world," says Nathan.

"The stay may be a little longer than expected this summer daddy," Cindy Lou admits.

"What do you mean a little longer?"

"Can we talk about it over dinner?"

"Oh no, we have to talk about it now. This could be a game changer."

"Jon you know the girls are more than welcome to stay however long they want," adds Melba.

"Now Melba, do you really want to disappoint the workers? Not just the workers, what about the animals? It took a month before the chickens started to lay eggs again and what about what they did to the fishing pond? We did not sell one blue fish at the market. Those girls practically turned our farm into a Dr. Seuss playground."

"You know very well green eggs and ham have been sold in restaurants around the world Jon. You have eaten them yourself."

"Melba when was the last time have you heard of a blue fish? I am listening. Now I will be dog gone it if those girls turn that farm upside down again."

"Brother must you overreact," snickers Nathan.

"Nathan, I would not be surprised if you were behind all the shenanigans that transpired last summer."

"It was all in the name of fun. The dye wore off in no time."

"Well fortunate for you the workers have a sense of humor."

"It is something that you seem to be missing."

"Daddy, uncle please do you have to start again. We still have my graduation to attend. Can the both of you please remain civil until we return to the farm?"

"What do you mean *we*?"

"I will explain later daddy. Let's go girls, make sure the lights are out in the house."

Everyone begin to leave Cindy Lou's home.

"Close the door, please someone," instructs Cindy Lou.

"Where is the lock?"

"Come on daddy, I know you must be hungry."

Cindy Lou begins to escort Jonathan to the car. Jonathan hesitates to allow the girls to race past him and get into the car.

"Who is going to lock the doors," Jonathan asks.

"Daddy this is a safe neighborhood."

"That is great but you still have to lock the doors."

"I agree with you on that dear brother. You can never be too safe."

"The neighbors will notify the cops if anyone enters the house," she answers.

"Where is your husband?"

"Dad you had to ask. Can we talk about him later?"

"I see you want to enjoy dinner. I understand baby girl. We can talk later but we will talk."

The girls are in the car eager to get to the restaurant. Nathan climbs in the driver's seat of his car while Cindy Lou accompanies him in the passenger seat. Jonathan checks to make sure the children are secured in their seats before he closes the door. He continues on to his automobile where his wife waits. He turns the ignition and sits for a minute.

"What are you thinking about?"

"Did you not find it strange that he is not anywhere to be seen?"

"Who is he Jon?"

"That coward she married," Jonathan huffs. "He could not wait to get her away from New York when they married."

"I noticed Jon but I am sure that she will fill us in when she is ready."

"If he thinks he is going to leave my baby girl with three children to rear by herself he has lost his mind. I never liked him anyway."

"What did you say Jon?"

"I said that I never liked him anyway," he squint his eyes. "He always looked passed you when they came to visit. That was a clue that he was not right for her. But you insisted that it was her decision whomever she falls in love with."

"I still think that is correct Jon. If your father never came to the hospital when he was called we would not be together today."

"Nonsense, I was going to come for you when the farm was in full operation; besides I had no idea that you were pregnant. I am still angry that you hid the pregnancy from me."

"Jon you appear to be intelligent, you mean to tell me that you had no idea that I could become pregnant without using any form of contraceptives?"

"You were my first what was I supposed to know? Nathan did not have a clue himself and I could never bring myself to ask mother about sex."

"What about your father or even Arthur?"

"I would have had to bring you home to meet the family and I did not know how they would accept our love. I guess it was meant to happen since my parents experienced the same fears."

"I would have never guessed that your mother was African. It is unbelievable that Nathan and you are twins."

"My life truly amazes me. I would have it no other way."

Jon leans over to plant a light kiss on Melba's cheek.

"Let us get to the restaurant before the miniature tornadoes destroy it."

Melba giggles to herself while she gazes out of the window.

"You know that Nathan and you were no different. I think you two brought this on yourselves."

"What do you mean by that Mel?"

"Well do your remember the time that you faked you own death?"

"Of course I do it was a lesson he needed to learn. I nearly broke my neck when he removed the planks from the basement stairwell."

"It was nothing short of you placing a saucer size tarantula on top of Nathan's head while he drove us to the University one morning. He literally wet his pants Jon."

"And he should have. He could have killed me," Jonathan sulks.

"And you could have killed us along with those poor innocent pedestrians. You two are unbelievable and I think this is payback for everything you did to your parents as children."

"Did God have to multiply it times three?"

"Believe me putting up with you two was not easy."

"I am sure I was not that awful."

They arrive at the restaurant and Jonathan surrenders to valet parking.

"Really Jon you used to say valet's were rip offs."

"It would be my pleasure if they lost this tuna can on wheels. For years I have wanted an excuse to get my truck out of storage."

"Jon I thought you had gotten rid of that old piece of junk."

"Are you out of your mind woman? That is a vintage truck."

"So where have you hidden it?"

"I will never tell."

"I am pretty sure it sits somewhere near while it wastes away."

Never Underestimate The Power of A Secret Place

"We made a lot of memories in that truck including our son," Jonathan quips. "There they are over to the left."

The triplets wave them in the direction of their table. Betty sits at the table while she rests her head on Nathan's shoulder. The triplets sit across from them while Cindy Lou and little Nathan sit further to the end of two tables that were joined together. Melba and Jonathan take their place beside Betty and Nathan and across from Cindy Lou.

"How do you feel Betty?"

"A lot better now that we are off the road."

"I think we will fly back," informs Nathan. "It will be easier on Betty."

"Well who will drive the girls back?"

Jonathan squints his eyes at Nathan.

"You better not think about it!"

"Calm down daddy something will work out. Let us order. I cannot wait to eat."

An hour later after desert has been served and everyone appears to be satisfied; Cindy Lou stands then begins to tap her wine glass with her spoon to demand their attention. Everyone looks in her direction.

"I have an announcement to make. I know it is everyone's expectation that I will graduate with a degree in Medicine but I have actually earned a degree in Agriculture."

"Did you hear that Melba? I expected her to attend NYCU to pursue a degree in Medicine."

"And what do you have to say Jon?"

"That is what I expect in return."

"Daddy it is more complicated than that."

"What do you mean more complicated? I could have easily paid for a tutor."

"No daddy that is not what I mean."

"Explain while I listen."

Never Underestimate The Power of A Secret Place

"You do not have to explain anything baby. A degree in Agriculture is important just like degree in Medicine. If I can remember someone left home to pursue their own dreams in Agriculture themselves despite earning a degree in Medicine. Do you happen to know who that someone may be?"

"Now Melba you cannot compare apples to oranges."

"What do you mean apples to oranges? It is all the same."

"Let me explain woman! Farming is a subservient career for a woman. There is manual labor involved that a woman would have to endure on a daily basis."

"Well daddy, I am very capable of facing the challenges to become a farmer. I am sorry if I have disappointed you."

Jonathan sighs, "You have always made me proud since the day you were born. How about we talk this over later and just enjoy the evening. You have a big day ahead of you."

Jonathan stands with his glass lifted.

"I would like to make a toast."

The others stand along with the triplets in their chairs.

"I want to make a toast to my most beautiful, strong willed daughter."

Everyone tip their glasses around the table then take a sip. The girls begin to giggle to themselves.

"Somebody check their cups and make sure they have not gotten into the wine."

"Jon," Melba gasps in amazement!

"You never know with those three. It is possible."

Everyone return to their seats then they begin a low chatter among themselves.

"Where is your husband," Jonathan asks.

"Is daddy coming," asks Lacey?

"I hope he will attend the ceremony."

"What do you mean hope? Are you having marital problems?"

Never Underestimate The Power of A Secret Place

"Daddy I really do not want to go into this right now."

"Alright, when do you think is the right time?"

Jonathan leans closer then he begins to squint his eyes.

"Jon you are prying."

"I do not pry. I just want to know what is going on with my daughter."

He raises his brows at his wife.

"Well I hate to be a bearer of bad news but we need to get these girls to bed," Nathan interrupts. "Tomorrow will be a busy day."

"I don't want to go to bed," sighs Lindsay.

"This is not a debate young lady," insists Jonathan.

"Take it easy brother. Okay girls we have to get home like the dragon said and I will read you ladies a bedtime story."

"Uncle," the girls respond in surprise.

"Whaaat?"

"Look at us."

"I see all three of you. What is the point?"

"We are too big for bed time stories. Can we watch television?"

"Not at all; I want you girls well rested for tomorrow's festivities," Nathan demands.

"Mommy lets us watch television before bed," they harmonize.

"I am not your mommy," Nathan sings back. "Push in your chairs. There are people in line for this table."

Everyone begin to push their chairs to the table while Jonathan pays the waitress. The waitress takes a moment to look at his Diner's card.

"I will get your receipt."

Minutes later she returns to hand him his receipt to sign.

"Thank you, sir."

"No thank you for your impeccable service."

Never Underestimate The Power of A Secret Place

Jonathan takes a long look at the waitress. Her skin is a dark mahogany, large brown eyes with beautiful long lashes and full lips.

"Come on daddy," directs Cindy Lou while they begin to walk towards the entrance. "It is not polite to stare at the waitress."

"Her eyes look so familiar. Matter of fact she resembles Angie quite a bit."

He turns to look at the waitress while Cindy Lou guides him out the resturaunt.

"Are you still searching for Angie? But daddy I thought…" her voice trails off after she witness the tears form in his eyes.

"I will never give up."

He looks straight ahead then walks out of the restaurant into the cool night air. The streets are filled with cars but the walkways are clear. He begins to peer through the glass window of another restaurant at the people dining there when he walks by. He observes that they appear to be separated by race. The Africans are grouped nearer to the exit. They appear to talk and laugh among themselves. He shakes his head and returns his attention to Cindy Lou.

"We have to talk after you put the girls to bed. I can wait on the porch. Do you want your mother to join us?"

"She already knows daddy."

"Why am I always the last to know," he shouts. "I am the man of the house and I should know everything going on under my roof."

"Daddy I do not know if you have noticed but you are getting angrier with each passing year."

"I am not angry. The older I get the less patience I have for foolishness."

"Daddy you have become an old angry man."

"What did you say?"

"It is the truth daddy."

Never Underestimate The Power of A Secret Place

"Do you still love me?"

"Daddy, I will always love you and mother loves you too."

"Oh I know your mother loves me. I have her wrapped around my finger."

"What did he say?"

"Daddy says you got him wrapped around your finger mother."

"You do not have to save me. I can handle your mother."

"Hurry Jon before the girls fall asleep."

"Here I come. Keep them up or we will have to haul them into the house."

"Daddy!"

"Well just look at them. You got three middle ankle biters."

"Bye daddy, see you when we get to the house."

"Okay, who wants a peppermint?"

"I do," they all sing.

Cindy Lou climbs in the car before Jonathan closes the door. Jonathan walks over to his car and climbs in then looks at Melba.

"Is there something you need to tell me?"

"I have no idea what you are talking about."

"You know how it makes me feel when you hide things from me."

"Jon, this is not the time to get emotional."

"It makes me feel incompetent as a father and a husband."

"Jon the doctor said that the next heart attack may kill you if you do not calm down."

"I will calm down when I can hold my baby girl again."

"Jon you will have to accept the fact that Angie is with us in spirit."

"With all my heart I want to believe it but something tells me she is out there. We have got to get to the house. I want to hear what Cindy has to say unless you want to continue to break the vows of our marriage."

"And vow would that be Jon?"
"To obey your husband until death do us part."
"How about obey your wife until death do us part?"
"I have done everything you have asked of me."
"So you have stopped smoking?"
"Except that."
"You have canceled the search for Angie?"
"Except that."
"You most certainly have not gotten rid of that old truck you call the blue racer."
"That too."
"So you have not been obedient yourself Jon."
"May I tell you why?"
"Please do."
"I remember the day the doctor prescribed me castor oil for my occasional irregularity. But you decided to invent you own way to prescribe the medicine. You secretly forced me to take a dose every morning with my orange juice. Do you remember that? I thought you were trying to kill me."
"Oh Jon that was just one mishap; you have survived worse than that."
"It was only by the grace of God. I would have never thought my own wife would turn against me."
"Is that what you think?"
"I sure do."
"Well then, see if I hide you from the girls this summer."
"You would not leave me at the mercy of my enemies would you?"
"I sure will."
"I guess I retract my statement."
"Do you mean your statements?"

Never Underestimate The Power of A Secret Place

"Of course sweetheart; I meant statements with an 's'. And any others that I may utter from here on that may offend you. Now how did I do?"

"You outdid yourself mister."

"Well here we are. You can help Cindy get the girls to bed and I will wait on the porch. Let me see how Betty is doing before they drive off."

"Okay honey it will only take a minute."

Jonathan slides out of his car and heads around to the passenger side to open the door for Melba. Melba has already stepped out of the truck.

"Now woman! Why do you not allow me to open the door for you anymore? You used to love it."

"I can manage for myself."

"That women's right movement is going to your head."

"Would you like to retract that statement?"

"I thought I was paid up for some time to come."

"Do not short change yourself mister."

Melba walks away with a smirk.

"Will he ever learn?"

Jonathan walks toward Nathan's car.

"As the old adage goes, you cannot live with them and you cannot live without them. Are you sure you cannot stay a little while?"

"It is up to Betty she does not feel well."

"I will be fine."

"Are you sure honey?"

"I am sure, besides it is too early to turn in."

"I will get a pitcher of cool water and a few glasses. You two can join us for the bombshell Cindy is about to drop."

"Brother, I think you will like what she has to say."

"How would you know? Am I the only one who does not know?"

Never Underestimate The Power of A Secret Place

"Basically, you are too dramatic. She is afraid that you would over react if she told you what she was going through."

"Nonsense, I am the most balanced father she could ever have."

"Please let us join them on the porch and we shall see."

Jonathan walks around to the passenger side of the car and helps Betty to her feet. She is frail but well rested. Betty wears a multi-colored scarf that covers her bald head and outlines her face. Her eyes are large, round and the softest brown. Skin a smooth pecan brown. Nathan exits the car and joins them.

"Is it too cool out for you honey?"

"No I am just fine. Stop fussing over me. I have survived my last round of radiation. It is just a matter of time before I regain my strength."

Both men escort Betty onto the porch. Jonathan eases Betty into a cushioned chair.

"How is that?"

"Just fine Jon. You are such the gentleman."

"I am glad someone appreciates me."

Nathan and his wife sit in the loungers while Jonathan and his wife are seated on the wooden porch swing.

"What is taking Cindy so long? I am beginning to get sleepy myself," yawns Jonathan.

"Why don't you just turn in for the night," Melba suggests.

"Well I guess I will."

Before Jonathan can stand to his feet Cindy Lou exits the front door in her graduation gown.

"I just wanted my family to be the first to see me."

"I am so proud of you Cindy."

"Thanks uncle."

"Now what does that scarf say?"

"Daddy these scarves are a part of the graduation regalia made in Africa. Is it incredible daddy?"

"Of course it is and so are you."

"I am sorry I did not graduate with honors. I hope I did not disappoint you."

Cindy sits between her mother and father on the swing.

"Do you think this swing is sturdy enough to hold the three of us?"

"Jon what are you trying to say?"

"Yes, daddy it is."

Jon begins a slow rock while they sit in the cool breeze of the night.

"So you have a landlord?"

"Yes daddy. I plan to move back to Nathan's Place after graduation."

"Is that so? I thought you despised Nathan's Place."

"Daddy, I love my home but everything changed with Angie's abduction. I wanted to experience life on my own at least once."

"So you are a representation of the prodigal daughter I suppose, except you will bring three more of you home."

"Daddy, have you ever wanted to leave home and travel the world?"

"Of course but I am a man. You are a woman and people take advantage of women when they wander around alone in this world. Now look at what happened to your sister. You had to add misery to the fire by leaving the very place where I knew you would be safe."

"Daddy I left to follow my husband."

"Could you have said no? And furthermore I had no idea you were married. If anyone should have known it should have been me."

"Grandfather gave us permission to marry. I was pregnant and I did not want my child to be fatherless."

"Well where is he now?"

"He is here in Oklahoma somewhere. We are divorced. He did not honor our marriage vows."

"Now where have I heard that before," asks Melba.

"I think Cindy has the floor if I am not mistaken," demands Jonathan.

"So I took the refund from NYCU and applied to an agriculture program here."

"Why here?"

"Well my grades were too low to apply at any of the other nearby colleges. This was my opportunity to redeem myself. A few months after I gave birth to the triplets then marriage went downhill. When the girls color began to change he became abusive and accused me of cheating.

"He simply could not accept your African lineage," Jonathan replies.

"I finally called the cops after he continued with the abuse and the girls and I were removed from the home."

"Honey what did you do?"

"Mother I did not do anything."

"Mel what made you think she did anything wrong?"

"Normally the abuser is removed from the home."

"He refused to leave the home so they asked if I would leave mother. I was able to file for divorce and I was given sole custody of the girls. He continued to harass me and refused to financially support the girls. I met another single mother in the process and she lived in city of Langston. I moved to her place for safety and so that the girls could have someone to play with on occasions. I felt like I was at home so I applied to the University which was in close proximity to the family residences."

"Why did you not come home?"

"I was ashamed."

"That is understandable."

"Jon," they all gasp.

"What am I to say?"

"Just be quiet and listen for once in your life," instructs Nathan.

Cindy continues.

"I applied to the University and was accepted on a conditional admission."

"What is that?"

"I signed an agreement to remain in good standings academically with the University. After I requested my transcript from NYCU the financial aid office informed me that they would send my refund from the account that was set aside for my tuition, fees and housing. I was able to apply it to my educational expenses here to support myself and the girls. Uncle Nate bought me a car and paid for the insurance when he visited a few years ago."

"Here we go," says Nathan.

"Now daddy, Uncle Nate happened to get my information from the financial office of NYCU somehow."

"Well to be truthful Betty's sister Vivian was the actual person that contacted Betty to tell her that Cindy was in Oklahoma. She was not legally authorized to give her Cindy's address but she was able to give the University's address. So I drove up and within no time I was directed to Cindy's residence."

"You mean to tell me brother that you did not have the decency to tell me where my daughter was living?"

"I felt that it was Cindy's obligation to tell you. Besides she is right on the nose. Nathan's Place resembles the University's community in many ways. In that respect we have continued for the most part to embrace our culture and traditions that laid the foundation for Nathan's Place. Sometimes the culture of an institution can shift for many reasons beyond their control but as for Nathan's Place we are able to maintain our culture and traditions due to our ability to be a standalone entity."

Never Underestimate The Power of A Secret Place

"Just think even with the factory closure we are still able to maintain our existence with the retail businesses we have established. I am proud to say we have become self sufficient. Everyone has a talent or skill that produces a harvest to maintain the existence of Nathan's Place. My brother everything that we have endured was not in vain. God had a purpose for everything. Mother and father would be very proud of us."

"I am certain they would be. Even Arthur has taken a turn for the better."

"How is Uncle Arthur daddy?"

"Since father's death, with the closure of the factory and his divorce he has made his home at Nathan's Place. It really feels good to have my brothers with us. My prayer is that one day Angie and you will return home soon."

"Daddy," whines Cindy Lou.

"I know what you all have accepted but I will not give up on God's promise."

"Well daddy maybe half of your wish is about to come true."

"What is that?"

"The girls and I are coming home."

"What do you say now? Do you necessarily have to bring the girls?"

"Jon, you cannot be serious."

"Where are we going to put them?"

"They can live with us. They are your only grandchildren Jon."

"No they are not. They are his!"

Jonathan points to Nathan.

"He has taught them every trick in the book to rub my hide raw."

"It is all in the name of fun brother. You should ease up and enjoy the girls while you can. They will soon be grown and the shenanigans will be a past time."

Never Underestimate The Power of A Secret Place

"I cannot wait."

"Daddy you have allowed the loss of Angie to interfere with every aspect of your life."

"No I have not."

"You have too!"

Everyone begin to shake their heads in affirmation.

"It is not the loss of my baby girl that troubles me. It is the fact that everyone discounts the vision God revealed to me. Do you remember Nathan the day that I revealed to you my dream that you were hung from a tree on dead man's road? I told you to take another route did I not?"

"Yes brother I remember."

"I remember the day as if it were yesterday. Sampson, Charles and I drove to dead man's road and found you dangling from a rope. It was Charles that shot you down just in time do you remember?"

"You have got to be kidding me. Jon you have become delusional," argues Betty.

"Show her! Show her the evidence," Jonathan shouts.

"Nathan you told me you ran into a clothes line."

"Betty I did not want to you to worry. I wanted you to come and live at Nathan's Place. I knew if I told you what really happened to me you would not come at all. Brother I believe you. I have lived with you all my life and you have envisioned some of the most profound events that have come to light. I will continue to believe that one day Angie will come home."

"It is our hope as well daddy," Cindy Lou insists.

The calmness of the night falls around them except across the street where there are dark figures that appear to be rambunctious. Someone appears to bend down as if to tie their shoes and a few of the figures appear to dance. Music resonates afar off but not loud enough to interrupt the Johnson's while they gather.

"Quite energetic neighbors you have."

"Yes daddy, I really do not have any complaints except for the occasional loud music."

"So is that why you do not lock your doors?"

"No daddy the locks were installed after I moved in. So I became accustomed to not lock the doors. I have lived here in the city after I completed my degree since December so I moved to find work until I walked across the stage. It was so important to me to participate in the graduation ceremony and to have my family here. I have not had any problems here. Really I haven't."

"Well let me see what problems you are not having now."

Across the street a police unit has arrived. All the figures have vanished. Jonathan has taken the liberty to acquaint hisself with the ongoing situation. Jonathan approaches the officers.

"You called sir?"

"I most certainly did not."

"There has been a disturbance call in the area," reports one of the officers.

"Well my family and I have been gathering at my daughter's home and everything has been calm for," he glances at his watch; "approximately the last hour or so."

"This area is well known for drugs and crime. We have kept watch on this particular house for quite some time."

"And how so," Jonathan asks.

"This house is a nuisance to the neighborhood sir."

"What makes this house a nuisance officer?"

"The teenagers that live here have a lot of time on their hands with nothing to do. It is a recipe for trouble."

"And how do you plan to approach this situation may I ask?"

"If we catch them breaking the law we have to arrest them."

"What if they do not break the law what will you do?"

"Our hands are tied until they do, then it becomes our job to take care of it."

"Sounds like you have it all figured out."

Never Underestimate The Power of A Secret Place

"Yes sir we do."

"Have a good day gentlemen."

Jonathan begins his way back to the porch where the others look on.

"What is going on," Melba asks.

"The matter does not concern you," replies Jonathan.

"I knew I should have come with you."

"That is my point exactly."

Jonathan leans back in the swing and places his arms around his daughter and his wife.

"Well I guess it is time to turn in we have a busy day ahead of us," replies Melba.

"Nathan can we ride with you back to the motel," asks Jonathan.

"Jon I think I will stay with Cindy and the girls."

"Be my guest, I need all the alone time I can get."

"Really Jon, I will be more than happy to give you all the alone time you need when we get home."

"Now that the ankle biters are coming to stay my quality time will become nonexistent anyway."

"Where have you been mister?"

"Now Melba this is not the time to air our dirty laundry."

"Okay mom, dad can we change the subject?"

"Goodnight baby girl. I will see you in the morning. Mel, I will see you in your dreams."

"Daddy!"

"More like in your own dreams mister, replies Melba."

"This goes on and on and on Cindy; you may as well get used to it," Nathan interjects.

Nathan lifts Betty out of her lounger and starts in the direction of his car. Nathan eases his wife into the passenger seat. Jonathan gets in the backseat of the car.

"Betty I will ride in the back seat for you any day. Mel would most definitely have to ride on the hood."

Nathan shakes his head.

"You wonder why the dog house is your second home."

"Brother one day you will understand."

"That is something that I hope will never happen."

They both chuckle.

"Were you honest when you said that you believe Angie is still alive?"

"Brother who knows you better than I?"

The ride to the motel becomes quiet just for a little while.

"Do you remember the day Sheriff Badeaux rode onto the property with his men?"

"Yes I do."

"For a brief moment I thought we were left alone to fight that battle. The workers disappeared among the trees, quarters, everyplace you could imagine. My first experience of the Africans running for safety was after we purchased the farm over thirty years ago. It puzzles me that the Africans still run today. Could it be possible that they have inherited a genetic or environmental predisposition?"

"Brother we agreed that we would only challenge the obstacles set before us. This is not the time to grapple with the past."

"It appears to me that this is a matter well over due for a challenge, but if you say so brother."

Nathan pulls up to the front entrance of the motel to drop Betty off.

"I will go in and reserve a room for Melba and me."

Jonathan opens the door while Betty eases out of her seat. The pavement is bricked and leveled with precision. When they enter the small lobby Jonathan begins to look for a seat for Betty.

"Why don't you sit right here while I check in."

Never Underestimate The Power of A Secret Place

Jonathan reaches the appointment desk and there stands a young white male with blond hair and a fair tan.

"Welcome to the Benford Motel, do you have reservations?"

"I am sorry to say that I do not."

"Well let me check to see what we have available."

The young man begins to review his registration book while Jonathan attempts to peek over the desk.

"Well we have a double available for two. The remaining available rooms are suites."

Nathan enters the motel.

"What floor are you on Nathan?"

"He reaches for his key and looks at it."

"The second floor room two hundred-fifteen," Nathan answers.

"Where is that double room located?"

"It is located on the third floor room three hundred."

"Well I guess that will have to do."

Jonathan reaches into his pocket for his wallet to retrieve his Diner's card. He then searches both pockets and returns to search his wallet.

"I know that cannot be. I just used the Diner's card at the restaurant."

"Did you lose it?"

"I am quite sure the waitress returned the card then I placed it in my wallet like always."

"Well I can take care of the bill."

"Of course not," Jonathan pulls out another card. "I never leave home without an emergency card. Here you are young man."

"Thank you, sir. I will need some form of identification."

"Of course if you will give me just a minute."

Jonathan searches his wallet again and he is unable to find his license.

"Now this is ridiculous."

"I just think you have begun to age and you can longer remember where you put things brother."

"Well I am just older than you by two minutes younger brother."

"Excuse me did you say that you two are brothers?"

"Yes we are. Matter of fact we are twins."

Jonathan and Nathan begin to laugh to themselves.

"Here you are."

The clerk observes the two in shock. He takes Nathan's license and credit card to complete the transaction. He hands the receipt to Nathan who signs and returns it to the receptionist. Afterwards the clerk hands a copy of the receipt and a key to Nathan.

"Check out time is noon and we ask that you check out here at the front desk. If you should decide to remain another day please make the transaction by nine o'clock am to reserve your room. If you need anything my name is Peter and I will be on duty until seven o'clock am. Valerie will be the morning reservationist and she will be happy to take care of you."

"Thank you again Peter for your impeccable service."

"We have a bellboy available if you should need his service."

"Thank you, but I packed light for this trip," replies Jonathan.

"Goodnight sir."

"Brother you left your luggage in your car."

"I will be fine. I can just borrow some of your clothes."

Jonathan winks at Peter. The three enter the elevator. Nathan pushes the number two button then the number three button. The elevator begins its journey to the second floor then stops. The doors open to a clean lobby with interior walls and carpentry in earth tones that extends to the left and to the right.

"I will see you in the morning brother. We can head to Cindy's early to get a jump start on the children then you can get dressed before we make our way to the University."

"That sounds like a plan, goodnight you two."

"Hey," Nathan places his arm between the elevator doors to prevent it from closing.

"Make sure you report the card lost first thing in the morning."

"It will turn up somewhere."

"Anything can happen with a credit line of ten thousand dollars. I will make the call myself. Goodnight brother."

The door closes and the elevator resumes its journey to the third floor. The door opens and Jonathan finds himself in a lobby somewhat like the one he witnessed on the second floor. He observes the arrows on the wall. Rooms three hundred and twenty five to three hundred the arrow points to the right. Jonathan begins to walk in that direction. He passes room three hundred-twenty five on his left then three hundred-twenty on his right.

"I imagine all the even numbers will be on the right. I am correct three hundred and sixteen, three hundred and ten, three hundred and four, stairwell, three hundred; this is my destination. This motel does not appear to be large enough to have so many rooms."

Jonathan reaches his room then turns the key in the lock. He enters the room and it smells of a light scent of cigarette smoke. *The smell of cigarettes is just what I need to trigger my urges he thinks.* The carpet has been neatly vacuumed in a diagonal pattern; it is a warm chestnut brown and the bedding décor matches the furnishing. A cherry oak dresser and headboard compliments the warm tones of the décor. Jonathan opens the hutch to reveal a television encased inside.

"This is every man's dream to be up close and personal with his favorite western. I may never leave this room for the rest of my life."

Never Underestimate The Power of A Secret Place

After a short time Jonathan falls into a deep sleep when his motel phone rings and he jumps. He hesitates to answer the phone then he looks at the clock; it is nine o' clock in the morning. He then pulls the receiver to his ear.

"Hello," he whispers then he peers to his left then his right.

"Brother I have contacted the Diners credit card company to report you card lost. They will have to report it stolen so that you are not responsible for any other purchases. Are you certain Melba does not have it because if so she could be detained for unlawful possession?"

"It would serve her right if she did take it. Now she has a budget she has to abide by and that is final."

"Brother do not get carried away. I will let you know what I find out until then get cleaned up and don't you dare turn on that television. We have to get over to Cindy's for breakfast. I shall see you in a few minutes."

Jonathan places the phone receiver in the cradle and reaches for the television before he lies across the bed. Click, the television is now on. Jonathan begins to view his favorite western program before he drifts back to sleep. Click. The sound of the television blares loud but Jonathan has a keen sense of hearing. Nathan's attempt to startle Jonathan has failed. Jonathan pretends to sleep while Nathan cowers over him. All of the sudden Jonathan grabs Nathan and places him in a choke hold.

"I would put an end to you if it was not for the love I have for Betty."

"I am at your mercy brother."

"Is that so?"

"Yes, just name your price."

"First of all you will not teach my granddaughters any more of your shenanigans."

"It is done."

"Second, you will no longer make me look like a terrible husband around my wife and family from this day forward."

"Brother that is all you. I have told you on so many occasions to shut your mouth, but every time you place yourself at a disadvantage. Besides," Nathan wiggles out of the choke hold. "It is your fault that we are outnumbered."

"How can that be?"

"You have the twins and now the triplets. Because of you the odds are against us. You may as well deal with it. Get up we have to get you to Cindy's to get dressed. You know how they are about timeliness."

"I am ready as we speak."

"You better not be or it is going to be a huge bug tussle when we get to the house."

"I like to ruffle their feathers, let's go."

"Turn off the television."

"That is what the help is for."

"Mother would be very disappointed in you."

"Why did you have to bring mother into this?"

Jonathan reaches for the television and pushes the off button. He gazes at the screen and whispers, "Paradise does not last always."

"If this is your idea of paradise Mel has sold herself short. Come on you have to get dressed. We do not want to be late."

"I bet your watch when we get there not one soul is prepared to go."

"No thanks, father gave me this watch and I plan to hand it down to Todd."

They begin their walk toward the elevator. While they wait for the elevator Nathan looks down at his watch.

"Is it broken?"

"No, I just wonder if Todd would actually appreciate something this sentimental."

"Why wouldn't he?"

"He has never appreciated anything I have done for him. Maybe I have given him too much."

"You are an excellent father Nathan. Sometimes you can do all you know how to do and they still get off track."

"He is my only child. What could I have done wrong?"

"Nathan, I have never told you this but I am jealous of the relationship you have with my daughter and grandchildren. I just cannot make that connection with them."

"Brother you have always been awkward with women. Even while you dated Melba you were clueless. I am surprised your marriage lasted this long."

"I think she loves me."

"I know she loves you. There is no way any woman would put up with the things you have put her through."

The elevator opens and a teenage couple is in a corner engaged in a heated kiss.

"Never mind us we are just passing through," Jonathan speaks aloud.

The couple continues without any attempt to avoid embarrassment. Soon the elevator reaches the ground floor and the brothers' exit.

"Now that is what I am talking about," says Nathan.

"What do you mean?"

"The remark you just made."

"It was an innocent remark. What troubles me is the way the two of them carried on without any respect for the public."

"It is not our business."

"Last I checked dear brother I am a member of the public."

"I give up you will never change."

"You talk like I am a nuisance."

"For goodness sakes you finally got it."

"How have I been a nuisance?"

"I will give you an example. Do you remember the night Betty and I were alone in my bedroom?"

"Do you mean the night you hid Betty in your bedroom without father's knowledge?"

"Yes, and you entered without an invite. You sat down at the foot of the bed which embarrassed Betty to no end."

"She should have we just buried mother and there you two were committing fornication when you should have been grieving."

"Did you ever consider that it was the way I mourned the loss of mother?"

"No, frankly I never made that connection. To tell you the truth I just wanted to ruin the mood for the two of you. That is why I threatened to tell father of your foolishness."

"And I threatened to kill you."

"You did and somehow I sensed the threat of danger then retreated to my room."

"Sometimes I have to take drastic measures to get your cooperation."

"Why do you think father revealed the truth that we were fraternal twins? Why did he hide it for so long?"

"Actually the secret was a blessing for us."

"How was it a blessing?"

"You were able to hide in your secret place to maneuver us both through our social, academic and business aspect of our lives. Look at it this way; if we both resembled the African race we would have faced many challenges to become this successful if at all."

"You are correct. I was quite stunned to hear that Arthur's blood line was associated with white slavery. It is a myth that slavery was only the African's torment. Every race on earth has experienced some form of bondage although not to the extent of the Africans. What most amazes me is to know that Charles and

Thomas are brothers. It is quite remarkable that Charles being a quiet and gentle man could be related to Thomas whose heart contains so much greed and malice."

"You have to remember that their environment shaped them, brother."

"That may be true. Charles came to New York with his mother as slaves and received his freedom when he was child. He was quite protective of his mother. It seems that Thomas decided to continue in the business of slavery like his father."

"It was quite profitable in those days you know," reminds Nathan. "Just think years after slavery was abolished the mindset continued for almost another half century. What is more profitable eternal life or the riches of this temporary existence?"

"You know you must always quote the bible verbatim."

"I will leave that to you."

"You should God warns against the adding and taking away of his Holy word."

"I apologize," says Nathan.

"Is it forgiveness that you seek?"

"If so, I am not alone," replies Nathan while he looks at Jonathan.

When they pull into Cindy's drive the neighbors are gathered across the street on their front lawn. Jonathan gets out of the car and heads toward them.

"Brother, please do not get yourself killed," Nathan yells.

Jonathan waves him off after he crosses the road.

"Good morning gentlemen; how are you?"

"Who is this weird dude talkin to?"

"I noticed a police unit at your residence last night."

"Oh, so you the cat that ratted on us."

"Not at all, I actually come in your defense."

"Yo daddy, why do you care about us all of the sudden?"

Nathan reaches the group and stands beside Jonathan.

Never Underestimate The Power of A Secret Place

"Please let me introduce myself. My name is Jonathan and this is my brother Nathan."

Jonathan extends his hand to one of the boys. They all look at him in amazement.

"You seem stunned."

"Yo daddy that is yo real brotha?"

"It is unfortunate but he is my brother. We have the same mother and father and we are also twins," Nathan reveals.

"That is cool dude," exclaims the boy in the red shirt.

"I can dig it," says Jonathan.

"Man that is unbelievable."

They all begin to shake hands and the boy in the red shirt leans in toward Nathan for the famous hand shake but Nathan fails at it. The young boy looks at Nathan as if he has seen a ghost.

"So what bring you in our neck of the woods?"

"Well my daughter will graduate from college tomorrow."

"Yeah, we be watchin that chick."

"Excuse me," replies Nathan.

"Dude don't flip yo wig. You know we makin sure nobody cop a feel. She got some colored kids so I know she would like a cat like me."

Jonathan leans forward.

"I have no idea what you just said but that is my daughter and I would advise you to stay away from her."

"Calm down daddy yo. You don't want me to freak out."

Another boy with a larger than life afro steps close and leans in. Jonathan and Nathan take a step back.

"My intentions were to ask you how I could help you make a better life for yourselves."

"Yo cat what makes you think that you can come over here and judge us?"

"Well after you left last night I met with the police and they pretty much think you boys are trouble. But I see great potential in all of you. Let me tell you a little about myself. I am from Louisiana born in New York City. My brother and I moved to start a farming business. When we arrived although slavery was deemed unconstitutional years ago we still met resistance with some slave owners."

"What do you mean resistance?"

"I mean that there were some people that wanted to continue slavery because it was profitable to them. They made a profit off the misery of the Africans."

"Yo cat, I am not African. I am colored."

"So be it but there were people who look just like you who were killed for running for their freedom."

"Yo man, you was a slave owner?"

"Never would I be a slave owner. I was able to hire many of the Africans to work in our business in New York and at the farm in Louisana."

"So you the fat cat around here huh?"

"Not exactly, the farm is very successful due to the collaboration of everyone. You know my first experience in Louisiana was that of the slaves who ran and hid from their former master. Even though slavery was illegal there were those who continued to hunt after their former slaves. Many of them hid on the property that I purchased to farm. All of them possessed skills and talents that would benefit the business that my brother and I created so we hired them. That was over twenty five years ago. Now everyone is free to go where ever they wish and buy or sell whatever they want. Today they are independent members of society."

"Like I said man why is yo lips flappin?"

"Well it appears that history continues to repeat itself in some form. For some reason or another you continue to run. From what I have no idea."

"We split cause we don't wanna go to jail."

"Well if you obey the law you should not have to run."

"It don't matter dude. You can be walkin down the street mindin yo own damn business and the fuzz gone still mess with you."

"So every time you see the police you are going to run."

"Right on. You never know what they got up they sleeve."

"So you do not trust the police?"

"Daddy-O, I don't trust white people."

"Why don't you trust white people?"

"No matter what we do they still get hairy. If somebody robs a store they automatically think a cat like me did it. Like don't no other race do no wrong."

"So what can you do about it?"

"Nothing, we can't do nothing but what we been doin."

"What is that?"

"Split we have no choice but to split."

"What can you do to make yourself profitable?"

"You mean like sell drugs?"

"No that in of itself is a form of slavery."

"Dude our hands are clean. Still ain't nobody gonna give us no job."

"I ask you again. What skill do you possess?"

"You mean like washin dishes?"

"Whatever type of work that will allow you to earn wages to support yourself."

"I can cut some hair. Show him man what I can do."

The boy with the afro leans over so that Jonathan and Nathan can examine his barber skills.

"Why aren't you in a barbershop somewhere?"

"Cause man you got to have money to have a barbershop. Besides they ain't gonna hire nobody like me."

"Tell me why not."

"Because yo; I am a flake."

"What is a flake?"
"I am a lost cause yo."
"Who told you that?"
"Nobody I just know."
"What have you done to make your dream come true as a barber?"
"Yo cat. I cut hair at my house but every time these cats come around the fuzz show up. They try to frame us for drugs and nobody gonna give you a chance with no drug charge."
"I tell you what if you can produce a diploma that states that you have completed general education then I will help you to get training to become a barber."
"For real daddy-O?"
"For real."
"Lay it on me."
"Here is my business card. Keep in touch."
"Yo daddy-o what about me," says the boy in the red shirt.
"What can you do to support yourself?"
"I like to work with dogs."
"What do you mean?"
"I know how to take care of them and train them not to go in the house."
"So where is your dog?"
"They took him from me."
"Who took him from you?"
"The pigs."
"Why?"
"Everybody was complainin that my dog was vicious."
"Why don't you get a job to work with animals?"
"Cause man, my old lady says I can't have a job until I stop smoking."
"So you are smoking cigarettes?"
"No dude that stuff can kill you."

Never Underestimate The Power of A Secret Place

"What are you smoking?"

"Dude everybody smoke maryjane around here."

"Do you mean marijuana?"

They all nod to confirm. Jonathan and Nathan both look at each other.

"Why do you smoke?"

"Cat just look around you; everybody is bummed out. You would smoke too. They ain't gonna give me my dog back."

"You think so?"

"Dude I know so."

"When will you complete your education?"

"I got one more year."

"Here is my card. I tell you what I want you to do for me and what I will do for you. First of all stop smoking maryjane. Also you must complete high school with grades no lower than a 'C' and third respect your mother."

"Oh my old lady gets much respect. She all I got. So what I get out of it?"

"I will bring you to the farm and train you to work with my horses."

"Brother, I really think you are taking this too far," says Nathan.

"A deal is a deal. I will fulfill my part if you will fulfill your part."

"Yo cat you got a deal."

"Here is my card."

"This card is clean."

"You can call me anytime you wish."

"You a cool cat yo."

"Now tell me your name."

"It is puppy. That is my nick name; my real name is Shawn."

"I will refer to you as Shawn."

"And your name is?"

Never Underestimate The Power of A Secret Place

"They call me Bug but my real name is Jimmy."

"It was nice to meet you. What about the rest of you?"

The others shake their heads no, "We cool" they remark.

"Well then you have my information and I hope to hear from you soon."

"So we can call you anytime?"

"Anytime you want to talk."

Shawn and Jimmy lean forward and give Jonathan a partial hug.

"You one cool cat," says Shawn.

"I am very proud to have you as my daughter's neighbors."

"Don't sweat it. We heard about your other one. That is the pits. It is weird how a white and black person can make babies in different colors. I hope you find your daughter dude. She just might be right under your nose. It be like that sometimes."

"I agree, it be like that sometimes," mimics Jonathan.

"Here we go with another cliché that you are going to butcher to pieces. Brother it really does not become of you to speak slang."

"I will see you in the near future gentlemen. Good day."

They both turn to walk back to Cindy's home. Once they approach the house everyone waits outside with unpleasant looks on their faces. Jonathan climbs onto the porch first and looks around.

"Looks like I better get ready."

"You have fifteen minutes Jon. Cindy has to line up for the processional," Melba reminds him.

"I will not be long; I just have to change."

"You will be doing more than that. You could use a good shower."

"Nahh, I showered just the," his voice begins to trail off.

"Just when papa?"

"Oh, none of your business; I will not be long."

Never Underestimate The Power of A Secret Place

"Papa needs a bath," Lindsay chides.

"I do not!"

"Oh yes you do and you will get in that shower mister," directs Melba.

"I could not WAIT to be an adult and make my own decisions. I never imagined things would never change."

"Papa you don't stink to me," says Cidney while she looks up at Jonathan.

"You are my little angel. How about we get some ice cream and sit by the pond when we get home, he whispers."

Cidney nods affirming his invite.

"My girl you got a date."

Jonathan heads toward the bathroom.

"Sweetheart will you bring me my clothes?"

"That old hoot will not get me in that bathroom alone with him today!"

"Why not granny?"

"You are too young to understand. Cindy take your father his things into the bathroom, yells Melba. Old dirty hoot is up to his tricks."

"Mother, why do you and daddy have to be so dramatic?"

"You try to live with that man. He is a nut in a shell all by himself."

"Where are his under garments mother?"

"In your room they are all laid out for him. He can use your robe to get to your room."

Cindy Lou enters the bathroom while Jonathan showers.

"Daddy she yells, here are your things. You can use my robe to get to my room."

Minutes later Jonathan exits the bathroom with Cindy Lou's pink robe wrapped around him. He parades himself around the living area where they wait for him. The girls and little Nathan begin to giggle when he shakes his rear end. Even Melba had to

49

Never Underestimate The Power of A Secret Place

laugh at the sight. Nathan shakes his head after Jonathan exits the living area.

"Did you see his hairy legs and big floppy duck feet?"

They all begin to laugh out loud at the thought of him. Everyone continue to wait for him to get dressed. He reappears in five minutes well dressed. Melba stands from her seat and approaches him.

"Now this is the handsome man I married."

They kiss longingly.

"Ugh," the girls sigh.

Then they begin to sing.

"Granny and Papa was sittin in a tree, ki-s-s-i-n-g."

They begin to laugh. Jonathan smiles and winks at them.

"Well we must go so we can get good seats. I will have to pick up Betty," says Nathan. "Okay who rides with me?"

"Little Nathan can ride with Melba and I," says Jonathan.

"So you are going to stick me with the girls?"

"*It be like that sometimes♪,*" Jonathan sings.

"No problem we can use this time to master our plans of destruction for this summer."

Lindsay and Lacey nod their heads in agreement. Jonathan looks to Cidney who gives him the wink and he smiles.

"I will always have an ace in the hole. Let's go young man."

Little Nathan walks toward Jonathan with his arms folded and a frown upon his face.

"Why do you look so unhappy?"

"I want to ride with Aunt Cindy."

"You do say?"

"Angel would you like to ride with papa?"

Cidney skips to his side and reach for his hand.

"That's my girl. We shall meet you at the University."

Melba and Jonathan leave the house with Cidney in Jonathan's arms. Jonathan opens the door to the driver's side and place

Never Underestimate The Power of A Secret Place

Cidney in the middle. He then walks around to the front of the car while Melba gets in.

"Well are you going to shut the door Jon?"

"Whatever happened to women's rights?"

"Never mind you old hoot."

Jonathan hurries to the passenger side and reaches for the door.

"I can get it myself," yells Melba then she slams the door.

"Do you have to get your panties twisted in a knot?"

"You mister are the most unpredictable, pig headed man I have ever met."

"Now there you go with the name calling. Remember the pastor said to speak highly of your mate and that was not highly at all."

"Mother can you guys get along for one day," Cindy asks.

"Whatever makes you happy baby girl. Today is your day and we are going to make the best of it."

"Thanks daddy we have got to get on the road."

Jonathan circles the car and hits the hood to startle Melba.

"If you get in this car Jon I am getting out."

"How do you expect to get to the ceremony?"

"Without you mister!"

"Be my guest, Angel and I will ride together won't we sweetie."

He leans in and whispers in Cidney's ear.

"We can stop for some ice cream on the way."

Melba leaps out of the car and walks around to Nathan's car while she shakes her head.

"I cannot take it any longer he is driving me crazy."

"Mother this is why I am coming home with you. So that I can relieve you of some of the stress you have with daddy."

"I believe your father has lost his mind. Angie will never come back and I am tired of the nonsense that she is out there somewhere. We have her remains and we will give her a proper burial when we return."

"Mother things will work out you will see."

"I hope so I just cannot take it anymore."

"Okay, everyone lets load up the car. We will have to stop to get Betty."

"There is one more thing I forgot to do. Just give me a minute to contact the charge card company one more time before we leave."

"What is wrong with your charge card uncle?"

"Not mine your fathers. He has lost it or it was stolen."

Nathan and Cindy Lou run back into the house and Nathan picks up the phone, dials the number then leans into the receiver.

"Hello. This call is in regards to an account that I have with you. You can look under the name Nathan Johnson or Jonathan Johnson which ever you prefer. Yes, thank you. She is searching for the account. Excuse me can you repeat that? Really! That is unbelievable. They are in custody? Oh, she is in custody. I will make sure I do that within the next hour. Thank you for your time."

Nathan returns the receiver to its cradle.

"The suspect has been arrested for possession of the card. They say that the suspect made several purchases at the same location and they were able to retrieve the card. It was a colored woman and the store owner suspected that she had stolen the card. Someone has to go to the county jail to see if we can identify her, but it will have to wait until after the ceremony. Do not tell your father or we will have to restrain him. So far he is convinced that Melba has his card."

"Are you serious uncle?"

"Your daddy is very imaginative. However, Mel has begun to spend a lot of money. I think it is her way to release stress. Hurry, we need to load up everyone."

Never Underestimate The Power of A Secret Place

"They are already in the car uncle."

"Good we can get on our way."

A few hours later they arrive back at the house.

"That was a wonderful ceremony Cindy. I have never experienced anything like it and the choir was phenomenal. They have such lovely voices," comments Melba.

"Yes they do mother. Daddy how did you like it?"

"It was a beautiful ceremony. I fully appreciate the premise on which every Colored University was founded."

"Would you have attended a Colored University daddy?"

"I do not see why not. God created an inclusive world. How about we get something to eat at the restaurant we visited last night?"

"Sure daddy whatever you want."

"Brother we have to stop by the county jail and identify the person who has stolen your charge card."

"Who stole my charge card? You must be mistaken money bags has the charge card."

"What did you say Jon?"

"Mom, please do not start again; I want to have a nice evening."

"For you I will but when we get back mister you are in the dog house."

"Just the way I like it."

"We will see that you do," Melba grimaces.

"Cindy where is the county jail?"

"It is down town daddy. Can we just let the legal system take care of it? I really do not want to be stuck at the jail house all day."

"Justice has to be served Cindy."

"I know uncle but does it have to be today?"

"It is up to your father."

Never Underestimate The Power of A Secret Place

They arrive at the County Jail and both men step out of their vehicles.

"Brother I can take care of it. It may be someone in need of assistance. We cannot charge someone who may be struggling to survive," Jonathan justifies.

"I will go in with you brother. Just in case you get the bright idea to bail all the criminals out of jail," he whispers.

Jonathan looks back at the vehicles and yells, "We will not be long!"

They enter the building to approach a counter enclosed with bars that separate the clerk from the public.

"We are here in regards to a stolen charge card," Jonathan reports.

"Your name," the clerk asks.

"Jonathan Johnson."

"Please take a seat a deputy will be right with you."

They both take a seat.

"I can get the girls this may take a minute."

Nathan leaves and brings the family into the building. After some time the children become restless. Nathan turns to give them a warning and within seconds they sit down in their seats on command.

"How did you do that?"

"Do what?"

"Get them to sit still and be quiet."

"I am in charge and they recognize it."

"We shall see how long that lasts."

"Mr. Johnson please approach the counter," directs the clerk.

Nathan and Jonathan appear at the clerk's counter.

"We need you to identify the suspect if you can. Please follow the deputy at the door to your right."

They both look to their right at a bald, pale man in uniform. They nod at each other before they enter the door propped open by

Never Underestimate The Power of A Secret Place

the deputy. Nathan stops without warning which causes Jonathan to walk into him.

"What did you do that for?"

"He has to escort us."

The deputy eases by them into the narrow bright lit hall. He stops in front of a room that has a table with two chairs positioned on each side. He motions for them to enter into the room. A young woman hands the deputy what looks like are pictures. The deputy motions them to sit down but there is only one chair on their side of the table so they both stand. He begins to speak.

"I have mug shots of the suspect who we believe may have stolen your card. We do know that this is the person that used the card to make purchases."

The deputy assembles the pictures in a row to face Nathan and Jonathan. Jonathan bends down to examine the pictures. Jonathan places his head on the table and begins to rock back and forth.

"Oh my God this has got to be her? Oh God please answer my prayers today."

Jonathan begins to sob and Nathan pulls the chair out and guides Jonathan into it.

"Oh God please, I beg of you please, please. I cannot take it any longer."

"Can you tell me her name," asks Nathan.

"I am sorry but I cannot disclose that information."

Jonathan raises his head to hand Nathan a picture with tears gliding onto the table.

"It is her; I know it is. I recognize my daughter when I see her; look at the birth mark. It is her please God let it be her."

"Deputy?"

"Deputy French."

"Deputy French my niece, his daughter was abducted in Louisiana about twenty years ago. My brother has not given up his search for her. She looks very much like her mother. There is a birthmark underneath her ear like her sisters. She was eight years old when she was abducted and sold into slavery. Is there any way you can confirm whether or not this person is his daughter?"

"My supervisor will have to take over this case. It will take a minute."

"Take your time sir. We appreciate any assistance you may provide."

Nathan pulls the other chair around and sits next to Jonathan then wraps his arms around him.

"I believe brother that your vision has come true. You said that you saw her behind bars and she was close to your shoulder in height. I pray that this is the end of your journey."

There is a soft knock and Melba enters the room. She looks at her husband leaning over the table sobbing. Nathan hands the pictures to Melba and she falls into the wall. Nathan jumps to catch her but he is too late. A loud thud permeates the room. Deputy French looks in, "Is everything alright?"

"Yes," Nathan answers.

Nathan eases Melba into his seat. She leans over and lays her head on Jonathan's back while he continues to cry. Nathan opens the door and soon the whole room is filled with the family members. The pictures are passed around to Cindy Lou. For the first time in twenty years she sees her twin sister. In her heart she knows that it is her.

"When can we see her?"

"We have to speak with the supervisor to confirm that it is Angie."

After twenty minutes of calmness the door opens to a tall Caucasian officer who enters the room.

"Excuse me my name is Detective Latham."

He looks around them and begins to speak to Nathan.

"So you have reported that your daughter has been abducted?"

"No it is my brother's daughter."

Never Underestimate The Power of A Secret Place

Jonathan stands to extend his hand. They shake hands it seems for an eternity.

"And you are?"

"Jonathan Johnson."

"Mr. Johnson the suspect that we have identified with the stolen card is colored."

"Yes sir I know, she is my daughter."

"Do you mean your biological daughter?"

"That is what I mean. Let me explain Detective Latham. This is my wife and twin brother; here is my daughter's twin sister; and these are my granddaughters."

"Is the suspect aware that you are her family?"

"We have no idea we have not met with her yet."

"Well how do you know she is your daughter?"

Cindy Lou turns her head and raises the picture next to her face.

"That is remarkable but anyone can have a mark like that."

"Is there any way that we can meet her," asks Jonathan?

"I am sorry, unless you do not want to press charges we can release her then you can meet her outside."

"Well I do not want to press charges."

"It is your call. You will have to retrieve your belongings in the front," answers the Detective. "You all are free to go."

Everyone begins to file out of the room with Jonathan the last to leave. He feels a tug at his arm then turns to see who it may be. It is Deputy French.

"Come with me," he motions Jonathan further down the hall.

He places his finger over his lips to signal him to keep quiet. The deputy places a key into a metal door that opens into a small area. They walk a few feet further where there is another metal door with a small glass window. He then places a key into the lock to open the door that reveals two rows of jail cells. The room smells of mold and urine. He follows the deputy down the rows of cells that are empty and stop at the last cell. Inside a figure lays on a cot facing the wall. The deputy shakes his keys.

"You have a visitor," he announces.

The figure turns around to sit upright on the cot.

"Come close so he can see you," the deputy orders.

She stands up then walks closer to the bars but not close enough that she can be touched.

"Where are your parents," Jonathan asks. "Where are you from?"

"I don't know mistah why you askin me all these questions?"

"Do you have a family?"

"Why you wanna know? If you ain't gonna press charges then leave so I can get back to my baby."

"I will help you if you help me."

"What do you want from me?"

"About twenty years ago my daughter was abducted."

"What do abducted mean? What do it have to do with me?"

"Just listen. She was eight years old when she was taken from us. We lived in Louisiana it is south of here."

"I know where Louisiana is that is where I'm from."

"Well you look just like my daughter."

Jonathan pulls a family portrait from his pocket. The very one he used to post throughout the state of Texas and Louisiana.

"Bummer for some reason these people look like somebody I know."

"What is your name?"

"My name is Brandy Badeaux. My husband is at home with our son."

"What is his name?"

"Timmie, why you getting so deep man?"

"Is his father Thomas Badeaux?"

"Maybe why you askin man?"

"He just died a few months ago."

"How did you know?"

"Because for quite some time I thought that he had something to do with my daughter's abduction."

"Well Mistah, I don't know nothin about no girl bein abducted. The sheriff says that if you ain't gonna press charges then I can split. So you can just lay it on me right now."

"I will make a deal with you. You can call your husband and have him bring your baby. Give me a chance to talk with your husband. Only then will I drop the charges."

"He is gonna come anyway to get me so you can see him then. Just hang loose."

She walks back to the cot and flops down.

"I will have to take you back to the briefing room for now," the deputy explains.

"Will I be able to meet with her husband when he comes?"

"He will have to approve the arrangements."

When they reach the briefing room Jonathan asks, "Can I have some time alone?"

"Yes sir, take all the time you need."

Jonathan enters the room then sits down at the table. He bows his head and he begins to pray in a low voice… *"Divine creator, I come to you with a humble and heavy heart. You have never failed me in all of my days. I confess I am a terrible husband, father and grandfather. I fail at it miserably I will have to admit. I do not deserve your mercy or your grace but I come to you anyway. Because of your awesome power I know that you can make the impossible become possible. Father I come to you unworthy of your blessings to ask that you will fill her heart with your love. Please return my child to me. I ask in Jesus Holy name, Amen."*

Jonathan begins to weep. Meanwhile Nathan has been given permission to visit the suspect. He approaches the cell's bars.

"You know your father loves you. He has searched for you since the day you disappeared. Why must you take your father through this?"

"Uncle Nate he said that if I ever left him he would kill my baby."

"So you do know who I am?"

"Uncle I can't lose my baby."

"Who is the father?"

"He is the father."

"Is it a boy or a girl?"

"He is a boy."

"Timmie will have hell to pay. How old is he?"

"He is two months old."

"Why did you leave your other son?"

"What other son?"

"There is an eight year old boy that was brought to us after Sheriff Badeaux's death."

"Uncle ain't no tellin who that boy belongs to. When the slaves ran the Badeaux's kept their children so they would come back. But not everyone came back."

"So you were a slave?"

"Yes, but most of the time I cooked and cleaned around the house. Timmie wanted me for himself so he hid me from his father. His father tried to bed me so Timmie robbed him and we ran off."

"How long have you been here?"

"Just a couple of years, we ran after Timmie saw pictures of me in a store window in Texas. The pictures were everywhere in Texas."

"Why did you not call or run?"

"Because Timmie had all of the money and he never left me alone."

Never Underestimate The Power of A Secret Place

"Timmie has got to be the same age if not a few years younger than your father and I."

"I guess so he colors his hair all the time."

"Do you want to leave him?"

"Uncle, that was a ditzy question to ask."

"Answer me," Nathan yells!

"Yes, I want to ditch him," she cried out. "But I can't because we are married."

"We will see about that. Did you get that Charles?"

"I got every word Nate."

When the door opens Nathan and Charles exit the jail chambers.

"I need to speak with you two in the briefing room along with Mr. Johnson."

Detective Latham escorts them to the briefing room where Jonathan waits.

"Charles, how are you? What are you doing in Oklahoma?"

"I just happened to pass through and met up with Nathan to take care of some personal business."

"It is good to see you again brother. Do not be a stranger."

"The family and I are headed down for the ceremony," says Charles.

"I look forward to your return."

"I have to see Melba and Betty before I leave."

"Of course they are in the lobby."

"Mr. Johnson I need to brief everyone on agency protocol," informs the detective. "We will detain Mr. Badeaux when he arrives. The child will be taken into custody until the case has been resolved. I was able to contact the investigator on the abduction case. Because of the complexity of the case we cannot release your daughter or grandchild until the investigator arrives. He is in route to our station as we speak. This may take a few days to unravel. All I can do is ask that you be patient with us. Your wife and daughter have been escorted to the cell to reunite with their relative; afterward I will have to ask you to leave the premises while we book Mr. Badeaux."

The deputy enters the room and whispers something to Detective Latham.

"I was just provided some updates to the case. The minor has been taken into custody this very minute. Mr. Badeaux has also been detained. Because your daughter was a minor at the time of her abduction we find it necessary to place your daughter at another facility."

"Mr. Johnson will you allow the county to file the charges against your daughter for unlawful possession of stolen property? This will allow us to detain the suspect and possibly file the charges against her husband if she admits that she committed the acts under duress. It depends on their cooperation, but we hope that Badeaux will accept a charge of kidnapping. We are aware that other crimes were committed against your daughter. She is a very strong lady. When we took her into custody it is common practice that we examine the detainee for any identifying marks. I have to admit I have never experienced anything like this in my life. Your daughter reported that she was whipped when she attempted to escape her abductor. She has the marks to prove it. She also admits that there was an unsuccessful attempt to lynch her when she was a young girl. She reports that someone by the name of Todd retrieved her from the rope before they fled. While they were in flight the gentleman was shot and left in the field. She reports that she has not seen him since that night. Do you happen to know who this victim may be?"

"I have a son named Todd but he cannot be dead. I am positive he is deployed somewhere in the states."

"When was the last you have heard from him?"

"It has been a few years ago. We had an argument over his desire to enlist into the armed forces. It must have been at least five years ago. He was just twenty- one years and was entering his last year of college. He must have encountered Angie while in route to New York on dead man's road. That explains why he never enrolled. All along I thought he was angry at me. I figured he would call me when he cooled down."

Jonathan embraces Nathan and weeps. Nathan is in total shock. Unable to connect to his emotions he sits motionless with a distant blank stare. Jonathan releases him and shakes Nathan.

"Are you alright brother? Todd gave up his life for my baby girl and for that I am most grateful."

"If I had not argued with him that day he probably would still be alive."

"It may be in God's design that he saved Angie. I am sorry it resulted in the loss of your only son."

"Angie has informed me that Little Nathan is not her son. She has no idea who he could belong to; maybe a slave that ran and left her child behind."

"So he is orphaned?"

"Maybe so, I have no idea but that does not change anything the adoption will be finalized except."

"Except what?"

"I want to adopt him as my son."

"You have a heart of gold brother."

"Maybe this is my second chance to get it right. All things happen for a reason and according to God's purpose for my life."

"That is very true dear brother. I have always admired how you bounce back in the face of adversity. You never cease to amaze me."

Meanwhile in the jail chambers Melba, Cindy Lou and Angie Lou are huddled close together with their arms extended around each other. Angie Lou resembles her mother's complexion but her facial and physical features match Cindy Lou's.

Never Underestimate The Power of A Secret Place

"You know daddy never stopped looking for you. He has been so angry since you disappeared. Daddy had a mild heart attack after he was told that you were dead. Uncle Nate and Uncle Charles had the remains exhumed and they are being held at Nathan's Place until we return."

"Momma what made him think it was me?"

"Your baby doll was in the grave with the remains."

"Momma it is Todd's remains in that grave. I put lady bug beside him so he won't be alone. Todd was on his way to New York when he found me. I was choking when he begun to unwrap the rope away from my neck. Then I heard a loud boom and Todd fell on top of me. It was Timmie he shot him. He put me in Uncle Nate's old truck and hid it in some bushes. Then he told me that he was going to bury the body. Sometimes Timmie is cool headed and sometimes he is mean. He tied me to the steering wheel for a long time. I cannot remember how long but he brought me food and water. He tried to touch me sometimes but I fought him. When he came back he had Todd's bill folder. There was a check in it to NYCU and Timmie said that he was going to cash it. But he couldn't so he took money from his father's safe and we left Louisiana in Uncle Nate's truck. We still have it. I have Todd's bill folder too."

"How will we tell Nathan," Melba asks.

"Mother we will figure something out," answers Cindy Lou.

The detective reappears. He looks to be in his early thirties, tall, slender with coal black hair. He introduces himself.

"My name is Detective Latham and I will return you to the lobby area."

He escorts Melba by her elbow to the adjacent hall. Soon they are reunited with the children who are being entertained by the female secretary. The girls sprint towards their mother while little Nathan is fixated on a book that Betty reads to him. Jonathan along with Nathan enters the lobby and approaches them.

Never Underestimate The Power of A Secret Place

Jonathan's eyes and face are red. Cidney runs to Jonathan and wraps her arms around his legs. He rubs her head then looks to his wife. Lacey with her sister Lindsay surround their grandfather and embrace him. He looks in amazement at the compassion they bestow upon him.

"I actually think they like the old man."

"Jon they do love you."

"Yes daddy, they have always loved you. Get ready to leave everybody we have to find a diner to feed these little ones. So what will it be?"

"Juanita's," the triplets yell.

"Who is that?"

"It is an ice cream shop and diner. Daddy the girls love it there."

"Then Juanita's it shall be. It may be just what we need."

The cars pull into the parking lot and within seconds the door to Nathan's car opens. The kids begin to jump out from the car one by one. The last to exit is little Nathan.

"He looks like a defeated little boy," sighs Jonathan. "If he plays his cards right he may never be tied up and left at the mercy of the triplets."

Melba giggles and Jonathan turns to look at her in amazement.

"*Oh golly Miss Melba♪,*" he sings.

She turns to look at him while she opens the door.

"Keep dreaming mister."

She eases out of her seat and lands with both feet on the ground.

"That women's right nonsense is going to ruin the world," Jonathan yells!

Melba closes the door with all her might. Nathan walks over to Jonathan's car while he rolls down the window.

"Brother for once can the both of you bury the hatchet?"

Never Underestimate The Power of A Secret Place

"I think she loves to hate me," replies Jonathan. "Sometimes I think that is what drives our marriage. Somehow I just keep reeling her back in; it is that Johnson charm brother."

"Fortunate for me it must have skipped me."

"Maybe I should tell you more often how much I love you. You mean so much to me brother. I am very elated to share this journey with you. I cannot for the life of me, understand how you can be so compassionate after all you have been through."

"Our parents did provide the most nurturing environment to dwell in terms of what others who look like me have had to endure. For the most part because I was told most of my life that I was adopted I never took anything for granted. I felt that at anytime I could be orphaned. It haunted me that one day I could be without the comforts that I have enjoyed my entire life after mother passed. Somehow I thought mother felt the same because of her preparation for my future. It was never my wildest dream that our relationship would continue to thrive to this extent. I imagined you to become well known physician or literary writer."

"Well it explains everything since we are twins who share the same biological genes. I never could have imagined my life without you. I felt your sadness, pain even your fear like it was my own. Arthur made some shameful remarks about the connection we shared. I initially thought he was envious of our relationship. It explains the deception he created within our family. He was very successful to divide the family on every level. I did not think I could have invited him into Nathan's place after the confusion he had created within our family. To take responsibility for his actions was the least he could do if he expected to become a dweller among us. We have made some tough decisions to maintain the sense of community and cohesion among the dwellers. I have the same expectations of Arthur. It will take him some time to adjust. Our community does not mirror mainstream society. But I will not tolerate any passive aggressive nor

Never Underestimate The Power of A Secret Place

destructive behaviors from Arthur. If he does not acclimate to our culture and traditions he will be asked to leave. It has taken so much of our energy to redirect the maladaptive behaviors many of our family members have been taught. Arthur has had every opportunity to develop into a well balanced individual. There is no excuse for his behavior to continue as it was."

"Brother we must join the others before I starve to death."

Jonathan climbs out of his car to join Nathan before they walk into their first Juanita's diner.

"Well it seems the women are focused on the children so I will focus on our order," says Jonathan.

"Welcome to Juanita's; are you ready to order?"

A tall girl approaches the counter with curly brown hair and freckles scattered along the bridge of her nose.

"Let me see now I will have a hamburger with a cola."

"Would you like anything else?"

"Make that two," Nathan chimes in.

"Yes, make it two hamburgers and two colas."

"Will that be with mayonnaise or mustard?"

"Nathan?"

"It doesn't matter, I am starving here."

"Mayo will be fine."

"Would you like french fries with your order? We have the best fries in the state."

"You do now? I will try an order."

"Make that two," Nathan adds again.

"He will pay for the order," Jonathan points to Nathan.

Jonathan leaves the counter en route to the table where the women sit.

"Where is everyone?"

Melba nods in the direction of the crowd.

"They are giving away free ice cream to the children. It is going to ruin their appetites," she sighs.

Never Underestimate The Power of A Secret Place

"Not mine," Jonathan claims while he invades the crowd of children.

"We will just have to take the meals to go," Cindy Lou decides.

Jonathan returns with an ice cream cone in hand.

"Jon, do you always have to act like a clown?"

"Trust me it is not an act," adds Nathan.

"If I am, I have a few tricks up my sleeve ready for you when we get home Mel."

"Daddy, you can be so repulsive."

"Really, well you must consider the millions of people who have been repulsive since the beginning of time."

"Like who Jon?"

"Look around you this world did not populate itself."

"Daddy you are so…"

"So what Cindy now as much as I do not want to accept it even you have been repulsive."

"Forget it before you get him going," insists Melba.

Everyone returns to their food.

"How am I supposed to sit in this seat? I am a man Melba I require elbow room."

Jonathan begins to wrestle in his seat.

"Goodness can we eat without a bug tussle please!"

The girls return to their table then dive into their meals.

"We will have to reserve a room for tonight," Jonathan informs Melba.

"I can stay at Cindy's."

"Daddy you can stay at the house."

"I don't mind if I do."

Everyone stop to look at each other.

"What did you say Jon?"

"Daddy you are more than welcomed to stay at the house."

Never Underestimate The Power of A Secret Place

"If you plan to return to the farm Cindy why have you not begun to pack?"

"Daddy we do things different now. The house was furnished when I rented it. All of our belongings have been packed and sent with Uncle Ch…"

"Greyhound it was sent by Greyhound," Nathan interrupts.

"I think Cindy has the floor. What did you say? And do not tell a fib to your father," Jonathan winces.

"We need to get home detective Latham will contact us in regards to Angie's status. I am relieved they have him in custody," Melba interjects.

"Daddy we have to remember that Angie could have been dead. Maybe his lust for Angie kept her alive."

"I do not understand how she can be the subject of so much ridicule because of the color of her skin and also be the object of someone's desire. My Angie Lou turned out to be beautiful just like her mother."

"Daddy she was always your favorite."

"Not necessarily pumpkin. People accepted you no matter where we went but Angie was always at a disadvantage."

"Like myself," interjects Nathan. "Brother advocated for me on every end. I felt like he wanted to save me from the world."

"Not necessarily from the world brother but from those that dwell in ignorance. For the life of me I will never comprehend how others can view you and me as two separate species. It is pure illogical to me. One thing we must all remember; there will come a day when God's truth will be revealed to us. Not my truth or your truth. We will no longer be able to hide behind our foolish ways nor will we be able to deny his truth and for that we will all be judged."

"The girls are getting restless. I need to get them home so they can run off some of that energy."

"Jon go start the car and I will clean the tables."

"Will do is there anything else can I do for you?"

"No that will be all."

Jonathan maintains his gaze at Melba.

"Daddy you are staring at mother?"

"I cannot believe how much Angie resembles you Melba."

"Daddy I just realized where I last saw Angie."

"Where?"

"At the restaurant, she is the waitress that took your charge card."

"So what do you all have to say for yourselves?"

"Here he goes again. Sweetheart I know you are a big dreamer and I have always been there to support you. I think at some point you stopped believing in yourself and also the vision God had for you. I still believed but I think I became impatient."

Melba pulls Jonathan's face to her and kisses his lips. Jonathan leans back with a grin until his entire face turns red. Everyone begins to giggle at the sight of him until he turns and walks away.

"I think we embarrassed him."

"Cindy your daddy embarrasses himself," Nathan adds.

They all begin to laugh while they clear the tables.

"Everyone accounted for?"

"Everyone is accounted for," Cindy Lou confirms.

"Then it is time to move out."

Nathan pulls out while Jonathan trails behind. The neighborhood is quiet when they pull up. Everyone exit their vehicles before the girls run towards the back of the house.

"Where are they going?"

"To the backyard daddy where the swing set is."

"Who keeps watch over them while they are back there?"

"Sometimes I sit on the back porch while they play."

"That is where we are headed."

Never Underestimate The Power of A Secret Place

"You will have to grab the chairs and bring them around to the back deck daddy."

"No problem, Nathan we can stack those loungers on top of each other before we carry them around back. You grab the head of the loungers and I will grab the feet. I think it will be easier to get them to the back deck."

When everyone has reached the backyard they enter into a well manicured yard with a small swing set along with a deck. The area is serene nestled within a crowded urban neighborhood. The wooden fence stands tall which offers privacy.

"You really have a nice place here Cindy are you sure you want to leave? Nathan's place has changed quite a bit since you have been gone."

"I am ready to go home to my family. I miss everyone along with the family gatherings."

"I am very happy that I made it a place you want to come back to."

"In a half hour or so the kids should be ready for bed," Cindy whispers.

"Good idea let me know if you need my help."

"Brother, it is for you," Nathan yells from inside.

Jonathan looks at Cindy Lou then walks in a fast pace into the house.

"It is Detective Latham he has some good news and some bad news he says."

"What is the bad news?"

"Detective Latham will have to discuss that with you."

Jonathan walks down the hall to the living area. His heart begins to race. He pauses before he places the receiver to his ear.

"This is Jon."

"Mr. Johnson this is Detective Latham the investigator is unable to make it to Oklahoma County. This will delay the proceedings because we must have the legal document of probable cause. Now we can interrogate Mr. Badeaux with the possibility of a plea bargain that may result in a first degree murder charge in the death of Todd Johnson. We can also offer him a lesser charge of 1st degree manslaughter if he cooperates. The kidnapping charge will stand no matter what he admits to because we have found your daughter in his possession. I must commend you for your commitment to find your daughter's abductor otherwise we would never have met on these conditions. I have taken a written statement from your daughter. I will meet with Mr. Badeaux to secure a confession within the next hour. My hopes are that the plea deal will expedite the process. That is normal protocol when we attempt to resolve the case in the least amout of time. I will get back with you once Mr. Badeaux accepts a plea deal but at this moment he will be charged with first degree kidnapping in which he could serve the minimum of twenty years. I cannot give you a time frame in which this process will unfold; I can only advise you to stay near the phone for any updates."

"I appreciate your help Detective Latham."

"I will do everything in my power to expedite this case. Please get some rest. Goodnight."

Jonathan places the receiver onto its cradle. He continues to sit on the arm of the sofa and before long he drifts into a deep meditation. Melba steals close to him and wraps her arms around him.

"It is almost over honey just be still and know that he is God."

"I feel like my chest is about to explode."

"Are you in any pain? Can you breath?"

"No I just feel like I am about to lose control."

"CINDY," yells Melba. "Bring me some water. Your father does not feel well."

"What is the matter daddy?"

"I just feel like I cannot take this anymore."

Never Underestimate The Power of A Secret Place

"Daddy it is almost over. Angie will be coming home soon. We can stay here until we have gotten it all straightened out. We will not leave until Angie and her baby are with us."

"Take a deep breath Jon. Do you feel any chest pain?"

"No honey, I am just tired of this nonstop foolishness."

"Daddy it is what you make of it. If you have faith that God has brought you to this point then know that God will give you victory."

"I know Cindy."

"But daddy you do not act like you know it. You behave like Angie has just been abducted. You should rejoice. Have you called Nathan's Place to let them know that Angie has been found?"

"I have to do that. They will intercede on Angie's behalf."

"Call home right now daddy, here is the phone daddy please call home."

Jonathan dials the number. The phone begins to ring on the other end.

"Hello, Nathan's place."

"Mother?"

"Yes is this Jon?"

"Yes mother it is."

"How is everything son?"

"We found Angie."

"Son come home you have had another one of your spells."

"No mother we found her."

"Well who are we preparing for burial?"

"It is Todd. Yes, mother it is a long story. Todd was killed in an attempt to save Angie."

"No son you are mistaken Todd is here."

"There? You have got to be mistaken mother. Have you been drinking again?"

"Here speak to your uncle."

Never Underestimate The Power of A Secret Place

"Hello Uncle Jon."

"Todd?"

"Yes sir it is me."

"Where have you been?"

"I enlisted when I left home. Now I am a Master Sergeant in the Air Force."

"Why did you not contact us?"

"Dad said that he would not have anything further to do with me if I enlisted."

"Wait a minute; hold on do not hang up."

Jonathan covers the receiver.

"Go get Betty and brother while I stall him on the phone. Thanks for holding Todd."

"Is mom near?"

"Yes she is do you want me to get her?"

"Yeah, I heard she has cancer."

"She had cancer Todd."

"I heard you can never get rid of it."

"Who told you that?"

"A friend of mine."

"What does he do for a living?"

"He is a soldier."

"Does he have any experience in the medical field?"

"Uncle he could have heard it from a reputable source."

"Here is your mother and don't you dare share that nonsense with her."

"Yes sir."

"Here she is."

Jonathan hands the receiver to Betty.

"Hello son?"

"Yes it is me."

"Did you ever think about your parents? You had us worried about you. We thought you were dead."

"Uncle Arthur told me,"says Todd before he is interrupted.

"I do not give a damn what he says. I am your mother. You owe me the respect to call and let me know how you are doing."

"But mom I am grown."

"You will always be my child and you will answer to me for the rest of your life."

"Yes ma'am."

"We will be home in a few days and don't you dare go anywhere. Do you want to speak to your father?"

"Does he want to speak to me is the question."

"You are pig headed just like your uncle."

Jonathan looks perplexed. Betty hands the receiver to Nathan. Nathan takes a deep breath.

"Dad?"

"Yes son I am here."

"I am a Master Sergeant in the Air Force."

"I know."

"You know?"

"Yes, I received documents that detailed what process would be taken if you were killed in the line of duty. It was your signature so I assumed you had enlisted. That was five years ago what have you been doing since then?"

"I have been enlisted since the day I left. When I was recruited for my first mission I signed the release to have my remains forwarded to you. I came home to get your permission to commit another two years."

"Why does it matter now?"

"Because Dad I want to include you in all my decisions from now on. I really want to come home. I have a wife and a daughter that I want you to meet. I cannot wait to see everyone. Oh, Angie too. It is unbelievable how God has restored our family."

"Yes it is."

"Dad I also want to tell you that I am an Ordained Minister. I have earned a degree in Divine Ministry during my mission. I now serve as the Chaplain for the Air Force."

There is a pause.

"Dad?"

"I am here son."

"What have you got to say?"

"I am sorry."

"Dad you do not have to apologize. I am your son and you have every right to be concerned with by wellbeing. There were times when I wished I should have listened to you. But here I am safe at home again and from the looks of it I may never leave again."

"I will see you when I get home son."

"See you soon dad."

"I love you son."

"I love you too dad."

Nathan places the receiver on the cradle. He lets out a sigh of relief then pulls Betty to him.

"He is alive. Amen God is great! When I get home I am going to shake the rocks out of that boy's head."

"Not before I do," adds Jonathan. "Who is with the girls?"

Jonathan races down the hall. Frantically he looks for the children then from out of the corner of his eye he catches a glimpse of them.

"Little Nathan they are right on the edge of the house."

"Papa," they scream.

"What?"

"You ratted on us."

"I did no such thing."

"How dare you. Jon you will have hell to pay if you keep this up," warns Melba.

"I did not imagine anything would change anyway."

Never Underestimate The Power of A Secret Place

"Well it makes no sense to dig a deeper hole for yourself."

"Bedtime everyone," Cindy Lou yells.

"You heard that Mel it is time for bed."

"Stop it you old hoot."

"You know you love me."

"Daddy, please not in front of the girls."

"Who do you think taught me to say that?"

"Really daddy you are going to blame it on the girls."

"Well they did."

"You are going to get it," Lacey sings.

"Unlike you three I am an adult and I can say whatever I want."

Jonathan licks his tongue out at them then squints his eyes.

"Mommy," the triplets yell.

"Get ready for a bath. Pay no attention to your papa. Daddy, do you have to encourage the girls?"

"It is the least I can do."

"Mother, how do you put up with him?"

"I ask myself that every day."

"It is because you cannot get enough of me."

"Nate please get your brother."

"Brother trust me on this, you will ride Greyhound back to Louisiana if you keep this up."

"I rode up here in that contraption you call an automobile and I will suffer myself to ride it back home. My Angie will love to spend some time with the love of her life."

"We will have to follow close just in case she tries to bail," whispers Nathan.

"Unlike the others I have always had a special relationship with Angie," whispers Jonathan.

"What did you say Jon? Why do you always have to stir up strife? Is that a statement you want to retract?"

"Maybe so."

"Are you unsure mister?"

"Yes I want to retract that statement."

"I thought so."

Betty smirks at Melba while she nestles in her seat.

"How about drinks everyone?"

"Sure brother can you bring me something to relax? Not too much we have some important matters to discuss," Jonathan informs him.

"What do we have to talk about," asks Melba.

"You know Mel."

"No, I do not Jon."

Jonathan eases into the lounger next to Melba which was meant for one. Melba attempts to push him away.

"Daddy leave mother alone."

"This is *my* wife and I suggest you mind your own business young lady."

"Jon will you stop it."

"Stormy weather♫," he sings.

Everyone begin to laugh hysterically.

"Jon please!"

"That is what I intend to do."

"Goodness."

"Sit down you are not going anywhere you sweet chocolate morsel."

"Here we go. Jon have you been drinking again?"

"Of course not, love is in the air ♫," he sings.

Jon places his arm behind Melba's head so that she can relax.

Nathan brings out a tray of drinks and offers everyone a glass except Cindy Lou.

"Where is mine?"

"Someone has to keep an eye on the ankle biters," answers Jonathan.

Never Underestimate The Power of A Secret Place

"Daddy the name calling is uncalled for, besides they are your grandchildren."

"Must I repeat myself again? They are HIS grandchildren."

Jonathan points to Nathan.

"I will be happy to take them."

"What do you mean? You have already taken them."

"Can we change the subject? What did the detective say daddy?"

"Well... hold on that is the phone again."

Cindy Lou runs to answer the phone.

"Hello, Hello."

She returns the receiver to the cradle then waits in hope that it will ring again.

"Why do you stare at the phone?"

"Whoever called hung up before I could answer."

"Do you mean to say that if you stare at the phone long enough it will ring again?"

"No daddy. You can be so ridiculous sometimes."

"Come outside it will ring when someone decides to call."

They both return to join the others on the deck. Jonathan reveals the conversation that transpired with Detective Latham afterwards they sit in silence.

"We better turn in tomorrow will bring a new day. Just leave everything I can clean up tomorrow," instructs Cindy Lou.

"Nonsense it will take me no time at all."

"Mother it is not that much to clean."

"Let her be everything has to be clean before bedtime. She has not changed."

"I can get the rooms ready mother."

"Sweetheart we can get a motel room."

"No daddy I want you to stay here. The detective will contact you from this phone."

Never Underestimate The Power of A Secret Place

Cindy Lou enters the living area highlighting the arrangements for the night.

"The kids are in the triplet's room. Little Nathan has his own bed because to be quite honest he looks hairy to me. Uncle Nate and Aunt Betty can take the guest room. Daddy you can sleep in my bed with mother."

"No I can take the sofa; Cindy you can sleep in your room with Mel."

"Jon you know how your back acts up."

"Oh, one night will not kill me. Besides I could use a good massage when we get back Mel."

"We will see when we get back to the farm."

"I cannot wait."

"Daddy, mother how do you put up with him?"

"It is only by the grace of God."

"Here are some blankets for you."

"What is this?"

"Blankets to keep you warm daddy."

"The blankets are in girly colors."

"Of course daddy, I have three girls. What do you expect?"

"I apologize just hand me a pillow. I will be just fine."

"Here you are daddy."

"Of course now what is this?"

"It is a pillow."

"It looks like Angie's old pillow."

"Does everything have to be about Angie?"

"Sweetheart I did not know you felt that way."

"What way?"

"Do you resent your sister?"

"No daddy of course not, but Angie has been the center of our existence ever since her disappearance. Can we get back to normal?"

"By all means baby girl we can. Can the old man have a hug?"

Jonathan embraces Cindy Lou tight when she tries to pull away his grip intensifies.

"Daddy let go."

"Just a little while longer; it has been a long time since I have held you in my arms."

"Daddy this is enough already."

"I say when it is enough. Unforgettable♪," he begins to sing.

"Ugh, daddy please let me go."

"Alright then but we must have daddy time when we get back to Nathan's place."

"Daddy I never like to fish that was Angie's daddy time."

"Well you make the call and it is whatever you want on Cindy's daddy time."

"We will see daddy."

"Yes we will pumpkin. Give daddy a kiss."

Cindy Lou plants a kiss on his forehead after he bends down.

"Goodnight daddy."

"Goodnight baby girl."

Jonathan rests his head on the edge of the sofa while his feet dangle over the other end. Cindy Lou gives him another kiss on his forehead.

"I know you love your daddy," says Jonathan.

"Righto daddy," Cindy replies.

It is now morning and the triplets have been up for quite some time. Cindy Lou calls Juanita's to order breakfast.

"I need five complete breakfasts plates with everything also let me have four kid breakfasts with orange juice. Does the complete breakfast come with coffee? Great how long will it take? Okay, that is fine I understand. What is the damage? Fine I can smooch off my uncle he is good for it. You are welcome."

Never Underestimate The Power of A Secret Place

Cindy Lou places the phone receiver in the cradle and notices that the girls have surrounded their grandfather.

"Girls how long have you been up? Leave papa alone let him sleep. Oh my goodness! What have you girls done?"

"Granny said we can do it, answers Lacey."

"You painted his nails too?"

"Is he pretty mommy?"

"Cidney he is going to be so disappointed in you. Come with me into the kitchen. Girls follow me and help me with breakfast."

"Okay mommy; papa gonna like it," says Lindsay with a smile.

"We will have to see girls."

"Oh," screams Cindy. "Daddy you are awake. Let me help you get cleaned up for breakfast. I will get you a facecloth and…"

"I can take care of myself," argues Jonathan. "I am not that far gone yet."

"You look pretty papa."

"What does she mean by that?"

"Daddy, just stay right here and let me get a facecloth."

"I can imagine what they have done."

Melba enters the living room.

"Hurry someone get my camera," Melba yells. "I have got to get a picture of this."

"Mom please do not get daddy started this morning."

Melba runs to the back.

"I bet she was in on it. I knew it. That woman has allowed the enemy to infiltrate our marriage."

"Daddy, mother had no idea."

"She was in on it. I am all alone in this battle. But not for long I assure you. I may have lost this battle but I guarantee you I will not lose the war."

Snap, snap the camera flickers.

Never Underestimate The Power of A Secret Place

"I do believe that I bought that camera for you myself. I never thought you would use it against me."

"Stop being so dramatic Jon. You have taken so many pictures of me while I was asleep."

Melba begins to remove the makeup from Jonathan's face.

"Of course I did. You look so beautiful when you are asleep and so does the ankle biters. Sometimes that is the only time that I can have some peace and quiet."

The phone along with the doorbell rings within seconds of each other.

"I will get the phone and somebody can answer the door," Jonathan orders.

Everyone starts to scatter in different directions. Cidney reaches the phone before Jonathan.

"Hand papa the phone sweetie."

Cidney raises the receiver to Jonathan.

"Thank you angel now I want you to go and join your mother."

Jonathan takes a deep breath.

"Hello, yes this is Mr. Johnson. Of course we can get there in about an hour. Yes Detective we will see you soon. Brother," yells Jonathan. "We have got to get to the jail house this very minute. How soon can you get dressed?"

Nathan appears in the hall still in his night clothes.

"Give me about fifteen minutes."

"But I have breakfast daddy."

"Sweetheart I appreciate it but we have to get to the jail house."

"You better get dressed."

"I am dressed."

"Jon I have laid all your clothes on the bed; please wash up."

"I will wash up but it makes no sense to change clothes when I look perfectly fine."

"Daddy can you please try to be presentable."

Jonathan gets down on one knee. Cidney runs into his arms.

"How does papa look?"

"You look pretty papa."

"Did you hear that it was out of the mouth of babes."

"I give up," says Melba.

"Me too," says Cindy Lou. "Come on little ones the food is here get ready to eat."

Everyone except Jonathan makes their way to the dining area. Can someone get me a cup of coffee for the road?

"I can bring it in just a second daddy."

Jonathan walks to the bathroom where Nathan gets ready to shower.

"Boy you would think you were going on a date."

"Brother it never hurts to be presentable."

Jonathan ponders over the group of toothbrushes then finally just grabs one.

"I hope that is your tooth brush."

"I have you know everything in this house is mine."

"You do not impress me at all brother."

Jonathan takes a final spit then rinses the tooth brush before he places it back in its original place. He splashes water onto his face and grabs a towel without looking. He brushes his hair back with his fingers while he looks into the mirror.

"You are one handsome guy."

"Oh thank you brother I appreciate the compliment," Nathan says from the shower.

Jonathan leans over the toilet then pushes the handle down.

"Brother," Nathan yells. "Why do you have to be so immature?"

Jonathan exits the bathroom refreshed then walks to the living area. Cindy Lou stands at the entrance with his coffee.

"Thanks baby, he plants a soft kiss on her forehead."

"Is Uncle Nate okay?"

"Of course he just happened to see his reflection in the mirror."

"Daddy!"

"It is the truth. He looks quite frightful in the mornings. I do not know how Betty does it."

Jonathan sits on the sofa with his legs crossed and looks to be without a care in the world. Cindy Lou walks into the dining area then leans toward her mother.

"Mother has daddy always been like this?"

"Ever since I have known the old hoot he has been like that."

"Why did you marry him?"

"Because he is the most loving, unselfish man I have ever met. Is he crazy? Hell yes, but I love me some crazy him."

"I heard that," says Jonathan. "You are going to regret every word you said."

"I already do Jon; I already do."

Melba looks up before she could realize that Jonathan is standing behind her then he plants a soft kiss on her neck.

He whispers, "I will be back. I think we are going to tie up some loose ends on Angie's case."

"Well I want to come."

"No stay here just in case things get hairy. It does not make any sense for all of us to go to jail."

"I have told you time and time again if you get arrested again I will not bail you out."

"Woman you will tear the bars off the jail house to get me out."

"See if I do."

"You know you cannot live a day without your knight in shining armor," he winks.

"Daddy, where did you learn that?"

"I learned it from the girls."

"Girls, where did you learn that from?"

"From the bedtime stories Uncle Nate reads to us."

"Now you see how he has filled those girl's heads with that foolishness."

"Jon go on please have a seat."

"Go on daddy, uncle should be ready in a minute."

"Sometimes I wonder if you are the fruit of my loins."

"Daddy, please go have a seat until uncle is ready."

Nathan enters the kitchen.

"Uncle, will you please take daddy with you NOW?"

"After I have some breakfast then we can leave."

"Breakfast, brother bring something along I will drive."

"Can you put something together for me Mel?"

"Sure Nate."

"So that is how it works?"

"Daddy you never eat breakfast."

"You never have Jon," Melba agrees.

"That is beside the point. You treat him far better than you treat me."

"How Jon? I have practically raised you. You would be dead by now if I did not tell you which way is north."

"I am quite capable of raising myself."

"Here is a sandwich Nate. Would you like one honey?"

"Of course not you know I do not eat breakfast."

"Why do I ever try?"

"Because you must obey all of your vows Mel, I have told you so many times but you do not listen. Betty never behaves this way with brother."

"I must leave you to your own devices brother," says Nathan before he leaves the dining room.

"Jon, that is because she is not married to you. You probably would not live too long married to Betty."

"Just like you I would have Betty wrapped around my finger."

"Go daddy, uncle is in the car. Hurry before he leaves you."

"He cannot leave me I got the keys."

Jonathan wiggles the keys in front of them.

"Daddy hurry so that we can find out if Angie will be released today."

"You are right I have to stay focused. I shall return."

"Please do not remind us."

"I heard that," Jonathan replies before he leaves out the front door.

Jonathan quickens his pace toward the car. Nathan sits in the car devouring his sandwich.

"I cannot wait to get this over with it has begun to drive me mad."

"I understand brother how you must feel."

Jonathan starts up the engine then he backs out of the drive. He observes Shawn as he mows the grass while Jimmy tends to someone's hair.

"Do you think I could find work for them at Nathan's Place?"

"I can think of a couple of jobs myself brother."

"So can I," says Jonathan.

They both wave at the two before they drive away and the boys' wave back.

"I wonder if their father is in their lives, questions Nathan. It is unfortunate that the slaves were bred for their physical attributes. The damage may be irreversible."

"I am almost quite sure it is. Bondage is the most dehumanizing system invented by man. May God have mercy on us all."

"We are not responsible."

"I beg to differ," says Jonathan. "Nothing with such magnitude can exist without a unified force. Doing nothing makes one guilty along with those who commit the atrocity."

"Why have you become such an advocate for the injustice of the Africans? Is it for Angie's sake?"

"No brother it is for my own. Had not God deemed it necessary to clothe me in this skin I consider my secret place. I too would have suffered the ill begotten horrors of greed and hate. I too am of African descent although sometimes I forget."

"That is a sign of old age my brother."

"I am sure it is not a road that I will travel alone."

The brothers look at each other then begin to laugh. They continue on until they arrive at the County Jail.

"It is remarkable how quiet it is for a Sunday afternoon," Jonathan observes.

Both men now stand before the barred counter in wait for someone to arrive.

"Hello," Nathan yells. "Is there anyone here?"

"Maybe someone forgot to lock up like you sometimes do."

"Why must you be so judgmental?"

"I just state the facts. It appears that the loss of one's memory can be a quite bit unsettling."

Nathan begins to walk toward the entrance.

"Brother someone approaches," says Jonathan while he motions Nathan to return.

He looks through the bars but no one appears. Jonathan glances at his feet.

"Please do not leave me now brother."

Nathan places his arm around Jonathan.

"I will never leave you brother. Even despite the fact that you are one major annoyance to the family. We should take a seat it is going to be a long day."

The brothers' sit in silence and after fifteen minutes someone approaches the counter.

"May I help you?"

Never Underestimate The Power of A Secret Place

"Yes," Jonathan jumps from his seat. "I am here to see Detective Latham."

"Does he expect you?"

"Yes he is expecting us."

Jonathan also points to Nathan. Jonathan's heart rate begins to increase. His cheeks begin to turn red. He bows his head to pray in silence.

"*Lord I know you are omnipotent. I stand on your promise that my baby girl will return to me today. I thank you in advance. Hosanna Lord.*"

He takes a deep breath then to his left a door opens and a woman appears in uniform. Her hair is dishwater brown her eyes are a sky blue. Jonathan passes her after he gives her a nod. Her large frame blocks most of the entrance. Nathan grabs the door then motions for her to go ahead of him. She takes him in then walks off to leave him behind. The woman points to the briefing room where they met the other day. Jonathan is already seated in the same seat he sat the day before. Nathan stands then paces the small area he is allotted. Soon Detective Latham enters the room. He closes the door behind him before he motions Nathan to take a seat. Deputy Latham sits on the edge of the table opposite of the both of them. He looks as though he has not slept all night.

"I must advise you that during the interrogation of Mr. Badeaux he experienced a massive heart attack in which he did not regain consciousness. I have been under investigation myself in regards to my practices during the interrogation. The body was expedited to the coroner's office to be examined for any possible physical injuries that may have occurred during the interrogation. In my defense there were no findings. The examination was extended to reveal that Mr. Badeaux's abrupt death was the result of massive heart attack."

"I am sorry that you were subjected to that type of treatment," replies Jonathan.

Never Underestimate The Power of A Secret Place

"It is departmental protocol. Fortunate for us the court proceedings have been terminated. We were unable to legally take your daughter's child into state custody. The child was returned to his mother just a few minutes ago. I am sorry that you had to wait while we examine the child before we return him to the custody of his mother. Not only will we release your daughter but your healthy grandson also."

The deputy stands and extends his hand to both men who begin to weep.

Nathan pulls his brother close and whispers, "You have a son brother."

Jonathan wipes his eyes before he stands. He attempts without success to reserve his emotions but he begins to sob when Angie Lou walks into the room. She walks into the arms of them both for what it seems like eternity. Detective Latham takes the baby from the unidentified female secretary before she exits. He begins to sway the baby from side to side to calm the baby. Jonathan reaches in to pull the baby away from the detective. He holds him close while he pours kisses all over his face.

"What is his name?"

"Marlon."

"Marlon Badeaux?"

"No daddy it is Marlon French."

"He looks just like you daddy."

"I hope he gets some color."

"Daddy he is your color. I would have named him after you but Shawn's middle name is Marlon."

"Perhaps we can change it later," says Jonathan.

"No daddy. That is his name and you have to accept it. Can we split," asks Angie.

"Of course we can split," says Jonathan.

He kisses Angie Lou on the forehead.

"Do you have everything?"

"Yes, daddy I have everything."

They take each other in for a minute then embrace once more.

"I thought we were about to leave? The family wants to see Angie, we better get home," Nathan reminds them.

Detective Latham stands in the hall while they exit the briefing room.

"I just need a signature from you Mr. Johnson to acknowledge that we have released this young lady into your custody after her lengthy abduction."

"Where do I sign?"

"Sign where the x is."

Detective Latham places the clipboard in front of Jonathan then hands him a pen.

"Let me take the baby brother."

"Not on your life."

Jonathan scribbles something legible on the paper.

"Thank you, I wish you nothing but the best for your future."

"Thank you Detective Latham for your hard work it is very much appreciated."

When they exit the County jail doors the skies blue overcast does not reveal a cloud for miles. The leaves rustle in the cool spring wind. Angie covers the baby's head with a blanket. Nathan climbs into the driver's seat while Jonathan takes the passenger seat. Angie Lou climbs into the backseat of the car.

"Give me the baby daddy."

"He is safe with me."

Jonathan examines the baby for his birthmark.

"Yes, there it is; he is a Johnson."

"Of course he is brother."

"Why have you not begun to drive?"

"I cannot turn the ignition."

"Why can't you turn the ignition?"

"It requires a key to turn the ignition brother."

Never Underestimate The Power of A Secret Place

"Oh, hold the baby."

Jonathan searches his pockets then retrieves the keys. Nathan returns the baby to Jonathan before he starts the car. He backs out of the parking lot at a slow pace.

"How do you feel about Timmie's death," Jonathan asks.

"I am sorry he died but I do not want to ever see him again."

"I am sorry I could not find you but I looked everywhere I thought you could possibly be. I searched every inch of the Badeaux's property but I could not find you."

"Daddy I was there. They placed me in an open grave and covered me with dirt. I thought I was going to die but Timmie dug me out then he hid me in the barn after everyone left. When his father found out that I was still alive he tried to hang me."

Jonathan stares straight ahead.

"I have some good news, Todd is alive."

"No daddy he is dead; I saw Timmie kill him."

"Baby girl that was not Todd it was someone else."

"But it was Uncle Nate's truck. I am sure that it was not Uncle Nate."

"I have no idea who he is either. He deserves a decent burial at Nathan's Place that is for certain."

"We still have the truck at our place."

"That old truck still runs?"

"Yes, uncle it was our home for a long time."

"How long have you been here?"

"We have been here a couple of years. I began to work at the restaurant to pay for our room. Timmie left to go home not too long ago to get more money. Then when we got back we got a place of our own."

"Did you try to get away when he went home?"

"No, he took me with him. He never leaves me alone. Before I had the baby he would sit outside of the motel in the truck and watch me clean rooms. Then when I had the baby he kept the baby

Never Underestimate The Power of A Secret Place

while I worked in the restaurant. He said that he would kill the baby if the authorities ever came to look for him."

Nathan pulls into the drive.

"Uncle, slow down."

"What is it?"

"I need to get out."

"For what?"

"Umm, I know that cat."

"Which one?"

"He is the one who is cutting the grass."

"Shawn," Jonathan asks?

"How do you know his name?"

"I met them a few days ago."

"He offered to bring him to Nathan's Place and give him a job," interjects Nathan.

"Oh, daddy you have a heart of gold."

"And that is the way it is."

"Oh goodness," Nathan sighs.

"Let me out daddy."

Angie climbs out of the car.

"Give me the baby."

"What for?"

"I want him to see his baby."

"This is his baby?"

"Yes daddy did you think it was Timmie's?"

"I guess that was my conclusion."

"Timmie was afraid of me, I told him I would turn him in to the authorities so he would just touch me sometimes."

"Why did you have to tell me that," Jonathan winces?

"Oh, sorry daddy."

"I am very proud of you. I just want to ask you one question."

"Yes daddy?"

"Why did you make those charges on my card?"

"Brother!"

"I am just curious. Could you have just called?"

"Daddy I did call but every time grandpa Opio answered the phone he could not hear what I said, then granny Raffy got on the phone then granny Linda until I finally just gave up."

"You have to understand they have grown up in the ages."

"I hoped that you would come to the restaurant again to look for your charge card and license. I was almost right. Daddy I have to go."

Jonathan exits the car to watch Shawn who now has recognized Angie Lou.

"Do not stay too long the family wants to see you too."

A few days later…

"That was your mother they just landed in New Orleans. Todd should be there at the airport to pick them up. Is everything packed and loaded on the truck?"

"Yes daddy we are ready."

"I will ride with Uncle Nathan," says Cindy Lou.

"Are you sure ladybug? The three of us can ride together and catch up on some missed time."

"No daddy, Angie can ride with you so you both can catch up on missed time. Besides I think you will need some time to get to know Shawn."

"What is there to know?"

"Daddy!"

"One wrong move and he will ride in the bed of the truck the entire ride home. I do not want to hear it. That is my baby girl."

"Not anymore daddy."

"That young pup does not have a chance with me. I will have the triplets erase him from the foundation of this earth."

"Daddy did you not tell his mother you would take good care of him? Do you want her to come to Nathan's Place to look for you? You know how a mother is about her babies."

Never Underestimate The Power of A Secret Place

"She is pretty large; a force to be reckoned with. I just hope she enjoys that tuna can on wheels."

Jonathan waves at Jorene.

"I wonder if she could be related to your mother."

"You never know daddy."

"Well it is time to get on the road."

Jonathan climbs into the driver's seat of Nathan's old truck. He glances at Angie Lou and Shawn huddled in the corner of the passenger's seat.

"Mr. Johnson, do you need me to help you drive?"

"Nonsense this is a man's truck. Do you even have a license?"

"No sir."

"Then there will be no driving for you."

Shawn pulls Angie Lou closer then gives her a light kiss on the lips.

"I tell you what you drive the first leg of the trip," Jonathan orders. "At least you will make it half way."

Jonathan exits the truck; he walks around to the passenger side of the truck then opens the door abruptly. The two are engaged in a heated kiss. Jonathan grabs Shawn by the shirt and throws him to the ground.

"Let me make something very clear to you son. You will respect my daughter in my presence."

"I am sorry Mr. Johnson. I just love Angie that's all."

"Your daddy never told you to beware of the girl's father?"

"I don't know my old man "

"You will get to know me very well," Jonathan huffs. "Here are the keys."

Jonathan hops into the passenger seat then pulls Angie Lou close to him. She lays her head on his shoulder just like she did when she was a young girl. Shawn jumps into the driver's seat.

"Man this is nice."

"You like it," asks Jonathan?

"Yes sir."

"It is yours. I finally get a chance to get back at brother for all the shenanigans he conspired."

Shawn turns the key in the ignition of the truck. The engine roars until it turns into a low purr.

"Nice."

Shawn changes the gears before he pulls out of the drive. Jonathan waves at Jorene.

"Wave at your mother this could possibly be the last time she will see you alive."

"Aww naw Mr. Johnson, I plan to come back to get my old lady and my little brother when I get my own pad."

Jonathan smiles while he rests his cheek on Angie Lou's forehead. She snores into the crevice of his neck.

"I want to thank you for what you have done for both of my daughters."

"Ain't it crazy how I knew both of them even though I didn't know they were sisters. You know I was going to come for my son even if I had to get hairy with that old man. The night the fuzz showed up we were on our way to bust a move over to their pad. She was supposed to call me when he crashed but she never dropped a dime."

"It appears that everything was in God's plan."

"You know Mr. Johnson you don't talk like the white people around here."

"White people," Jonathan mocks.

"I mean you know the caucasian persuasion."

Jonathan shakes his head.

"I was born and raised in New York."

"How did you get way down there in Louisiana? Ain't New York at the top of the map?"

"I guess you can say that."

Never Underestimate The Power of A Secret Place

"Well lay it on me; you dig that's what cats do. We might as well be cool."

"Excuse me?"

"Don't sweat it. I'm just tryin to get to know you dude."

2
SEARCH FOR YOUR SECRET PLACE

"Well if you must know it all began in the early 1900's. Our intentions were never to become slave owners; quite naturally we have long anulled that notion. During my studies I read that slavery does not represent democracy."

Now the story begins…
"Brother you would not believe the atrocities that I have witnessed at the hands of our own brethren. It was as if I had visited hell," recounts Jonathan.
"Tell me once again your account of this treachery."
"While Nathan and I searched for the whereabouts of a cotton mill we encountered a rather wooded area that appeared deserted. I began to hear someone ramble at the top of their voice. I realized an auction was in place. When we drew near to the area I witnessed a group of men of our resemblance who appeared to be in deep discussion. There was at least one man and two children with their mother of African descent bound in chains on a platform huddled close together. The young lad had this faraway look on his face like he had seen a ghost. The woman wept like mad while she held tight to the young lad. The man looked forlorn while he

was turned for inspection. He said nothing in his defense. Our brethren approached the platform then begin to separate them. The woman lets out this awful scream. Then there was left the young lad on the platform. He just stood there and appeared horrified."

"Nathan begins his way through the trees which alerted the brethren of our presence. They approached Nathan with guns drawn to take aim at him. I rushed before him to make my presence known. They acknowledged me before they inquired about our business there. They asked if the negra was in my charge. I regained my awareness of our whereabouts. Slavery had not been entirely eradicated as I had imagined. I must be cautious of my discourse, I thought to myself. I replied, 'Yes brethren I am in charge of this negra.' Nathan does not acknowledge to me that he is in accord with my activities. I recognize that Nathan is intrigued with the young lad, so I ask the price of the young lad. The brethren refuse to give me an offer so I offer them a generous compensation for the young lad. They are baffled by the offer so I offer them a price for the young lass hidden behind a large oak tree. She looks frightened. I am at loss for words for she is the most beautiful blue eyed African that I have ever seen. Nathan takes notice of her but says nothing. My offer was meager for I do not know of my intentions for the boy; except to bring him to the orphanage. The brethren without hesitation accept my offer for the young girl also."

"Brother, are you telling me that have contributed to the purchase of a human being?"

"Brother I know what it may appear to you, but I had no other viable option but to shelter these little ones from the cruelties of slavery. I once read that often our deeds are a direct result of who we are. Therefore I considered the plight of the little ones. Nathan was very disturbed by what he witnessed."

"Would you be brother?"

"Of course I would but he has distanced himself from me. I thought I was morally justified to save those two but he differs with me. We never disagree on anything."

"Well there is a first for everything."

"I am quite sure there is but I thought I knew Nathan in more depth. He is not just my friend but he is like a brother."

"Only God knows the depth of a man's character. I am sure he will come around. Where is he?"

"He has taken leave for the day. His desire is to find a home for the little ones."

"I am sure he will."

"It is my prayer. Where is father?"

"He is in the study. Do not disturb him with your shenanigans. He is troubled with you already."

"What is the reason? Has he not encouraged us all to follow our dreams? Has he not inquired of us on numerous occasions, what is life without dreams? What do you think brother is it unreasonable that I wish to follow my dreams?"

"No, brother but it is very irrational to dream to become a farmer," he chuckles. "Why bother."

"I am an outdoorsman unlike you cooped up in this house to chase father's every beckon call. So, you consider a lawyer more profitable than a farmer? Is that what you have implied?"

"Of course not, who am I to imply that?"

"Both serve the common good. The cost of justice comes with a price just like every morsel that we consume," Jonathan challenges. "Is one more significant than the other?"

"It depends upon what you are in need of. Our desires are to bring equality and education to all would you not agree?"

"I agree. The burden rests on our shoulders to save the world; each of us in our own unique manner. That is our heritage; the hand we have been dealt."

"You can always trump the hand you have been dealt," replies Arthur. "I am sure you have at some point in your life."

"What do you insinuate brother?"

"Just that human beings are not perfect. We are unsound; prone to make mistakes or even to take detours like I have mentioned."

"Why are you so divisive in regards to my pursuits?"

"It is your selfish dreams that tear at the heart of our dear father. Is it enough that he has lost his wife?"

"You talk like there is no one to care for him. I can never replace mother and you know it. I am not a loss to our father. He will recognize that my endeavors will bring honor and wealth to our family."

"How do you imagine that will come to pass?"

"During my studies I have realized that we could increase profits in the cotton industry if we purchased acreage in the south to grow our own cotton then export it to other countries or import it to our own factory."

"Who would manage the farm? You have no knowledge of agriculture dear brother."

"I have read somewhere that we learn by doing. Nathan and I discussed it and…"

"Nathan," questions Arthur.

"Yes, Nathan."

"But he is a city boy; he never wants to get his hands dirty."

"That is not true he has taught the Africans to read and they have become quite fluent with the English language. They have become the most efficient workers in the factory."

"So when does he have the time to teach them? He works hours on end in the factory himself. He is our most knowledgeable machine operator trainer."

"Father has allowed him to teach the young lads at the orphanage. Father believes that education is the vehicle by which we engage with one another. It intrigues me the relationship Nathan and I share. We often do not say a word yet we communicate our thoughts very clear. I am amazed at our differences yet the likeness we share."

"Brother you have always strayed from mainstream."

"Please explain yourself."

"You never dwelled with your own kind. You are like mother. You both are eager to examine life far beyond its mere existence. I think that is why mother died so young, so rich and full of life. Father and I are quite different creatures. We accept life at face value along with its intriguing nature. We wait for the tide to turn to examine what it brings. Do not consider it an insult; it is just that we are cut from different cloths. Maybe that is why you feel the need to travel so much."

"During my travels I have gained the breadth and depth of wisdom to overcome ignorance. I can no longer judge others through the narrowed lens of my own experiences."

"That is my point you must determine the authenticity of your thoughts before you acknowledge them as sound."

"I am quite confident of my intentions; yet it reassures me to know that someone with likewise experiences have come to the same conclusion. Your disdain of my conquest for truth troubles me. You are a legal advisor; you should embrace my quest for truth."

"I just advise you against the road traveled by mother. You will spend yourself empty in attempts to save the world."

"Can we return to the subject at hand?"

"Be my guest."

"Many of the Africans have complained about the factory. The tireless long hours to spin the cotton into thread can be exhaustive. The odor from the dyes tends to make the women ill and the northeastern weather wears on their bodies. Some simply cannot acclimate to the harsh winter months. Nathan mentioned that many of them are acquainted with agriculture. We are financially capable to secure enough land to increase the supply of cotton for our factory. We will become self sufficient to produce, manufacture and market our own product."

"It sounds inconceivable but will we be able to manage a farm and the factory? Where will we get the replacements?"

"I have discussed it with Nathan and he suggests that we secure the slaves that are auctioned in the south. We can transport them to the orphanage where you my brother can legalize their rights to freedom. Father will allow them to receive an education at the orphanage so that they are prepared for a better life. Our mother will be proud to know that the orphanage will be used as an instrument for more than shelter for the less unfortunate. We can allow them to determine if they want to live in the city or work on the farm. Of course we will have challenges once they return to the south. I am certain you can finagle your way around the legal system to maintain their rights to freedom. I trust God will meet their needs."

"Am proud to say you are my brother. Hurry now, do not waste any time send for father."

Jonathan retreats to his father's study.

"Father, may I interrupt?"

"Of course you may. How was your expedition? Before you begin I want you to know that Veldka had informed me of your intentions to venture out. I was not open to her suggestions but nonetheless I would like to honor my wife's wishes. I assumed that I was aware of the family's financial estate but to my surprise Veldka revealed accounts that contained finances she secured for your business venture. You do not only have my blessings but also the monetary support for this venture. I would like to hear more of your plans for the investment if you will."

"Yes, father. You are aware that I have travelled with Nathan this harvest season to secure cotton for the factory and during our excursion Nathan revealed to me a partnership that he would like to secure with our family."

"You are aware that Nathan is family."

"Yes father but I do not think that Nathan is quite convinced himself. Now with the passing of our dear mother he finds it difficult to accept the fact that he has been legally adopted."

"He does not appear to accept me as his father if I should say so myself."

"No father he just has a preference for mother like myself. Everything appeared to be a trivial experience to share with you in comparison to the delight you take with Arthur."

"Are you to imply that I displayed favoritism among you?"

"No father, however we felt that our interests appeased mother more than you. You have been an excellent father to us all."

"Why do you think Nathan never comes around anymore? I rarely see him at the factory."

"I think he grieves the loss of our mother."

"Aren't we all? Enough of that, now why are you here?"

"To present my proposal to you father for approval."

"Nonsense you have Veldka's approval. It is all you have ever needed."

"No sir, it would mean the world to me to have your blessing."

"When have you ever needed my blessing until now?"

"Always father but I never wanted to disturb you. Mother was always available to the children. That was her mission to give all children an opportunity for a better life. It is because of you father that she was able to continue to care for all the freed children. It was your support that provided the children with the means to survive."

"Father I have read in my studies not long ago that when a people is free of inhumane treatment the human race advances."

"I have always taken pride in your thirst for literature Jonathan. That was your Rafael's doing. Nathan the same he is very knowledgeable of politics. He possesses the tenacity of a world leader."

"Yes father he does. He is the reason this proposal will be successful."

"Tell me more."

"Well father, I must mention that Nathan invited me to travel with him to purchase cotton for the factory. In doing so we became entangled with the idea to raise cotton ourselves. We examined the process to harvest cotton during our journey while we were hired to work in the fields."

"Whatever happened to the funds that Veldka provided Nathan for the business venture?"

"We were not exactly honest with the plantation owners; we appeared poverty stricken. Our plight was lifted when I received a notable invitation from the Master of the plantation. Unlike Nathan although slavery has been deemed unconstitutional he was placed in a slave quarter. Nathan worked in the fields among the cotton pickers while I oversaw the fields upon a stallion with rifle in hand. It pained me to think if I would be forced to make use of it and it occurred to me that I am a man of honor and it is upon that honor I should consider the outcome of my decisions. It reminds me of my moral obligation to be mindful of the snares set before me. Although my brethren may not count my actions against me it is still my heavenly father's judgment that rests upon me. Much to my avail I was relinquished of my duties without an incident. Nevertheless one morning I witnessed the Master's dealing with a minor offense. It was reported that a freed man stole food from the field. The fieldsman determined his punishment to have the freed man taken to the slaughter to have his hand dismembered. It was the most unbearable sight I have ever witnessed. I have often wondered why we set pitfalls before our brethren and I have read that one does it to elevate himself in hopes that his brethren will be abased. I have found that it eludes the most noble of us all.

Father, it is not the act of fieldwork that is the death of man but the system of bondage itself."

"How so son?"

"Well father if a man toils in a land that does not yield profits for himself how true will he be to his trade? A man must yield a return on his efforts to be genuine to himself and his trade. The slave master has emptied the Africans of their merit. How long can anyone live in such degradation? I am appalled at the very thought of slavery. Never will I purchase a human being to enslave in which God has fashioned into a free creation. How did mankind inherit such ignorance?"

"Please continue with your account of the events."

"Forgive me father. No one appeared to concern themselves with the well being of the freed man; while he bled profusely I became afraid for his life. I completed the severance of his hand from his wrist so that I could proceed to decrease the loss of blood. I then bandaged the wound. May I offer my graciousness to you father for your investment in medical school; forbid that your investment should be for not. I continued to hear the freed man's piercing cries throughout the night. It was required of him to continue his duties regardless of his condition the following day. I found myself unable to take it any longer. I insisted that the master render medical treatment to the freed man. I informed him of my origin and also my intentions to report him for his vicious acts against a freed man."

"What was the outcome?"

"The master's order was that I be removed from the plantation without threat or harm. Nathan was surprisingly removed also without harm. More investigation of the cotton farm operations was much needed. Nathan was distraught himself with the turn of events. He fretted the entire journey of our return to the city. The only joy that I have seen in his eyes is the two youth that we brought with us on our return. He spends quite a bit of time with them like they were his own."

"Son I believe that Nathan has a connection with the lad."

"How so father?"

"He was once a child of a slave himself before your mother took hold of him."

"What did you say? Nothing has enlightened me more than what I have experienced in my travels south. I never could imagine how any two human beings could treat one another so savagely without even a cause. Not once to consider our creator's purpose for each of us. It disgusts me more even today the concept of slavery."

"How so son?"

"It puzzles me that biblical teachings reveal God's distaste of bondage in the early testament if I am not mistaken."

"You are correct."

"Throughout biblical literature there were revelations of many incidences of various inflictions in which people were liberated. And it puzzles me that many decades later with our profound reverence to religious obedience we have somehow misinterpreted God's revelation in regards to slavery. I remember a story told to me when I was a lad. God's intent was to bring the Hebrews out of bondage of ungodly men. Although God's existence was apparent among most of the people it was the blatant disregard of Pharaoh and his followers that led to the destruction of Egypt. We represent a similar mindset that will eventually ruin the world's chances of living in God's promises today."

"How so Jonathan?"

"The Hebrews became indoctrinated to the lifestyle of the Egyptians. They lived in those conditions for thousands of years if I am correct."

"Yes please continue."

"I have come to the conclusion that it was God's quest to renew their minds and spirits with true wisdom. What intrigued me the most was the mindset the Hebrews developed while they were in bondage. Their desire for the lifestyle of the Egyptians outweighed their need for a relationship with God. It perplexes me that bondage is the vehicle that drives destruction for all mankind."

"Do you suggest son that we are all doomed to destruction?"

"I am afraid to say we are."

"Nonsense son we are Godly men ourselves."

"Have we ever been challenged to defend our allegiance to our God? Not at all, we have only experienced the luxury to acknowledge God. Those who perceive a God that is so abstract that they believe he can produce a tangible existence in their lives such as freedom from bondage it's they who will more likely reap the promises of God than those of us who never made that connection with God. It is for those of us that I have concern. I am most certain that it will be impossible to regain the reins of bondage in any form if it ever were to be."

"Jonathan, why does slavery trouble you so? You were so far removed from its existence."

"Father, we are all fallen men bound by one flesh and one spirit. If one perish we all perish, when will you ever learn?"

"I know more than I ever want to know Jonathan and that is more than enough for me."

"Mother never spoke of Nathan's parents to Arthur or me. We both assumed that Nathan was orphaned at birth. There were so many families that resemble our racial dynamics here in New York. I did not think that Nathan actually knew his biological mother."

"He is very aware of his mother's identity and his brother Nathaniel."

"I do not remember mother mentioning any siblings of Nathans'."

Never Underestimate The Power of A Secret Place

"Veldka took Nathan quite often to visit his mother before she died. She was a frail little girl that Veldka found in a boarding room of one of the African factory workers. They were afraid that she would die so they called for your mother. Mary, his mother did not have wages to pay the doctor so Veldka sent my father to visit Mary. He found that she was with child and would die if she did not receive adequate medical attention. Of course Veldka placed her in the finest medical facility until Mary could recover. Soon she delivered the child but she was too ill to care for him. You were yet a month old. Veldka was engorged with milk which allowed enough milk for Nathan and you. The both of you would embrace each other while you nursed. You both were inseparable throughout your youth. Nathan's mother requested to see him often. Veldka took him to the hospital when she requested to see him. She held him for hours before she gave him the name Nathan. Mary asked your mother to care for him until she was well. But when her health took a turn for the worst she insisted that Veldka release Nathan to her sister's family. It was unfortunate for they did not have enough room for another child. When the hospital officials realized that Veldka had taken custody of Nathan they forced her to place her name as legal guardian of Nathan. Your mother had the natural and adoptive birth certificate for Nathan. She gave them to him before her death. Veldka informed me that he shredded the natural birth certificate. He is very angry that his father left his mother alone to die. I imagine the death of Veldka has annihilated him. He has begun to protect himself from further loss. He just needs time to heal then you shall have your brother back to his everyday mischief."

"My hope is that it will be soon, father."

"Now tell me your plans son."

"Father there is an estate in Louisiana that I would like to purchase to produce cotton for the factory."

"Louisiana? Can you not consider any other state besides Louisiana? Why so far?"

"The soil is filled with rich nutrients to grow cotton. Our intentions are to harvest our own cotton and transport it to the factory to be processed. We can separate the seed from the cotton then store the highest quality seeds to be sown for the next harvest. I will train the farmers to collect the seed with the least damage then place them in a cool dry place for storage. I plan to make an offer for a plantation north of New Orleans in a few days."

"Please do not allow me to hinder your travels. Have a safe trip."

"Thank you for the encouragement father. It means everything to me. I must find Nathan to share the good news."

Jonathan leaves his father study in search for Nathan.

"Brother, please wake up. I must speak with you in regards to our plans to purchase the plantation."

"Brother I trust you with my life," answers Nathan.

"How foolish it is of you not to take interest."

"Not now brother allow me time to grieve for our mother."

"When will you be done with it?"

"How callous can you be? It is our mother who is no longer with us. She will never return to us again."

"I understand but I have come to accept the loss of our dear mother. She remains with us in spirit."

"Please leave me be."

"I must tell you something."

"Can it not wait brother?"

"I must tell you before I forget."

"You must get our head examined."

"I will brother but for now I must tell you my dream."

"I am listening."

"Then face me so that I know that you are sincere."

"Sincerity resides in the heart."

Never Underestimate The Power of A Secret Place

Jonathan climbs over Nathan then lies down so that they are face to face.

"Brother your hygiene is not quite up to par."

"Never mind that I have something marvelous to share with you."

"Tell me if you must."

"I had a dream brother."

"You do say."

"Please brother it is vital to our success."

"Carry on."

"In the dream I begin to walk along a long dark hall. In my arms there was a baby of my complexion and a young lad of your complexion who walked along side me. All of the sudden, I heard the sound of a train barreling down my road. I say to myself, is it conceivable for a train to travel along a gravel road? I exit the house in search of the train and I appear to be positioned on the roof of the house. Yet I stand on the front terrace. From there I have an aerial view of the properties that surround my house. On the outskirts of the property it appears the grass has been ripped from the earth. There are trees of various heights and widths encircled around the other properties. Some of the trees are tall some short but for the most part the tops of the trees have been cut away. Where there were once houses are now empty lots and the debris was nowhere to be found. It appeared that a tornado had ripped everything from its foundation. I observe the damage to the property that surrounds my house. I take notice that the number of livestock had multiplied even though I knew not the previous number. The gardens were overturned where it revealed seeds that were previously planted; they too had multiplied. The vegetation was beyond belief in vibrant colors of green, red and yellow. Everything appeared to be lively in comparison to the other properties. Then a voice spoke to me and it said, 'Where are you enemies now?' "I have no idea what to think of this revelation."

3
NOT JUST A PHYSICAL PLACE

In Louisiana...

"Well Mistah Johnson had ya gotten here soona you'd be sittin real pretty on that ole Gourdeau's plantation. Now here is what I can do fer ya. If you will look down yonder, you see that ole barn," Mr. Rey points.

"That tin roof on stilts? How can you tell that once was a barn Mr. Rey?"

"Please use yo imagination, it is located next to a beautiful pond; not too far fo yo cattle to water. You can stock it if ya like. Theres a lot of benefit from this here piece of land. Now look ova yo shoulda to yo far right. That slave quartas is included in tha sale of this property. There is tha last slave quarta. It is a historical site if ya really think of it. Of course that big house is tha most attractive home in tha parrish. This could be income a producin property if ya know what I mean? Now tha price is mo than reasonable considerin tha draught an all. I put a no trespassin sign on that old barn so ya don't have no problems with them gypsies."

"There are gypsies here you say?"

"For years, ya see when tha slave ships come through the port most of this land was farmed by tha slaves. I'm sho ya know the history of tha south."

Never Underestimate The Power of A Secret Place

"Please do tell."

"Well ya see afta slavery been outlawed many of the Africans squats here an now we have this lot we call gypsies. They has they own medicine, they own language, they own food an religion. They use ta meet on occasions unda that there tin roof ta have ceremonies befo we took control of tha property. When them gypsies was baptizing in that there pond I tell ya tha fish would jump outa there nearly touch tha sky. We tries ta fish that pond but nothin comes up. Ole Gourdeau used ta sell fish in town; fresh catfish, croupie, bass, ya name it. But everythin done dried up when he died. It's a shame nobody can farm this land like he could. He neva tole a soul how he done it."

"No wife, no children jus him. When he died we had no choice but ta take control of tha property. Tha land produced tha highest quality produce aroun these here parts. But no soona we took control everthin dried up. Jus like that. It's been said tha gypsies put a curse on this property an no one has been able to pull a decent crop since. Tha last three owners left that property in less than one harvest season. No one is interested cept you. Now that I done tole you tha history an all are ya still interested?"

"Well, I would consider your offer if you gave me a price. I am definitely interested in the house. It is a lovely piece of work."

"Well, Mistah Johnson, I am willin ta throw in tha barn, an tha quartas fo a reasonable price."

"Mr. Rey again, please will you give me a price to consider."

"Mista Johnson everythin is a package. Nobody wants nuthin ta do wit this here property an I am willin ta give it ta ya fo tha same price tha big house goin fo. Now, do I have a deal?"

"You have a deal. I will need my attorney to review the deed before we proceed further with the sale of the property."

"Attorney?"

"Yes sir, I have to make certain that this is a legal transaction."

"Mistah Johnson whateva it take ta make tha sale, I am willin ta do. How soon can ya attorney git here?"

"Will this afternoon work for you?"

"That is fine can ya meet me in town at tha Royal Bourbon Café?"

"That will be fine, noon it is Mr. Rey?"

"Noon it is."

After Jonathan enters his car he views the properties that surround the Gourdeau Plantation. He soon realizes that the vegetation on the property that he is about to purchase appears to be stagnated. The vegetation has not begun to revive even with the onset of spring. It appears to mourn the death of its former proprietor. The other properties reveal vibrant new buds. He takes a last look at the house with its alluring nature. Jonathan drives back to the motel. He enters his room to find Arthur in an intense examination of a document.

"Arthur can you meet with Mr. Rey and I to seal the deal on this house?"

"Are you sure?"

"Of course I am sure this is the one. The price is a steal. I have no intentions to reveal my plans for the property. I am sure this is the right choice. I need you there to review the deed to make certain everything is legitimate. Mr. Rey has included the slave quarters adjacent to the property along with a barn that is nestled along a beautiful pond. There is also a wooded area in the purchase. Something tells me that it is too good to be true. Be sure to comb through this one with a fine tooth comb. I will pick you up before noon; by the way thank you for meeting with me on such a short notice."

"Where are you off to?"

"This is a very important investment. I want to review the property once more before we make a final decision. Can you make arrangements at the Royal Bourbon Café and make sure you secure a private section."

"That should give me time to find something to wear," says Arthur.

"Must you take this so seriously?'

"Well it is a very special occasion. I want to look presentable."

"I should swing by around eleven thirty is that enough time?"

"Yes brother I will be on standby."

Jonathan returns to the property once again. He wonders to himself, *is this place really cursed? Why is the vegetation dead at the start of spring? Maybe there was a hard freeze. Then again the property is elevated at the top of a peak. That does make ecological sense. How will I ever revive this land? It is possible that the nutrients have been depleted if crop rotation was not adhered properly. What am I getting myself into? Please lord, send me a sign. I will trust you until the very end.*

Jonathan raises his head in time to observe a figure in the near distance. He does not know whether to be on guard or to welcome him. *Gypsies, yes it is most likely a gypsy. Well this shall be my first encounter with a gypsy. I must keep my hand on my gun just in case. Who knows where I am? Did I mention to Arthur that I would return to the property? I must be more careful next time.*

Jonathan greets the stranger.

"My name is Jonathan Johnson it is nice to meet you."

Rayborn approaches the tall, pale white man with caution.

"Good day suh, my name is Rayborn."

"Please to meet you Rayborn. Do you know anything about this property? It is my desire to purchase the home."

"Yes suh, I do. Masta Johnson was tha masta but he die then masta Gourdeau took ova. That theres masta Gourdeau's house an theres that last of tha quartas."

"What do you mean by quarters?"

Never Underestimate The Power of A Secret Place

"Suh this here is a plantation. Behind tha big house is quarta's fo tha slaves ta live. This quarta is where masta Gourdeau's helpa lived. Ms. Rosa Lee was one of tha main helpa's in tha house. She ran tha big house fo masta Gourdeau but she dead. In tha night some mens they come on horses an set fires ta all tha quartas. They set fire to Ms. Rosa Lee quarta but it burns out. Tha slaves take to tha woods ova yonder an make a place fo themselves."

"Tha Johnson family be here in Louisiana a long time an buy slaves to work tha land. Afta young masta Johnson dies masta Gourdeaus say he wanna buy some land an start him a farm. Then he buys tha big house an this here plantation in Badeaux Parrish. He ask us slaves to stay wit him an git tha land ready fo plowin. We build some mo quartas fo us slaves an we build a barn so we can worship. When masta Gourdeau came ova us slavery was no mo. Masta Gourdeau teach us to read an write. He say he want us to understand him. Miss Wilamae teach tha younguns ta read and write. Miss Doris teached the field hands to read an write. But we cain't let tha town people know. We has ta burn our books if we knows tha town people lettin on. We learns ta read tha bible too. When ole masta Johnson was tha ovaseer we cain't talk or sang. That's cause slavery still alive. So we jus hum. Sounded like sweet music. We like farmin an we likes tha country life just plain an simple."

"You were Mr. Gourdeau's slave?"

"No suh. I was too ole ta work tha field when masta Gourdeau run tha place. I mighty proud ta say I works fo tha young masta Johnson. He nothin like his papa. His papa a evil man but I was too young to know. He ran dis property like a plantation. No one quarreled wit him or he sent em away. He marries tha sherrif's daughter an ran da Missus back to her family befo long."

He raise his two sons befo sendin em up north to be educated. The youngest boy came back to be wit his pa. That was what tha family agree ta. Tha first time oldes masta Johnson come home he took Eric up north wit em. Eric come back afta a time wit gifts fo all tha slaves. He don't look an talk tha same no mo. He say up north a place wheres people lives togetha an git along. He says they talk different an was many colors up there. He say tha houses not like tha quartas everybody got one of they own. Nobody went outside ta... ya knows what I mentionin ta say. He says everybody like one family an helps each otha. Theres no masta up there an tha young ones git a good life. He says oldes masta Johnson smiles at him, says good morning an he say glad he come. Eric say he gotta flat an can take two mo slaves so they git to workin. He says if ya sick tha doctor come see bout ya. When he left he took Miss Scarlet and Mr. Leonard. We suspected they be likin each otha so they go togetha. Miss Scarlet come back ta the farm afta Mr. Leonard die. She say her chile up north but she don't know wheres. She too old ta work in tha field so young masta Johnson built her a bigga quarta to look afta tha chilluns that lose they ma an pa. Ever since then a slave or two been goin up north."

"Afta young masta Johnson pass away I'se hopin to go up north but everythin done died wit young masta Johnson. Mistah Johnson are you some relations ta young masta Johnson?"

"Not that I am aware of. How can I reach you later? I would like to hear more about the history of this plantation."

"I'se livin in tha woods wit my common law wife an my sista."

"What is your wife's name?"

"Her name Zaneta, my sista name Jessie. It was tole to my common wife that there quarter was hers but they take it away. That there roof is where we has worship but they take it away. So we stays in tha woods ta ourself in case they comes afta us. They gonna have a fight on they hands if they do."

"Mr. Rayborn I have a very important meeting can I call you later?"

"No suh, we got no way ta call nobody. I can watch fo ya from tha woods. The slaves can see tha big house from tha woods but nobody see us. We watch ova the big house for masta Gourdeau."

"Well look for me later today. I may have some answers for you in regards to the quarters."

They both shake hands before they depart their separate ways.

"Arthur, hurry or Mr. Rey will think we have backed out."

"Jonathan I have waited for you for quite some time. It is not my fault this time that we are late. I will never forgive you if we miss this opportunity."

"Do not worry Arthur they are so hard pressed to sell we can practically name our price."

"Are you sure of that?"

"I am positive just let me do all the talking."

Arthur and Jonathan enter the Royal Bourbon Café. Patiently Mr. Rey sits in a secluded booth. The table is a cherry oak wood with a polished finish; there sits a neat stack of papers on the table beside Mr. Rey. Mr.Rey has ordered a bottle of wine and glasses for the occasion.

"Jonathan," Mr. Rey stands to greet them.

"Good afternoon, this is my Attorney Arthur Johnson."

"Good afternoon, Mr. Johnson."

"Mr. Rey you can drop the formalities we are practically neighbors. Now if we can get to the order of business; do you have the deeds?"

"They are laid out right in front of you."

"Give me a minute to review the deeds. You can order our meals in the meantime."

"Of course take your time," Mr. Rey responds.

After Arthur has reviewed the deeds he takes a sip of wine then clears his throat.

Never Underestimate The Power of A Secret Place

"Uhmm, I have reviewed the deeds to the property in which I have found a discrepancy in the amount of acreage of the property. Mr. Rey this deed does not mention somehow the acreage to the east and southwest of the property to include the pond. It was somehow extracted from the most current deed. The original deed reveals the property to include the big house, sixty three acres of farm land, the pond adjacent to the big house and the barn located south of the pond. For some reason the previous owners altered the deed due to a probate sale but I have yet to review the court documents. Until then, I will have to advise you not to enter into contract for the sale of the property until all deeds related to this property are recovered."

"My, my, my, Arthur such big words. Do you intend to say that the Gourdeau's property is off the market?"

"Not exactly, what I intended to say is that this deed that has been presented to me is not the most current deed. The property being sold to you should include the acreage with the last standing quarter, a pond, a nearby barn and acreages east of the barn. Somehow those details are excluded from this deed which I will need proof that you are about to purchase what the deed says you will purchase."

"Is that so?"

"Yes it is so; Jonathan, I would advise you not to follow through with this purchase until you reconcile the deed to include every item mentioned in the offer."

"Where do we begin?"

"Well it is going to be a lengthy process. We have to review court records to determine if any previous deeds to the property reveal when it was divided. Generally this happens when there are multiple siblings who have decided to divide the property. Or possibly the owner has specified that the property be divided among his beneficiaries."

"How long will this process take? We are anxious to seal this deal."

"Well it depends on what is on record at the court house. If the family followed the probate process to divide the property then it will be relatively easy. Otherwise it will require contact with the previous owners to find out when the division occurred and if those parties are staking claim to the acreages in question. Mr. Rey may I ask at what point was the property divided?"

"Well Arthur I wouldn't know. The last owners have lived on this property fo about a month. Mistah Gourdeau left tha slaves on tha property too."

Jonathan interrupts, "Do you mean to say the freed Africans?"

"No I meant what I said," Mr. Rey replies sternly. "Now some was slaves even afta slavery was ova. Well, that goes fo Ole man Johnson's plantation he neva let slavery die."

"So he denied them their freedom?"

"I wish it was so, Ole man Johnson died an his son took ova. Young Mistah Johnson caused so much commotion givin them slaves they rights every nearby Parrish refused ta trade an sell ta em. That didn't stop him one bit. The gypsies who squatted in town bought from him jus like tha towns folk. When young Mistah Johnson died then come tha droughts. They hung aroun so long it nearly sent most of tha farmers packin. Some of em hired a man ta tell em what crops ta grow jus ta keep from losin they land. All tha while tha Johnson's plantation was tha most producing farm in Badeaux Parrish."

"Mr. Rey that cannot be true; the soil on the Johnson's property appears to be depleted of its natural resources."

"Maybe that was tha straw that broke tha camel's back. I am sho that tha property was yieldin quite a crop befo Mistah Gourdeau's death. Within a year tha property went completely downhill. There was three takers fo tha property; afta tha first

Never Underestimate The Power of A Secret Place

taker evicted the gypsies from tha property then tha problems started. Its been said that tha property was cursed by tha gypsies."

"How long has the property been in this condition?"

"It was doin pretty well uptil tha time tha sheriff ran off the gypsies. The very next day when tha takers went ta move in they say that everything withered away even tha cattle."

"Even the cattle you say?"

"Yep, we figured they was poisoned."

"Poisoned by whom?"

"Tha gypsies, ain't ya been listenin to what I said?"

"That cannot be possible," replies Jonathan. "You give them far too much power."

"I guess ya ain't heard of witchcraft."

"You cannot be serious?"

"I sho am. I give ya a year an you will see what I been talkin about."

"Enough of this nonsense, I will be at the courthouse first thing in the morning to research court documents. Is there anything else that I can do to assist you Jonathan?"

"No Arthur, please whatever you can do to expedite the process. I will do what I can on my end. Well, this ones on me gentlemen," says Jonathan.

"Oh no, I cain't let you do that. I have ta pick up tha tab; I have a feelin this gone be a ongoing affair."

"I will let you know when I find out something Mr. Rey."

"I appreciate ya Arthur an have ya a safe trip ta tha courthouse."

"I will good day Mr. Rey."

On the drive back to the motel…

"Arthur what have we gotten ourselves into? I just wanted to purchase a farm to start a business."

"For goodness sakes Jonathan do not listen to him. You have the favor of God. If he has guided you to this farm then it is in his purpose for you. Has God ever steered you wrong?"

"Well no, maybe you need to see for yourself. There is something about this place that does not make sense."

"Take me to the place. We can pray while we are there and maybe God will send us an answer."

"That is probably the best advice I have had all day."

On Jonathan's way to the Gourdeau's plantation they drive past a tall figure dressed in blue overalls with a plaid shirt rolled up to his elbows. Jonathan stops the vehicle.

"What is it brother," asks Arthur.

"He resembles the gentlemen that I spoke with earlier today about the property."

"Jonathan you know how you are with names."

"Understandable but I must at least see if it is him."

"Can you remember his name?"

"I remember his last name is Johnson so I will just go with that."

Jonathan waits until the figure approaches the car.

"Umm, Mr. Johnson?"

"Who wanna know?"

"It is I sir, Jonathan."

"Yes suh."

Rayborn stops in his tracks. Jonathan exits the car and begins to walk towards him. He extends his hand for a handshake.

"Where are you headed?"

"Up to tha quartas ta check on tha property. Nobody suppos'd to know cause I ain't suppos'd ta be there."

"Oh you do not have to worry it is none of my business. Can I give you a lift?"

Rayborn looks perplexed.

"Can I give you a ride?"

Never Underestimate The Power of A Secret Place

"The law says we cain't ride wit white folk. Only somebody give us a ride is masta Gourdeau. Nobody eva tries."

"Well Mr. Johnson…

"Rayborn that's what they call me all my life."

"Rayborn, please ride with me up to the Gourdeau's plantation. We can finish that talk we started this morning."

When both men enter the car Jonathan introduces Rayborn to Arthur. They both shake hands then smile.

"Where to Rayborn?"

"Jus unda tha tree ova up yonda."

Once Jonathan reaches his destination Rayborn climbs out of the vehicle.

"When can I meet with you to talk about the history of Gourdeau's plantation? I would like to come into the woods to meet the others?"

"Suh, this is our secret place. Nobody come here but us. I meet you ova there when tha sun meets tha top of 'em trees."

Rayborn points to the trees across the road.

"Do you suggest in the morning?"

"Yes suh. In tha mornin it is."

"Have a good day Rayborn."

Rayborn nods before he disappears into the woods. Jonathan and Arthur return to the motel.

"Just about every home is equally exquisite as this one. Who knows the cost of maintaining such a place? How can one justify a family of four who live in such lavish accommodations meanwhile two families live in a squander of a domicile like the quarters? It is visibly inexcusable."

"We cannot fix the world's problems Jonathan."

"No we cannot but we can do our part by doing right by those around us."

"Jonathan you may be taking on a larger fight than you can ever phantom."

"I am up for the challenge. I am ready to face anything that comes my way."

"Are you done?"

"No I am not done. I have not begun to start. Just wait until we settle in; the first challenge is to build walls to that barn so they can worship in peace."

"You are going to build the walls?'

"Even if it kills me!"

"I had the notion that maybe you intended to say you were going to have a carpenter build the walls."

"Arthur, do not underestimate me. You know very well what I meant."

"Calm down Jonathan save your energy for the journey. I have a feeling it is going to be a long one."

"Is there a possibility the big house may have heirs to the property that we are not aware of?"

"It is possible. I believe that Mr. Rey may have concealed some valuable information. What do you think of these gypsy people he described Jonathan?"

"Arthur all I know is that God is my fortress. If he is for me no one can be against me. We both share experiences from the years we volunteered in the inner city. If that did not kill us then either will this. I can count on both hands the number of times I prayed for my safe return to our family. That was not an easy area to work but it has made my faith stronger than ever. It also helped me to understand that we all have something in common. Once we found what it was that we had in common we used it to bond with the youth. Before I knew it I became the most influential music teacher whose brothers built their first church with an indoor lavatory. We mentored many of the youth in that church. They learned to fund raise themselves so that they could travel to other churches in the city and do the same. I really believe that we were living on purpose. My hopes are that we will bring the same liveliness here. I think that we have a lot to offer the gypsies."

"What if they do perform witchcraft? How are we going to deal with that? Our commonality with the inner city kids was our belief in God. This witchcraft is a totally different concept. Are you sure we can handle it?"

"We could possibly win them over to God."

"What if we do not?"

"Then we will have to find a common place that will bring us together. God has never failed us yet."

"Remember we have to get here when the sun meets the top of those trees."

Arthur begins to laugh heartily at the idea and Jonathan sighs.

"Whatever that means," replies Arthur.

"What was that?"

"It is nothing Jonathan. You really should have stayed at the motel."

"I have just as much right to be here as you do. I am the one who will have to live with the gypsies. We can discuss this in the morning Arthur. Goodnight!"

The early morning sun peeks through the trees when they arrive at the Gourdeau plantation. Jonathan parks under an oak tree across from the woods. It is dawn and they wait to meet Rayborn.

"Will you put the gun back into the compartment before it accidentally discharges?"

"Jonathan I can handle a gun better than you can any day of the week. It was I that shot that copperhead between the eyes when he came after you."

"Arthur it was pure luck."

"I agree you are fortunate to be alive."

"Arthur let us not indulge in the past you are a great brother."

"Don't you ever forget it Jonathan."

"Somehow I believe I never will."

"Let us see here. The sun is at the top of the trees just like he said. Well what do you know? It looks like someone comes our way. I see one no two figures. Zaneta is a pretty large woman."

"Arthur it is not nice to throw stones. Put on your false face Arthur here they come."

"Mista Arthur, Mista Jonathan this is Zaneta my common law wife."

"Is there some place where we can all sit down to discuss the Gourdeau's property?"

"Mista Jonathan we ain't allowed on tha Gourdeau's property. The sheriff gonna put us on tha chain gang if he catch us."

"What about under that metal roof?"

"No suh that's part of tha Gourdeau's property."

"How about we go back to our motel room? Is that alright with you?"

"Jus let tha town people knows we is wit ya."

"You should not have any problems. I can guarantee your safety."

Everyone enters the vehicle. Jonathan drives away from the plantation in route to town. They arrive at the motel which looks more like a cottage.

Rayborn whispers, "Suh this ain't no motel; dis somebody's house."

"Rayborn this is a Bed & Breakfast. It once was someone's house however they rent out the rooms to earn money."

"Yes suh, I neva heard nothin like it."

"Well you learn something new every day. Let us enter in through this door. It will lead us to our room."

Jonathan leads them through a hall to the first door. Once inside they enter a sitting room with pale yellow walls and high white baseboards. Large portraits of floral sceneries hang neatly throughout the room. The floors are cherry oak hard wood with

Never Underestimate The Power of A Secret Place

floral tapestry runners that lead to the other rooms. There are two chairs on each end of a long cherry wood table. A gold sofa covered in velvet face a large picture window. The window reveals painted statues of jockeys on race horses throughout the well manicured lawn. There is also a sculpture of a cross above the bird bath with a stream of water flowing from a spigot. A bird takes flight toward the cool water to take a dip then takes flight again. A hummingbird expeditiously travels from flower to flower to feed on its nectar. It is a serene view for the visitors. The adults settle down around the coffee table before Jonathan leaves the room. He returns with a pitcher of cold water, glasses and a tray of cookies. Everyone sits in silence until Rayborn begins to speak. He reaches for a glass and pours himself some water.

"Soon slavery was ova an not too long afta ole masta Johnson sick. My mammy livin in tha big house to keep it runnin. Some say my mammy take care of ole masta Johnson til his dyin bed. Young masta Johnson took ova tha plantation an gave all tha slaves they freedom afta his pappy dies. We all say he too young to run a farm but he say he do right by us who stay. Only three left. Two of em come back; they say no one will give em they freedom. We still has our quartas, food fo our chilluns an a place ta go worship ta our God. Young masta Johnson gave us tha barn on paper. He say it's a secret place fo us. Sometimes he sit near tha pond on tha otha side listenin to us hum. Ole masta Johnson neva let young masta Johnson come ta tha barn. Call it a barn cause if tha towns people know we worshipin they kill us. They burned down tha ole barn afta young masta Johnson die. Then we goes ta live in tha woods befo they burn down everythin."

"So there are quarters in the woods?"

"Yes suh, afta they burns down tha quartas we has nowhere ta go. We moves to tha woods. They tries to come in on us an they git caught in tha traps. They neva come ta tha woods agin."

"When did they set fire to the quarters?"

Never Underestimate The Power of A Secret Place

"First time was afta young masta Johnson die they just burn some of em. Then some time afta masta Gourdeau dies in tha field they burn some mo. Zaneta do ya rememba?"

"I rememba roun the harvest season,"

Zaneta continues the history of the plantation.

"Masta Gourdeau went huntin wit masta Badeaux. He trusts us wit tha farmin cause he say it is our farm too. Masta Gourdeau git bit by a snake checkin on his traps one day. Masta Badeaux say slaves cain't ride on tha horse. So masta Gourdeau dies in tha field befo da worka come ta tell us da news. Rayborn's mammy went ta tha horse ta see him."

Rayborn describes the event, "She wailin afta him like he her own son. Tha horse pull back an jump in tha air. The horse hoof hit my mammy in tha head an she die too. Jesse was too young ta know so we hide it from ha. We bury my mammy an masta Gourdeau ova in that plantation cemetery where young masta Johnson an tha rest is buried. Tha doctor come ta see masta Gourdeau ta make sho he dead. Then theys try ta drive us out of tha plantation but we stay. We don't know nowhere but here."

"Masta Gourdeau don't believe in no God. He say he only believe what he see. Befo he die a log roll off da wagon an fell on masta Gourdeau. It crushed his legs sumptin awful. We think he might not eva walk no mo. He neva walked like tha rest of us eva agin. Some town people was mighty mean ta him. Masta Gourdeau neva like goin ta town only if he had too. He walked wit a terrible limp an sometimes he in awful pain but he neva say a word. He keep around tha chilluns most of the time. Teachin em how ta read an write. Masta Gourdeau don't mind long as tha field work done. Masta Gourdeau love books an give some ta tha younguns. Most us knows how ta read, write, sew, cook, hunt an fish just like any regul'r folk. Some of tha workas who went up north wit oldes masta Johnson go ta school. They sent books down fo tha younguns; jams, flour and cloth ta make shirts an trousers fo us. Masta Gourdeau say everythang ours. He take care of us like we his own family."

"Rayborn do you know any gypsies around here?"

"No suh. Tha town people say we gypsy; say we worship tha devil. They say we worship fire an hell. We make fire ta cook our food, fo light an ta keep warm. Most people do suh."

"I understand Rayborn. How can I contact you when I hear something about the property?"

"Well suh, we keep watch ova tha trail next ta tha big house. Tha only trail in an out of tha plantation. We knows everythin that goes on roun there."

"You mean to tell me that when I met you the other day you knew I was there all along?"

"We knows ev'ry time somebody come ta tha big house. We is watchin."

"How many of you are in those woods?"

"Mens, women, an chilluns? I reckon bout thirty folk suh."

"You don't say. How long have you all lived in the woods?"

"Befo tha last harvest come they run us off tha propr'ty. Most us went back ta tha quartas ta git our b'longings befo they set tha fires. Some of tha workas livin in that woods befo masta Gourdeau die. He buys tha metal ta build a place so nobody burns it down. When they took ova tha propr'ty da rest of tha workas went ta live in tha woods. Tha roofs is cov'red wit mud an leaves so tha metal cain't shine. We come out only in tha day ta cook. We hunt at night an lost two mens by mistaken em fo game. We buries em in tha woods fo now; waitin til we go back ta tha prop'rty an bury 'em wit tha rest our folk. We want our dead an alive ta stay together. Even da folk up north bring they dead ta bury wit our dead. Masta Gourdeau an young masta Johnson buried here too."

"Where is the cemetery located?"

"Ova by tha barn, tha land aroun tha barn is where our dead buried. We knows where everybody is; one day we gonna mark tha graves ta say who is who. We afraid fo now cause tha town people huntin afta us."

"If we find that the Africans are the owner's of this very property you can do whatever you wish with it."

"Yes suh, but who gonna make it right? Nobody owe us nothin."

"Do not fret, I hope Arthur can give us both some answers."

"Arthur he workin fo us too?"

"Yes Rayborn somehow we are in this together. If I cannot legally buy the plantation he will pretty much know who owns it. I feel like God has brought us together for a reason."

"Yes suh. I prays dat God send us a man like masta Gourdeau. Somebody who ain't gonna turn they back on us."

"I will never turn my back on anybody if I can help it. How about we order something to eat?"

"Would you and Miss Zaneta like to share a meal with us?"

"Yes suh, we don't mind."

"What do you like?"

"We eat jus about anythin suh."

Arthur call the kitchen and order a meal for four. Tell them to put it on your bill."

Arthur gives Jonathan a stern look.

"Is there anything in particular you would like to order Jonathan?"

"I am not particular just order something decent."

"Arthur, Miss Zaneta just informed me that she does not know who her father is. She also says that that her name is Johnson. Is that strange?"

"No Jonathan if they were slaves they often were given the surname of their master. Some were not allowed to even wed."

"That is unfortunate."

"Yes it is."

"Miss Zaneta have you ever met your father?"

"No suh, my mammy neva say a word bout my pappy. She ain't allowed ta have a man come ta tha quarta cause she was ole' masta Johnson's slave hand. I knows she has a boy an ole masta Johnson sent him wit a man an woman up north. My mammy say she hope he has a good life, betta than we havin."

"Do you know his name?"

"Donald, he born da same time young masta Johnson born. Mammy say she made enough milk fo tha both of 'em ta feed. She say young masta Johnson was dying away when ole masta Johnson sent him ta her. She say da Missus left tha plantation neva ta be seen again. My mammy raised her boy an young masta Johnson togetha like they kin."

"Your mother raised the master's sons also?"

"Yes suh, when young masta Johnson big enough he went ta tha big city an come back ta tha plantation cause he fretted ta come home. Ole' masta Johnson took 'em ta tha big house an he fretted ta go back ta tha quartas. My mammy say he fret all night til she come ta tha big house in tha mornin. She say he fret so much ole' masta Johnson moved my mammy ta do big house but her boy cain't come. One day tha oldes masta Johnson came fo Miss Doris an Mista Otis. They was good ta each other an theys keep an eye Donald. They say they take him too so he can git educated. Ole masta Johnson gave Mista Otis money ta take her boy an say he send fo him when he ready fo tha field but he neva send fo 'em. When young masta Johnson big 'nough to run tha farm he built a quarta close ta tha big house. My mammy say I was born in tha quarta an ole' masta Johnson come ta see me. He say she can keep me cause I'se black as tar like my mammy. He ask who tha daddy she say she don't know. Ole' masta Johnson raise his hand ta beat my mammy cause he say she lyin; she say she tole tha truth. Young masta Johnson hears my mammy screamin fo ole' masta

Never Underestimate The Power of A Secret Place

Johnson ta stop cause he say he gonna ta beat it outa her. Young masta Johnson runs ta her quarta ta see why all tha screamin. He hit ole' masta Johnson wit da butt of tha rifle in tha head. He got a mark ova his eye. He tells ole' masta Johnson neva touch his mammy agin or he kill 'em. He tells young masta Johnson no black mammy can have a white boy. Young masta Johnson say she tha only ma I know an I ain't gone let you run her off. Ole' masta Johnson neva come ta tha quarta no mo. My mammy still run da big house wit me wrapped round her. I learnt to clean, cook an serve from my mammy. I loves ta sang an my mammy like ta write songs fo me ta sang. If there was somethin ta sang bout I sang bout it. Even ole' masta Johnson grew ta likin my sangin."

"One rainy mornin I git up ta go ta tha Big House. I'se wait fo my mammy cause we walk togetha ev'ry mornin. I calls her name but she don't say nothin. I goes to my mammy's bedside an calls her name but she still don't say nothin. I climb ova her to see her face an she look like she be sleepin."

Zaneta begins to weep quietly.

"Her face soft an warm but she ain't breathin. I git Miss Scarlet cause she see afta all tha ailin workas. She shakes her head an just looks at me. She say go fetch young masta Johnson. I goes to tha big house but they say young masta Johnson he in tha field. Gals ain't suppose ta go ta tha fields but I goes anyway. I feels hurried inside so I git ta runnin. Young masta Johnson on his horse lookin down on tha workers in tha cotton fields. I call his name but he don't turn ta me. So I stands real still an yells wit my big voice. Young masta Johnson's horse stand up on his two hind legs nearly knockin him to tha ground. He look at me an says gals cain't be in tha field. 'Ya knows it Zaneta,' he tole me."

"I tell young masta Johnson come ta tha quarta cause Miss Scarlet calls fo him. He rides past me an I can feel tha wind rush by. They say he comes ta tha quarta an he fell ova my mammy. He don't talk ta Miss Scarlet he just start moanin a horrible moan

Never Underestimate The Power of A Secret Place

deep down in his soul. No one could quiet him not even ole' masta Johnson. They say I'se too young to know what went wrong wit my mammy. Young masta Johnson digs her grave down by da barn; took 'em three days. They bury my mammy down by tha barn an no field work dat day fo no body. I understand then about my mammy."

"Young masta Johnson take me ta Miss Scarlet quartas; she ain't got no room fo me. She takes care of chilluns that got no mammys' or pappys'. She old an bent ova; some say she blind but she see what she wanna see. She keep a stick wit her an can strike ya fasta than a snake. When she let out this scream young masta Johnson come runnin no matta where he at; we's younguns try ta scream like Miss Scarlet but young masta Johnson neva come. He love Miss Scarlet like he loved my mammy. Miss Scarlet cook his meals afta my mammy die. She knows what he like an how he like it. My mammy teach Miss Scarlet how ta cook fo him even though she be tha youngun. I run back ta my quarta an young masta Johnson let me stay. He say this is yo quarta, I make sho of that."

"Nobody come to my quarta jus' him. He come one day an give me a pap'r an say put it in a secret place. He say this my quarta til tha day I die. When I come like a woman he bring Rayborn an say he my comm'n law husband. I don't knows nothin bout no husband so we jus look at each otha. Miss Doris come down ta take me up North but I tells her I stay. She say I have a brother doin well wit a family. I don't go cause I don't wanna be no burden. Young masta Johnson give us a day to make ceremony fo me an Rayborn. All da worker give gifts fo our quarta, we hum an dance then Rayborn an I jump tha broom ta make it right."

"What do you mean by jump the broom?"

"When tha man an woman jump ova tha broom at tha same time we believe we go into anotha life togetha."

"I have never heard of that before. Is that some kind of gypsy tradition?"

Never Underestimate The Power of A Secret Place

"Mista Arthur we ain't no gypsies. Our people come here from Africa. We cain't talk our language cause town people say it gypsy talk. It ain't gypsy talk, no suh."

"Rayborn I know you must have family here besides Zaneta."

"Yes suh, I do. When tha oldes mastah Johnson came fo my pappy ta work in tha big city, I stay an work in tha fields. They say I'se a good field hand an young masta Johnson need me."

"Who is your father?"

"They say his name Otis. We figure they was my mammy an pappy gone ta tha big city wit Zaneta's brotha. I'se reachin manhood an I see Zaneta walkin ta tha big house wit her mammy since she a babe. Young masta Johnson make me ova see tha cotton fields cause I'se young an strong. He promised ta send me to my pappy when I git old'r. But oldes masta Johnson neva sent fo me. I'se runnin chores fo tha womans in tha big house mostly haulin tha meat ta tha house fo cookin. Zaneta, she becomin a woman an sometimes I carry her wares ta her quartas. Young masta Johnson don't like men's comin aroun Zaneta's quartas. Say she too young fo beddin so I jus help her from time ta time. Miss Scarlet has otha plans. She my mammy since I was a boy an she knows me well. She say I can take care of Zaneta if she can git in young masta Johnson's head. She say maybe young masta Johnson was keepin Zaneta fo his self. Nobody eva seen young masta Johnson beddin in town or beddin a negra. He nothin like his pappy ole masta Johnson. He kind to all. Miss Rosa Lee raise him that way. But he don't pay any mind ta womens, not even when he come tha overseer of tha property. All tha workas love him; some of tha chilluns calls him pa. Them that don't know they pappy. He mark tha tree fo tha younguns an show 'em how ta mark tha tree every harvest season, cause most of us don't know how old we is. Young masta Johnson get us ta marryin. He say Zaneta needs a husband ta look afta her. He send fo mistah Kyle ta come up ta tha barn an tells us if we want ta live in tha quartas like man an wife we has ta get married like mans an wife. Zaneta and I been thinkin we's married all this time befo' they tells us it got ta be on pap'r."

"Who told you that?"

"Tha sherrif tells Zaneta afta he take tha property tha first time. They waits til I come off tha boat an ask me if Zaneta my wife; I say yes, an they say show me tha papers. I say what papers. They say you ain't married if ya ain't got no pap'rs. Then they tole' us ta leave tha property."

"Did you sign any papers the day you were married?"

"No suh, we jumped tha broom like tha othas."

"Do you think Mr. Johnson kept any records?"

"Oh no, suh, Ole masta Johnson neva allow'd us ta marry. He beat us if we caught near tha womans quartas. He only allow'd us ta bed every now' n then; when workas got low."

"What do you mean by low?"

"Sometimes we lose workas cause they git sick an dies. When plantin season come we low on workas. Ole masta Johnson makes some of tha men slaves bed wit womans slaves ta keep warm in tha winta and make babies. Sometimes babes come in tha harvest season an tha womens have tha babes in tha field. They keep workin while it nursin. We have some babes ta die in tha field. That was tha only time young masta Johnson stop work. He let us bury tha babe. We back ta work tha day afta. That is tha only time there ain't no field work when somebody die."

"My goodness the resilience these people possess amazes me!"

"We don't know no otha way. One day a worka birth her babe in tha field but she too young ta know ta clear its mouth so it choke an die. Young masta Johnson right there lookin on an he have a old worka take her ta tha quartas to rest. Tha same young worka her belly full agin, she look scar'd. She have no mammy ta look afta her so he sends her ta Miss Scarlet's quarta ta live. Tha young

Never Underestimate The Power of A Secret Place

worka she births anotha babe in tha field again but this time young masta Johnson have tha midwife come ta tha field an help take tha baby. Tha babe don't cry this time agin an tha worka she in tha field bent ova like she mournin. Young masta Johnson ride his horse ta tha quarta wheres tha babe is; he watchin tha midwife rub on tha baby. She a rubbin like she tryin to rub the skin off the babe. She keep rubbin tha babe then she blowin in tha babes mouth. Tha babe start coughin an she bring da babe back ta life. The babe cries an all tha workas in tha field is sangin an laughin. Young masta Johnson say, 'Thanks be to God.' Tha young worka go ta her quarta so tha babe can nurse an knows it mammy. Young masta Johnson allow tha worka ta stay wit da babe til it strong. He makes sho' tha docta see tha babe an it gonna have a good life. Tha babe stay wit an ole mammy til it can walk."

"Afta masta Gourdeau took ova he allow his workas ta talk when we wit him. He teach his workas ta go ta town ta trade an sell. Town people don't like that we talk business wit 'em. That's how masta Gourdeau make sho' everythin go like he want. If they cheat one of his workers's masta Gourdeau neva put up no fuss. If we wrong tha town people he make sho we make it right. Sometime they don't tell da truth but masta Gourdeau still make it right wit 'em. One day we go to town theres a masta takin his slaves off his wagon. A slave git off tha wagon an falls to tha ground by a towns lady passin by. She screams an tha masta say, 'what ya doin negra?' He says, 'I'se just fell that all suh.' The masta shot him dead. Masta Gourdeau he troubled so he tells tha slave masta, he a free man, 'you breakin tha law by killin a free man.'

The slave masta spits on tha ground an say, 'Who gone do somethin bout it?' Masta Gourdeau say, 'I make sho you pay mista.' Anotha day go by an a lot of folk at tha big house. They mostly white mens who look mighty impo'tant. They say tha masta was put on a chain gang fo shootin tha slave cause it a law

Never Underestimate The Power of A Secret Place

against killin a freed man. Somethangs change when masta Gourdeau was tha overseer. Some of tha slaves come ta tha Johnson plantation ta work an we finds some of us kin. Some goes up north an we neva sees 'em again. We ain't scar'd no mo. Masta Gourdeau allows us ta sing so we worship."

"And what do you sing?"

"We sing, ♪We trust you Lord, ♪We trust you Lord.♪ We trust you Lord!"

Zaneta sings a chorus of the song.

Jonathan replies, "You have such a smooth velvety voice."

"Everybody say I sing like my mammy. She used to hum to young masta Johnson when he was a babe. When he begun schoolin he teach my mammy ta read. She write tha songs an sang 'em ta him in ha quarta. She sang, wade in tha wata sometimes. She learnt ta read tha bible some befo' she die, cause young masta Johnson read ta ha, Zaneta relishes. The Bible tells us ta love our neighbor, do good an good come back to ya. He say tha bible say obey yo mammy an pappy an you will live a long time. Tha slaves say they don't know they mammy an pappy."

"I'se rememba anotha day we went ta town an I was tradin cattle, says Rayborn. Tha farmer say I promised him two steer fo a milkin cow an I only deliver one steer. He say I stole from him an I go ta tha chain gang. Masta Gourdeau is wit da women tradin they vegetables while this is happenin. So I send fo masta Gourdeau, but tha sheriff he takes me away befo he can git ta me. In da middle of tha night masta Gourdeau come ta wheres I at but no body there fo him ta speak ta; so he wait. Next mornin tha sheriff come an he say he holdin me fo tha chain gang ta come so I can pay fo tha steer I stole. Masta Gourdeau looks at him long time then he cocks his rifle an points at tha sheriff. He say, 'I know what I tell my worka ta say an he only say what I tells him. I'se sends two mo steer to Farmer Boudeaux fo his trouble but I'se takin my worka back wit me.' He say to da sheriff, 'You okay wit

Never Underestimate The Power of A Secret Place

that?' Tha sherrif says, 'Whateva you say Mista Gourdeau.'
"Masta Gourdeau pulls me on tha back of his horse an we ridin away. He stops tha horse and turns tha horse aroun an then say, 'Tell my ma, I'm doing good fo myself.' 'I will tell her brotha,' says tha sheriff. Masta Gourdeau points his rifle at tha sherrif an close ta shootin his head off. He tells sheriff Badeaux, 'You neva be no kin ta me.' We rides back ta tha property he says he gone die soon. He says he gone change some things. He say he gone build dwellins fo tha workas in tha woods so they can keep watch ova tha property. That way nobody come ta take ova tha property. He says tha quarta b'longs ta Zaneta. He says he signs paper for tha barn an tha land round tha barn and gives it ta me an ha chilluns so they has a place to worship of they own. Tha woods his property too so he makes me tha overseer ta tha woods to protect tha property. Some workas takes they b'longings ta move. They knows tha town people want tha Johnson plantation. We's gonna fight fo it. He says oldes masta Johnson come down an bring big city talkin people wit him ta make papers on tha property. So nobody can stake claim. Masta Gourdeau signs da paper so nobody say dat young masta Johnson do wrong by him. He asks me if tha workas gonna leave? I'se don't know I tells him. He says 'help me ta make 'em stay or tha farm have ta be sold then wheres they gonna all go?' "I says I talk ta tha workas."

"Whatever happened?"

"We troubled but we all stay 'cept two workas. They say they free an they gonna find work. But they comes back Moses and Aaron, they says no work out there. Tha towns folk troubled cause tha slaves done gone no one ta farm tha land. Moses say ain't no farms producin, no one to plow tha fields. Masta Gourdeau sends Moses up north cause he say he run again an he might take mo workas wit him. Tha day masta Gourdeau die there was heavy spirits roun tha property. Mostly cause no one know what gonna happen ta us. We believes masta Gourdeau cause he ain't gone teach us no wrong; we do right to each other an tha towns people no matta what they do ta us. Sometimes they throw rocks at us an spit at us but we pay no neva mind cause we know God is watchin."

"Do you ever wonder why the town's people treat you this way?"

"Sometimes an sometimes it don't matta cause our God says we all made like him. We figure some people don't like God so they troubled inside."

"Did there ever come a time that you wanted to fight back against the towns people?"

"Yes, Mista Jonathan all tha time. We comes from our country wheres ya fight ta protect our land an family. So, when we comes here an they tells us we cain't protect nothin we think somethin wrong. We come togetha in our tribes cause we protect our tribes that way. We keep power in our tribes. When we come ta this country we come togetha fo our masta but when we try ta protect our tribe on tha plantation tha masta beat us. We don't know what they say an why they beat us. So we do nothin an they beat us agin. In our country when tribes go ta war we know we fight fo somethin wit meanin. Here they say we cain't fight fo nothin. We have no power ova our lives. But we believe our God be wit us here; he neva leave us. We hum, dance an cry out ta God. He brings us peace ta see anotha day no matta what eva it brang."

"When masta Gourdeau dies, he give us power ta fight fo our property. He gave us mo rifles ta protect tha property. The town people don't know we watchin in tha woods so they run away like they see a ghost when they come ta take tha land. Masta Gourdeau tell tha workas ta run tha farm. He say this be our home too. Young masta Johnson gone; masta Gourdeau gone; Miss Rosa Lee an Miss Scarlet. We got too many chilluns to care fo Mista Jonathan. We pray day an night everythin be alright. We put trust in God we ain't gonna lose tha property. Miss Badeaux says she comin fo what hers. The oldes masta Johnson come wit his men ta tha property an sent Miss Badeaux away. He say she lost her rights ta tha property when she married tha sheriff."

"Do you happen know where I can find the sheriff?"

"Yes suh, Sheriff Badeaux property is ova there."

"Did you mean Mr. Rey?"

"No suh, he not tha sheriff no mo tha towns people run him outta town. Masta Badeaux is da Sherriff. They say Sherriff Rey tha reason da slaves run."

"I think I know where to find him, thanks for your help. I think we can get the property assigned to its rightful owners very soon. Let us eat before this delicious food gets cold."

Everyone has finished their meals and continue their conversation.

"Well it was nice to meet the two of you. How about we take the both of you to back to the trail?"

"Yes, suh that is fine wit us."

On their drive back it is a warm late afternoon. The dragon flies busily scurry along their disorganized paths. Jonathan observes the look on the town's people faces when they drive by. Many seemed perplexed like they have never seen whites and blacks enjoy an afternoon ride. Jonathan decides to wave at an onlooker that he passes by but to his surprise the greeting is not returned.

"Rayborn, do you mind if I stop here for a moment?"

"No suh, take yo time we in no hurry. We never ride in a automobile befo."

"I will just stop in and top off my tank."

When Jonathan pulls in the service station the attendant diligently begins to clean his windshield. He leans in and observes the occupants of the car. Jonathan extends his hand out of his window to hand the operator cash. He does not accept it. The attendant returns his cloth to his back pocket then begins to walk into the station's office. He begins to converse with another man in the office and he looks in their direction. Still no one approach the car to offer services. Jonathan gets out of the car; it is then that both men approach him. The attendant that cleaned the window earlier begins to speak.

"Suh, we don't carry on wit folks that mix wit tha gypsies."

Jonathan replies, "I am sorry to who do you refer to as gypsies?"

"I am referrin to them gypsies in tha back of that automobile; we don't serve 'em."

"Well sir, I can provide evidence that I own this automobile. I am more than happy to pay for your services."

"Yo money ain't welcomed here long as ya take company wit them gypsies."

"I see well can you tell me if there is another service station near that I may patronize?"

"Nearest service station is twelve miles outa town that way, the attendant points west."

"Your hospitality is greatly appreciated. What is your name?"

"They call me Mista Lanue an yourn?"

"My name is Mr. Jonathan Johnson."

"Theres a hardware store comin ta build down tha road in that very location ya gettin gas. Are ya any relations ta tha store owner?"

"Why do you ask?

"Well fo one darn thing it's goin ta take my business."

"Well Mr. Lanue your refusal to service me seems to be an open invitation to take your business."

"The Johnson's an I had a good understandin. He brought me lots of business wit those trucks he brung through here. If it weren't fo this here station he cain't transport his cotton outa here. Ya understan we have rules aroun here. Once they know ya takin company wit them gypsies ya ain't gonna git this towns business or any surroundin Parrishes fo that matter."

"Well I guess we will have to see about that."

"Ya damn right we will."

"Good day Mr. Lanue."

Jonathan returns to his car and drives away. They leave a cloud of dust to cover their exit. Jonathan absentmindedly drives along the trail which leads to the woods. He has never been that far. He is curious to meet the other Africans.

"Rayborn just tell me when to stop."

"This fine right here suh, neva has a automobile come this far."

"Do you mind if I meet the other Africans?"

Rayborn looks at Zaneta.

She answers, "Mista Jonathan only in da daylight."

"I can just park under this tree if that is okay."

"Yes suh Mista Jonathan. It is mighty hard on Zaneta legs so she don't come out much."

"I think I can make it."

"How far is this trail?"

"Ya gotta go deep in da trail befo ya git ta da dwellin."

"So it is downhill?"

"No suh, uphill. Our dwellin is lil ways up tha hill."

"Arthur did you bring a change of shoes?"

"I was not prepared to hike up a mountain. This has turned into an adventure of some sort. I will look in the extra bagage in the trunk there has got to be something I can change into."

"What about these?"

"Those are my lounging shoes but I guess they will have to do."

Arthur changes his shoes before they continue into the woods. It begins to get dim even though it is mid-day. There are sounds that come from the dark places. Rayborn makes a sound that mimicks a bird. He turns to Jonathan, "We has to let da othas know dat everythin is safe." A tall dark muscular man steps onto the trail from out of nowhere. The Johnson's leap back alarmed at the sudden appearance of this figure. Rayborn introduces them.

"This is Joshua, he watch's ova da woods."

"Goodness, I did not know he was near us."

"We's all round ya Mista Jonathan jus cain't see us."

"Is that why it is so dark in the woods?"

"Yes suh, we protect our family, our property an da woods protect us too."

"What happens if someone gets in here?"

"We take em an cova they eyes then we ties 'em up til they is weak an cain't fight no mo then we takes em to da road down yonda wheres they can be found. They neva comes here no mo cause they neva see our faces. They say they seen a ghost or gypsy like ya say."

"So, you do not shoot them? Do you not have guns?"

"Yes suh. But masta Gourdeau tell us neva kill nobody til ya in danga. We use our rifles ta hunt."

"How much longer do we have to go?"

"We is here, welcome ta our dwellin."

When Jonathan enters it is dark and he is unsure of where he is. He becomes confused so he asks to sit down.

"Yes suh, right here."

Rayborn retrieves a stool with an embroidered cloth seat. He eases down unsure of how low the stool is. Rayborn offers Arthur a stool also, similar to Jonathan's. He sits down with confidence. Rayborn squats down near them on the dirt floor and lights a lantern. The light is so soft it accentuates the figures around them. Jonathan is able to recognize each of their silhouettes except one. Jonathan observes a figure from the corner of his eye.

He asks, "Who is there?"

The figure steps forward and it is a child.

"Hello darling, what is your name?"

"My name Effie, masta."

"Effie you can call me Jonathan."

"Yes suh masta Jonathan."

"No, No Effie just Jonathan."

Effie looks confused.

Rayborn reports, "He ain't no masta he just a regul'r man."

Everyone begins to laugh at once.

"It is nice to meet you. Rayborn by any chance do you have any lights or running water?"

"No suh, lights bring trouble ta us. We fetch our water at night by tha pond."

"I am pretty sure there is plenty of well water at your finger tips with the pond near here."

"Prob'ly so we ain't dig that deep befo."

"Well you can now just let me make contact with a few brethren. I will see what we can do. Of course, I do not want to make any promises until we settle the probate on the property."

"Suh what a probate?"

"A probate simply gathers any documents that pertain to the deceased owner of the property. In this case if it is Mr. Gourdeau; we need to know if he has a will that describes how he wants his estate divided. After my attorney research court documents he will make contact with the remaining surviving family members. We should be able to determine if your rights are legitimate."

"How long it gonna take?"

"I am not sure but from what you have told me we can go straight to the documents filed at the court house. I promise I will keep in touch and when I learn something I will meet with you the following day. Make sure you look for me every day."

"Mista Jonathan I'se pray ya git our prop'rty back soon, replies Rayborn. We all prayin."

Never Underestimate The Power of A Secret Place

When the Johnson's begin to return to their automobile the darkness drops behind them with each step they take. They reach the car to notice the sun's glare in the bright blue sky. There is not a cloud in the sky while the birds fly with caution from tree to tree. They squawk at the visitors to alert the others of possible danger. Arthur climbs into the car and locks his door at once.

"Gosh it is such an eerie feeling; feels like someone has watched our every move."

"They very well might be. This is their home and they want to protect it."

"I do not know how I feel about the woods so close to our home."

"Well you better consider it carefully. There is a possibility that the nearby quarter will belong to Zaneta. The barn will become a place where the Africans will meet each Sunday."

"I think I want to reconsider this property. Maybe there is too much controversy with this property. I wonder where we will fit in with the town's people and the gypsies."

"We will fit in fine, says Jonathan. You have worked in New York's inner city community and now you question if you fit in?"

"Jonathan in all honesty it is not the same. We had a lot in common with the inner city children their goals were just misaligned. This is a different animal we must consider the challenges."

"Explain yourself."

"For instance their vernacular is decades outdated. Not to mention their knowledge of human rights. Where have these people been?"

"Arthur by far it is not their fault that they have been isolated from main stream society. You must understand that they have learned the culture of the Americans in this region. If anyone should be ashamed it should be us. Whatever happened to your tenacity to make a difference in this world? If you thought for one minute that we have come to a place in our lives where we can retire to indulge in the lavishness this world has to offer, you are sadly mistaken. It is required of you to live out your purpose on this earth until the day you die."

"Really brother? You are only interested because there is a profit to be made."

"That is not my motivation."

"Then what is?"

"This is something bigger than you and me, Arthur. I feel that God has brought us here for a purpose. It is no coincidence that we are here."

"Well if this deal does not fall through we will need a plan B."

"And plan B is what Arthur?"

"Plan B is to find a nice cottage in New Orleans near the Louisiana shores. I want to live life to its fullest."

A few days pass before Jonathan hears a word from Arthur. He finds his way back to the Johnson's plantation and waits. The sun's translucent ray shine upon Jonathan's face and awakens him to see the sun peek over the trees. He looks around but does not see anyone. He begins to pull himself up in his seat only to recognize a figure perched under a large oak tree near the entrance of the woods. Jonathan grabs the papers on the passenger's seat before he exits the automobile.

"Good mornin suh," says the gentleman before he rises to his feet.

Jonathan recognizes him it is Rayborn.

"I hope that I did not disturb you."

"No suh, ya welcome ta come any time."

The men shake hands once they are in arms reach.

"I have some unsettling news. Are you aware that Sherrif Badeaux and Mr. Gourdeau are brothers?"

"I'se mention it when we met befo."

"So you understand that the property's owner were the Badeaux family."

"He owns jus bout ev'ry plantation in da parrish."

"That is not true."

"I am now the owner of this property and I would like to make a concession with your wife."

"Yes suh."

"I have here a written legal document that states Zaneta owns the quarter along with an acre of land that surrounds the quarter."

They both look in the direction of the quarter. When their eyes meet Jonathan can see what appear to be tears in Rayborn's eyes.

"You may live there for however long you like. Your children will inherit the property and any of your future descendants. I hope that I have not let you down."

"No suh. We got jus what we been askin fo."

Jonathan extends his hand for a hand shake instead Rayborn wraps his arms around him.

"I'se most gracious suh."

"Any time my brother."

"But I ain't yo brotha Mistah Jonathan."

"Rayborn we are all created one in Christ."

4

A PLACE OF NEW BEGINNINGS

Eight months later...

"Ahh, Brother you have arrived safe and sound. Were there any hardships?"

"Absolutely not our travels were filled with exquisite wonder. Once we reached our journey into the southern states there was not a soul among us. It was like our Lord had cleared the way."

"So who have you brought with you?"

"I have with me Salonia our headmaster from the orphanage. She will be most suitable to teach the youth. Her husband Blanton will accompany her to assist with the establishment of the school for the youth."

"That explains the extensive luggage we have incurred. Then there is Christine she has experienced difficulty transitioning to the factory work or the thought of losing a prize such as myself. I am certain that everyone will enjoy Christine's exquisite culinary cuisine and her lovely vocals."

"Of course you will brother."

"Jonathan I had nothing to do with Christine's decision to retreat. She is an adult woman who makes her own decisions."

"You will never convince me brother. Am I not your right hand man?"

"Oh, you know me too well but none the less father will not approve of our union.

"Jonathan has father's opinion ever prevented you from your pursuit of Melba?"

"Of course not but this converstion he must never hear of."

"You have no worries dear brother."

"Now who are these young ones?"

"They are not as young as you think brother. All of these youth range in age from thirty-eight to forty-one years of age, Nathan smiles. You must know that they each have their documentation of freedom therefore by no means will they serve as slaves on the farm."

"Boys, enough of your shenanigans," Linda insists.

"Of course brother we are all equal partners in this endeavor. Each of us will experience great loss if this plan fails; therefore I want them to know they are equally invested in this venture."

"You have my word that I will not betray you or those that you place in my care. My honor to God, my love for mother and you will never waiver."

"You have never deserted me brother even when our dear father insisted that you do so. You have been a brother like no other brother; I can not phantom any other."

"Nathan you must know that your decision to continue in New York cut me deeper than you can ever imagine. We were inseparable, what has changed since then?"

"My true love is with child; I could never forsake her for you."

"I understand brother love is a mysterious creature. It crosses all boundaries of race, religion, ethnicity, and class. If anyone should know it should be me. However my will to commit is quite unimaginable."

"When you find the right love your resistance will subside."

"If only it were true for me. I will never gain my father's approval; his death is the only light I see."

"Do not consider such darkness my brother. God has a way to make the unthinkable a reality. One day my brother, one day your heart will surrender but for now enjoy your freedom to venture it does not last forever. Now for the young ones please care for their safety. The lad is an ordained minister in accordance with New York ordinances; now that may be another matter here in Louisiana."

"Well I tell you this to be true, we will make known to the U.S. Congress any suffrages placed upon our workers. They will maintain their rights to freedom under my leadership. Our association with our remaining union soldiers will serve us tremendously to preserve democracy. Would you agree dear brother?"

"Only God secures our future. It is the mere obedience to God that requires man to walk with integrity."

"So true it is my prayer that there are more with us than against us. Let us eat brother my return will be a lonesome one."

"My hope is that your stay is lengthy for I have longed for your companionship."

"You were always the needy one. You behaved as though we were joined at the hip."

"I wonder if you had not arrived what would be the result of me."

"On what basis do you question your existence?"

"Arthur has always been father's most prized possession. I imagine that my deformity reminds him of his own limitations."

"You are much healthier than I. Very athletic not to mention your vast knowledge of literature," says Nathan.

"His only conversations with me were (in his father's voice) 'Where is your brace? Must I remind you of your limitations? Why do you continue to chasten yourself?' He has never inquired of my well being. He has never mentioned the medals or the literary awards that I have acquired. He has not the slightest clue that it was I that has passed the Bar exam for Arthur after he failed it twice."

"So why have you not exposed the truth?"

"What good would it do to divulge my brother's failure? We are both of the same cloth. If one of us fails we all fail. You were once very committed to our family yet you appear to be so distant from us now. Especially since our mother's death; tell me why now?"

"Mother was my only connection to the family; now that she is gone I feel the need to branch out."

"My hopes were that you will be my partner in this endeavor."

"Brother, I am your partner but now I must attend to my love and the newest member to our family. You will understand when you become a father. Are you not honored to become an uncle?"

"I am beyond honored. Yet my only hopes are that I will be a better father than my own. My desire is to marry someone like mother. My chief apprehension is that I will father a child with scoliosis like myself. Would my father accept him? Will I ever earn my father's acceptance? It is a question I want answered."

"Brother let us not dwell in misery. Look before you, here a future with more success than you can ever imagine. Focus on your future for the past will never come again. Mother depends on us to fulfill her dreams to become humanitarians. I believe God will do a great thing in you; greater than your brother will ever achieve, encourages Nathan. It will be because of you that the family business will expand beyond comparison to any competitors on the market. It is only because of your vision to bring equality to the forefront of America's consciousness among all brethren. "Jonathan do you realize it is your perception of your own physical inadequacies that has caused you to embrace those less fortunate than yourself? You could have easily have chosen another maiden but you did not because you embrace the downtroddened. You have never questioned our relationship; most of all you have always enjoyed the company of those different from yourself."

"You know our brother has considered our acts unnatural. Nathan do you remember when you would entwine your hands with mine while we were nursed?"

"Yes, mother cherishes that picture you know."

"You have slept with me on stormy nights when I was terrified. You have eaten from plate, worn my clothes, and bathed with me. You are closer to me than my own brother yet we look so different."

"Jonathan you have denied yourself of friendships, activities, many opportunities because of me. You have studied with me late in the night so that I would progress in school along with you. Never did you consider my deficencies. It was my dream to have a farm and live a simple life. It was also your mother's desire to secure my future. Your dreams were to become an acclaimed literary writer or a doctor; so far from where you are now. You only pursue this endeavor to support me. Please do not deny yourself of your own dreams for my sake. I feel indebted to you for your steadfast loyalty."

"Nathan when you presented this idea to mother I was very gracious that you inquired of my appraisal. I am quite competent enough to manage a business and write literature simultaneously. My dreams are to become a business partner with you; my true brother. You have been apart of my family since birth. I have never confided my thoughts toward you but every night I thank God that you are my brother and my friend."

They both embrace.

"Enough of this foolishness like father would say. What shall we eat today?"

"How about we test Zaneta's culinary skills? Her food has its' own flare."

"Whatever it is I am sure I will be pleased."

"Zaneta has exquisite culinary skills. Shall we continue to the dining area brother?"

"Of course to the dining area we shall depart."

They both stroll to the big house while they ponder the renovations needed to prepare for the newcomers.

"This is a very enormous mission. I can not imagine how we will be able to staff the farm with the workers we previously predicted," questions Nathan.

"You are absolutely correct. There has been an ongoing evacuation of the former slaves since the Civil war. Daily I have met with former slaves who desire to annul their rights to freedom to work and occupy here. I have approximated fifty freed men, women and children who dwell in the woods south of the farm. I can not for the life of me turn them away. I have furnished them with the necessities they will need until the quarters are updated. I plan to allow five of the nineteen quarters to remain on the farm for the overseers of the property. The others will be uprooted and transported into the woods where they can have a place of their own. The acreage allows me to place multiple septic tanks along the outer edge of the farm. Our attempt is to prevent the possibility of contamination to the soil."

"Do you see that barn over there? It could possibly become a school or church for the workers. I have not conceded on the arrangements yet. There is room for their cemetery and a pond for baptismal."

"How did you come up with this?"

"A few of the former slaves described their previous arrangements. I asked them what they would need to live happily and be committed to work hard."

"Do tell!"

"Their requests were quite simple. Somehow the Africans were able to educate themselves to a degree. I have asked many of the Africans if they would prefer to return to their native country.

Never Underestimate The Power of A Secret Place

One African stated that they have lost their heritage. Their country is not the same to them now than before they left. They have lost their identity and must create a new one here. They are in need of a place to call their own; a secret place that protects them from their known and unknown enemies; a place where they can erase the nightmares of slavery. They feel they must reach that place where they can conquer their feelings of fear. I suppose they cannot heal the scars of their past until they have conquered their fears."

"Have you agreed to their concessions?"

"I have made no mention of my intentions yet. Are we not partners? Your counsel is required in regards to the operations of the farm. I have always consulted with you on matters that affect the both of us. You are a great judge of character. Shall we meet with our potential stakeholders later this afternoon?"

"Of course we shall, after a fine meal and much needed rest we can forge forward with the preparations."

"I will notify the group to be available this afternoon and tea will be served on the terrace while we consider our options."

"This is the most breathtaking view of the countryside. It amazes me everyday. Just over a month ago this land was barren. The vegetation was dead without any hope to ever revive and now we have expansive fields of green acreage."

A wonderful display of magnolia trees nestled among the low lying azalea bushes. The oak trees hover over the hills while the moss seeps from its branches below the blue sky. Various wild flowers and berry bearing bushes perched along the trail portray like escorts to the big house. The road winds up along the large spread that reveals a beautiful white plantation mansion at the end of two rows of weeping willows that disguise the entrance of the mansion. Along the mansion's walkway leading to the front entrance where begonias are placed strategically in terra cotta pots. The spacious terrace traces around the exterior of the entire house

Never Underestimate The Power of A Secret Place

where rocking chairs and tea tables are lined along the front of the mansion. White stone pillars stand erect from the east to the west near the rear of the mansion it reveals an area covered by a red clothed canopy above round tables with matching chairs neatly arranged along the edge of the terrace. The rear of the house faces the north and there lined neatly in four rows are the quarters. The partially burned and weathered quarters are where the slaves once lived on the plantation. Advantageously planted within the rows of quarters were three weeping willows, full of life they bow to pay homage to the dwellers of the quarters. The yards were impeccable with its walkways outlined by the normal traffic of the dwellers. Each quarter identical with its tin roof and decades of paint washed from its wooden surface. The gray outcast of the quarters compliments the green lawns with graveled pavements to create a sense of dignity even amongst the least of them. Northeast of the quarters where several oak trees stand unorganized but utilized for a clothes line. Wooden tables with benches and extremely large metal wash pans stacked underneath each of the tables. It appeared to be an area designated for the women to entertain daily gossip while they tend to the laundry. The mansion and the quarters are centrally located at the apex of the hill which overlooks scattered sites of the nearby plantations. Many of them appear to be abandoned with neglected fields for the upcoming harvest.

    Jonathan begins to prepare for the arrival of the machinery to plant the cotton. Nathan researched techniques which required the least amount of physical labor that will produce the highest quality of cotton. Storage of the cotton for transit to New York was Nathan's primary concern. Contractors were hired to build the most efficient storage facility for the cotton and other commodities. The acreage wrapped around the entire mansion from the west to stretch north then circle east to end south of the property. Below the twenty feet of rocky terrain is a road that

Never Underestimate The Power of A Secret Place

encircled the Johnson's Plantation. Many trespassers found it difficult to maneuver the terrain which rendered their attempts to enter the property unsuccessful. There is only one entrance onto the Johnson's acreage just beyond the adjacent wooded area which became the lookout for unsuspected or uninvited guest.

Jonathan recognized the need for individualism when he envisioned the workers housed in the woods. His intentions were to separate work from home. Therefore he created an atmosphere of privacy with also the permission to separate work duties from personal time. Everything had its rightful place with its own purpose like the workers suggested. Hours later the Africans begin to gather on the lawn near the quarters.

"Let us assemble with them to make offers for employment. We need workers right away to get the farm prepared for the planting season," suggests Jonathan.

Jonathan and Nathan returned to the back lawn of the mansion where they are greeted by the New York workers already assigned to their post and prepared to meet the Africans. Without regards to their attire they all appear that they could possibly be related. Nathan clears his throat to muffle the idle whispers among the group.

"It is my pleasure to introduce myself. I am Nathan Johnson and this is my brother Jonathan Johnson. We are one third of the property owners of this farm. There is Arthur Johnson who you will meet from time to time on the property while he tends to the legal operations of the farm. Then last but not least Mr. Opio, Ms. Rafael and Ms. Linda. Our goal is to produce the finest quality products to sale all over the world. We would like to offer a generous package to include fair wages, equal treatment, health benefits and housing benefits. I will now hand the platform over to Jonathan who will discuss your concerns and our expectations for employment."

Never Underestimate The Power of A Secret Place

"Hello everyone, I could not be more delighted to share this business venture with you. This is not our first business venture. Our family operates a cotton mill up north that is very successful. A few of our workers from the factory have made the decision to come south to invest with the startup of the agriculture aspect to raise cotton. So here we are and here you are. We want this to be an easy transition for everyone. This farm will become a home for all of us and we will blend into a large family. I have no intentions to become the "master" of the plantation. Suggestions have been made to name the plantation the Johnson's Plantation but I have decided to rename the plantation in honor of the person who invested their total inheritance in this endeavor."

Jonathan places his hand on Nathan's shoulder then announces, "The name will become Nathan's Place. I am proud to say we will finalize the documents in the near future. We will operate this farm like a business with everyone responsible for its success or failure. Nothing less than our best efforts will we expect from all that we offer."

"In regards to the requests you have made. We agree that under no circumstances should anyone work under the conditions you have mentioned in your request. This farms sole foundation is that of cohesion. We will not tolerate any form of degradation, humiliation, physical or emotional attacks from one another under any circumstance. We have on board three of our most knowledgeable leaders who you will mediate any conflicts experienced on the farm regardless of the person in question. I introduce to you Rafael, Linda and Opio our human resource team that will maintain the human relations component of the farm's operations. They will be the team that will assist with the human resource aspect of employment also any greviances on and off the farm."

"In reference to your request to your own quarter we have incorporated in your employment package the opportunity to purchase one of the quarters. The quarters will be relocated across the trail in that wooded area to your south. Each quarter is to be fitted with indoor plumbing and two added living spaces, some three. If you decide to purchase one of the quarters your must sign an agreement to make payments for the purchase of the quarter. Upon the completion of your agreement you will own the quarter for long as you wish. Any differences which may result among the dwellers that interfere with the operations of the farm will not be tolerated and will result in termination of the employment and housing contract. Are there any questions?"

A hand is raised.

"Yes, the woman in the dark head dress."

"How we buy our quartas if we don't work da farm?"

"We want the workers to love what they do and also have a home to come to at the end of the day. We have limited quarters for those invested in our business. If you do not have any interest in farming we do have a factory in New York where the cotton is manufactured for sale. If you feel that you may be interested in moving to New York we do have positions available. We can provide training and wages so that you can afford to live in New York. We will not house and feed anyone that does not invest in either of these ventures."

"How we git ta New York," someone from the crowd asks.

"Nathan will travel to New York within the next few weeks. Please meet with Linda, Opio or Rafael to review the job duties in the factory to determine if you are interested. We will not be held liable for anyone who deviates from Nathan's instructions throughout the trip to New York."

"Are there any further questions?"

"When we gonna start?"

"We can begin the process today. Your assistance will be needed to relocate the quarters. This is your opportunity to select the area where you want your quarter to be placed. Unfortunately all the quarters will be painted in earthly colors to camouflage their locations. Are there any more questions?"

"Why ya runs us off if we cain't git along?"

"We will suggest that you each reach a compromise those of you who may engage into a verbal conflict," explains one of the New Yorkers. "If you become physically combative you will no longer be employed as a worker or live in your quarter. It is at your request that we prohibit any form of degradation or physical abuse among other things. You have requested to live in a respectful and safe environment. We will honor your request but we expect you to honor your request also. The consequences are harsh but you will grow to appreciate a quality way of life once you have experienced it. Are there any more questions?"

"We calls ya masta Johnson?"

"Allow me to reiterate our relationship. This farm will run like a business. You will be workers no longer slaves. I understand that many of the landowners have not given up your rights to freedom quite easily. I must inform you that we will abide by the Constitution of the United States. If this eases your concerns any further for the record I am no relation to the previous owners. We will address everyone by their first name; you may deviate at your convenience ONLY with the permission of others. Are there any more questions?"

"If theres a man an he has two families which one he dwell wit?"

"I will leave that to the families to decide. The man will have to make arrangements that all parties can live by. We will also have Opio who to begin to officiate marriage ceremonies to eliminate any future problems. Bigamy is prohibited in the state of Louisiana. Only, and I repeat ONLY shall the initial marriage documented be considered legal all others are void. Opio will work in concert with our legal team in New York to document live birth certificates for everyone."

Never Underestimate The Power of A Secret Place

"Now I will discuss the reconstruction of the quarters that are to be relocated into the wooded area across the trail. I have hired a land surveyor who informed me that there is reasonable space to house all of the nineteen quarters and its inhabitants. However I have decided to maintain five of those quarters to establish a common market place. It will consist of a place to buy and trade wares at your request. A dining hall of the finest foods the world has to offer. Last but not least an infirmary for the sick. The marketplace will be stationed there west of the barn, Jonathan points. The barn will be refurbished into a place of worship for those of you who wish to attend. Opio is an Ordained Christian Minister and can officiate all services within his expertise. It will be an honor for the all workers to select the title of your sanctuary collectively. However, your participation is not required."

"The quarters that will be relocated to the woods will be yours to purchase. You may choose the location of your choice since there is adequate space for atleast thirty additional quarters. Some quarters will be modified to house larger families. The builders will instruct those of you who wish to learn the trade of carpentry. You will use those skills to maintain the quarters in addition to build add-ons as you grow. The wooded area is an enormous amount of acreage. You should be very conscious in how you care for it. The groundwork has already been laid for indoor plumbing our next step is to organize the quarters so we can fit the lines to meet the septic tanks. We will need your assistance to complete this operation."

"The most important venture into this project is to protect the woods. There will not be any removal of the trees for any reason unless they absolutely must come down. The trees are for your protection. They will disguise your whereabouts from any obtrusive forces. Your quarters will be upgraded with exterior brick walls for protection. The woods are a dark place. It would be in your best interest to keep it that way. There will be some dreary days and some beautiful days it depends on the weather. You must conform to your living enviornment and you will be well protected. I have learned that the woods are inhabited with wild animals. That is an advantage for you to preserve wildlife. I am an avid hunter myself it would be a great pleasure to hunt with some of you in the future."

"Tomorrow morning when the sun meets the top of these trees we will begin the excavation of the quarters to relocate them to their designated areas. Once all the quarters are all in their rightful places a team of volunteers will be available to help reconstruct the quarters."

"Masta Johnson."

"It is Jonathan, please refer to me as Jonathan it is my request."

"Jonathan what is a volunteers?"

"It is in reference to my colleagues who serve as philanthropists."

"What Jonathan attempts to explain to you is that he has class mates who attended the University with him in New York City. The University is considered an institution of higher learning. Which is beyond formal education which most of you may have experienced."

Nathan and Jonathan glance at each other in an awkward manner.

"I will say it again we will begin at early morning sunrise. Breakfast will be served in the barn. There will be accommodations for the families to lodge there until the project is complete. I have cans of paint so that you may mark the location of where you want your quarter stationed. Please locate an area that has been cleared to accommodate your quarter. We have uprooted the least amount of trees possible. Please make certain the mark is recognizable on your plot also the quarter you have selected. We will assist you so that the process will go like we planned. The quarters furthest from the entrance will be stationed first then we will work our way downward. Are there any questions?"

"Now I must have your attention to the instructions as we begin this journey. I need each of you to gather in a group with your prospective families."

The families begin to form small groups.

"Thank you for your cooperation. I see we have twenty-two families that is excellent. Now I need one person from each family to approach the table to select a can of paint then return to your family then each family must select the quarter that they prefer."

"The first family to reach the quarter of their fondness will be the owners of that quarter. Do not be afraid, off you go now."

The families began their walk towards the quarters. They look inside to inspect the interior of the quarters. Many of them are similar however some appear to be more recently rebuilt. There are some with fire damage and some weathered from the rains. Most important they are very sound structures that can withstand the upheaval of its contents. The families stand near their quarter of choice with signs of satisfaction. There is one family who appears to have selected a smaller more worn quarter. Nathan approaches them to inquire about their selection.

The woman of the group replies, "Dis here our quarta eva since we been here."

"But ma'am you may choose any quarter of your desire."

"Dis da one we desire."

All the children nod to confirm her report. Nathan scratches his head and assesses the family's dynamics. There are four males and two females to include the mother.

"Where is your father?"

"He gone to find freedom an neva come back."

The family's mood seemed to darken while Nathan looks on.

"Well I imagine your father will be very proud of your new home once he returns. Be of good cheer I assure you he will take great delight in your new home."

The young girl turns to her mother then giggles.

Nathan asks, "What do you find so delightful?"

She buries her head into her mother's waist.

"May I ask what is your name little one?"

"Estella."

"What a pretty name. Who are these fine lads?"

"What a lad?"

"A lad is a young boy or man."

"This my brothas Morgan, Cottrell, Carlton an his name Donell."

"Who is this beautiful woman by your side?"

"She my mammy."

"Tell me her name."

"Her name Delia."

"It is my pleasure to meet your family Delia."

Nathan kisses Estella's hand before she shyly pulls away.

Jonathan approaches, "Brother have I not warned you in regards to the advances upon my love?"

"You must be mad Estella would never find interest in the likes of you."

"Or would she?"

They both approach Estella in a teasing manner and cheer her to choose one of them.

"So dear Estella, who do you find with the most charisma?"

Nathan points to himself.

Jonathan remarks, "Do not kid yourself; it is clear that she chooses me."

"Do tell Estella?"

Estella appears to concentrate then points to Jonathan. Nathan pretends to be offended and asks, "Why him?"

She replies, "My mammy says he a good masta."

"I have known Jonathan all my life and never within that connotation."

The brothers embrace each other before they say farewell to the family. They begin their venture back to the front of the crowd. There are two rows of tables clothed in white linen with a display of cool beverages and food. Underneath the oak tree is an assembly of tables and chairs for everyone to gather. Children prance among the adults to view the selections.

"Please everyone help yourself to whatever you wish. We will continue our journey to the woods to mark your lots after you have eaten. Enjoy everyone!"

The brothers withdraw to the terrace to look over the blue print of the wooded area.

"We could easily conquer this project today if we maneuver the family with this blue print. It is an exact replica of the property therefore we will have no need to parade everyone around the grounds. Each can place their mark on the blue print to match their mark on the quarters. We will then begin to uproot the quarters for removal. The families can begin to disband their current dwellings to make room for the quarters that we will begin to relocate tomorrow. I suggest we set a goal at three relocations per day. Allow at least a week for completion before the carpenters begins."

"Jonathan are you certain they can handle all the hard labor it requires?"

"I have over fifty of our faithful fraternity brothers who would love to invest their time into this project. It will be a great experience for them. Now let us get these quarters assigned before night falls."

"Um hmm,"Nathan clears his throat.

"Everyone, I hope you have enjoyed the refreshments. Now we will begin the assignment of acreage in the woods. We will begin with the lots along the entrance way. Are there any takers?

Never Underestimate The Power of A Secret Place

Yes, the lad in the suspenders; please approach the blueprint to claim your lot with the same marks that you placed on the quarter. Let me see it appears that you have made an 'x' on the quarter. Now you will place that very mark on the blueprint directly on the lot of your choice. Very well you have made your selection. May I have another person from their family come forward? Now what is the mark that you have placed on your quarter? Another x; my, my, my. I believe we have a problem Jonathan."

"Yes we do, what do you suggest?"

"I have no idea where to go from here."

"I have an idea."

"Yes, Opio please do tell."

"Perhaps we can provide each member of the family with two square cards with their surname written on both. They shall place one on the quarter of their choice and one on the blueprint."

"That sounds reasonable. Mother please gather some paper and writing utensils. Now everyone, please take a pencil and inscribe your surname on both of the cards that we provide to you."

After a few minutes has passed.

"Now someone from your family will place the card inside the quarter of your choice after you have pinned your card to the blue print. Very well now, someone from each family please come forward to pin your card on your chosen lot located on the blueprint. You have selected this lot am I correct, Badeaux is the name?"

The man nods to affirm his choice.

"Now pin it on the blueprint somewhere that suits you."

The man pins his card on the blue print.

"Very well, this shall be the place where your quarter will be relocated. May I have the next person?"

A young boy hands Jonathan his card with the name Badeaux printed on it.

"Nathan!"

"Yes brother?"

"Once again our plans have been stymied. Mr. Badeaux, am I correct?"

"Yes suh."

Jonathan turns to face the crowd.

"Will all the Baddeaux's please raise your hands?"

Over half of the Africans begin to raise their hands; men, women and children.

"How can this be that they are all related? It cannot be so brother."

"My brother it was customary that slaves take the surname of their masters."

"That has got to be the most selfish act known to man."

"I believe so, if I must say so myself. So how shall we press forward?"

"I have not the slightest clue. Are there any suggestions how we should proceed to reallocate the quarters?"

Linda steps forward to speak.

"It appears to me that we have only one family that has some sentimental connection to one of the quarters. This will allow us to relocate the other quarters according to family size. Possibly we can place one quarter at the entrance to serve as a safe gateway for the families. Thereafter the families can select the quarters. Nathan I think that will be the most negotiatable plan for everyone. Do you agree?"

"Quite naturally, the families can determine their selections once the quarters have been relocated. Now we must plan for the most exhaustive part of the reconstruction. We need assistance to clear the lots for the quarters. We will also need workers to mark the lots so the truckers will know where to reposition the quarters. Can I depend on any of you?"

Everyone in harmony says, "Yes suh."

Never Underestimate The Power of A Secret Place

Jonathan smiles at the eager group hopeful not to discourage them.

"The staff will make arrangements for food and temporary lodging until the quarters are ready to inhabit. We will house many of you in the barn. There is enough camping equipment for all. Women please bring your belongings to the barn and create a space for your families. The men will camp around the barn to secure the area. We have plenty of oil for your lamps. There are some wool blankets for cover during the cool nights. You may now dismiss yourselves to prepare for the night."

The families disburse to collect their belongings. Jonathan, Nathan along with the staff board the wagon. With its double wide bed loaded with food and camping equipment they begin the ride down to the barn. They pass the families who merge along the trail which leads to the barn located west of the woods. Many of them appear to be tired but full smiles adorn their faces to reveal a sign of hope.

The wagon stops along the trail east of the barn. Men, women and children begin to move their belongings to the barn while the brothers sit on the bed of the wagon to continue their talk.

"Oh, how I wish for the paved streets of New York. How strange is it to live in a moment where two states seem worlds apart? There is New York with all its luxuries and diversity versus Louisiana with its natural resources struggling to overcome its fear of difference, Jonathan ponders. Why do we reject God's flawlessness yet we fail to recognize our own imperfections?"

"I am puzzled by the thought myself brother. My hopes are that we will come to our senses before it is too late. By the way we should prepare for the night; morning is yet a breath away."

"I think I will dwell with the workers this evening, says Jonathan. It will be good to establish a bond with the men early as possible."

"That is a very good idea."

"I think I will join you with our new brethren."

"Nathan, you are so needy."

"Needy you say? Was it I that struggled with the monster in the closet in my childhood?"

"Fair enough Nathan, but it was mother who tended to your every beck and call. She hardly soothed me in sickness because of you."

"Oh brother, you know mother loved you more; you are the only son of her flesh."

"Yes but you were like a prize to her; her pride and joy."

"No, I cannot imagine that to be so."

"She yearned to reveal her true identity but feared that she would destroy father's reputation prevented her disclosure. It continues to astound me that I have not revealed any signs of my African heritage. Father was very careful not to disclose my birth so that it would not to reveal mother's passing for white. He could have easily chosen not to wed. He was not forced to marry her unlike what we were originally told. Mother became impregnated well into the marriage. It must have been pure love."

"Of course it was brother. Mother is the most beautiful woman in the world. She has the most beautiful blue eyes with long bronze curls. I did find it strange that she often tanned very easily in the summer months. She reminds me of the golden angel perched on the mantel in grandfather's study. How long before he knew of her true ethnicity?"

"He said that he knew all along because her father was a worker in grandfather's medical facility."

"What did grandfather think of it?"

"It was he that encouraged the marriage."

"How do you know?"

"Mother revealed that she pretended to be impregnated to force father to wed her. She then took on the care of Arthur whose parents abandoned him. Grandfather's wits got the best of him then he encouraged them to marry. Of course father was able to obtain Arthur's birth certificate then have it altered to his satisfaction."

"Jonathan I have heard enough of your foolishness."

"It is father's story. He says that grandfather procured the adoptions of the children in the orphanage to keep the siblings together. Often the courts would separate the children to esablish a home for them. I once heard that Arthur had a sister that was adopted by a wealthy family but he has limited recollection of their kinship. Father has the original birth certificate of them both and presented the documents to Arthur when he left for boarding school."

"What was his reaction?"

"His initial thoughts were that father relinquished his rights. Father reassured him that the opportunity was so that he would have knowledge of his sister."

"Do tell, did they ever reconcile?"

"Yes, his sister's adoptive parents agreed to the union. For some time they were reunited during our summer camps but eventually they parted ways."

"Why have I not met her?"

"Nathan you have my brother."

"I would have some recollection of Arthur's sister."

"Try to recall the memories of Sharon while she accompanied us during the summer camps."

"Sharon Ahh, my first love!"

"Nathan she was ten wise years to your five meager years of existence."

"I shall have to say she was impressed by my athletic attributes."

"Or it was your numerous injuries that captured the attention of all the sympathetic lasses."

"Nevertheless it served its purpose."

"What shall that be Nathan? I can recollect many occasions that your deception got the best of you. My most remembrance is of Betty a woman who will not be denied."

"Ahhh, yes my Betty I used to think of her. She was not fond of my numerous lady callers."

"If I remember your lady callers almost cost you the acquaintance of a scolding hot breakfast one early morning."

"I remember that day so well."

"It serves as a reminder to always serve your acquaintances with a long handle spoon or you shall end up with egg on your face."

Both begin to laugh aloud!

"So what became of *your* Betty?"

"From what I understand she is with child now."

"Do tell whoever fathered this child must be an incredible man. I could never imagine how you were able to even peek into the good graces of such a remarkable woman."

"If you must know Jonathan, that incredible man is none other than me."

"You must be mad dear brother. Betty is such an exquisite and beautiful young lady. There were many eligible suitors before you that would be considered miserably to meet her father's criteria. Her father will eat you alive if what you say is true!"

"Let us just say that mother's love for me spared my life."

"How so?"

"She was first to know that Betty was with child and somehow our mother was able to confide in Mr. Wellingsworth. He insisted that we marry right away. Mother has her way with people you know."

"Why was this not ever disclosed to the family?"

"Father and mother were present at the ceremony."

"What ceremony? Am I not your brother and are we not inseparable?"

Never Underestimate The Power of A Secret Place

"Indeed you are but mother's passing overshadowed every aspect of my life. Of course I was going to tell you but the pain of losing mother became unbearable. Are you aware that mother and Mr. Wellingsworth are sister and brother? Betty was adopted by Mr. Wellingsworth."

"I had no idea. Why is there so much secrecy among us?"

"It was mentioned that mother escaped from slavery and never gained her freedom. She traveled to New York along with her father and brother. At the time her brother was still in his youth and able to gain his rights to freedom but mother was past the age of redemption. Mr. Wellingsworth was adopted into a wealthy family while mother became a helper in the orphanage."

"So that is why mother was so dedicated to keeping the orphanage open."

"Yes, Nathan but it was grandfather that provided the finances to keep it open. Grandfather often visited the orphanage to provide medical assistance until his death. Father often assisted him and upon one particular visit he found a beautiful young lady hidden in the cellar. He inquired about her well being and she revealed that she was a slave that escaped with her father. Then it was common for whites to be slaves also, so father never questioned her race. The headmaster of the orphanage fell ill afterwards and the orphanage was threatened with closure. Father revealed the possibility of a young lady at the orphanage who could continue to manage the orphanage. When grandfather met mother, he was convinced that she possessed the tenacity to keep the orphanage open. Grandfather donated a large sum of money to continue the operation of the orphanage on her behalf. To gain her rights to freedom father agreed to marry mother disguising the obvious that he was in love with her. Grandfather gave his permission for the union before his death. Father invested a portion of his inheritance into the factory and mother moved into the estate with father as husband and wife. The orphanage gained supports from many of

Grandfather's colleagues who continue to provide medical care and financial support for the orphans. Mother was able to gain access to the records of the adopted orphans to find that her brother was adopted into the Wellingsworth family. The Wellingsworth remains a financial partner for the orphanage until this day. Mother's brother name is Tony. He is an alumnus of ours. He served in the World War I. A few of his Army brigade's officers attended mother's funeral in his honor."

"So he is still alive."

"As we know of to this day; it will be a joyous occasion to meet him."

"Indeed it will."

"We have become poor managers of time. We must secure the blankets to the post so that the women and children can settle in. We can camp here with the men tonight. There should be enough blankets for everyone. Here, here, gentlemen. Now let us begin to set up camp near the women and children tonight for protection. If we construct a camping area here then one there we will be able to keep watch over the barn. How does that sound?"

The men nod their heads in approval.

5

NOT JUST A SAFE PLACE

Once everyone has settled Nathan gathers a wool blanket and burlap bag to settle in with the runaway slaves near the east of the barn. Jonathan gathers with the freedmen near the west of the barn. The campfire in Nathan's group had fully ignited which lights up the circle so that the faces of the men are recognizable. Nathan begins a round robin introduction among his settlers as an ice breaker.

"My name is Joshua, I has two boys, James and John an my boys mammy."

"Let me clarify Joshua you have two sons and a daughter?"

"No suh, she my boys mammy."

"Mammy you refer to as your mother?"

"Yes suh."

Nathan thinks to himself, this is an opportunity to set acceptable values for the Africans.

He stands, "Gentlemen please accept my most sincere apology but you have been misled in regards to the proper manner in which to address women. Throughout our journey together to build this legacy we will re-indoctrinate the proper language that will be practiced here at Nathan's Place."

"Brother we do not have the right to alter their culture, advises Jonathan when he reaches Nathan."

"Jonathan it is not the culture of the Africans to degrade their women with inferior descriptions. Never has it been for any tribes of Africa for that matter. These derogatory titles have been the source by which the African people have been labeled for years. It is a covert attempt to separate the African people from society. We must eradicate this mindset by which language is used as a weapon to alienate one another. If not, hatred will adopt this new method to destroy the powerless."

"Nathan again you have taken this matter too far."

"Have I brother?"

"Yes, brother the laws have changed. No longer will our brethren live in fear of physical or verbal torment. These acts of violence are unlawful for all men; American and African too."

"Jonathan there will never be a law able to change the heart of man. I believe there is only one type of human being, those that choose to do evil or those that choose to do good. There will come a day when hatred will transform itself into a form that will continue to spew evil among the powerless and defy the laws of tomorrow."

"How so brother?"

The others look on while the brothers continue.

"Please do tell."

"The bible speaks that the tongue is like a double edged sword."

"That is correct."

"My point is that if we continue the path to label human beings with undignified titles we will soon kill the soul. A wounded soul will either turn on itself or its society. I have never mentioned this before brother but in my youth I experienced verbal hatred and it bruised my spirit. If it were not for my faith in God along with mother's encouragement I would have taken my life years ago."

"But Nathan you were so cherished by the family we share. How could you feel that way?"

"Jonathan everyday I left home to face a world of new disappointments. It is because of God's hedge of protection around me that I made it this far. Their fears are my fears. Their reality is my reality. For you Jonathan you have been protected by the white complexion that your mother also sought refuge. This is my duty."

"Again, it is a shameful statement used by the slave owners when they apply the term mammy in regards to a mother. It is also the same as gal in terms of an African woman, young lady or girl is more appropriate. From this day forward we will no longer use those terms: mother will replace mammy; woman or young lady will replace gal; worker will replace slave; we will NOT use the term nigga, nigger, or masta from this time forward. I expect everyone to educate themselves to the proper manner in which to address one another. Am I clear?"

In unison everyone says, "Yes suh."

Jonathan heads back to his group.

"Now tell me are you both married?"

"No suh."

"Would you like to marry?"

"Yes suh."

"Then it shall be. What is her name?"

"Her name Esther."

"I see you all have biblical names."

"Esther's mammy she wit us too."

"So Esther's *mother* lives with you also."

"What is her name?"

"Her name Ms. Sallie."

"That is a very unique name. Brother you are next tell me about yourself."

"My name is Samson, I has no family."

"Is that so? Are you from around here?"

"My masta's plantations up yonder."

"Whatever happened to your family?"

"He sold my motha and fatha an young ladys."

"Samson when you say young ladys do you mean you have wife?"

"No suh, my sistas."

"How long ago?"

"Not too long suh."

"They say a white man an black man took one of my sistas."

"What does your sister look like?"

"They say she look like me but her eyes da color blue."

"You don't say. Now where do you think your mother and father may be?"

"They say masta Badeaux paid for 'em an now theys his slave. He lookin fo me but I don't wanna be a slave no mo."

"I see I am fascinated by your report Samson. Slavery is now unlawful determined by the U.S Constitution. You have nothing to fear brother you are a free man."

"They put a bounty on my head if they finds me they gone kill me."

"Murder my brother constitutes a crime punishable by law. I have access to an attorney who will document your freedom legitimately. He will visit here soon. By any chance can you tell me the name of your former Master?"

"His name Thomas Badeaux they's done name a Parrish afta him. He a powerful man."

"We shall see about that but another time Sampson. Tell me your story sir."

"My name is Levi, my chilluns wit they motha on tha Badeaux plantation."

"By any chance do you two know each other?"

"Yes suh, we runaway togetha."

"Interesting so you escaped together?"

"I went back ta tha plantation ta git my fam'ly but they say they is dead. Samson an his fam'ly run wit me but they git caught."

"I am sorry to hear about your loss. I must tell you that you will not have to run anymore. You are safe here. You all are safe here. Who is next?"

"My name Elijah my pappy run from tha Johnson's plantation."

"Did you mean to say your father, Elijah?"

"Yes suh."

"You were once a slave on this very plantation?"

"Yes suh."

"So tell me, why are you among the runaways and not with the freedmen?"

"When you run da masta beat tha ones dat stay. Sometimes kill they family so everybody too scared ta run. They turn on us; say we bring death ta da family. If we caught an brung back ta tha plantation nobody have nothin ta do wit us. We disgrace ta our people. We wanna die not come back ta tha plantation. When ya tired ya don't care if ya die so you run. Sometimes we say dyin is betta than livin in dis world full of hate."

"Hate is such a strong word Elijah."

"Yes suh, who ya know beat an kill tha one theys love?"

"You are very wise Elijah one day you will know what love is."

"I hope that day come suh."

"So do I Elijah."

"Now who are you sir?"

"My name Kyle an all my family dead."

"How old are you sir?"

"They say I'se one hundred years ole suh."

"One day Kyle I want to sit with you to learn of all your wisdom."

"I'se a slave boy suh what can I teach ya?"

"We all have something to learn from you sir. You are the most honored among us. Are you alone?"

"My comm'n law wife in tha barn suh."

"Kyle points to the barn."

"We ain't neva been apart."

"Please pardon the disruption but it will pay off in the long run. I promise that you shall see greater days, Mr. Kyle."

"Sir, please introduce yourself."

"My name Joel, I runs from tha chain gang."

"What is a chain gang?"

"When ya break da law ya do hard time workin da railroad."

"Why where you placed on the chain gang?"

"I beat tha masta's boy fo beatin my mammy."

Kyle nudges Joel.

"I means ta say motha suh. They take me ta tha chain gang. I runs back ta tha plantation ta my motha."

"How old are you son?"

"I'se don't know suh. Nobody know when I'se born."

"We can get access to the slave rolls. By law all slave owners must record the births and deaths of all their slaves then forward those records to the United States Registry. Somewhere there is a record of your birth and we will find it. What is that contraption around your foot?"

"I was chain ta anotha slave."

"Where is he?"

"He dead suh."

"How so?"

"He dies in solit'ry."

"How did you escape?"

"Afta he die I wait fo him ta waste away an pull tha chain off his bones."

"How long did that take?"

"Don't know suh."

"Dear God have mercy. I am sorry for the horrible sufferings you have experienced. Did you ever find your mother?"

"No suh."
"You are here alone?
"No suh, my wife in tha barn too."
"So you are married?"
"Yes suh. Tha overseer marries us on tha chain gang."
"I tole you they ain't marries ya tha right way."
"What ya know ole man."
"I know ain't no way ya git married on tha chain gang. Ya lower than a slave boy."
"Gentlemen, I will have an attorney to look into the matter. Do not worry yourselves with it now, let us surrender ourselves to rest."
"Mistah Nathan ya don't talk like us; wheres ya from?"
"I am from New York City. My mother was a slave in Mississippi before I was born. She fled up north to freedom. Of course she was never free."
"So freedom ain't true?"
"Yes it is but my mother died before she gained her rights to freedom."
"So yo papa raised ya?"
"No, I never met my father. I have no knowledge of him. I was adopted by Jonathan's family at birth. I wish I knew my biological mother. However, I was truly blessed with a devoted family, beautiful home and an opportunity for a quality education."
Jason stands up and speaks, "I wanna educat'n."
"You shall have that opportunity."
"I can go ta New York City ta go ta school?"
"If that is your wish Jason, only you can limit yourself."
"I go right now."
"Easy now lad you will have to meet with my staff to make the arrangements. Why are you in such a hurry?"
"They gonna kill me when they finds me."

"Nonsense, you are in a safe place. You have no reason to run anymore."

"What do ya knows boy? We neva stop runnin long as hate is alive."

"Believe it or not there are some people who are very compassionate."

"One these days ya gonna look hate in tha face."

"Mr. Kyle have ya ever looked hate in the face?'

"Yes suh."

"Tell me what does it look like?"

"Suh it look like death."

The quiet night falls around the group of men. The fire continues to flicker and releases traces of red sparks into the air. One by one the men begin to turn in for the night. Resigned to the truth of their reality; Nathan struggles to understand.

Sunlight breaks their sleep while they awaken to an enormous spread of breakfast entrees lined upon white crisp linen covered tables. There are enough seats for the women and children while the men stand among them. Everyone is washed up and prepared to enjoy their morning feast. Mingled among them is the staff from New York. They begin to share recipes along with stories about their experiences in Louisiana. The brothers observe from afar while they consume their favorite pastries.

"How was your night? You appear to engage with the men quite well."

"I must say their stories troubled me throughout the night."

"I am sorry that mother is not here to console you."

"I wished she were I would tell her how much I appreciate the life she afforded me."

"You must tell me what has troubled you so."

"How was your night brother?"

Never Underestimate The Power of A Secret Place

"Quite delightful I must say. There is a gentleman by the name of Junebug. He gave me an account of how the farm operated after the Civil war."

"Junebug is his name? Humor me if you must."

"I would rather you hear it from the horse's mouth."

They approach Junebug while he is wrestles with the canvas on which he slept. Jonathan motions for one of the ladies to take the cloths from him.

"Please place these with the others for tonight."

Two of the ladies take the canvas between them and fold it into a neat square. Jonathan guides Junebug away from the crowd then they begin to walk towards the trail. Nathan grabs a portion of food for Junebug before he meets up with them.

"Junebug you have met Nathan I assume?"

"Yes suh."

"Can you recount the story that you mentioned to me last night?"

"Yes suh."

"Junebug please describe the Gourdeau's plantation before we became the owners."

Junebug begins to describe the scenery.

"Now dis road leads ta tha back of tha big house where tha slave quartas is. Masta Gourdeau helped us ta build tha ones we see. Ova there we grows cotton fo miles an miles. Ya know we neva has boweevils til last year. They ate up tha crops ova night; went through 'em like a speedin train. Neva saw nuthin like it. Behind tha slave quartas was tha farmland fo tha veg'tables. The chilluns worked da veg'tables; theys easier on da hands an back. Then when they git bigga they come ova to work tha cotton. Everythin has a place of they own. That quarta way ovah yonder was where I lives befo'e masta Gourdeau dies. Then they took it aways. Says dat it b'long to masta Badeaux he's tha new masta. Myrtle told em dat she has her pap'rs they paid her no neva mind."

"Junebug, do you have a deed to that quarter?"

"Is that what you call it suh? I don't have no papers my Myrtle got em suh."

"Can we see those papers Junebug?"

"Well that be up ta Myrtle. She git mighty protectin of 'em pap'rs."

"Junebug I would love to meet your wife."

"I'se see if I can git her ta meet somewheres on da trail, she cain't come back ta this property."

"I can imagine why. Can you take us to where she is now?"

"No suh, she masta Badeaux's slave. He a powerful man. That her only home, if ya knows what I mean?"

"I understand, how about if we wait right here on the side of the road while you bring Myrtle to us."

"How bout in da mornin?"

"Well, I guess that will have to do. Can we meet you in town? Maybe we can get something to eat?"

"No suh, we ain't been ta town since masta Gourdeau die. We lost all our rights when he die."

"Junebug slavery is over it shall never return again," Jonathan reminds him.

"Suh, here slavery ain't gone they just hides it."

"What do you mean?"

"Well suh, we cain't sell or trade nothin in town like when masta Gourdeau was livin."

"Mr. Gourdeau?"

"Yes suh, Mistah Gourdeau. We stay in da woods outa sight so we don't bring no trouble ta us. I don't know how longs it gonna ta stay that way. We gettin mighty tired of livin dis way."

"Junebug we can meet you on the trail right here where we stand, is that okay?"

"Yes suh."

"Please bring your wife."

"Yes suh, I can meet ya when da sun reach da top of those trees." Junebug points to the wooded area.

"About what time is that?"

"I don't know suh, that's how we knows it time fo work."

"Well we will be here first thing in the morning."

"Yes suh."

"Now let us eat."

The men walk back towards the aroma of hot butter biscuits being released in the air. They look at each other then each begin to walk faster and faster before they begin to race to the table laden with eggs, biscuits, fresh bacon and ham.

"Brother how will we know when the sun reaches the top of the trees? I am baffled by that concept."

"Nathan, we will just have to wait and see. It may be senseless to us but to them it is how they survive in this world. It is so strange how there is such a great divide between those that have and those who have not. This world produces more than it can ever consume yet we have people who live a substandard life. What is most ridiculous is that we say we care but we let it continue right under our very nose."

"Jonathan we cannot save everyone."

"I agree, we cannot but what sense does it make to burn down the quarters without any remorse and then live in a beautiful home like this one?"

It is now another day; Nathan stirs while the sun peeks through the oak tree over head. He glances over to see if Jonathan has awakened to find him sipping a cup of tea. Nathan wrestles himself out of his blankets then he leans toward the fire to warm himself. He extends his hand to Jonathan so that he pulls him from the warmth of his blanket.

"We must get inside to freshen up. I think the sun has reached the top of the trees sometime ago. Let us hurry so that we may partake of a hot meal."

Never Underestimate The Power of A Secret Place

They race to the big house in attempt to throw each other off course. Nathan arrives first with Jonathan at his heels. They settle into their routine of horseplay while they wash up for their meal. When they finally sit at the table Linda and Raphael greet them with a cup of breakfast tea and hot biscuits.

"Do not eat too many biscuits your meal is almost done," announces Raphael. "You know the trucks will be here today and you will need a good hot meal to hold you until the mid-day meal."

"Why do you not keep a warm tray in the oven for us like you have in the past?"

"Because son we have small children to feed."

"Ahh, brother it seems that we are no longer important."

"You will always be important to us Nathan but these little ones are top priority."

"It is a part of becoming a man Nathan, one day you will understand."

"You will also *my* brother."

"Will the two of you ever end your quarrels?"

"One day mother when we become too old to remember what we were fighting about."

"I hope we shall see those days brother."

"We will Nathan we are inseparable."

Opio enters the kitchen.

"There is a couple on the roadside to see you," he reports. "They refuse to come in but would like to meet with the both of you."

"Perhaps it is Junebug and his wife?"

"I recognized the gentleman he may be one of the former slaves," reports Opio.

"We must hurry the trucks will deliver this morning."

The brothers rush to meet the couple. Myrtle is a robust, molasses colored woman with large brown eyes and lips to match. Myrtle's features remind Jonathan of Melba. He wonders to himself if they are somehow related. Jonathan greets them before he introduces Nathan. He shakes the hand of Myrtle while she looks curiously into his eyes.

Junebug begins to speak, "Befo' Mista Gourdeau die he give Myrtle these pap'rs."

"Junebug we neva calls masta Gourdeau mistah. Folks hear ya sayin that an they gone hang ya on dead man's road."

"It is alright Myrtle, murder is against the law. You are safe to say whatever you like."

"Ya see Myrtle's motha Ms. Sallie work in Mistah Gourdeau's house. Since slavery is no mo Ms. Sallie feel no need ta run. Many of da slaves on Mistah Gourdeau's farm say theres no need to run. Mistah Gourdeau paid us fair wages fo what we earns. We eat from da best of his crops an he allows us ta meet unda da ole tin roof to thank God fo our blessins. We ain't allow'd to talk at da worship jus like in da field. Town folk scared we'd put a hoax on 'em so they say we cain't talk to each other; only ta da overseer. So we moans when we sad an hum when we happy. It sounds like music that we be makin with our hearts. Sometimes it sound sweet an sometimes it sound low. Ya neva know what ya gonna get. They say ya could hear us down in da valley. It made da town folk unsteady. They say it brung bad weatha, sickness or even death. But they neva could say fo sho it was us."

"Ms. Sallie sometimes tends to da big house on Sunday mornins. When she did she hums da sounds of worship til it fill da whole house an that's a mighty big house. Soon all tha workas starts ta hum an its in da air It gets calm ova Mistah Gourdeau's property when we hums its like everythin be still. The pond settles down even if there's a storm brewin. Mistah Gourdeau sometimes sits on his porch or fish by da pond, but he neva caught anythin he jus listen to da workas hum."

"It seems like everythin on da plantation celebrates wit us. Sometimes we jump, dance, hum some pass out on da ground like

Never Underestimate The Power of A Secret Place

they dead. But ev'ry body fine when da worshipin is ova we neva lost a soul. Many people in town troubled bout it an tole Mistah Gourdeau ta put a end ta it. But he tole em, long as they ain't hurtin nobody they can keep hummin an moanin. Da worship place used to be a wooden barn but it been burned ta da ground many a times. Mistah Gourdeau put togetha some sheets of metal ta iron poles an put 'em da ground. Say, he cain't stand ta see us wit nowhere ta go ta talk wit our God. It be mighty funny cause Mistah Gourdeau ain't believe in no Gods. He say when he was a chile his motha sent him ta worship meetins. He was tole ta be good when he went inside but when everybody left worship they went about da day commenced ta being tha same ole rotten beings they was. When he got olda he stop goin ta worship meetin. He say he neva been back since."

"Now let's talk about the papers, do you have them with you?"

"Yes suh. But we needs to know that ya ain't gonna take away da only place we know ta be ours."

"Myrtle, if you have papers which say the quarter standing on that land is yours, I am more than happy to help you get it back. A man can only live in one house."

"Well suh, I believe that's what it say, my education ain't da finest. I do rememba Mistah Gourdeau tells my motha she neva have to worry fo a place to live. He say masta Badeaux has a will that says da same."

"May I see your papers please Myrtle?"

Myrtle slowly pulls the well maintained document from her bible then hands it to Junebug; Junebug hands it to Jonathan. Jonathan proceeds to read the deed aloud:

I/We <u>Mr. Timothy Gourdeau & Mr. Thomas Badeaux</u> the undersigned grantor (s) for a valuable consideration, receipt which is hereby acknowledged, do hereby remise, release, convey and forever quitclaim to <u>Ms. Sallie & heirs of Ms. Sallie</u> the following described real property in the City of: <u>Bouseau</u> the Parrish of: <u>Badeaux ,</u> State of: <u>Louisiana.</u>

Property #1 sec; Township 76; 5 acres, 1 quarter dwelling located east lots ; Property #2 sect 3;Township 76 to include 1 acre.

Executed on <u>December 27, 1910</u>, in the City of <u>Bouseau</u>, State of: <u>La.</u>

Assessor's parcel No. <u>1 76; 3 76</u>

"What do it says, Mistah Jonathan?"

"It says that you are the property owner of the quarter also the acre that surrounds the quarter. I think I may be able to help you get your property back. Are you on board?"

"Yes suh."

"My attorney will meet with you in a few days; you have the information we need. Can you trust me that I will work in your best interest Myrtle?"

"If masta Badeaux finds out he gonna kill me."

"Myrtle you do not have to go back. You are more than welcomed to stay here to claim your mother's property that you may have inherited."

"You gonna let me have tha property too?"

"Of course it is rightfully yours to claim."

"My chile she at tha Badeaux plantation an I cain't git her away from there."

"How did you manage to escape?"

"I'se tell masta Badeaux I'se go pick some pork greens fo dinna. I done already picked 'em an they is ready ta cook but he don't know no difference. He keeps my chile so I always come back."

"Myrtle you may return to your daughter. We will think of something. Gather your most treasured possessions then be prepared to leave at a moment's notice."

"Yes suh."

Both men walk away to discuss the matter in more depth.

"First thing first let us meet with Arthur to confirm the authenticity of the deed."

Jonathan walks into the big house then picks up the phone to call Arthur.

"Father, yes this is Jonathan by any chance is Arthur available? How are you father? Please excuse my indifference I have an important matter to discuss with Arthur. Hello brother how on earth did you not know that the Gourdeau Plantation has multiple proprietors?"

"Jonathan there is no possible way. I scoured the court records exhaustively. How could it be?"

"It appears that I have someone here who has what looks like a legal copy of a deed to the property."

"You don't say? Can you give me the filing number on the deed?"

"Tell me where is it located?"

"It should appear in the upper right hand corner. It could begin with letters or numbers."

"Yes, it is here. It reads LJ dash 110231901."

"Thanks, I should be able to access the records and go from there."

"Then what?"

"Well, we will have to determine if it is a legal document. If so, then the property will have to be relinquished to its rightful property owners. Then you may proceed to file a motion to have the documents recorded to display the correct information. If I am not mistaken the oldest brother of Mr. Gourdeau is still living. His name is Thomas Badeaux. I will attempt to make contact with him."

"Arthur, it may not be a wise decision. The woman who produced this document is a slave at this time to Mr. Badeaux."

"That is absurd slavery has been outlawed over a half century ago."

"Brother you must imagine that some of the slaves do not know their rights or are threatened upon death if they escape here in the minutest regions of the South."

"Well we must do something about that."

"What do you suggest dear brother?"

"I am positive that I can gather a few of our active soldiers to articulate the laws on the subject of the abolishment of slavery. It would be a pleasure to dust the cow webs from my uniform just for mere entertainment."

"Brother this is not the time for amusement lives hang in the balances."

"Do not fret Jonathan my intentions are of grave concern for those who are disenfranchised by no fault of their own."

"When shall we expect your arrival?"

"I will keep in touch. This is a rather large task since I must consider that we will have to travel by horse to reach you."

"Nonsense we have travelled by automobile since our initial journey to purchase the property. Has our finances dwindled to such meager means?"

"Jonathan sometimes I wonder if your common sense was narrowed by your indulgence of academic knowledge."

"This is no time for insults."

"I must reiterate the importance of a horse to its soldier. Nevertheless, I will keep in touch."

"I will have everyone take watch for your arrival."

"No need brother, the chatter will meet you long before our arrival."

"Tell father I send my love."

"Will do."

The phone call ends. Jonathan turns to Nathan.

Never Underestimate The Power of A Secret Place

"We need to get some history on Mr. Badeaux. Someone has to know something about him. My guess is that it would be Junebug. I hear the sweet sound of an engine. It sounds like there may be more than just one single engine."

They both approach the front entry way of the big house. Soon they witness a long line of wide bed trucks with shotgun houses positioned on each of the truck's bed. Nathan perplexed by what he witnesses then turns to Jonathan.

"Nathan after much discussion with our fraternity brothers we could not for the life of us allow anyone to continue to live in such deprivation. Grant has donated the lumber to build sixteen shotgun houses for the families when he learned of our plans for the quarters. The Freemans' are a massive family with many talents. Along with a few of our colleagues they were able to install indoor plumbing for each of the modules. Granted that they are substantially small they were manufactured upstate then shipped to the nearest port where they are now transported to this site. The modules will be stationed on the lots and modifications can be made to fit the family's need."

"Jonathan how can I thank you?"

"Brother it was not I but the generosity of our brotherhood. Many of them were astounded at the living conditions of the former slaves. It is not until you walk in another man's shoes that you grasp his plight. The men who built these homes dwelled in the quarters while they prepared the property for the sewage lines. A few of the men who once lived in the flats downtown have found it difficult to imagine that humans beings have lived in such deplorable conditions."

Tears begin to stream from Nathan's eyes once he observes the expressions of the former slaves; somehow they appear to be cognizant of the event. The brothers begin to race to the meet the driver of the first truck.

Never Underestimate The Power of A Secret Place

"I can not allow him to see the sign post before it has been set in place. Please Lord this is my gift to him, he must not know," Jonathan thinks.

Jonathan reaches the truck out of breath as a warning he places his index finger over his lips. The truck driver nods to acknowledge that he understands. Jonathan leaps onto the truck's footrest to search for the sign to no avail. He jumps down then approaches the second truck to ask the driver in a low voice, "Where is it?" The driver covers his mouth and he whispers to Jonathan that it is being transported in on its own truck. Nathan pulls himself up to the truck's window while balancing himself on the footrest.

"It is good to see you Grant. Can you tell me what is going on?"

"I will have to leave that to Jonathan, I don't want to steal his thunder if you know what I mean."

"Yes sir he can be quite a nuisance at times."

"Shut her down," yells one of the truckers.

Grant turns the ignition off to allow the truck to shut down. Nathan jumps down before Grant exits the truck. Careful to measure his steps Grant leaps from the truck.

"There was a time when I could do that but not anymore son."

Nathan smiles, "Mr. Grant don't be so hard on yourself."

"Call me Grant. We are family."

The truck drivers come together in a circle along with Nathan and Jonathan.

"Now there is enough cleared space to back the trucks onto the site to unhitch the modules. The first modules to settle will be the largest ones. There are six. Three will be stationed on the farthest southeast of the entrance also two on the farthest southwest. Once we have those in place the eight smaller modules will be stationed north of those modules with four on each side of the entrance way. Each module has wheels for relocation if necessary but for the most part the modules will be stationed where we have marked the lots. Are there any questions?"

"There are only six modules, where are the others?

The smaller modules are in route. We expect them to dock this afternoon."

"How long has it taken you to develop this project?"

"I would have to say after you purchased the property. Once Jonathan viewed the property he had it in his heart that everyone deserves to have their own home. A few of the fraternity brothers came on board and it grew to one hundred men to collaborate on this project. The trucks, fuel, material and manpower are all donated."

Jonathan smiles with gratitude while Nathan begins to weep.

"Why the tears brother?"

"This has really been the most remarkable experience. I am so moved by the generosity."

"Brother to serve our community has been in our blood for generations."

"If I must say your father and grandfather laid the foundation for many of our businesses, Grant replies. I must also say your dear mother fought hard for our future. She provided us with the opportunity to be adopted by compassionate families. We just want to reciprocate the goodwill."

All of the men huddle up to embrace Nathan.

"Enough of that! I am not a child anymore."

"For goodness sakes, there is nothing immoral about men who show affection to one another once in a while. Okay now let us get to work. We need a marker man to lead the movers to the site of the first lot. Junebug," yells Jonathan. "Can you assist us to guide the homes onto the lots?"

"Yes, suh, I don't mind if I do."

"Please make sure you stay in sight. We must have mod two pulled forward while mod one is moved onto lot one on the farthest southeast quadrant. Let's go everyone please clear the way for the trucks. Junebug when you guide the truck along the trail make sure you can see the driver from the rear view mirror. Do not lose sight of him and do not allow him to lose sight of you."

"Yes suh!"

Junebug begins a slow trot towards the trail. He turns around to get in the view of the driver like he was told while the truck backs onto the trail. The truck begins to edge toward the lot while Junebug guides him through the terrain. Junebug directs him to the east when he reaches the farthest lot to the trail. The truck's wheels begin to spin when it swings out left to inch the house onto the lot. The driver pulls forward a few feet before he puts it in reverse in an attempt to get past the resistance. With more firmness the truck backs onto the lot with success. Junebug waves at the driver to stop afterwards the driver places the truck in park. He jumps down to determine how much space he will need to set the module in place. Junebug was very precise with his directions.

"Good job Junebug. Now all I have to do is release the connections from the module to the truck then turn this knob until this anchor has disappeared into the soil. You should see the yellow markings when you press this leveler down to anchor the module. While you anchor the module I will secure the wheels so that the module will be a stand alone."

"Yes suh."

The trucker returns to inspect Junebugs work.

"Excellent work Junebug. You can call me Charles."

"Yes suh, Mistah Charles."

"No, just Charles will be fine. How about you climb up front so we can get the next module transported onto its lot?"

They both climb into the cabin of the truck then Charles starts the engine. The truck begins to vibrate once Charles drives away from the lot. The module settles on the lot.

"Oh, we cannot forget to lock the wheels."

Never Underestimate The Power of A Secret Place

They both jump down from the truck while Charles pulls the leveler down to lock the wheels. Both sides are locked before they return to the truck and begin down the trail. Nathan directs the first truck to turn south along the trail to exit the property. Junebug appears to look perplexed then signals to Charles to stop.

"Don't worry I will pull over to the side. You will have more room to work with before it is over."

Charles notices a sign of relief on Junebug's face.

"Junebug are you okay?"

"Yes suh, I jus cain't leave da plantation."

"Why can you not leave the plantation?"

"If we caught from da plantation they gonna kill us."

"Who will to kill you?"

"Da towns folk say we da reason da town is wastin away. They mighty angry since da slaves left da plantation."

"Junebug you should never fear for your life if you obey the law."

"Everybody don't think that way Mistah Charles."

"Then they should be fearful for their lives. Those that live by the sword die by the sword."

"Yes suh, Mistah Gourdeau always say ya reap what ya sow befo' ya leave dis earth."

"Mr. Gourdeau sounds like a good man."

"He was a mighty good man, suh. Mistah Gourdeau was very kind and neva lift his hand ta hit nobody. We always had enough ta eat; no reason ta steal from Mistah Gourdeau."

"Whatever happened to him?"

"One day Mistah Gourdeau was out in tha field an a copperhead bit him. A worka an Mistah Badeaux was wit him but da worka was too ole ta lift him on his horse. Mistah Badeaux say da slave cain't ride horses. When da worka git ta da property an tole somebody he was dead. A few of da workers buries him right on da Gourdeau plantation. Mistah Gourdeau gave his word dat he keep da farm runnin if we doin our share. But Mistah Badeaux came up ta da property an took a few of da workers wit him. He promised 'em freedom but he tha sheriff an he says nobody free in Badeaux Parrish. We been hidin eva since."

"It is unfortunate that a good man like Mr. Gourdeau had to die senselessly. Well we better get back to work. We expect the arrival of the last modules this afternoon."

Both men jump from the truck. When they reach the entrance to the woods two of the six modules have already been placed on their lots. Junebug resumes his position behind a truck in the process of backing a module onto a lot in the woods. The path appears to be completely clear of debris to allow the truck to inch back with ease. Junebug guides the driver toward the lot with expertise. Nathan motions for Jonathan to join him.

"Looks like we may have a driver for the farm," says Nathan. "We will need drivers to deliver the cotton to the factory once it has been harvested."

"Do you think he will leave his family for those long trips up north?"

"It is possible."

"We might want to consider Joshua and Sampson for those positions. I would rather have two on the road for safety measures."

"What could possibly happen?"

"I do not want to take any chances Nathan."

"What are you afraid of my brother?"

"I am afraid of the evil doers of this world."

"Aren't we all?"

All five modules are secured on their lots. The completion will entail indoor plumbing and electricity.

"When will the laborers arrive?"

Grant signals for Jonathan to join him. Nathan approaches the group while they pretend to discuss the plans for the smaller homes. Nathan leaves the group to inspect the modules in the woods. The men return to their initial conversation.

"The laborers will begin to construct the entrance for the farm. We will have to keep Nathan distracted until the project is complete."

"How much time do you think this will take?"

"Before we can mount the sign across the entrance we have to get the last of the modules onto the trail. We will have to move these trucks out then get back to the docks to meet the next shipment. That way we can connect five of the modules and have them on the property before sundown. The last five will have to be secured on the trucks until we can move them to their lots. Time is money so we will have to get this next set of modules stationed on the trail within the next few hours. We do not have much day time so time is of the essence. Get the trucks back to the docks after they have been unloaded. We must return to the docks to hitch the next load within the hour. Charles can you take Junebug under your wings?"

"I got him."

"Teach him how to operate the truck."

"It will be my pleasure."

"I have two more men that will need to be trained to operate the trucks. But for now we will begin with Junebug."

"Hey Junebug," calls Charles. "Climb in we have another load to pick up at the docks."

"Suh, I appreciate ya offerin but I betta stay here at da plantation."

"It is your boss's request. He wants you to learn to operate trucks."

"No suh, I neva operate a truck in my life."

"That is why I am here to teach you. For right now you can just watch me until you get the feel of how it drives before I put you behind the wheel. The Johnson's own a fleet of trucks. There is enough back roads around here to get you the experience to operate your own truck."

"Mistah Charles suh no disr'spec but we ain't allowed in town."

"Who ain't allowed in town Junebug?"

"The slaves suh they say they hang us if we come to town."

"First of all Junebug slavery is abolished. Do you know what that means?"

"Yes suh I do but those just words. Nothin changed around here."

"Well I be damned!"

"No suh, you done nothin wrong. You a good man Mr. Charles a good white man."

"Junebug stay right here. I will be right back."

"Yes suh."

Charles approaches Jonathan while he has taken on the duty to guide the trucks onto the lot.

"Jonathan may I speak with you for a moment?"

"Just a moment Charles," Samson he yells.

Samson comes within seconds.

"Samson, can you take over from here?"

"Yes suh."

"Make certain to stay in the driver's view so that you both can see each other."

"Yes suh."

"How can I assist you Charles?"

"I can not seem to convince Junebug to accompany me to the docks. He is concerned with his safety."

"You have to understand Charles that the reality of freedom has not manifested in the minds of the former slaves. Not to mention many of the slave owners in this region. Slavery has only taken a back seat here. In my opinion we must eradicate it at its very core."

"What do you suggest?"

"Do not worry with Junebug at this point we must continue with the reconstruction of the woods. We have a delivery truck in the warehouse to train the drivers also Nathan is a very experienced driver. He can train someone to drive for the farm."

"Jonathan I would be more than honored to stay behind to train your drivers."

"I appreciate the offer but it would place Phyllis at odds with me if I accept. She is very protective of the time she spends with you."

"Sometimes I question the validity of that statement."

"You are a cherished man in your household Charles. Any man would love to be greeted by the love of his life along with those beautiful girls of yours when he gets home."

"It is far more complicated than you think Jonathan."

"Oh, I can only imagine."

"One day my reality will become your reality."

"Soon I hope."

"Well I must get to the docks to retrieve my shipment."

"Have a safe trip Charles."

"It is my intention."

Charles starts back to his truck where he meets Junebug.

"Well Junebug you are more than welcome to ride with me to the dock. I can promise you that you will be safe with me."

Junebug hesitates for a minute.

"Did you hear me Junebug?"

"Yes suh, I jus hope I come back alive."

"You have my word that you will return in the same condition that you left here. Hop in and let us get to the docks. You stay in the truck and you must not leave for any reason."

"Yes suh."

Charles begins his drive down the trail to the main road. They approach the entrance where men pour cement on the west and east end of the trail. Some of the men are Caucasian and a few were African. Junebug asked if they were slaves. Charles reports that all the men were free. They begin their journey onto main road to town.

"Slavery has taken on a whole new nuance for me since I have visited Louisiana. I meant to say that slavery was legal up north more so than it was in the south. However the respect for humanity was more apparent than it is here in Louisiana."

Charles glances at Junebug.

"I would never justify slavery by any means. During my lifetime I have witnessed many barbaric accounts that I wish not to mention."

They continue on the main road when Junebug directs him to a narrow road that will shorten the trip. There are tall oak trees with long branches that reach beyond the road. It makes for a cool shade for those that travel this road. They continue to travel the narrow road then all of the sudden they come upon a rope dangling from a branch in the middle of the road. Charles stops the truck and looks at it for a moment. His cheeks begin to turn red. Charles reaches under his seat to pull out a short handle gun with a long nose. He checks the chamber before he places it between his backside and his trousers. Charles climbs out of the truck then walks toward the rope. All of the sudden he hears movement to his right. He acknowledges he is not alone. Charles glances around before he reaches for the rope. A figure appears beyond the oak tree to the right of him. Charles slides the gun from his trousers to release a bullet into the chamber. The figure leaps behind the oak tree when Charles aims in his direction.

"Identify yourself. I SAID identify yourself before I shoot."
"My name is William."
"Reveal yourself this very minute."
William steps from behind the tree.
"Place your hands above your head and continue this way."

Charles directs him to come closer. Junebug observes from the truck before he eases down in his seat. He does not want to be recognized. William approaches Charles once he lowers the gun in front of him.

"What is the meaning of this?"

Charles grasps the rope and yanks at it in hopes it would fall from the tree.

"What is the purpose of this rope hanging here? ANSWER ME," Charles yells!

"I'se tole ta hang it so the negras won't settle here."

"What negras?"

"Tha negras on da Gourdeau plantation."

"How dare you to consider such a heinous plot against another human being."

"Everyb'dy knows dat dis dead man's road."

"You foolish man, you continue to live in the past when the past is no more."

William begins to laugh. "Ya mus be new aroun here. This Sheriff Badeaux's Parrish an da civil war ain't gone change nothin."

"Is that so?"

"Yes suh an we gone hang a negra tonight an ain't nobody gone do nothin bout it."

"You say tonight William?"

"Yes suh."

Charles aims his gun at the rope in the tree; it sways at the mercy of the wind. The gun fires then the rope falls to the ground. Charles places the rope over his shoulder. William reaches for the rope.

"I do believe dat belongs ta me."

"Can you prove it?"

"Yes suh, right there is my pa's initials."

"What is your father's name?"

Never Underestimate The Power of A Secret Place

"Thomas Badeaux."

"Well this rope has three initials branded on it, so I guess it's mine. Now I do not know you and I am sure you do not want to know me. It would be in your best interest to face east; continue in that direction until you are out of my eyesight. If you should so happen to turn around I will fire my gun in your direction with the hopes that a round reaches you right between your eyes. Do I make myself clear?"

"Yes suh."

"Carry on."

William turns around to begin his way eastward. He hesitates while he contemplates whether to turn around.

"I would not do that if I were you. I am a man of my word," he yells!

Charles enters the truck. He places the rope on the floor. Junebug cowers in his seat. Charles extends his hand to comfort him.

"You have nothing to worry about. I promised to keep you safe."

"That's masta Badeaux's son he a powerful man."

"Everyone has to abide by the same laws Junebug there are no exceptions."

"They gonna hang a slave tonight."

"What makes you think so?"

"This hangman's road an most time ya walk down this road ya gonna find a slave hangin to they death."

"What do you do about it?"

"We cut 'em down an bury 'em."

"Does anyone get arrested for the crime?"

"No suh it ain't no crime ta hang a slave."

"When will you learn slavery is no more?"

"Nobody changes ova night suh."

They continue to travel the road until it comes to another main road. Junebug's posture begins to relax while he gazes at the scenery. Charles hesitates before he speaks.

"What frightened you the worst the rope hanging from the tree or William?"

"Myrtle an my chile at Badeaux plantation. If Mistah William was ta see me he kill 'em wit out blinkin his eyes."

"You must be mistaken."

"No suh, there ain't no law against killin a slave. Specially a runaway slave like me."

"When will you learn that slavery no longer exists?"

"Suh, I been running so long it jus my nature; I might not eva stop runnin."

"You have got to be kidding me."

"Mistah Charles they say I run when I was a babe. They say they know I'se gone be a runna. They say I run like a stallion. I ain't been caught by da slave masta yet."

"Is that right?"

"Yes suh!"

"How about I teach you to shoot?"

"Suh slaves cain't handle no guns."

"Why not?"

"It jus da way it is."

"So how do you expect to protect yourself?"

"That's why we run Mistah Charles."

Silence falls between them when they enter the entrance to the docks. Once again Junebug eases down in his seat. He peeks out of the window to watch Charles make preparation to connect a module to the truck.

"This has not been accomplished before but I figure we can move two of these modules to the farm at once."

"Yes suh."

Charles climbs in the driver's seat then he starts the engine.

"We will have to take it slow but I think we can kill two birds with one stone if we are careful."

He eases the truck onto the main road when the modules start to sway along the width of the road.

"Junebug how much do you weigh?"

"I don't know suh. I'se guessin bout two hundred."

"Junebug we have to get some weight on that second module so it does not get away from us; now I want you to ride in the back if you do not mind."

"No suh, I neva mind."

Charles eases to the right side of the road to avoid the moss ridden bayou.

"Here climb out over here. I want you to ride in that module."

Charles points to the last module loaded on the truck. They walk to the back of the module to unlock the door. Junebug climbs in then he looks around.

"Now you will have to hold on because it is going to be a bumpy ride you hear? If you have any problems wave your hand out this window. I will pull over to check on you."

"Yes suh."

Charles returns to the truck then he pulls back onto the road at a slow pace. Junebug holds on and braces himself before they turn onto the narrow road that leads to the farm. The road is covered with large clumps of hardened soil. Junebug loses his grip only to become tossed around what appears to be the kitchen. He grasps the sink for leverage so that he can return to an upright position but he is unsuccessful. He looks around to locate something that will support his weight. He attempts to gain proximity to a window but the truck comes to an abrupt stop. Junebug begins to propel forward to the floor. He remains on the ground while he listens to voices in the distance. He hears the truck's door creeps open then shut. Junebug crawls to the window nearest to the front of the module. He peers through the window to see Charles standing with a rifle in his right hand along with his left hand on a smaller gun nestled in the back of his trousers. There are three men in front of him. There is also a woman kneeling down on the road in front of a rope already prepared with a noose. The woman sobs into her hands making it difficult to see her face. Something compels Junebug to open the door and climb down from the module. He approaches Charles to whisper in his ear.

"That is my Myrtle."

"Who do you have with you," Charles asks.

"Just some negra dat done tried to run."

"Is that so; what do you plan to do with her?"

"Well we sure ain't tendin to marry her now is we?"

"I do not know for sure. Now brothers I do not want any trouble you understand?"

"Understan you ain't *our* brother. Now how bout ya jus git along so we can finish our business?"

Charles points the rifle at the rope then fires. The rope falls from the branch.

"I will get along after you release that woman to me so we can get on our way."

"Cain't do that she our propr'ty."

"That is not up for discussion. Now I am going to count to three and the only people I want to see on this road is that woman, Junebug and I."

"Ya mus don't know… One, who we, Two, is…Three."

Charles pulls the trigger then he shoots William in his right leg. He goes down to the ground and grabs his leg. The other men begin to run. Charles rests the rifle on his shoulder before he walks over to Myrtle. He helps her to her feet then he hands her his handkerchief. She looks up at him in disbelief. Junebug has not moved an inch but continues to watch William.

"Ya remember this gal, we still got June Lee at da plantation. Ain't no tellin what we gon' do ta er."

Never Underestimate The Power of A Secret Place

Charles points the rifle at his head. "I got an idea. Get to your feet. You are riding with me back to the farm. If anything happens to June lee you can kiss your soul to damnation."

William gets to his feet. He limps with caution to the truck.

"Junebug I want you to take this rifle. Hang it outside this window here. If anyone comes near us you aim then pull the trigger. You hear me?"

"Yes suh."

"It is easier than it seems. Let the butt of the rifle rest against your shoulder like this, then aim. Once you spot your target pull the trigger. It has a little kick back but you will do fine. Now let me see you try."

Junebug places the rifle in his right hand; he allows the butt of the rifle fall against his shoulder.

"Now aim at that tree."

Junebug points the rifle in the direction of the tree.

"Now fire that sun of a gun."

Boom! The rifle fires off to jolt Junebug back a step. He hits the tree dead center. Charles walks over to the tree then places his finger in the hole for proof.

"Are you sure you never fired a rifle before?"

"No suh."

Junebug's aim turns in William's direction. Junebug begins to shake angrily. Charles places his hand on Junebugs shoulder.

"Easy now Junebug; I know how you must feel but we got to do this the right way."

"Suh they got my chile."

"Junebug we are going to get her back alive I promise."

Junebug hesitates to lower the gun. Charles rubs his arm then he looks at William.

"Junebug take your wife back to where you were. I will have William ride with me. He can serve as ransom until we get your daughter back to safety."

Charles, Junebug, Myrtle along with William arrive back to the farm. The brothers hurry to the truck to meet them.

"What do we have here?"

"It looks like we have caught us a live one."

"You do say?"

"Fortunate for us we were able to intervene before they could attempt murder. We have one of Badeaux's sons for ransom. I say we get over there right now before they sacrifice the little girl. Samson!"

"Yes suh?"

"Bring that truck on down."

"Yes suh."

Samson jumps into the farm truck then pulls up next to Charles' truck. Jonathan and Nathan carry William to the bed of the truck while all three climb aboard.

"Look into that compartment and get me a rag."

"It has oil on it."

"That is fine. No need to waste our time on him. I need a couple of guys to come with me and bring your rifles."

They all approach the truck.

"I need some of you to stay to protect the farm."

Three of the men jump onto the bed of the truck with their loaded rifles and extra ammunition. Charles climbs into the driver's seat while Junebug jumps in the passenger seat.

"Are you sure you want to do this."

"That's my only chile Mistah Charles."

"I understand."

Charles starts the engine. He yells at the men to hang on. He eases onto the main road which is covered with dirt and rocks. Dust rises around him while he heads in the direction of the Badeaux plantation.

"Mistah Charles, do ya know wheres ya goin?"

"Pretty much Junebug; I want you to be ready if I need you."

Never Underestimate The Power of A Secret Place

Charles pulls up to the big house on the Badeaux plantation. Sheriff Badeaux is there on the porch dressed in uniform. His two sons are at his side with their rifles pointed in their direction. Charles exits the truck then begins to walk in quick steps toward the Sheriff.

"Charles!" Jonathan yells, "Don't be foolish."

Before Charles could stop himself he is face to face with Thomas Badeaux. Charles breathes heavily while sweat pours from his face.

"I am going in there to get June Lee and you better not stop me."

Charles marches past him to enter the house. His sons stare in amazement.

"Papa are ya alright?"

"What do ya think I'm jus fine."

Charles exits the house with June Lee in his arms. She clings to Charles with all her might.

"If I ever see you again it will be too soon."

Charles walks to the truck then eases June Lee in the seat.

"Go to your papa. Fellas," Charles yells. "Get your rifles and take every freed man, woman and child on this plantation."

"Papa are ya gonna let him do dat. Jus take our prop'rty an all."

"Shut up!"

"You better listen to your father before I have you sentenced to the chain gang."

"My pa is da Sheriff here in Badeaux Parrish if you ain't heard."

"Not only have I heard but I don't give a damn."

Charles anger escalates before he realizes it he steps toward the younger son then raises his rifle.

"If you open that trap one more time, you will never see the light of day again."

The men gather the children and women from the back.

"Where are the men?"

"They have run for their freedom."

"They left the women behind to fend for themselves? I am going to beat some heads together when I get back. Are there anymore?"

"Looks like that is it," says one of the truck drivers.

"Nice doing business with you. Grant get us out of here," yells Charles!

He tips his hat before he jumps on the back of the truck's bed before it pulls out. They continue to watch the Badeauxs' carefully while they exit the property with guns still drawn and ready to fire at a moment's notice. Once they enter the trail to the farm calmness floods the entire area.

"Where is everybody?"

"They is everywhere."

"What do you mean I do not see a living soul?"

Junebug waives his hands and all of the sudden the workers appear to come from nowhere.

"What on earth is going on here?"

"We learns ta hide in our secret place."

"No kidding. That has got to be the creepiest thing I have ever seen. You will have to show me that trick one day."

"Yes suh."

The men jump from the bed of the truck and begin to help the women and children down from the bed.

"I cannot believe what just happened. Charles have you lost your senses," asked Jonathan? "You could have been killed."

"I despise everything a man like that stands for. My mother and my sister and I were enslaved until we escaped. I did not think we would make it out alive. The orphanage took me in and cared for me. The orphanage could not take my mother so your grandfather gave my mother a job in the kitchen. I went to school until I got a job in the factory. Then one day your father gave me my first route. I disappointed him when I took off in the truck to look for my sister. I was gone for days but when I came back your father gave me another chance."

"Whatever happened to your sister?"

"She was sold to a Madam. When I saw her she did not look the same. She made a place for herself there. Mother and I have made New York our home. If you can survive the mean streets of New York City you can survive anywhere."

"I never would have imagined that you were enslaved."

"Why not?"

"Look at you, you are white.

"Slavery is not about race. It is about greed. Besides, every race has been enslaved to some degree."

"I agree. We have to become determined to eradicate slavery. The fight must continue. We can expect retaliation in the coming days," says Jonathan.

"I will be here."

"No Charles you must get back to your family."

"We will all be here until the soldiers arrive. We can man the post just like they can. No argument fellas."

"How many did we free from the Badeaux's plantation?"

"There are four women and eight children."

"We will just have to make due. Nathan please inform the women that we have more mouths to feed."

"Oh no brother, I will allow you the honors. I have had enough excitement for one evening. I am going to take this beautiful blue eyed girl to Samson to claim. He is right she resembles him from head to toe."

Nathan gets on one knee before he extends his hand to the young girl. She is hesitant to come but is pushed by one of the other children into his arms.

"There now, you do not have to be afraid. What is your name?"

She remains silent.

"Does anyone know her name?"

"Her name is Brea," one of the women reports.

"Brea, what a beautiful name; please come with me I have a surprise for you."

"Make sure she eats Nathan."

"I will make sure of that."

Nathan walks with the young girl to the big house. He opens the door then takes her by the hand to the kitchen. She follows close behind him until he reaches the oven and he opens it.

"Get out of there," yells Linda.

Nathan jumps straight up and pulls the little girl behind him.

"I know what this must look like."

"Of course you do. What do you have behind your back?"

"I have no idea what you are referring to."

"Get away from that oven before I give you a thrashing you will never forget."

Linda approaches him and she reveals a strap in her hand. Nathan pulls the girl in front of him to shield himself.

"You should be ashamed of yourself using this poor child to protect yourself. How did she get here?"

"She is one of the slave children we rescued from the plantation today."

"Nonsense this is Jasmine."

"No mother her name is Brea."

"You have got to be kidding me she is the spitting image of Jasmine."

"I thought so myself. I suspect one of the workers to be related to her also. It would not surprise me if many of the slaves are related in some way. Some ways we may not want to know."

"How unfortunate," sighs Linda. "I know she must be hungry."

"You do say? To be honest that is the purpose for which I came to the kitchen. I know you have treats in the oven like you always have in the past."

"When have you known us to hide treats in the oven?"

"Ever since I was a young lad you have hidden treats in the oven."

"But you are no longer a young lad."

"Indeed but this young lass deserves a taste of your delicious treats."

"We will be the judge of that Rafeal interjects. Now go and we will tend to the young child."

"Surely I can not just leave her alone with you two."

"And why not," questions Linda.

"I believe you have frightened her. You are safe Brea they are really delightful ladies once you get to know them."

"Nathan if you remain in this room one more second you will need to seek safety from our wrath."

"Mother I never…"

"Run Nathan their patience has run its course," yells Opio.

"I think you are correct."

Nathan hurries to exit the kitchen to make his way outside. Nathan runs down to the barn where tables are filled with various foods. Many have already begun to eat while the truckers look on.

"Why have you not joined the others?"

"We can wait until they have eaten."

"Nonsense there is plenty; we have more than enough to feed everyone."

Samsom walks over to the men then he extends his hand to them.

"Come eat wit me my brotha."

"Who can say no to that," asks Jonathan.

Never Underestimate The Power of A Secret Place

"I humbly accept your invitation," Charles answers.

They all get in line while more food is placed on the table. Once they have been served they sit among the former slaves under the tree. Junebug points to Charles.

"We mus thank him. He save my family," Junebug whimpers.

"It is something we do every day."

"Not everybody like you Mistah Charles."

"Oh there are millions of men like me."

"No suh. Not even wit us. I neva seen a man do what ya do today. We run because we afraid. Fear chase us down like animals. But Mistah Charles you ain't let fear chase ya. Yo love is strong. Yo love chase fear away. There was a time when we love dat way too."

The former slaves all nod.

"But every time we die. Every time! One day I wanna love like ya an neva fear no mo."

Tears coast down the faces of the crowd. Junebug begins to hum. The women begin to hum. They grab the hands of those next to them. Before long everyone begin to hum. Then all of the sudden a soft voice begins to sing:

"♫I trust you Lord; ♪ I trust you Lord; ♪ I trust you Lord; ♪ I love you Lord; ♫I love you Lord; ♪ I love you Lord."

Everyone begins to sway side to side until the young girl stops singing.

"What a beautiful voice June Lee."

Everyone claps and before long she has a standing ovation. June Lee runs to her mother then hides her face in her mother's chest.

"I hate to be a bearer of bad news but we will need to make plans for this evening," says Jonathan. If you have not noticed our family has grown larger. We will need to divide responsibilities among ourselves to keep everyone safe. I would like to have two volunteers to secure the entrance throughout the night. Every four hours we will need to relieve those on guard at the post. Do I have any volunteers?"

All of the men raise their hands.

"I have a remarkable group of volunteers to choose from. Samson, Charles if you two would secure the post tonight I would appreciate it."

"You have picked the best men for the job."

"Steven, Aaron can take the next rotation to secure the entrance."

"Mistah Jonathan, suh?"

"You can call me Jon, asks Moses"

"Yes suh. Can I go wit my brotha?"

"Of course, all three of you can manage quite well together," he winks at Steven.

Steven is the son of a prominent physician in New York. He often volunteered at the orphanage with Jonathan and Nathan. They were sometimes referred to as the 'Three Musketeers.' Of his five siblings he is the most successful. Often he would donate his used clothing to the boys in the orphanage. Sometimes they were not worn at all just something he felt like doing. His brothers often taunted Nathan about his skin color. Steven was always apologetic for his sibling's behavior. Never did he invite Jonathan or Nathan to his parent's home. He spent many sleepless nights in horseplay at the Johnson's home. Steven often stated that he wish that he could switch places with Arthur. Steven extends his hands to the twins but instead the twins wraps their arms around him.

"We is family," says Aaron.

"Yes sir we are family."

"I need one more team."

Junebug raises his hand.

"Are you sure Junebug?"

"Yes suh."

"Then all I need is one more person."

Myrtle raises her hand.

"I am sorry Myrtle we need you here with the children."

"I don't trust nobody wit my Junebug's life but Nathan."

"Nathan it appears that you have been nominated."

"You do say."

"Ms. Myrtle I will make sure that Junebug returns to you safe and sound."

"If ya don't ya sho gonna have ta ansa ta me."

"Me too," adds June Lee.

"That is a lot of pressure; I do not know how I will manage."

"Do I smell a chicken brother?"

"Of course not *brother*," mimics Nathan. I will be there Junebug ready to serve my country."

"Really brother?"

"Unlike you, I will put my life on the line for my fellow brethren."

"What a small price to pay."

"Enough you two we have to get settled in," Charles insists.

"That is correct everyone but before we do we need to welcome our newcomers."

"Ladies if you can help the newcomers settle in the barn. I know it may be crowded but with your patience we should have all modules in place by tomorrow."

"Jonathan can I speak with you for a moment," asks Charles.

"I have a moment what is your concern," asks Jonathan.

"The gate is expected to be delivered in the morning so that we can have it assembled. Nathan will have to take the first shift to secure the post to guarantee secrecy."

"I understand please make the necessary arrangements."

Charles approaches Nathan while he assists the others to gather blankets for the night.

"Nathan I will need you to take my shift tonight."

"Of course I will notify Junebug and his wife of the changes," answers Nathan.

"That was easy," Charles admits.

"Junebug," he yells. "Come here for a moment there has been some changes."

"Yes suh Mistah Nathan."

"Junebug, if you call me Mister one more time."

"Yes suh Nathan."

"Now that was not so hard was it?"

"No suh Mistah Nathan."

Nathan wipes his face.

"We have to go man the post. Ask your wife to get your things so that we can leave now. I will get us a rifle."

"What about Myrtle?"

"Can she handle a rifle?"

"Yes suh she sho can."

"I will bring three rifles then. Meet me at the post."

Junebug rushes to get Myrtle. He stops at the blanket that hangs to separate the women from the men.

"Myrtle," he calls.

A young girl peeks from behind the blanket.

"Go git Ms. Myrt."

The girl nods then disappears. A woman appears at the entrance.

"I'se need Myrt."

She nods then disappears. Another woman appears at the entrance. Junebug shakes his head and begins to walk away. June Lee comes around the corner of the barn and almost crashes into Junebug.

"Wheres ya goin?"

"In there papa."

"Tell yo motha I say come right away."

"Yes papa."

Never Underestimate The Power of A Secret Place

June Lee disappears behind the blanket. A few minutes later Myrtle appears with June Lee not far behind.

"We go ta protec tha post now."

"Ya sho Junebug?"

"Mistah Nathan say we go now."

"What we gon do wit June Lee?"

"She stay here cause they come fo her."

"Ya sho Junebug there sho is alot of folk lookin fo a pallet ta sleep on."

"I'se sho."

Jonathan comes around the corner to secure the premises.

"Is everything alright?"

"No suh. We goin to tha post an we don't knows what ta do wit June Lee."

"She will be fine. I will take her to the house and she can stay with Ms. Rafael. You will like it there. You two go ahead and I will take June Lee."

Myrtle becomes motionless when Jonathan takes June Lee's hand which causes Jonathan to become uneasy.

"I will tell you what I can do. Wait right here."

He turns the corner and in less than a minute he reappears with Rafael at his heals.

"This is Ms. Rafael and she will care for June Lee just for a short time."

"June Lee say hello to Ms. Rafael."

"Hello," says June Lee.

"There is another little girl up there waiting for me," says Rafael. "Would you like to go meet her?"

"Yes ma'am."

"Well it looks like I will be busy tonight. I will put it on your tab son."

"Ahh, I already owe you my life what next?"

"Your first born will do."

Jonathan looks puzzled.

"I do not expect to start a family in the near future."

"Son I am a very patient woman I can wait."

Rafael walks away with June Lee while the others look on.

"Is she a good woman?"

"She is a very good woman. You will not have worry about anyone being offensive to June Lee in her presence."

"Junebug I have ta fetch my b'longins," says Myrtle.

"What b'longins?"

"Tha belongins I brung wit me."

"It can stay here it safe here."

Myrtle looks at Junebug surprised at his statement.

"I'se go git my bible."

"Hurry Mistah Nathan is waitin."

Myrtle disappears behind the blanket once more. She returns in a split second with her bible and a shawl. She hurries alongside Junebug on their way towards the entrance of the farm. The road is dark but they are accustomed to the night. They reach the entrance but Nathan has not made it. They both enter the woods to camouflage themselves from potential intruders. In silence they sit and wait. Nathan inches toward them unaware that they have hidden. Junebug by accident rustles a tree limb. Nathan drops two of the rifles then points one in their direction.

"Who is there?"

Junebug stands to reveal himself. Nathan lowers his gun.

"What were you thinking?"

Myrtle pulls Junebug close to her.

"I'se sorry masta."

"No Junebug call me Nathan. I am a man just like you."

"Yes suh Mistah Nathan."

"Come here my brother. You must be very careful; I could have killed either of you."

They embrace for a moment.

"No suh, we wanna live."

"It is my hopes likewise."

Nathan picks up the other two rifles then hands one to each of them. He motions to them to retreat to the woods. Nathan bends the young trees so that they continue to cover their hiding place.

"Sit on the branches but you must be still so that we do not to alert the enemy."

They all position themselves so that they will not to shift the branches. Myrtle wraps her shawl around her shoulders.

"Myrtle you know you do not have to do this," says Nathan.

"I ain't seen my Junebug in a long time Mistah Nathan. I wanna stay wit him."

Nathan looks into her eyes and a tear nestles in the corner of her eye.

"Myrtle your family is more than welcomed to stay here forever."

He leans over to kiss Myrtle on the forehead. Junebug sits motionless.

"Junebug I am sorry I do not want you to think I am disrespectful to you."

"Suh she my wife not my prop'rty."

"What do you mean by that?"

"Masta give me a wife but she his prop'rty."

"Junebug you must believe that you both are free. Myrtle is no one's property."

"Yes suh."

"Please forgive me I will never touch your wife without your permission."

"Yes suh."

"Mistah Nathan."

"Call me Nathan please."

"Nathan, I been thinkin all night long an we hopes dat ya can git our quarta back. Junebug worked on tha boats an he don't mind payin fo tha prop'rty if we has to. Tha quarta been ours eva since we can rememba. We don't mind helpin on da farm cause we knows this farm ova an unda. We can work on somethin fo us so we both can have what we want."

"Myrtle that sounds awful nice of you. Would you like to know if you own the property?"

"Ta tell ya da truth Mistah Nathan I'se afraid if we fight fo it we lose everythin. We ain't neva had no say in nothin."

"You have rights Myrtle. Sometimes you have to get somebody to represent you to be heard."

"Nobody r'present slaves Mistah Nathan. Nobody but masta Gourdeau; he always look afta what we needs. When we sick he sent fo tha bes' doctor in town. Some nights afta closin time he take us ta town so we git whateva we want. Nobody says no ta masta Gourdeau. We mighty blessed when he was livin. It seems like our God forgetin bout us sometimes. We in those woods livin like scared rabbits. Everyday we think they gonna burn us out. Don't know wheres we gonna go next. We got cannin to last thru tha next winta an wild animals fo huntin in da woods. We been prayin real low ta our God ta save us. We used ta hum an dance ta our God so he will ansa our prayers, heal us, an bless our crops but we scared cause they gonna kill us."

"Junebug, do you mind if I ask you something about your God?"

"No suh."

"What is the name of your God?"

"God."

"God?"

"Yes suh."

"Can you tell me something else your about your God."

"Yes suh, way befo' we was born God made tha whole world. He made tha animals, tha woods an us too. God's son name Jesus. We raise our hands up high ta show our God we thank him fo everythin good an bad. Masta Gourdeau allow his workers a day ta go ta tha barn an worship ta our God. He say he like us hummin it makes him feel good inside. Sometimes we be prayin fo him an his land ta keep givin ta us so we can live."

"Shhh, someone is near. They appear to come from the farm. It must be Charles; for the sake of humor let us deceive him. Be very still."

Nathan searches for a long branch then with care snaps it from the tree while Charles and another figure approach them. Nathan extends the branch to almost touch the shoulder of Charles which causes Charles to turn and see who is behind him. When he recognizes that he has been tricked he then decides to scare them. Charles pulls his rifle to his shoulder then releases a bullet into the chamber. Nathan drops the branch and stands with his hands in the air.

"Please do not shoot it is I."

"Reveal yourself before I am forced to shoot," yells Charles.

"Charles please do not be foolish it is I," cries Nathan.

Charles lowers his gun in laughter. Jonathan is on his knees in tears.

"Would it have been humorous had you killed one of your own? I think not."

"This time brother you will learn to keep your shenanigans to a minimum."

Junebug and Myrtle exit their spots with smiles on their face.

"How dare you put them in danger too. This should serve as a lesson to you. We shall see what mother and the others have to say of this."

"Must you indulge in my shortcomings?"

"If there are lives at stake then the answer is yes. You may return to the others; they expect your arrival soon."

Jonathan and Charles look on while the three of them make their way back to the barn.

Never Underestimate The Power of A Secret Place

"Is there any way I may interest you in a cigar?"

"I am not much of a smoker but I hear it is a dishonor to decline such an offer."

Charles pulls a cigar from his pocket then breaks it in two. He hands Jonathan his portion of the cigar. Charles then reaches in his pocket to pull a small box of wooden matches. He retrieves a match before he returns the box to his pocket. He lifts his left foot to strike the match and a small flame appears. He leans to Jonathan who takes a drag of his cigar then he turns the flame to his cigar and lights up. They both retreat to the area where Nathan and the others were hidden.

"This is such a marvelous idea."

"The cigars," ask Charles?

"Of course not this hiding place."

"It is a brilliant idea. Who would suspect anyone to hide here?"

"The both of you come out of there!"

"Did you say something Jon?"

"Not I."

"I said come out of there this very minute!"

A voice shouts from the trail.

"That sounds like mother."

When Jonathan eases out of the brush Rafael begins to shake her fist at him.

"What would your father say if he knew you have such a terrible habit?"

"But mother I," his voice trails off.

"Do not mother me your father wants to hear from you. He has called now hurry."

"Yes mother please do not tell father. I promise I will not do it again."

"Hand it over!"

Never Underestimate The Power of A Secret Place

Jonathan bends down to put the cigar out on the road then hands it to Rafael.

"Hurry along your father expects you."

Charles attempts to remain perfectly still.

"You may as well come down. I know you are in there."

Charles turns his rifle down then steps down from the brush. His cigar has been defused and hidden in his boot.

"I expect better from you Charles."

"Ms. Rafael he is an adult now. I can not ruin his life any further than it already is."

"Where did he get the tobacco from?"

"I have no idea."

"You don't say."

"Yes ma'am it could be any of the men here."

"Except you is that what you tell me?"

"Yes ma'am. I will keep an eye on him from now on."

"You do that. Now who will keep an eye on you Mr. Charles?"

Charles begins to scratch his head.

"Carry on I must get back to the house."

"Let me walk you Ms. Rafael."

"Oh, don't pleasure yourself I will be fine."

"Yes ma'am."

Charles nestles back into the brush on the trail while Jonathan is on the phone with his father.

"But father I had no idea that she was pregnant. Of course I know it is illegal to marry her. Yes sir, we will figure something out once the farm is established. You mean this very moment? No sir I am not trying to amuse you sir. I will expect your arrival. Goodbye sir."

"It sounds like someone has had their bottom handed to them on a silver platter," smirks Linda. "What have you gotten yourself into this time?"

Never Underestimate The Power of A Secret Place

"Where is mother?"

"She should be on her way."

Jonathan runs his fingers through his hair while he paces the floor of the living area. The door opens and Nathan enters.

"What is it brother?"

"Nothing that concerns you, where is mother?"

"The last I have seen she was headed up the trail. She was not delighted with you I must say."

"I am sure she does not know."

"What is it that she could possibly not know?"

"This is not the time Nathan. I must find mother."

"Oh look who needs his mommy," jokes Nathan.

"Brother this is a serious matter of the utmost concern."

Rafael enters the living area then gives Jonathan a stern look.

"Mother it is not what you think."

"When did you begin to use tobacco Jonathan?"

"Oh brother that is such a terrible habit."

"Nathan this is not the time for your shenanigans," shouts Jonathan.

Nathan raises his hands and steps away.

"What is the matter with you son," asks Rafael.

"I overheard Jonathan mention that someone is pregnant," reports Linda.

"Mother can we talk in private."

"It is a little too late for secrecy; spill the beans."

"I had no idea mother."

"Jonathan! Tell me what is going on this very moment."

"It is Melba she is with child."

"Are you certain?"

"Possibly."

"Son what do you mean possibly? Either Melba is pregnant or she is not; it is that simple."

"She never spoke of being with child."

"How far long is she?"
"Father says that she is expected to deliver next month."
"Jonathan you can not possibly be that naïve."
"Mother I do not know what happened."
"I am sure you must have noticed that her midsection began to protrude."
"Mother there is so much of Melba I honestly did not notice."
"What did he just say?"
Nathan snickers, "I can not wait for father's arrival."
"Your father is coming here?"
"Yes mother."
"Are you certain he is on his way here to this very place?"
"Yes, mother to this very place, I am afraid."
"Son I will not keep you from your father's wrath. When shall we expect him?"
"He is due to depart from New York tomorrow morning."
"Come Linda we must prepare for Mr. Johnson's arrival."
Linda shakes her head.
"Nathan has never brought me such heartache."
Nathan smiles then nods to Linda.
"Do not be too sure of that they are two peas in a pod Linda," says Raphael.
The ladies hurry upstairs chattering among themselves.
Nathan looks at Jonathan in surprise.
"Was father disturbed by his findings?"
"No, he is livid. Apparently someone from the hospital called him in for an emergency. Father says that he imagined that someone had mistaken him for grandfather but they were certain that it was him that they needed. When he arrived Melba was in the examination room. Father and the physician met with Melba who was very tearful. She reports to the doctor that her parents have prepared to send her away. She was then asked who fathered her child and she reported that it was I. Father says that he

expected that this would happen because I was so secretive about our relationship."

"Well it serves you right."

"How so brother I do not deny my responsibility in the matter. Had she been truthful to me we could have married if it were not against the law."

"Do you imply that you would have married Melba in New York without father's approval?"

"My love for Melba transcends the influence of others."

"Then why have you not mentioned to father of your relationship?"

"Because I was afraid he would demand that we end our relationship. I had no idea that I would relocate to another state to start a new chapter in my life."

"So what do you expect from this?"

"Father and Melba will arrive in the next few days. He will expect us to marry somehow and Melba will reside here. Who will provide the medical attention we are not equipped to care for an impregnated woman."

"Brother you will have to deal with that yourself."

"I need to speak with mother."

"She is upstairs disappointed at the confusion you have created."

"I will speak with her in the morning."

"Wise choice my brother. Goodnight. I must turn in tomorrow brings a busy day."

Jonathan continues to stand in the middle of the living area confused by his latest news. Opio enters with his hands in his pockets.

"Your father is very disappointed in you son."

"I cannot fathom why he hid his relationship with mother just as I have with Melba," answers Jonathan.

"It does not justify your actions son."

"What am I to do? I do not posses the knowledge to raise a child. We simply cannot deliver a baby here. The nearest hospital is an hour away. He would not leave her here to die would he? Why must he punish me so?"

"Relax Linda and Rafael both are midwives. The child will be well taken care of."

"What about Melba?"

"Melba will also be taken care of. You must gather yourself together it is an extraordinary event. I suggest you speak with Rafael in the morning when her spirit is light."

"I agree."

"I must return to the others to keep watch over the women and children."

"If it matters at all you will be a great husband in addition to a great father."

"My hopes are that you are right father. I truly hope you are right."

"Goodnight son."

"Goodnight father."

Jonathan exits the house with slow even steps while he begins his walk to the barn. The night air is cool while the stars shine in the dark sky sprinkled among the trees. Children run wild in chase of the many fireflies at their mercy. Jonathan places his hand on the head of a young boy. He speaks to them, "It is now time to turn in children." They return to their parents to prepare to settle in.

"I am amazed."

Nathan approaches Jonathan.

"Of course you are these are not your little ones. To raise your own children will be the difficult task. Just think of the hardships you have placed upon mother and father. You will without a doubt have your work cut out for you."

Never Underestimate The Power of A Secret Place

Nathan begins to walk away in humor to himself. Jonathan stands in the night's coolness while he meditates to himself.

Dear God, please do not forsake me. You know my love for Melba. Forgive me of my sins. Bless my child to be healthy unlike myself. Please do not burden us with scoliosis for it is a terrible condition. I am most gracious that you have brought Melba back to me. Please God place a wall of protection around my family while they travel this way. Also place a wall of protection around this farm. I pray that you broaden my borders and strengthen my stakes and let no evil overtake us. Amen and Amen.

Tears begin to stream down his face.

"Thank you Lord for I feel your presence."

Jonathan walks to the stone nestled above the pond. He observes everyone while they prepare to turn in. He feels a presence behind him then he turns to see who it is and it is Rafael who has a blanket in her arms.

"Mother please join me."

He extends his hand to ease her onto the stone. She sits beside him while he places his arm around her to warm her.

"It will be good to have a baby of our own in the house."

"I thought you would be disappointed in me."

"No son babies are a bundle of joy. I have always hoped to be a grandmother one day."

"Mother I was surprised when you accepted our business proposal."

"Stephen will be stationed out of the country for awhile so I needed something to keep me busy."

"How is he?"

"He writes ever so often."

"He says that when he returns he is going to steal you away from me."

"You both will always be my sons."

"I am most gracious that you came. It is your scent that I will always remember."

"After your mother delivered Nathan you were a difficult delivery. I was the first hold you."

"Mother are you certain that mother birth Nathan *and* I?"

"Jonathan I think that is a talk you must have with your father."

Jonathan looks puzzled.

"Maybe I have said too much."

"Mother if anyone would know it would be you. But you are right this is a discussion father, Nathan and I must have."

"I must turn in so that I can prepare breakfast in the morning."

"Of course mother, allow me."

Jonathan eases Rafael to her feet then gives her a gentle kiss on her forehead.

"I love you mother."

"I love you too son. Goodnight, I can make it back on my own."

Jonathan returns seated on the stone to enjoy the view. He notices that Rafael has left the blanket for him. He makes a pallet for himself on the stone's surface. Soon he is approached by Nathan.

"Mind if I join you?"

"Of course not your company is always a treat."

"Do you fret father's arrival?"

"I must say I do."

"For whatever it is worth I am very delighted to see him. It has been quite some time. Unfortunate for you but I can not say the same. Brother you must remember that we are no longer under his roof. We no longer have to strive to appease him."

"It is not that. I love my father."

"So do I."

Never Underestimate The Power of A Secret Place

"I did not leave home to rid myself of father. I still need his guidance. Most important I still want him in my life. We are all successful and educated men. Nothing compares to the wisdom that our father can provide whether it is our natural father or our spiritual father. The hardships that he has endured will one day be our own. It is all in God's design. Of all the biblical stories mother read to us the one that fascinates me most is the story of Noah."

"How so brother?"

"If I remember correctly there was a messenger going throughout the city to warn the townsfolk to prepare themselves for the great destruction."

"Ahh brother now I remember this particular story."

"There was a man who was obedient to God; because his children were obedient to him they were the only family spared from the great destruction."

"Yes it was their obedience that spared their lives."

"The bible says to obey your parents so you will live long upon the earth. It is my prayer that I fulfill God's word."

"Do you suppose you may start today? You have not been the ideal son you know."

"What do you have to say for yourself?"

"I did marry Betty our son is of legitimate birth."

"If it were legal would I have not done the same?"

"Brother who knows you are such a scatter brain at times."

"I have disappointed father."

"I am sure he has disappointed his father at some point in his life. Do not be so hard on yourself."

"Do you not love father?"

"I love him very much but I have perceived him to be more of a caregiver than an actual father. My prayer is that I will someday know my biological father."

"My hope is that your prayer will come true dear brother."

They sit in silence. After a while they soon drift off to sleep. Jonathan is awakened after someone begins to tug at his hair.

"Why must you torment me so," he asks.

"Breakfast is served."

He opens his eyes to see Rafael hovering above him.

"Wash up before you touch a single biscuit."

When Jonathan raises up he notice that Nathan has already joined the others. Jonathan gathers his blanket before he heads down the trail.

"Jonathan!"

"Yes mother?"

"Come and wash up this very minute."

"You know that Nathan will devour everything I love."

"Do as I say son, come wash up."

Jonathan races to the big house and through the front entrance. Rafael meets him on the terrace when he exits the house.

"Go back into that house and clean up."

"But mother I have."

"Nonsense there is no way you have cleaned up that fast."

"But mother," he interrupts.

"Don't mother me. I have a warm plate in the oven for you."

"Mother you are an angel."

Jonathan leans in to kiss Rafael just before she steps back.

"Don't you dare before you have cleaned yourself up."

"Yes mother."

Jonathan runs back into the house and retreats to the bathroom. After he has cleaned up he enters the kitchen. The aroma of warm biscuits and fresh bacon fills his nostrils. He races to the table to take his seat. Rafael retrieves a plate filled with his favorite breakfast treats to include the bran muffins that he sourly despises. Jonathan places the muffins aside before he begins to eat.

"Jonathan?"

"Yes, mother."

"What must you do first?"

"I know mother but I am famished can they wait?"

"I tell you what, you must eat one now and I will allow you to eat the other later."

Jonathan stuffs the muffin into his mouth and begins to chew with vigor. He opens his mouth to reveal to Rafael that he has eaten the muffin.

"Good boy. I hoped that you would have grown to like the muffins."

"Maybe if I were not forced to eat them I would love them."

"It is for your well being. You have never been regular since you were a child."

"Do you have to remind me?"

"I want you to remember the logic behind the practice."

"The interpretation my brother is quite simple."

"Do tell."

"You are for the lack of a better description can be full of crap at times."

"Mother will you sit there and allow him to speak of me in that manner."

Rafael stands up from her seat and she kisses Jonathan on the crown of his head.

"There are times son when it very well may be true."

Nathan burst into laughter.

"Even your own mother will not deny it."

Jonathan continues to devour his food while he pretends to ignore Nathan. A loud noise comes from outside. The brothers jump to their feet.

"Where are the rifles?"

They are with the men by the trail.

"We must join them."

They race outside to observe the trucks pull in the last of the module homes. Chaos is everywhere. The former slaves begin to rejoice at the sight of the trucks. They start to dance wildly along the trail. Some begin to chant, "Praises ta our God fo he is mighty." They continue to repeat the chant over and over again.

"Is that the only chorus line they know?"

"Perhaps it is."

"Then we must get some someone to direct a choir right away."

"That would be Stephanie's expertise."

"Can you be sure she initiates that project?"

"I most definitely will brother."

6

A PLACE OF ABUNDANCE

They begin their journey along the trail to find Junebug and Samson at work. They initiate the orders to the truckers where they should place the modules. Jonathan is advised to gather the children so they are not in harm's way. Instead Jonathan joins them and dance among the women while Nathan looks on and begins to laugh. The others surround them soon to become onlookers.

"What is this?"

A light rain begins to fall and everyone stop to take notice.

The rain is much needed but not now.

"Tha rain is comin,'" someone shouts.

"We must get the modules on the lots before the great rain comes."

The women shoo the children into the barn while the light rain continues. The men return to unload the modules on the lots. The grass and trees appear to devour the moisture so rapidly as not to waste a drop while life embraces the vegetation around them.

Hours later dusk is near and all of the modules have been placed on their lots. The trucks begin to line up to return to the dock. Everyone is encouraged to follow the last truck down the trail. Soon they come upon the entrance. There stands erected between two posts to reveal a black steel brazened sign "Nathan's Place." Everyone stop in amazement at the sight. Tears begin to stream down the faces of Jonathan, Nathan, Rafael, Linda and Opio.

"Today begins a legacy of many great things to come," says Jonathan.

A low hum permeates among the former slaves. The sound becomes charged with emotions while the soft rain lifts during their walk back up the trail. The flower's petals burst open while the blades of grass sway in the light air. It is a noticeable change from their initial walk to the entrance. It appears that life has been consumed by the land once again. The stars guide the families to their destination where they settle in for the night.

"I think it would be suitable for all the families to take possession of their homes tomorrow," advises Jonathan.

"I agree why wait any longer? The plumbing and electrical connections will take some time but we can manage until then."

"We can make the announcement tomorrow morning. It will be a memorable occasion. Dust off your old camera we will need to document this journey."

The brothers return to the area where they slept the night before. Rafael brings blankets along with an evening bite.

"How is the food supply?"

"Your father will bring a list of things. Fortunate for us there has not been any waste. There is plenty of food left over."

"We plan to celebrate tomorrow."

"You plan to celebrate what?"

"To celebrate the birth of Nathan's Place."

"Tomorrow will be more than just a celebration, says Rafael. Your father and Melba are expected to arrive. We have the room ready for Melba to deliver."

"Deliver? Deliver what?"

"The baby Jonathan you are going to be a father."

"It can not happen now I am not prepared for a family. There is no way we can have a baby at this point in my life."

"Brother now is not the time to make that decision. The deed has been done."

"Actually the deed was done many times."

"Son please you must be more respectful."

"I am sorry mother. I was at a loss for words."

"Now that you have admitted to your wrong doing you must now take responsibility. Get some sleep because tomorrow will be a hectic day. Goodnight."

"Goodnight mother."

"I did not expect them to come so soon."

"Father must have come ahead of the shipment."

"So it seems. Get some rest. I pray that tomorrow is a pleasant eventful day for you just as you have made for me today."

"I would not share this day with no one other than you brother. Goodnight."

The next morning…

The sun shines through the leafy oak trees. Tiny glitters of light pierce through to Nathan's face. He raises his head to look for Jonathan who has already left for the morning. Nathan glances down at the barn where the others gather for breakfast. He raises himself to his feet and begins to fold the blankets neatly before carrying them to the barn area along with the others. Everyone appear to be in good spirits. He searches for Jonathan but he is nowhere to be found. Nathan grabs a biscuit from a tray and walks toward the big house. When he enters the house is filled with several people. Out of the corner of his eye Nathan can see his father while he rests in a corner chair. The others appear to be medical personnel from the hospital. There is no sight of Jonathan or Rafael. He hears Linda's voice in the kitchen then heads in that direction. Nathan enters a kitchen filled with people whom he recognizes from New York. Linda looks up from the table to point Nathan upstairs. Nathan retreats upstairs to Jonathan's room where he hears voices in the background. Nathan knocks then he opens the door with caution. Inside Jonathan sits at Melba's bedside. Nathan steps in to see Melba propped with several pillows underneath her head and feet. Her torso appears enormous compared to the pregnant bellies he has seen before.

"Nathan, how are you?"

Nathan steps a little closer to get a better view.

"Very well how are you?"

"With the exception of my condition I am doing pretty well myself."

Nathan turns to look at Jonathan and it appears that all the blood has drained from his face. His ghost like features troubles Nathan because he has never witnessed his brother this distressed before. Jonathan rubs Melba's feet while she rests.

"How far long are you?"

"I am due any day the doctor says."

"That can not be true unless you conceived early in our relationship. Are you certain that I am the father?"

"Brother," Nathan screams. "Have you lost your mind?"

"I understand his apprehension I should have told him when I first knew. You were so excited to begin your new life on the farm. I did not want to deny you of the opportunity," explains Melba.

"There is no comparison to this experience. The farm could have been postponed until the baby arrived," replies Jonathan. "Are you comfortable?"

"A little, sometimes I feel this tightness then it goes away."

"I will get mother."

"That is unnecessary Nathan it may be indigestion. She appears to be very full. What did you eat today honey?"

"Jonathan I am pregnant," says Melba.

Never Underestimate The Power of A Secret Place

"I understand but that can not be the entire baby."

"Brother, allow Melba time to rest. The long trip can be tiring."

"I guess you are right."

Jonathan gives Melba a light kiss on the lips.

"Are you aware that we are getting married?"

Melba nods to confirm his question.

"My hopes are we will marry before you give birth."

Jonathan rises up from the bed after he gives Melba one last kiss on her hand. She grimaces with the increase of discomfort.

"Do you need anything?"

"I am fine, please send for my mother."

"Your mother is here?"

"Yes she came with us."

"What about your father?"

"He is here also."

Jonathan's face turns white as snow. He appears to panic and returns to his seated position beside Melba.

"Are they aware of your condition?"

"Of course Jon look at me. Do I not look pregnant?"

"Well you were always a large woman."

"What is that supposed to mean."

"Brother let us leave Melba to rest. I think that is best."

Jonathan leans forward to kiss Melba but she presses his face away from her with his hand.

"Leave Jon before I do something I will not regret."

Jonathan gradually rises from the bed before he turns to leave he asks.

"Are you sure there is no other suitor besides myself?"

Nathan grabs Jonathan's arm and pulls him outside the door. He gives the door a firm push to close it behind him.

Nathan returns to Melba and kneels at her bedside.

"Please forgive him. I believe he is in a state of shock or it could be that he does not possess any discretion. I always knew brother lacked common sense don't you agree? Are you in any pain?"

"Somewhat can you please call for my mother."

"Relax, I will return with her soon."

"When Nathan opens the door Mrs. Meril bursts into the room."

"Are you alright sweetheart? Are you in any pain?"

"I think the contractions are a minute apart mother."

"Son, please call for the midwives."

Nathan quickly exits the room. After a brief moment Rafael and Linda enter the room with Jonathan at their heels.

"Close the door behind you."

Jonathan closes the door with urgency. Linda and Rafael rush to each side of the bed to comfort Melba. Meril moves close to the head of the bed to hold Melba's hand. Jonathan stands at the foot of the bed to observe the event. The bed covers are pulled to the foot of the bed to expose Melba in her nightgown. They raise her nightgown to further expose Melba up to her waist. Jonathan stands in utter belief while he observes everything unfold. Linda inserts her hand into Melba's cavity to determine if the baby's head has crowned.

"I can feel the head."

"Already?"

"Yes son, please get the doctor."

"Yes mother."

Jonathan continues to stand in place.

"Son, I said get the doctor!"

"But mother I must witness the delivery of my first born son."

"Jonathan do not argue with me!"

Mr. Johnson enters the room.

"What is all the commotion about?"

Never Underestimate The Power of A Secret Place

"We need the doctor she is close to giving birth."

Mr. Johnson leaves the room. He soon reappears with the doctor. The doctor places his satchel on the nightstand then orders the men out of the room.

"You will be nothing but a distraction. Hurry the baby will be here soon!"

Both Johnsons exit the room.

Outside of the door there are three large chairs that have been placed in the hallway by the workers. Melba bellows a loud moan.

"Mother please stop the pain! Mother please! Please help me mother, Oh God."

Tears begin to form in Jonathans eyes.

"Father we must pray."

"Good idea son."

Nathan and Jonathan kneel before their father while the workers place their hands on their shoulders.

"Father please," asks Jonathan.

Dear Lord, we come to you humbly to make our request known. Please bless us with a healthy child. Keep your loving arms around Melba throughout this journey.

"Oh, God please help me, Melba cries."

Mr. Johnson pauses then Jonathan continues the prayer.

"Please Father bless my family that we may be a testimony of your greatness. Amen."

The room echoes of Amens. There is a lot of movement in the room after Melba bellows a long moan. The doctor can be heard encouraging Melba, "Just one more push now relax." All of the sudden the cry of a baby is heard along with the loud sigh from the midwives. There is silence for a long time and then the door creeps open. Rafael enters the hall with a bundle in her arms. Everyone looks in surprise when she hands the bundle to Jonathan.

"What do I do with it?"

"*It* is your daughter, hold her silly."

Jonathan uncovers her face. Her eyes are a soft brown, skin a touch of honey and hair the color of caramel. She begins to suck her fists hungrily.

"Pass her around so that the others can hold her."

Jonathan places her in Nathan's arms. He places his finger in her tiny fist. Her grasp is tight.

"She is going to be a very strong baby girl," says Nathan.

Jonathan motions for Nathan to give her to their father. Mr. Johnson opens his arms ready to receive her. The door opens again.

"Rafael you must come now," Linda whispers.

"What is the matter mother?"

"Stay here, I will see."

Rafael and Linda disappear behind the door.

"Oh, please mother," cries Melba.

Jonathan jumps up then steps toward the door but his journey ends there. His heart races but he is afraid to enter the room for what he may witness.

"Come on, give it all you got. That's it slow," the doctor encourages Melba.

All of the sudden the scream of a baby is heard behind the door. Jonathan looks perplexed then he turns to his father. They all glance at each other.

"It can not be."

"You are the father of twins, brother. Congratulations!"

The workers hurry down the stairs humming happily to themselves. Before long all the workers hum in jubilee. Rafael enters the hall once again with a bundle. Jonathan now sits in his chair in disbelief. Rafael lowers the baby in his arms.

"It is a girl, son."

Jonathan removes the blanket from the baby's face. He witness a smooth mahogany skinned baby with eyes and hair the color of coal. Her hair is curly unlike her sister's whose is straight. Nathan stands over him to peek at the baby.

"Brother she is amazing."

"What is it son," asks their father.

Nathan takes the first baby from Mr. Johnson before Jonathan hands him the second baby. Mr. Johnson takes a look at the second baby then looks to the boys.

"What is so amazing?"

"Father one appears to be African while the other appears to be Caucasian."

"Why does this fascinate you? Boys, there is something I must tell you please have a seat. You both are also twins. Your mother and I are your biological parents. Arthur was adopted at an early age."

"Why the reveal now father?"

"I prayed that your mother would tell the both of you before her death."

"Why was it so forbidden to tell the truth?"

"Your mother was once a documented slave. It was illegal for us to marry. We were able to find a loop hole that would allow us to wed. When your mother delivered we were shocked to see the difference in skin color between the two of you. I questioned her whether you two were fraternal twins. She denied it completely. You will have to believe me. I had no idea that your mother was African. I assumed that she was one of the poor white's that was subjected to slavery."

"What are we to do now?"

"You must get married so that you can name the babies."

"Melba and I will share in the pleasure of naming the girls. Nothing will compare to this moment."

"Oh yes there is dear brother. Be patient something will come along."

"Let us get the girls to their mother so that they can nurse."

"Father I will take the babies in."

"Are you sure son that you can handle them both?"

"Mother I want to be the first to carry both of my daughters."

Mr. Johnson carefully places a baby on one arm then Rafael places one in his other arm.

"Are you sure Jonathan?"

"Please open the door."

With measured steps Jonathan walks into the room where the women continue to care for Melba. Mrs. Meril rush to his side to take one of the babies.

"I can manage please."

He approaches the bed then eases himself next to Melba.

"Sweetheart, open your eyes."

Melba opens her eyes to see her daughters for the first time.

"Did I tell you that you appeared rather large earlier? I am quite sure this is the reason."

"Son, give us the babies; we must prepare them to nurse. Please give us some privacy."

"They are my babies also are they not?"

"Son, this is not the time."

"I want to be present with my children at all the milestones in their lives."

"Oh, it is coming," moans Melba.

"Please not another baby."

"Just bear down the afterbirth will come easily."

"The what," asks Jonathan.

"Take the babies he is about to pass out."

"Nathan!" Linda yells.

Nathan pokes his head in the room.

"Yes mother?"

"Please take Jonathan with you."

Nathan looks at Jonathan with a grin.

"Brother haven't you seen enough? This is the very reason you never pursued medicine."

Everyone laughs while Nathan guides him out of the bedroom.

"There have a seat. One day you will learn to listen to the women."

Jonathan eases back into his chair. He glances across the room at his father who is asleep.

Jonathan thinks to himself…

Why does fear drive us away from the very one we desire to love? I must be a better father than my own. I will not allow work to consume me only to distance me from my children. One day if I should have a son born with scoliosis, I will love him unconditionally.

Jonathan nestles back into his chair and like the others he drifts off to sleep.

7
A PLACE OF REST

Six years later....

"Good morning daddy."

"Good morning baby girl. What did you bring us?"

"For me I got a biscuit with syrup and you get a pile of bacon."

"That's my girl. Did your mother see you?"

"No daddy she is folding the clothes."

"Where is your sister?"

"She is there with mother."

"Good my hopes are that we can have some peace before it is time to do the chores."

They both sit on the stone while they skip rocks across the pond.

"Here is a big rock daddy."

Angie Lou hands the rock to him.

"For heaven sakes what is this?"

"It is a rock daddy."

"What is all over it?"

Angie Lou shrugs her shoulders.

Never Underestimate The Power of A Secret Place

"Looks like syrup to me. Just look at you. Hurry now eat the biscuit before your mother sees you and find out that you have been in the oven this morning."

"I'm done daddy."

"Alright now I am going to dip you in the pond. I want you to wash your hands."

Jonathan takes Angie Lou by the back straps of her overalls. She spreads her arms like an air plane about to take off.

"Don't drop me daddy."

"I will not let you fall baby girl make sure you rinse your hands well. We must never have any evidence."

"Jon what are you doing with my baby?"

"Lets come in for the landing."

"Really Jon! Why can't you just be a normal father?"

"I thought I was being a normal father," Jonathan yells.

"Angie come inside," requests Melba.

Angie Lou walks towards the big house in a rush.

"What is that all over you?"

Jonathan winces while he waits for the answer?

"I don't know mother I was just sitting there being good."

"I know and it just happened."

"Yes mother how did you know?"

"It sounds like something your father would say."

Jonathan stares straight ahead to pretend he is engrossed in an important matter.

"Keep it up Jon. You will be in the dog house tonight; just one more of your shenanigans."

Jonathan thinks to himself, "*I will have to save it for later. I shall never go to the dog house on an empty stomach again. I have learned my lesson.*"

"Good morning Jonathan," waves one of the workers.

"Good morning! It is a beautiful day isn't it."

"Yes suh it is."

"Where is your wife?"

"She comin later."

"I see, you know we are scheduled to ship her shawls to New York to be sold today?"

"Yes suh I tell her."

Jonathan scratches his head then yells, "I really need her today, it is of great importance."

"She a bit unda the weather."

"Under the weather, he thinks? She is a very vibrant and healthy woman. What could possibly be troubling her?"

Jonathan continues to sit while the workers walk to the farm to begin their day. He occasionally waves at the children who begin to make their way to school. Jonathan stands to his feet then begins his way down the trail ever so often someone passes him on their way to their respective place. When Jonathan enters the woods daylight begins to drift behind him. He nears the module of Ben who shares it with Sista. He knocks softly.

"Sista," Jonathan shouts.

"Yes suh," he hears from behind the door.

"May I come in please?"

"Yes suh."

Jonathan turns the knob then gives the door a gentle push.

"Sista I need to speak with you about your shipment."

"Mistah Jonathan can it wait for one mo day? I promise I get to it."

Jonathan looks around the room it is very orderly. Bare of the essential furniture.

"Sista I have heard from the others you have been beaten by your husband. Is it true?"

"Suh please I don't want no troubles."

Jonathan continues to stand with the door open.

"Sista turn and face me please."

"Suh, Ben don't mean no harm."

"I will be the judge of that. Please turn so that I may see you."

"Yes suh."

Sista begins to turn around but because of the dimness in the room Jonathan is not able to view the bruises on her face.

"Please take a step forward so that I may see you clearer. Can you open the curtains also?"

Sista walks to the window to open the curtains. Immediately Jonathan observes that her clothes have been torn from her body to reveal a partially naked woman. Her complexion is dark but despite her color the bruises are visible. Jonathan turns and walks out of the quarter then returns to close the door. Jonathan quickens his pace towards the big house and into the kitchen where the ladies chatter about recipes.

"Mother where is father?"

"Hush before you wake the little ones."

"I need father it is a very important matter."

"He is in the study. What is it son?"

Jonathan exits the kitchen to look for Opio in the study. Opio's attention is focused on the various stacks of papers on his desk.

"Father may I take a moment of your time?"

"Yes son how can I be of assistance?"

"It is of grave importance can you please accompany me to care for one of the workers."

"Of course I can come now."

Opio follows Jonathan to the kitchen where he requests the assistance of Rafael and Linda.

"Mother, please just follow me I will explain later."

They follow close behind him while they begin their way down the trail. Jonathan enters the woods and comes upon the module where Sista lives. When Jonathan enters the module Rafael pinches him.

"How dare you enter someone's home without their permission."

"Please mother this is not the time."

The others enter to find no one present.

"Son, why have you brought us here?"

"It is Sista you must see her now. Sista," Jonathan yells!

"Yes suh," she answers. "I be there."

Sista enters the room dressed with her hair combed. She appears to be fine until Jonathan gestures for her to stand near the window. Linda and Rafael gasp when they witness the bruises.

"Who has done this to you?"

"Ma'am I don't won't no more troubles. I already has more than I can handle."

The women wrap their arms around her and guide her towards the door.

"Where are you taking her?"

"We will take her to the big house where she will be safe."

"We must speak with Ben before you do," insists Opio.

"He will just come back only to beat her again."

"I am certain he will not be back," adds Jonathan. "Stay here until I give you further instructions."

Jonathan and Opio reach the big house where Jonathan retrieves a rifle.

"What is that for?"

"I want the women to be protected. Mother can handle this very well. She is not afraid to use it."

"Do you think we will have to resort to such violence?"

"If necessary I will do whatever it takes to protect the women and children. The men can fend for themselves."

Nathan appears before them.

"Nathan take this rifle to Sista's home. Make sure you place it in mother's hands."

"Yes brother," says Nathan, he leaves the big house.

"We must find Samson to assist us in this matter."

"Are you certain that he will assist us?"

"It is he that informed me of this matter."

"How long have you known?"

"Not very long besides I did not want to jump to conclusions."

"That was very wise of you. Samson should be caring for the cattle."

Jonathan and Opio search the farm without drawing suspicion to themselves to find Samson in the field. His boots are covered with slop.

"Samson," Jonathan waves him in his direction.

Samson approaches him dressed in overalls. His large physique almost bursts through the seams of the cloth.

"Opio be sure to order appropriate sized work clothes for the workers. We may have to have them tailored."

"Yes suh," says Samson after he approaches the two men.

"I need your assistance in the matter that you brought to my attention the other day. Will you assist us to remove Ben from the property if he is found guilty of beating his wife?"

"Yes suh."

"How did you become aware of this matter?"

"Sista is my motha's sista."

"So you are related to Sista. Why did you not bring this to my attention earlier?"

"I'se scared you might separate us."

"You do not have to be afraid any longer; we are all family here. Samson please locate Ben will you? I want you to bring him to the Meeting Place where we do our business. I will have the women gather his belongings."

"Jonathan you are very serious about this matter."

"It is unacceptable for a man to beat any woman. I must make it very clear to all the men here."

When they enter the Meeting Place Mr. Kyle is carefully reading over a document.

"Good day Mr. Kyle," Jonathan greets him.

"Good morning suh."

Mr. Kyle tips his hat when Opio enters the quarter.

"How are you Mr. Kyle?"

"Ready ta begin tha day?"

"Mr. Kyle we have a sensitive matter that requires our attention."

"An what is that?"

"We have come upon a matter that concerns Sista. It has been brought to my attention that she has been beaten by Ben."

"That is comm'n among tha slaves. That is how they keeps 'em in line."

"Mr. Kyle with all due respect, from this point forward any man that beats his wife or any woman for that matter will be removed from this farm."

"How he suppos'd ta train her?"

"A woman is not an animal. She is a human being just like any man."

"That's not what ole masta Johnson say."

"Once again I will remind you slavery no longer exists. We will live like civil members of society. No one on this farm will use their power to influence control. We are all law abiding individuals and will all suffer consequences if we break any law or rules for that matter during our stay here!"

"Calm down Jonathan."

Opio places his hand on his shoulder.

"You must remain calm."

Jonathan realizes that he has begun to shake uncontrollably.

"Please forgive me Mr. Kyle."

There is a knock at the door afterwards Samson sticks his head in.

"Mista Jon, here is Ben."

"Will you both please step inside?"

Ben enters nervously. He is motioned to take a seat. The other men remain standing except Mr. Kyle who remains in his seat.

"How are you," Opio greets Ben.

"I been doin mighty good Mista Opio."

"Are you aware of why we want to meet with you?"

"No suh, not at all."

"It has come to our attention that you have beaten Sista."

"Yes suh. She my wife an I keeps her in line if she get outa line."

"What do you mean by get out of line?"

"Sometime she don't do what I tell her. I tell her don't talk ta the other women cause they brings trouble."

"What kind of trouble?"

"Women's don't mean no good when they's git togetha suh."

"What makes you think that?"

"That's what the masta say. Keep your woman next ta you and she won't cause ya no troubles."

"Explain to me what kind of trouble?"

"Well suh, sometimes they hide the chilluns when the masta calls for 'em. Tha masta beats tha man cause his wife don't mind."

"Why did you beat her this time?"

"Cause masta say to beat 'em sometimes an they's be no trouble."

"That is unacceptable here Ben. Under no circumstances will any man on THIS farm beat any woman. If it ever comes to my attention again that person will no longer reside on this farm! Have I made myself clear?"

"Jonathan you must calm down," warns Opio.

Nathan enters the quarter and looks around.

"What is going on here brother?"

Jonathan turns to leave the Meeting Place. He is overwhelmed with anger and becomes tearful. Opio joins Jonathan outside.

"Are you okay Jonathan?"

"He has to go father."

"Where son, where can he go? If he leaves Nathan's Place someone will lynch him.

"I can not bear the sight of him."

"Allow me to handle this. Do you trust me that I will make the right decision?"

"Yes father I do."

"Jonathan walks away to sit on the stone above the pond."

"Daddy," yells Angie Lou as she runs to her father. She jumps on his back when she reaches him.

"Horsey ride daddy!"

Jonathan leans himself forward and with one hand to the ground he then pushes himself up until he stands.

"Baby girl did you eat stones for breakfast?"

"No daddy," Angie Lou giggles.

"Where do you want to go to this time?"

"I want to see the chickens."

"Oh no, I can not let you chase the chickens today." How about we take a walk around the property? You can pick flowers for your mother and maybe she will forget her troubles."

They begin their journey around the property while Angie Lou picks wild flowers.

"Baby girl stand real still there is a snake nearby."

Angie Lou stands still like a statue.

"Daddy where is it," she whispers.

Jonathan picks a leaf of grass then gently runs it across her leg.

"Do not move."

Angie Lou continues to stand still. Jonathan hides the blade of grass behind his back.

"It is gone baby girl."

Angie Lou lets out a sigh.

"That was close daddy it didn't even bite me."

"That is *because*?"

"That is because God protects me from my enemies."

"Do not ever forget."

"Can we go down the hill where the rabbits are?"

"Not today."

"Why not daddy?"

"Because is not safe. I do not ever want you down the hill without me."

"Yes daddy."

"When can we go down the hill?"

"One day sweetie."

"When is one day daddy?"

"I will let you know when one day comes."

They continue their journey when Jonathan recognizes a trail that leads up to the property.

"So that is where they are trespassing."

Jonathan peers over the edge of the embankment; he realizes that the rocks have been removed to allow entrance.

"Baby girl jump on daddy's back."

Jonathan kneels down so Angie Lou can climb on.

"Oh boy baby girl, I think you are beginning to take after your mother."

"Plump and beautiful daddy?"

"You got it."

He grunts when he returns to a standing position. Angie Lou giggles while they start their way back to the big house. When he approaches the house Nathan stands at the back door of the house. Jonathan eases Angie Lou to the ground.

"Now go into the house so you can get ready for school. Give me a kiss… off you go. So what is the update?"

"Opio has decided to allow Ben to dwell in the barn until he has counseled him."

"How long will that take?"

"My hope is that it will not take too long. Sista will not be able to work until she has healed from her wounds."

"Who will counsel her?"

"It will be Linda."

"I can not think of a better choice. Did you know that there has been a path cleared to the farm?"

"No I did not."

"That explains the theft of our cattle. I think we need to request the assistance of our soldiers once more. They were very instrumental in the release of the remaining slaves. I was amazed to find that there were Spanish slaves. It benefited the farm well to bring them aboard. We have become more diverse. The commonality that we share is priceless. How many have left for New York?"

"Last I have counted twenty three men, women and children. My hope is that we do not overwhelm father."

"I am sure he will tell us if it were so. I shall return home in a few days."

"Must you go brother?"

"Of course Betty expects my return."

"When will your family settle here?"

"Todd has begun school. We both want the best education for him."

"We have the most knowledgeable teachers here Nathan."

"Are you sure of that?"

"I am sure the decision lies in Betty's hands. There is no question who wears the pants in your home brother."

"Unlike you my family enjoys my company."

"What makes you think mine does not?"

"You are practically thrown out of the house every day."

"It is only because I am outnumbered. If it were not for Opio I think they would try to kill me."

"Are you surprised?"

"Yes I am."

"You can not be serious. How often have you criticized Melba's weight? She is pregnant for heaven's sake."

"Pregnant you say? When did this happen?"

"Brother I am very concerned about you."

"Do you think I should be the first to know? I am the man of the house, the nerve of that woman!"

"Brother, please do not create a scene with the women."

"Me create a scene? That should be the least of your concern. I have every right to know what is going under my roof."

Jonathan hurries toward the front of the house with Nathan close behind him. Jonathan eases into the front door and cautions Nathan to do the same. All of the sudden the door slams behind Nathan which causes Jonathan to jump.

"Who is there?"

Melba enters the hall to see who it is. She returns to the kitchen.

"It's nobody but Jon."

"What did you say woman?"

Jonathan enters the kitchen where a couple of the workers assist Melba with lunch for everyone.

"When were you going to tell me?"

"Tell you what?"

"That you are with child again," he sings. "When is the baby due?"

"I hope soon!"

"Why do you refuse to obey your vows woman?"

Never Underestimate The Power of A Secret Place

"Well it looks like I am not the only one. I have asked you to never smoke around the children and you continue to do so."

"First it was do not smoke in bed, then it was do not smoke in the house and now it is do not smoke around the girls. What do you want from me woman?"

"Disappear can you manage that?"

"If it pleases you!"

"Brother where are you going," asks Nathan.

"To smoke a cigar."

Later that evening...

"Aren't you brave mister?"

"Is there something I should be concerned about?"

"Maybe; maybe not."

"You know you have this presence of beauty that surrounds you tonight."

"Just tonight Jon?"

"For the most part tonight you know it comes and goes sometimes."

"Oh my goodness."

"What is it?"

"I think my water has burst."

"You mean you have wet the bed.'

"No Jon I am in labor."

"I am serious you have no doubt wet the bed."

"Call for mother, hurry Jon."

"You are serious aren't you?"

"Ohhh," Melba begins to moan.

"I assume you are."

Jonathan jumps from the bed and sprints down the stairwell.

"Mother please come this very minute!"

The halls light up before Rafael makes her way up the stairs.

Never Underestimate The Power of A Secret Place

"She must be in labor go tell Linda to gather hot water and towels right away."

Jonathan races down the hall to call for Linda.

"I have the towels help Opio with the hot water."

"Yes mother."

Jonathan hurries to the kitchen while Opio heats water. Jonathan paces the floor.

"I just found out that she was pregnant and now a baby will be delivered any moment. Do you think that this is just a bit too questionable?"

Opio shakes his head, "One day you will learn Jonathan."

"I believe somedays are a mystery to me and this is one of those days."

Linda enters the kitchen, "Jonathan come we need you upstairs." Her eyes appear tearful. She raises her hand to signal to Opio the water is not needed. Jonathan follows Linda up the stairs to the bedroom which seems like the longest journey. The door fully opens to reveal Melba in bed while she holds a bundle. Rafael speeds past Jonathan and the door closes behind him now they are left alone. Jonathan approaches Melba and sits next to her on the bed to find tears streaming down her face. He realizes something is wrong. She hands the bundle to him. The baby appears to be asleep.

"Is it a boy or girl?"

Melba turns to cry into her pillow. Slowly he unwraps the blanket from the baby. It is a boy. He turns him over in his arms to see the curved spine.

"Scoliosis," he whispers.

He returns the baby to face him it is then he notice that the baby's arms fall limp. He stares at his perfect face and wonders what is wrong.

"Melba tell me what has happened?"

"He is stillborn."

Never Underestimate The Power of A Secret Place

"Stillborn?"

Jonathan searches his thoughts for a definition before he processes that his son has died. Tears begin to flood his eyes. The door opens and Nathan enters the room. He is tearful when he kneels next to his brother then he rests his face onto the babies face and blows short breaths into the baby's mouth.

"Brother it is alright with me. Let him rest."

A whine comes from Nathan as he pulls back and sits on the floor.

The three of them remain still until the door opens this time it is the doctor. He hurries toward Melba to check her condition.

"Has she delivered the placenta yet?"

"No doctor," Rafael answers.

"We must deliver the placenta right away. Jonathan I am sorry for your loss; please allow me some privacy so that I can see after your wife."

Jonathan rises to leave the room with the baby in his arms. Rafael reaches to take the baby and he resists.

"Son we have to prepare him for burial."

Jonathan stands there in shock.

"Nathan take your brother and care for him."

"Yes mother."

Nathan wraps his arm around Jonathan and leads him down the stairs out of the house to the stone above the pond.

"Brother you must have a seat." Jonathan squats down and wraps his arms around his legs.

Angie Lou runs out of the house down to where the brothers are.

"Daddy, hold me daddy."

Jonathan's arms open to allow Angie Lou into his lap. She nestles her face into the crook of his neck before she drifts off to sleep.

"Jonathan allow me to take her to bed," encourages Nathan.

He holds her firmly.

"I will take her in a minute."

"Are you sure?"

Tears begin to flow from his eyes onto his cheeks then falls onto Angie Lou's nightgown. Angie Lou awakens to look up at Jonathan. She places her hands on his cheeks to catch the tears.

"Daddy don't cry, Mommy Rafy say our baby go to heaven. Are you happy our baby goes to heaven?"

Jonathan nods yes to confirm. He leans back to take a brief look into her eyes. She returns her head into the crevice of his neck then drift off to sleep again.

Lord, bless my little ones. I trust you with my whole heart and I release them to you, they are yours. Do with them whatever you please. I trust in your Almighty awesome power that you will always protect them. Amen.

The moon peeks through the trees at Angie Lou who is fast asleep. Jonathan leans forward to steady himself before he can stand to his feet. The cool breeze nestles on his skin and all of the sudden Jonathan looks around and the blanket is gone.

"What happened to my blanket? Thank you father, I know that it was your loving arms enveloped around us to protect us; for you are marvelous."

Jonathan pulls Angie Lou close in his arms for a moment before he walks toward the house. When he enters the house is dim and everyone is asleep in their warm beds. He walks down the hall to the twin's bedroom. It is very dim to be morning, he thought to himself. Jonathan looks at his watch but he is mistaken; to his surprise it is midnight. Jonathan places Angie Lou in her bed and wraps the blanket around her to secure her. He turns to Cindy Lou who is nestled underneath her blanket. He firmly kisses her through the blanket at the head of her bed. Before he returns to the hallway he hears a small voice.

"Daddy."

He peeks in, it is Cindy Lou. She slips her head from underneath the blanket at the foot of the bed. She smiles a weary smile before she vanishes underneath the blanket. Jonathan now stands over his wife who is deep in sleep. He sits down in a nearby chair to take his shoes off. He watches her sleep until she opens her eyes.

"I am so sorry Jon."

"It is not your fault it is all in God's design. However, I am angry that you hid the pregnancy from me."

"Jon how could you not know I was pregnant?"

"I just thought maybe you gained the freshman ten."

"Are you serious?"

"It can happen Melba".

"Jon we do not live near a college campus let alone attend college."

"It is a thought."

"No it isn't, just say it."

"What are you referring to?"

"My weight Jon you make constant rude remarks about my weight."

"Sweetheart those remarks will end today."

He climbs in bed and nestles close to Melba.

"I love you just the way you are. Why don't you sit by the pond with me anymore?"

"It is too uncomfortable for me. Maybe you can bring me a cushion to sit on."

"Mel you have enough cushion of your own."

"Goodnight Jon."

"I love you Mel."

Jonathan resumes to watch Melba while she sleeps. He rises from the bed and adjourns to the study reluctant to call his father.

"Good Morning father are you busy?"

"No son, how are you?"

Never Underestimate The Power of A Secret Place

"I want to be the first to tell you that I have a son."

"His name is Jonathan Johnson III. It is unfortunate but he was stillborn," he sighs.

"Son I am sorry to hear of your loss. How is Melba?"

"She is well. The services will be today."

"So sudden?"

"Yes father the pain is too much for us to bear."

"I will keep you in my prayers. I love you son."

"Father I must tell you that he was born with scoliosis. I prayed that I would never have a son to suffer such as I have. Maybe it was God's way of answering my prayers. In some ways I regret that I will never hear him cry or see him open his eyes."

"I am very proud of Nathan and you. You have blessed our family tremendously. I shall be there in a few days Charles will drive me."

"Father all is fine you do not have to trouble yourself. "

"But I want to it has been far too long. The girls have grown and I do not want them to forget me. I shall see you soon."

"Yes father we will expect you soon."

A low hum permeates every room in the house. The humming tugs at Jonathan's heart and he begins to weep. He walks toward the sound which comes from outside. He finds Nathan standing on the terrace while he watch the workers gather together at the grave site. Everyone is dressed in black.

He looks to Nathan, "What is going on?"

"They have begun to prepare for the burial."

"But we do not have a casket and we have to dig a plot."

"Brother come follow me."

The brothers walk at a snails pace to the barn.

"Melba would like to have the ceremony today. She feels up to it."

"Whatever she decides," says Jonathan.

Never Underestimate The Power of A Secret Place

They reach the barn and inside near the west wall a small casket sits upon a table covered with a white cloth. Jonathan maneuvers through the crowd to examine it. Inside is the baby clothed in a white gown. He looks to be at peace. Jonathan examines the casket which has been carved by hand. The lid of the casket leans against the wall, engraved upon it is the name Baby Jonathan Johnson III. The casket looks beautiful carved in fresh oak. Nathan reaches him and asks.

"Do you want to know who prepared the cover to this casket? She carved all night to have it ready for this morning."

"Who is the person that created this magnificent piece of work?"

Nathan spins Jonathan around to face Sista healed from all her physical wounds.

"How are you Sista?"

"I'm doin mighty fine Mistah Jonathan. Thank you so much suh."

"Sista that is what a man is required to do he is to protect the women and children."

"Yes suh, I believe it to be true."

"How is Ben?"

"He ain't come back to the house. Mistah Opio say it ain't time yet."

"Let me know if there is anything I can do for you."

"No suh, you done more than I hope for."

"Well thank you Sista for your fine craftsmanship. How about I get more wood for you so that you can build furniture for your family?"

"I'd like that Mistah Jonathan. I like to work with my hands."

The worker's hum has come to a noticeable silence. Opio stands behind the casket dressed in his clergy attire.

Jonathan turns to leave and hurries to his wife's side. He leads her to the stone above the pond then lowers her to the stone covered with blankets careful not to rush. He nestles down next to her and places his arm around her shoulder.

"Are you sure you do not want to join them?"

"I am too weak Jon."

"I understand my love."

Many of the women begin to weep. The emotions fill the air until it rises to meet Jonathan and Melba. Jonathan embraces Melba holding her with a firm grip while they weep. The mood begins to change to what feels like remnants of peace falling from heaven. When Jonathan glances down at the workers they have lifted their hands in the air. This goes on for quite some time before a light mist begins to fall from the blue sky. Jonathan looks up to notice that not a cloud appears in the sky. Everyone begin to walk to the burial site where the casket is to be buried. Two male workers have gotten to their knees to ease the casket into the ground. A few words are spoken then everyone bows their heads. There is a melody of amens before everyone embrace. They make their journey back to the woods. Jonathan observes the twins who hold hands with Rafael and Linda. A light rain begins to fall and Jonathan eases Melba from the stone. Nathan reappears to assist them while they make their way to the house. Once on the porch Nathan places his arms around Melba.

"Brother, go pay your last respects."

Melba glances at him and nods to confirm Nathan's directive. Jonathan turns and leaves to meet the workers at the grave. He hurries so that he can share in the ritual of his son's burial. Jonathan reaches the two males and to his surprise it is Mr. Kyle and Ben. They continue to stand above the grave staring down at the casket. Neither of the men says a word while they continue to look down at the casket. A slow rain begins to fall but still they do not move.

"Excuse me Mr. Kyle may I?"

"Yes suh I don't mind if you do."

Never Underestimate The Power of A Secret Place

Jonathan begins to shovel the dirt into the ground where the casket lies. The two men have not moved an inch but continue to stand like they are in wait for something to happen. Jonathan completes filling the grave. He joins the two who continue to look on then all of the sudden the birds begin to sing and the fish begin to leap from the water into the air. Everything becomes alive and vibrant. Ben and Mr. Kyle take up their shovels and begin to walk towards the barn. Mr. Kyle passes Jonathan then places his hand on his shoulder.

"Looks like you got yo'self an angel," Mr. Kyle replies.

"Thanks Mr. Kyle, Ben."

They both nod their heads and continue to the barn where they rest the shovels against the wall.

Jonathan makes his way back to the big house.

"Son, you are soaking wet. Go get out of those wet clothes."

The twins run down the hall to give Jonathan a hug. Angie Lou jumps in his arms when he kneels down on one knee Cindy Lou barrels in with a jump all her own. They fall to the ground and the girls begin to giggle.

"I think I broke a rib."

The girls lean back to look at their father with a serious stare.

"Go tell mother to come please I think something is broken."

The girls race to the kitchen to search for Rafael. Rafael quickens her pace then comes to stand over him with her hands by her side.

"Son if you don't get up off that floor you are going to regret it."

There is a sudden knock at the door. Jonathan turns onto his stomach to see who it is. He smells the aroma of apples and jumps to his feet. Rafael pulls him away before she answers the door.

She opens the door to a host of workers who have begun to bring various dishes cooked for the family.

Never Underestimate The Power of A Secret Place

"Why thank you! You shouldn't have this will be very much appreciated. Jonathan go change your clothes right this minute," she grimaces.

"Nonsense mother I am comfortable the way I am besides I am famished."

"And you will continue to be famished until you change those clothes."

Jonathan races up the stairs to the bedroom. He looks into the room at Melba who is in bed resting. With ease he steps in and opens the closet door to undress. He begins to search for a shirt and trousers then pulls them on.

"Change your under garments Jon," says Melba.

"Get your rest honey everything will be fine."

"Jon if you walk out that door I am going to tell mother."

"What does it matter?"

"You are soaked I am sure your under garments are too."

"If it makes you happy I will change."

"Thank you Jon and after you change, leave your wet clothes in that chair," Melba points to the wooden chair in the corner.

"You do not trust me do you?"

"Maybe I should just ring for mother."

Jon continues to remove his clothing and retrieves his underwear from the dresser drawer.

"The things a man endures to please his wife," he whispers.

"Did you say something Jon?"

"Get some rest dear do not work yourself into a rage."

When Jonathan reaches the lower level of the home the aroma of food over takes him. To his surprise the house is filled with many of the workers and their children. There is food everywhere of all varieties. Everyone chatter among themselves while some of the men shake hands with Jonathan. After he enters the kitchen he finds various dishes stored on every surface around him. Rafael, Stephanie, Zaneta and Linda prepare plates for everyone. He witnesses Nathan, Mr. Kyle and Samson who sit at the kitchen table and each of their plates are filled with various types of food. Nathan looks up for a moment then returns his eyes to his plate.

"Mother would it be too much to ask…"

Rafael cuts him off and opens the oven. She retrieves a plate filled with various appetizing foods while the men begin to make room at the table for him to join them. A sign of joy is written all over his face when Rafael hands him a fork.

"Do not eat until you make yourself sick."

"Mother must you disgrace me?"

"Son you are a disgrace to yourself."

"Where are the children?"

"They are on the back deck eating their meals."

"Where will the adults be held?"

"They are in the dining area."

"Is there enough chairs?"

"I do not have the slightest idea; go see for yourself."

"Brother it is a dishonor to our guest to indulge ourselves of the good deeds of others before returning the gesture ourselves," says Jonathan.

"Must we now? Our food will turn cold."

"You know that mother will take care of our needs."

The men rise from their seats to retreat to the back of the house and begin to remove the stack of chairs from the deck. Aaron and Moses follow suit. Soon the dining room has enough chairs for almost everyone. Some dine in the living area and along the halls. Everybody mingle happily among one another. Jonathan is satisfied with the arrangements and returns to the kitchen. When he sits down to the table Rafael returns his plate to the table. The others have already made it to the table and are almost finished. Nathan stands to gather his plate before he takes it to the sink.

"Has Mel eaten anything?"

"Yes she has eaten some time ago. I have put away something for later."

"Thanks mother you are fabulous," says Jonathan.

The girls race into the kitchen weaving through the crowd."

"Careful girls before you harm someone."

"Daddy may we chase the butterflies," asks Angie Lou.

"Yes you may and make certain you stay near the house. Do you understand me?"

"Yes daddy."

"That goes for every one of you!"

"Yes suh," says all the children. Their voices echo from the hall. Before he can return to his plate the children are out of sight.

"We will have to take turns watching over them. It has been sometime since we have secured the parameters."

"I shall be the first to serve my time. The walk will do me good," says Nathan.

Samson relinquishes his seat to Rafael who has prepared herself a plate. Linda now sits in Nathan's seat. Jonathan finishes and places his plate in the sink.

"Opio you do not have to stand; please take my seat."

"Thank you son."

"Mother I am most gracious for that incredible meal," says Jonathan while he wipes his hands with a cloth.

"Do not thank me the workers cooked all the food before we could start dinner."

"I must honor them for their kindness."

Jonathan steps into the living area and clears his throat.

"May I have your attention? Let me speak for my wife and myself when I say we are most gracious for your support during the loss of our son. I must tell you the generosity and love that you have bestowed upon my family today has overwhelmed me. Never in my entire life have I been met with such sincerity. It is an honor to be a part of your family."

"Mistah Jonathan."

"No please call me Jon."

"Jon suh, you a man with a big heart. It is so many of us and just one of you. You and Mistah Nathan young men, we hope you stay here for a long time."

"It is my hopes that Nathan's Place will continue here throughout the test of time and our very existence will exemplify the true sense of mankind dwelling together as one. Please stay however long you wish; I must rejoin my wife during our time of bereavement."

Jonathan exits the room and takes the stairway to his bedroom. The women begin to wash the dishes and clean where everyone once dined. The leftovers are far too much to store. Rafael begins to ration out meals to the workers. Many have their preference for foods that were prepared by one another. They share recipes and compliment each others dishes. The ladies continue to mingle a little while longer while the men return the chairs to the back porch. One by one they begin to drift to their homes with a light spiritual hum that seems to be carried away by the wind.

Jonathan eases into the bed next to Melba. She awakens to find Jonathan pretending to sleep next to her before she returns to a peaceful sleep. Moments later Jonathan sneaks a peek to watch his beautiful wife rest next to him.

"Thank you Lord for you created a beautiful woman just for me. It remains a mystery how someone like her could love someone like me. What have I done to deserve her? Please give me the wisdom to care for her as I should and the strength to protect her with my life. Hosanna Lord! You are worthy of praise, Amen.

Jonathan leans back into his pillow. He listens while the sweet spiritual hums of the workers drift into his bedroom. A release of tears begins to flow from his eyes and soon he drifts off into a deep sleep.

8

A PLACE OF REVELATIONS

Jonathan brushes sleep from his eyes before he rises from the bed. There she sits at the edge of the bed; Melba weeps into a pillow.

"Sweetheart please come to me."

He motions to Melba but she bends over into the pillow to weep louder than before. Jonathan jumps to his feet and runs to the door of his bedroom only to come face to face with Rafael.

"Mother I do not know what to do."

"Just hold her son she is grieving."

"Mother please come in," Jonathan motions Rafael to enter the room. "She needs *you* not I."

"Son go over there and hold your wife."

Jonathan turns and looks at Melba while she continues to weep. He turns around to face Rafael but she has disappeared. Jonathan shuts the door and kneels next to Melba near the bed. He wraps his arms around her and cradles his head into her neck.

"Are you hungry honey?"

"No Jon just leave me be."

"Are you sure? Maybe if you take a bite of something you may feel better. Everyone finds comfort in food dear."

"Jon please," Melba sighs.

Never Underestimate The Power of A Secret Place

"I can not leave you to grieve alone. I should join you to grieve the loss of our son. He is mine is he not? You know this is the second time that you have kept your pregnancy a secret from me. I have begun to wonder if it is I who fathered the twins to this day. Of course Jonathan III carries all the biological features of father and I so I can not argue that. It is Cindy that I am most concerned about. She appears to favor neither of us. Angie she possesses your beautiful dark skin and coal black eyes. She pierces my soul each time she looks at me. She has never spoken of my frailty at least not to me. She believes that I am indestructible. Sometimes I am afraid that I will fail her one day. Cindy has taken to Nathan. Quite naturally it was he that she grasped at birth. She claimed him; like I with Rafael. I will always have this bond with her for the rest of my life. Isn't it strange?"

"What Jon?"

"The bond that mother and I possess. It was told that Nathan was taken to another family to be raised. But in truth he was with mother and I was taken away. I was told that I was so feeble at birth. They did not think I would live very long. I nursed at Rafael's breast until I was strong enough to return to mother. Imagine that, Rafael's milk returned just for me; so that I could live. Maybe that is why I love her so. I fear the day when I will lose her forever."

"Jon?"

"Yes sweetheart."

"Do you ever fear that you will lose me one day?"

"Never, the thought of raising the twins alone is unimaginable!"

"Jon!"

"Sweetheart we have plenty of time before we shall ever have to face death. Although, there have been times when I think you have attempted to to take my life."

"Jon I need to rest."

"Can I get you something to eat?"

"Well if you must I am feeling rather hungry. Can you bring me a small portion of the baked apples?"

"Ah hah, so you are hungry. I will bring you whatever you like if it makes you happy."

"Jon I just lost my appetite."

"Did you really? I will bring it anyway just in case your appetite should return."

Jonathan eases from his wife's body and lifts himself from the bed.

Three months later…

"Brother I do not know how to say this but I must return to my family."

"Well if you must. Please brother, be ever so cautious I dreamed a dream last night. I can only recall the horror of it. You were found hanging from a tree on dead man's road. But of course we both know that God is our protector. I pray for your safe return."

"I shall return soon."

Nathan carries his baggage to the truck then places it on the bed of the truck.

"Charles," he yells. "Would you like to join me?"

Charles his shakes his head.

"It is too soon to return. There is so much work to be done. Nathan please look after my family and tell them I send my love."

"Nathan please make certain that you inform Phyllis that it is not I that keeps Charles from his family."

"Jonathan, Phyllis is very patient. She is anxious to visit the farm again."

Never Underestimate The Power of A Secret Place

"My hopes are that Nathan's family and yours will make Nathan's Place your home one day. Let us take pleasure in one manly hug before you leave Nathan."

The three of them embrace for a moment. Fear settles on Jonathan's face when Nathan pulls onto the trail.

"Nathan call home the moment you are near a telephone. Please keep me informed of your journey."

"I will brother. Do not fret, God is with me."

"Your rifle, keep it near."

Nathan waves from the truck while he travels along the trail to leave the farm.

"Charles when will the next truck load of cotton move out?"

"My hopes are that it will be in the morning."

"Who will drive the route?"

"My hopes rest on Sampson however I am still at a crossroads about who I will send with him. Do you think he is ready for his first long distance delivery?"

"Samson will be fine. My main concern is for the person that may get in his way."

They both begin to laugh.

"Let us check the load before we send them off. We need to ship as much cotton on this trip as possible. I can not believe this year's harvest. It continues to increase with each passing year. Father says that the factory receives more product than they have ever in the past. We will have to build another storage facility to keep the quality of supply at its peek. I never thought the farm would be this successful so soon."

"To tell you the truth I do not think it is the farm that drives the success."

"What do you think it is Charles?"

"I think it is God. I am sure the man upstairs is pleased with Nathan's Place."

Never Underestimate The Power of A Secret Place

"With all my heart I hope that is true. May God continue to dwell with us. Samson we will need to check the load before nightfall. Please gather several workers this will be a massive task."

Later that evening…
"That is enough for tonight get your rest for the long journey. Goodnight I will see you at day break or like the workers say when the sun meets the trees."

"Goodnight Jon."

"Excuse me Jonathan, have you heard from Nathan? Surely he should have made it to the Mississippi line by now."

"I will have to check with the others. Good night Charles."

Jonathan enters the big house. It appears that everyone has turned in for the evening. Jonathan knocks on the door of Rafael's bedroom.

"Mother? Mother?"

The door creeps open.

"What is it son is everything alright?"

Rafael ties the belt to her robe before she steps into the hall.

"I wonder if you have heard from Nathan?"

"No son let me ask Linda."

Rafael knocks at Linda's door. Opio peeks from the room.

"Yes, what is it Rafy?"

"Father, where is mother?"

"Jonathan now is not the time."

"I should think that I have the right to know what is going on under my very roof."

"Son if you should know Linda and I are married."

"When did this marriage occur?"

Rafael takes Jonathan by the ear then drags him down the hall.

"Now we are adults. We can manage our affairs without your permission."

"I dare say."

"You dare say what?"

"How long have you hidden this treachery?"

"Treachery? Jonathan you are ridiculous."

"We shall see what Nathan has to say concerning your shenanigans father and as for you…"

Rafael interrupts Jonathan.

"What about me son?"

Rafael places her hands on her hips and taps her foot.

"I will deal with you in the morning."

"Why all the commotion," Melba asks.

She leans over the balcony to get a better view.

"Jonathan has lost his mind again please help him find it before I have him committed."

"How dare you make such a foolish threat you just wait until I speak with brother. By the way has anyone spoken with Nathan today?"

"Not at all," they all shake their heads.

"Why is it your concern?"

"Well unlike you I am concerned with the well being of the family rather than the entertainment of foolishness."

Jonathan stomps out of the house and retreats to the module that Charles occupies. He approaches Charles who sits on a stool outside the module with Samson smoking a cigar. Charles makes a gesture to Jonathan to take a smoke but he declines.

"What brings you here Jon?"

"I am unsettled in regards Nathan's trip to New York. I should have heard from him by now."

"I am sure he will call in the morning."

Jonathan rubs the top of his head and looks around.

"I see the truck is ready to deliver the goods."

"Yes suh, we ready to get this over with."

"Are you nervous Samson?"

"I ain't afraid but I sho don't want let you down."

"You have nothing to worry about. We live and we learn by our mistakes."

"Come here Jon let me show you the lights on this truck. You can see for miles down the road in this thing. It is an impressive piece of equipment."

Charles, Samson and Jonthan climb in the truck.

"Samson get behind the wheel," orders Charles.

Samson and Jonthan exchange seats. Jonathan is now in the middle.

"Let's take a run."

"Where to?"

"Dead man's road," says Jonathan.

Samson looks at him.

"Mistah Jonathan, ain't nothin on dead man's road but trouble."

"Where are the rifles?"

"In the back," informs Charles.

"We are ready for trouble."

Samson starts the truck up. The engine roars before it reduces to a rattle.

"Turn on the lights."

Samson pulls the knob and the lights come on. He pushes the knob in and the lights turn off.

"What did you do that for?"

"To see if they work."

Jonathan and Charles glance at each other.

"Now pull onto the trail," directs Charles.

Without any urgency the truck edges on to the trail. The trucks vibration causes them to shake. The pot holes along the trail increases the movement in the truck. Jonathan begins to laugh at them jostle around in the truck. They both begin to stare at him.

"Have you been drinking again Jon?"

"Of course not Melba will kill me."

Samson turns onto dead man's road.

Jonathan continues to chuckle at the sight of them. Samson stops the truck and stares straight ahead. Charles and Jonathan follow his gaze. Before them a naked figure dangles from a rope.

"Continue forward," Jonathan yells.

"Faster!"

Samson drives within twenty feet of the body then stops the truck. Charles jumps from the truck and sprints toward the body raising his rifle.

"What is he doing," asks Jonathan.

"He is gonna kill him so he won't suffer no more."

"Do not shoot," yells Jonthan but it is too late.

The rope breaks and the body fall to the ground. Charles kneels over the body then jumps back. He recollects himself to hover over the body again and removes the noose from the body. Charles sits the body up; it is then that Jonathan recognizes Nathan. Jonathan begins to scream.

"No, No, please God spare my brother!"

Jonathan begins to shake uncontrollably. Samson sits next to him while tears flow from his eyes. He wipes his face with the back of his arm then gets out of the truck. He looks around the area then reaches in the truck for the rifle in Jonathan's hands. His grip is unmatchable. Jonathan continues to shake fitfully in the truck while he gazes at the two in the road. Samson walks away from the truck. He looks to his left then his right in fear that someone may appear out of the darkness. Samson reaches Nathan and examines his neck.

"He gonna be alright."

"How do you know?"

"He can still breathe."

Nathan gargles up small drops of blood when Samson raises his arms above his head.

"All he need is some air. He gonna live. I go get the truck Mistah Charles."

Samson walks back to the truck and climbs in. He looks to Jonathan who continues to shake. Samson wraps his arms around him and holds him for a moment.

"He gonna live; you save yo brotha from death. God tell you to come here an you obey God's word. Mistah Nathan gonna be fine. You gonna be fine Mista Jonathan."

Jonathan rocks back and forth while Samson drives the truck closer to the men. Samson joins Charles and Nathan once again.

"Where we gone put him?"

"In the truck."

Samson looks back at the truck while Charles attempts to get Nathan to his feet.

"Help me will you."

Samson pulls Nathan up and carries him to the truck. Charles looks around for any intruders before he cocks his rifle. Samson sits Nathan where Charles once sat then he closes the door. He takes the rifle from Charles.

"Where you going?"

"Right here," he points the rifle at the footrest of the truck.

Charles climbs into the driver's side of the truck and looks at Jonathan who is not aware that Nathan is next to him. Jonathan continues to rock back and forth while he holds the rifle. Samson climbs onto the footrest and takes hold of the inside of the door while Charles backs out. Nathan slumps over onto the dashboard and Samson peers into the truck to see that Jonathan's disposition has not changed. He looks at Charles who looks frightened himself.

"Just get me to the trail an we gonna be alright."

When Charles drives onto the trail Samson lets out a sharp scream. Within seconds men and women come from the woods to surround the truck. They begin to gather around the truck while the truck makes it way to the big house. Charles drives slow so that he does not hit anyone. The women reach into the truck to touch the brothers and the moans become so heavy that everyone from the big house and quarters come running down the trail. Samson stops the crowd he motions the women to take the city workers into the big house. They swarm around the women and the twins to build a hedge around them that guides them back towards the house. Opio makes it through the crowd to reach Charles.

"What is going on?"

He glances into the truck then steps away in shock.

"Samson says he is going to be alright."

"We have to get him into the infirmary without the others knowledge until we clean him up."

The truck pulls up next to the quarter where Charles lives.

"Put him in my bed. I will send for the doctor."

"The doctor is here."

"How is that so?"

"Somehow he was informed that he was needed on the farm."

"Where is he now?"

"He is in the truck with Nathan."

The men swarm around the truck to prevent any interruptions from the women. Linda angrily attempts to push through the crowd but finds herself bounced around only to return inside of the circle each time. Samson escorts Jonathan into the arms of Rafael who has become frantic. Rafael falls to the ground while she attempts to dash in Jonathan's direction. Jonathan reaches for her and they embrace.

"Son what is going on?"

Rafael looks into Jonathan's eyes he appears to be in a trance.

"What has happened?"

"He is in shock. The doctor will be here soon to see after him," says Opio. "Come on son."

Never Underestimate The Power of A Secret Place

Opio leads Jonathan into the house where Melba waits.

"Take him to bed the doctor will be up in a moment."

"What is going on," Rafael yells in panic.

"Just do as I say. I must call Mr. Johnson."

"What happened?"

"Enough," he shouts. "We have a crisis and I need you to take Jonthan upstairs until the doctor arrives. Samson!"

"Yes suh."

"There will not be any trucks leaving the farm until further notice."

"Yes suh."

"And Samson."

"Yes suh."

"Thank you for saving my boy's life."

"No suh, God has Mistah Nathan's life in his hands."

"You are absolutely right he does."

"This gonna make Mista Jonathan stronga suh. We prayin for him."

"Thank you Samson."

"Anythang else Mistah Opio?"

"I would appreciate it if you stayed near the house."

"Suh we ain't goin no where."

"Thank you Samson. You may leave."

"Yes suh."

After a short time there is a knock at the door. Opio opens the door and in steps the doctor.

"Dr. Waters welcome."

"Where is the boy?"

"He is upstairs let me escort,"

Doctor Waters interrupts; "I AM CAPABLE of finding my own way," he yells.

"GET OUT!"

Dr. Waters look up and Jonathan is there at the top of the staircase.

"Now Mr. Johnson please relax; how may I assist you?"

"You will not speak to my FATHER in that manner. Do you hear me," Jonathan yells at the top of his voice.

"Yes Mr. Johnson."

Dr. Waters steps backwards until he has reached the door then leaves.

"I will not allow even the minute disrespect to be hurled towards any member of my family."

Jonathan returns to his bedroom and closes the door behind him. Outside Jonathan hears the sound of someone humming. Not a hum of sorrow but a hum of peace and tranquility. Jonathan kneels at the bed unable to speak a word. He can not find the words to pray while he continues to listen to the hums of the workers. Soon his spirit becomes light and he is able to stand to his feet. He exits the bedroom and walks toward the stairs.

"Where are you going," asks Melba.

"I am going to care for my brother."

Jonathan now stands at the door of Charles's quarter. The door opens and he steps in and looks behind the door but no one is there. Nathan lies on a gurney on his back with his eyes wide open. Jonathan steps closer to him unable to utter a word.

"Brother," says Nathan then he reaches his hand out to him.

Jonathan takes his hand and holds it and does not let go. He stands there it seems like hours until he kneels beside his bed. It is now morning and Nathan sits up with his back against the wall. Jonathan awakens and looks in the direction of his brother.

"What are you doing here?"

"I came to see about you. Father is coming."

"Why?"

"He is coming to see about you."

"WHY," Nathan yells.

Never Underestimate The Power of A Secret Place

"He loves you."

"How can he love me when he denied he fathered me for most of my life?"

"Brother you have to understand."

"Understand what? That for lack of a better word he is a coward. How can he enjoy the luxury to deny any relationship to my mother, your mother and his children who are Africans? I have never been afforded that luxury any luxury for that matter."

Nathan rips the bandage from his neck.

"Not even the luxury to live in PEACE!"

They both sit in silence until there is a knock at the door. Linda enters with a tray of food.

"You must be hungry son. I have something soft and warm for you."

Nathan cuts her off.

"I am fine mother."

Linda pauses for a minute.

"Son, I never thought I would live to see the day any of my boys would lose their life. And for whatever it is WORTH," her voice breaks. "You are alive son; God saw it fit for you to see another day. Don't you dare become bitter. Rejoice and thank God that you have victory over death."

Linda places the tray on a nearby table. Jonathan stands and wraps his arms around her for a brief moment.

"Son, do not be angry with your father. He hid the truth to protect your mother. Your grandfather never married. He too was in love with a colored woman. There was not a chance back then that he would be allowed to marry her. She was my mother; Rafael and I. She was twenty six years old when they learned that she was not a child."

Linda smiles to herself.

"My mother was forced to leave the orphanage and she took us with her. Your grandfather took care of us even after my mother's death. He paid our living expenses and sent Rafael and I to school. Your father was an orphan that my mother grew fond of. Before she was forced to leave she asked your grandfather to look after him and he adopted him. Your father," she shakes her fist.

"Now history repeats itself again. Your father fell in love with an African girl in the orphanage. Except that she passed for white. When your mother became pregnant we were running frantic for months trying to figure out what to do with the two of you until a judge granted your mother her rights to freedom. Your grandfather got wind of it and had them married at his home. She was then able to care for the both of you. Your grandfather was threatened with imprisonment. Mr. Johnson was a factory worker in the very cotton factory that he now owns and to his surprise your grandfather's estate was left to him. It was only then that your life of comfort began. He was not a coward. He did whatever it took to keep his family together. You will respect your father when he arrives. Have I made myself clear?"

"Yes mother," Nathan replies.

"Mother I must say I find it quite intimidating that you would eavesdrop upon our private conversation," Jonathan replies.

Linda grabs Jonathan by the ear.

"Son this is not the time for your foolishness."

"Yes mother please forgive me."

Jonathan dances around Linda to free himself of her grasp. Nathan gasps for air while he laughs at the two. They all begin to laugh together.

"Your father should be here any day. He will bring your grandfather's colleagues from the hospital. Please shower them with your utmost respect."

"Yes mother."

Never Underestimate The Power of A Secret Place

"Jonanthan, Rafael has a warm plate for you in the oven. I will have someone bring it out to you. Preferrably Rafael so that she can speak with you about your behavior."

"Mother please forgive me for I believe I have lost temporary control of my senses."

"Without a doubt you have."

"Please do not tell mother."

"What is the worst she can do?"

"The bran muffins are far more than I can bear these days."

"Now if it were I," Linda begins.

"The bran muffins it is mother."

"Make sure you clean your plate."

"Yes mother."

Linda exits the quarter.

A few days later Jonathan sits on the stone to enjoy a peaceful early sunrise. A small garden snake slithers past his foot. He places his foot on the snake, grabs it and places the snake in his pocket. A few minutes later the girls come to meet him.

"Daddy today is our birthday."

"You do say? Now how old will you be?"

"We will be eight years old daddy. Have you bought our gifts yet?"

"Of course, I have one in my pocket this very minute. Cindy put your hand in there and pull it out," Jonathan directs.

Cindy Lou reaches in and pulls the snake out. She drops it before she runs away screaming.

Angie Lou begins to giggle, "Daddy is it mine?"

"I knew you would appreciate it baby girl. Of course he is yours and you must make sure it gets plenty of air. Show it to your mother she will take great delight in your new friend."

Angie Lou runs in the direction of the house with the snake dangling from her hand. Soon the door to the house slams shut.

Never Underestimate The Power of A Secret Place

Jonathan leans back on his elbows and all of the sudden there is a scream that resonates from the house.

"Angie Lou get that thing out of here!"

"But daddy said mother would take delight in my new friend."

"He did, did he?" "Jon," yells Rafael she shakes her fist at him when he glances over his shoulder.

"Looks like its going to be another day in the dog house just the way I planned it."

Jonathan sits up to observe a dust cloud coming from the entrance. He wonders to himself, *is this an ambush?* Everyone continue their way to the farm without any concern to the visitors who enter the property. Jonathan races down the trail until he meets the first horsemen. He recognizes him. It is Kennedy well known for his leadership skills at Summer Camp when they were children.

"Good morning to you. What brings you here?"

"We heard that one of our own is in need of our assistance. We are here to serve and protect."

"Thank you my brother, please carry on."

There are five more decorated men to pass him on horse back. He salutes them out of respect. Afterwards an automobile approaches with his father inside. A group of women accompany him also. The automobile stops and a man exits, it is his father. He walks up to greet him and they embrace for a moment. Mr. Johnson returns to his automobile to continue to the big house.

A second automobile pulls up and Jonathan peers inside. It is Phyllis, her daughters Stephani and Kimberli. Jonathan steps back in complete shock.

"Does Charles know you are here?"

"No Jonathan it is a complete surprise. I heard everything that happened with Nathan. Of course you know that I am a nurse; I just hope I can be of more help here. The hospital has granted me leave to be of service to you and your family. We just need some place to sleep."

"That will be up to Charles he is very protective of his family. Where is Sherri?"

"She is with your father. I will have to fill you in when we can have some private time."

Jonathan gazes off in the distance while he processes Phyllis's statement. "She is with *your father*."

"My life has begun to unravel," he sighs.

Jonathan makes his way back to the big house while Samson makes his way to the farm.

"Samson."

"Yes suh."

"I need you to alert the workers that there will be no work today. We are far ahead of schedule for this harvest. Tell everyone to please enjoy the time off."

Samson mimics the sound of a bird's call.

"You will have to teach that to me some day."

"Yes suh."

The workers begin to make their way in Samson's direction. They circle him then in silence wait for further directions. Samson waits while they continue to collect around him. Samson raises his hand sudden quiet falls among the crowd.

"Today we rest, the earth rest so we can heal from all the pain. Tomorrow a new day for everybody."

The workers make their way back to their homes. The children remain with their teachers for the day. On Jonathan's way to the big house he greets and hugs many of the workers. He feels the strength in numbers. When he enters the house the visitors chatter among themselves. He looks into the living area where he takes notice of his father enjoying a quiet conversation with Sherri. Jonathan motions for his father to come to him. His father looks perplexed.

"Father," he whispers. "It is urgent please come with me."

His father eases himself from his seat. Sherri appears to join him but decides to return to her seat when Mr. Johnson follows Jonathan to the back.

"Son, son what is your hurry? Can you atleast wait for your father?"

Rafael peeks into the hallway and Jonathan turns immediately to embrace his father.

"How was your trip father?"

"It was a rather lengthy one but I survived."

"Please join me in the study. I have some concerns that I want to address with you."

Jonathan takes a look down the hall at Rafael who is stares dangerously in his direction.

"Mother," he nods his head.

"Son," Rafael shakes her head.

They both enter the study and Jonathan closes the door behind them.

"What is it son?"

"It has been brought to my attention that Sherri has been spending time with you at our home."

"Yes, we have discussed living arrangements now that Arthur has married and moved out. Charles has a family also so we have found ourselves in need of each other's company from time to time."

"What is it that you suggest father?"

"Sherri and I have decided to reside together under one roof in a wholesome platonic living arrangement."

"I understand you to say father the two of you are not in love?"

"Son, neither of us have any intentions to marry now nor in the future. We have come to realize that we need companionship."

"That is a relief father. I do not know if I can digest any more calamity in my life today."

"I share the same love you have for your mother. There is no one on earth who could ever replace your mother."

"I agree father; let us join the others."

Mr. Johnson and Jonathan join everyone while they prepare for their afternoon meal.

"Mr. Johnson would you like something to eat?"

"I am famished Rafael whatever you have available will be fitting for these old bones."

"Mother may I," says Jonathan before Rafael interrupts.

"Your bran muffins are in the oven."

"Yes mother."

Jonathan continues to the living area to join the others.

"Where is Nathan?"

"He is being seen by the medical staff that came along on the journey."

"I will join them."

Jonathan enters the infirmary to find Nathan in the company of their childhood associates.

"Good afternoon Cassie?"

"Jonathan it is nice to see you again."

"The same here; brother I see you are in good hands. I hope that your health will be fully restored so that you can return to your *family*."

"Of course brother in case you did not know Cassie and Betty have worked together at the hospital for years."

"Yes we have developed a strong bond since Nathan has been here most of the time."

"That is excellent no worries here I suppose."

"Of course not brother."

"Then I shall tend to the children; school should adjourn here soon."

Never Underestimate The Power of A Secret Place

Jonathan leaves the two to their reunion.

"I have to get the girls before school ends."

Jonathan eases into his daughter's classroom in search for Cindy Lou. She sits diligently in the front of the class. He searches for Angie Lou and can not seem to find her. My mother warned that I was a very sly child and one day I would meet my fate. Jonathan asks one of the students on the back row.

"Have you seen Angie?"

"No suh."

Jonathan increases his pace as he walks to the front of the classroom where Mrs. Salonia finishes up the last few minutes of their assignment. He stands to face the children only to recognize that Angie Lou is not in the classroom. Cindy Lou looks puzzled to see her father in class. He walks toward Cindy Lou and whispers something in her ear. She then whispers in her father's ear. Jonathan abruptly stands straight then walks out of the classroom. He begins a slow trot then his pace begins to quicken. The workers who come for their children watch Jonathan disappear around the big house. A few of the men follow to assist him. Jonathan runs to the rabbit hole and he sees that the barbwire fence has been removed. He scurries down the terrain to see no one insight. Jonathan returns to the top of the hill to find many of the workers concerned about his actions.

"Has anyone seen Angie?"

"No suh," they reply.

Jonathan returns to the school house and approaches Mrs. Salonia.

"How long has Angie Lou been away from class?"

"Jonathan she did not return when the workers were released from work earlier today. Many of the worker's children did not remain in school. She was not alone she was with Lizzy."

"Are your sure?"

"I am sure they were in the field with what appears to be a baby chick or a rabbit."

"Thank you!"

"I hope that you find her."

"It is my prayer."

Jonathan rushes off to the woods to visit each of the worker's home to ask if they had seen Angie Lou or Lizzy but no one has. He is now at Castella's door and she opens before he could knock. She is very tearful when she opens the door. Someone supports her to prevent her from falling.

"Mistah Jonathan, Lizzy and Angie ain't here. We don't know where they is."

Jonathan steps backwards then stops.

"Where is Samson?"

"Right here suh."

"Samson have every man, woman and child meet me at the barn."

"Yes suh."

Samson billows out a call that can be heard for miles. Everyone begins to leave their homes and head to the barn. Jonathan walks with the crowd while he continues to search for Angie Lou. Everyone gathers together even those in the big house along with Nathan and his colleagues. Jonathan is too shaken to speak. Samson takes a chair from the barn and stands on it. He appears like a giant above everyone.

"Miss Angie and Miss Lizzy is missin. Look round here an don't stop til they is back with us. All the chilluns and womens stay here at the barn. Men get your rifle and boys go with your father."

The women and children squat in the grass. Many of the children have begun to cry. Soon the women begin to hum and everyone's spirit takes a nose dive. An hour later there is loud chatter on the northeast embankment that leads to a road below the

Never Underestimate The Power of A Secret Place

farm. There the workers are passing a little child up from one worker to another until she reach the top of the hill. Jonathan is anxious with hopes that it is Angie Lou. When the men place the child on the ground it is a tearful Lizzy.

"Where is Angie," he asks.

She points down in the direction from which she came. The workers begin to climb up the hill themselves. It seems like hundreds of them. Then the last one appears with a shoe in his hand. It is Angie Lou's.

"Where is she?"

Everyone remain silent.

"Lizzy say da sherrif took her."

"The Sheriff?"

"Yes suh, Sheriff Badeaux."

The hum becomes more of a plea for mercy and Jonathan begins to unravel. Samson raises one hand and everything stops; the humming, walking, talking and crying. One voice can be heard giving directions and it is Charles.

"Boys take the women and children home. Do not come out until we tell you. Every man seize your weapon it does not matter what it is. We are going to the Badeaux plantation and taking it by force."

"Suh we don't want no trouble Mistah Badeaux he a powerful man," says Junebug.

"Junebug our God is more powerful than any man on earth. Now let us go in and get our little girl back!"

Charles stops Jonathan in his tracks.

"I am sorry Jonathan you will have to stay here."

Jonathan grabs Charle's rifle from his hand and screams, "Night has fallen we must load up!"

Melba runs to Jonathan pleading him, "Bring our baby girl back."

"I will if it kills me."

Never Underestimate The Power of A Secret Place

Jonathan jumps on the bed of a work truck and the others follow suit. He looks to his left Nathan is beside him and to his right Samson stares straight ahead.

"Where is the driver?"

Charles hops in the truck then starts the engine. When he turns on the head lights there are six horses with soldiers in uniform. Jonathan strains to hold his composure while they head out. The horsemen are the first to reach the plantation. Charles turns off the headlights to conceal their arrival. Before Charles can put the truck in park every man has surrounded the property and made entrance to the house. Jonathan has his rifle pointed at Sherrif Badeaux's oldest son's head.

"If you do not release my baby girl I will kill him."

Timmie looks stunned. Everyone is yelling, kicking things over in search for Angie Lou. The younger Badeaux's and their visitors stay in the house.

"Take me to my daughter."

Timmie stands there and soon begins to urinate on himself.

"We ain't got yo colored gal. How bout you check the plantation down tha road," says Sheriff Badeaux.

He spits tobacco onto his floor then takes a seat. The men check the grounds to find a shallow grave that appears to be filled just recently. Charles grabs the Sheriff by the collar and pulls him outside.

"Who is in that grave?"

"That's a slave cementary."

"We took all your slaves."

The sheriff laughs at himself, "Aw no you cain't take all my slaves they my prop'rty. I have more slaves then you can count."

Charles pushes the Sheriff into the freshly dug grave. The men check every inch of the plantation before they load up for their next plantation intrusion.

Never Underestimate The Power of A Secret Place

It is early morning and the men are scattered along the trail that surrounds the barn. They are worn and weary. The women begin to take their shoes off while the children bring pails of fresh water. The scent of warm biscuits and bacon lingers in the air. No one seems to respond. Melba reaches Jonathan who is in a trance.

"Mother please call Jonathan inside."

"He will not listen dear I have tried. We will just have to pray."

The humming begins again and it feels of sweet assurance that all is going to be alright soon. The men begin to pick up their plates to eat while the women bring burlap bags and blankets to cover them. An hour later a mist begins to fall from the sky then heaviness fills the air that causes the men fall into a deep sleep for hours

"Jonathan wake up son! You were talking in your sleep."

"Mother I found Angie."

"No son it was just a dream."

"Mother please listen to me. She is hidden in a jail house. I am sure she is in a jail house somewhere. Please trust me mother."

"Son I trust you."

Jonathan rises to his feet to find Charles. He is under a tree smoking a cigar away from the others.

"Charles you must take me to every jail house in this parrish."

"I am ready."

He puts the cigar out underneath his boot. Once again the men load up in the truck to make their way to invade every jail house in the nearby parishes. Melba approaches the truck.

"Here take this."

"What is it?"

"It is a picture of Angie. Maybe… her voice trails off."

"This will be of great help."

"Wait let us pack some food for your journey."

The men wait until Rafael and Linda reach the truck with two large burlap bags of food.

"Please bring my baby home."

Jonathan leans down from the bed of the truck.

"Mother God has never failed me yet. He has shown me that she is in a jail cell somewhere. I will not stop until I find her."

FOUR years later…

Jonathan jumps from the truck and enters a Texas county jail. Ross Texas County Jail the sign reads.

"This will be our last stop on this journey. Kennedy ask that young man if you can post this picture in the window of his store? I figure we have covered almost the whole southern state of Texas. All we can do now is go home and pray."

Jonathan enters the jail house. There is one deputy in the entire building. He is leaned back in his chair with his feet propped upon the desk. Jonathan slams his hand on the desk. He leaves a picture turned face up. The deputy raises his hat from his face.

"How can I be of service?"

"I am looking for my daughter."

The deputy leans forward to glance at the picture.

"Well have you seen her?"

"Who's askin?"

Nathan and Kennedy enter the jail. They approach the deputy's desk with rifles in hand. The deputy jumps to his feet.

"You can check if you want."

He walks over to a steel door and unlocks it. A strong odor of mold exits when he opens the door. The hall is long and dark. It appears that no one occupies any of the cells. Jonathan enters and he hears a whimper.

"Is somebody in there?"

"You are welcomed to look."

Never Underestimate The Power of A Secret Place

All three men enter the hall and on either side of them are four cells along each side. Jonathan takes a step little by little while he peers into each of the cells until he has reached the last one on his right. Inside there is a small figure.

"Unlock this cell," Jonathan yells.

The deputy hesitates but pulls another set of keys from his pocket. He hands them to Kennedy. Kennedy joins the others while they try each key to unlock the cell. Finally they are able to pry the rusted cold bar door open. A colored girl unclothed wrapped in a blanket sits on a cot. The smell of urine and feces permeates the cell. Nathan covers his mouth with a handkerchief before he reaches for the girl. She whimpers louder.

"There, there I promise not to hurt you."

"Deputy," Jonathan calls.

Jonathan exits the cell then walks down the hall to the office area. He enters the area where the deputy once sat and he becomes aware that the deputy has fled. Jonathan rummages through the drawers of his desk to find a blood stained dress and one shoe. He stares at the shoe. Nathan appears with the young girl in his arms.

"Jonathan we must take her with us. I believe she has been assaulted."

The young girl appears to be five years old and very malnourished. They begin to exit the building while Jonathan grabs papers from the desk.

"What are you doing?"

"I must gather some kind of evidence so that we can report this inexcusable crime."

Kennedy gets behind the wheel of the company's truck while Nathan places the young girl in his truck between Jonathan and himself.

"We will have to stop somewhere and notify the authorities."

"We have just kidnapped an inmate. There is a possibility we could face criminal charges."

Nathan gets behind the wheel while Jonathan climbs in the passenger seat.

"We have enough food and water to last until we get back to Nathan's Place."

Jonathan and Nathan glance at each other then at the young girl before they pull away.

"Brother, we must stop somewhere to see after the girl," Jonathan instructs.

"What do you propose? What is the chance that we will be accused of her injuries? I am sure if I were to approach two men with a girl child who looks to be assaulted, I too would question their motives. I am positive we can make it to the farm so that we do not draw attention to ourselves."

"There!"

Jonathan points to a weathered shotgun shack alongside the road.

"Possibly someone there will be able to assist us brother," insists Jonathan. "Look there is a lad there. He is African. I am sure they could see to our needs. They will find your company most trustworthy. I will remain in the truck."

"Brother I beg to differ. When they witness her injuries they will most likely assume it may be one of us who committed the deed. We must remain cautious not to draw attention to ourselves," advises Nathan.

"Would you consider Ramona and Jason? They have known us since the conception of Nathan's Place. I am most certain they will not report us. We must become aware of the extent of her injuries. Perhaps they could be life threatening. Let us proceed to Ramona's before we return home. It is only a few miles out of our way you know. We should not consider it a burden, but a small price to pay for humanity."

The brothers continue with their travel to the home of Jason and Ramona. The road is so narrow only to allow room enough for one car. From time to time Nathan surrenders the road to allow the oncoming traffic to pass. In the south it was understood that the Negro driver would pull over to allow the white drivers to continue their travels.

"Brother pull over so that we may check our fuel levels," directs Jonathan.

Nathan pulls onto the grass; Jonathan climbs out of Nathan's truck then walks to Kennedy who has followed them in the company's truck. He reaches the truck and enters through the passenger door.

"Kennedy we will never reach our destination before night fall. I will need you to take over our journey to Ramona's and Jason's home. Nathan and I will follow close behind. This should decrease the number of surrenders we have experienced. I am positive the oncoming traffic will avoid this massive truck at all costs. How is our fuel supply?"

"I checked during our last stop," answers Kennedy. "We have more than enough on hand to make it back to Nathan's Place," assures Kennedy.

"I must tell you Kennedy. I am most grateful that you have joined our family. What brought you to that decision?"

"When we returned to New York I realized the effects of inequality in regards to women and it made sense to return to Nathan's Place. Angelica's experiences in the community due her Spanish heritage have caused us some heartache. When Angelica visited during the celebration of the birth of Nathan's Place, she made the decision not to return to New York."

"Are there any regrets?"

"Absolutely not one regret. Angelica quilts while the other women work at their crafts then afterwards I transport their wares to the New York stores to be sold."

"What about Ivan?"

"Ivan loves it at the farm. Before they came to the United States they lived on a farm. Their short experience in New York has been with the dwellers in the flats. Quite naturally this is like home to them."

"How did you two meet?"

Angelica worked in a tailor shop in the flats. I am frugal when it comes to my attire, so often I was in need of her services."

"That was a wise excuse; it appeared to ignite your desire to patronize Angelica's business."

"Jonathan it was not my intentions."

"No need to explain," Jonathan shrugs. "I trailed Melba for months before I revealed my intentions for her. It is our way as men to validate the quality of the woman we seek for a wife. Consider yourself wise. Now our destination has temporarily changed. We shall make a visit to the home of Ramona's for the girls' sake. You do know the way do you not?"

"I have visited their home quite often when I delivered lumber to the store."

"Excellent we shall be on way."

Jonathan returns to Nathan's truck.

"Do we have enough fuel for our journey?"

"I am certain we do. From this time forward we shall follow Kennedy's lead."

"Are you certain brother?"

"Do you not have faith in me?"

Nathan takes a deep breath before he starts the engine.

"Why do I ever bother?"

"Has your love for me waxed cold?"

Nathan re-enters the road behind the delivery truck then follows close behind Kennedy. The brothers hear a whimper and look down at the girl.

"She must have had a bad dream," suggests Jonathan.

"Something you know all too well."

"It appears that I have irritated you at some point."

"I am not irritated with you in particular. It is the women whom you irritate. When you irritate them then they irritate me. That is when I become irritated with you."

"Have you lost your mind dear brother? We have made a vow never to allow anyone or anything to come between us. They are simply emotional charged lasses, housed in an adult woman's body. You have to take charge or they will drive you mad. How do you think I manage to keep my wits about me?"

"Brother, I must inform you of some changes you can expect when we arrive home."

"I am listening."

"It has been brought to my attention that Melba and Cindy will be return home in a few days."

"You must be mad brother. Melba would not dare challenge my orders."

"You have to remember that they have been away for almost five years. I suppose they have become homesick."

"You have no clue in regards to the mind of a woman. You can never please them. How does she ever expect me to protect her when she does not obey my orders? Fine I will have to do what I do best."

"What is that brother?"

"I shall be forced to drive her away. Nothing gets under her skin more than my obnoxious behavior. She will soon wish she never married me."

"I think you have accomplished that already."

"Whose side are you on?"

"Well of course yours' brother. I would never betray my beloved brother."

"That is an excellent choice. It may become a little uncomfortable but I must do whatever it takes to protect my family."

"Have you considered that mother may not approve of your rash idea?"

"I have the mind to run them all back to New York and that goes for anyone who may get in my way."

"It would be very interesting to witness the results of your efforts."

"Do you think I could pull off this operation alone? Oh no, I am never alone. I expect your support along with the other men. The women shall not deter me from my purpose."

"What is your purpose?"

"Where have you been? My baby girl has been missing for eight years. I want her home where she belongs. Is that too much to ask for? I will not give up until she is home!"

"Brother please calm down. You have awakened the girl."

"Why are you so concerned about her? That should have been my Angie in that cell. Why has God deceived me? He promised me that I would find her. She will never replace my baby girl. I will not allow it."

Jonathan surrenders to tears. He weeps the entire journey to Ramona's home. On the edge of a grassy lot is the home of Jason and Ramona. The structure is painted white with a steel roof. The front entrance is adorned with a wooden porch and a swing that hangs from the foyer's beams. A pebbled road leads alongside of the house to the back where the field displays modules nestled vicariously on their lots. Kennedy pulls alongside the front of the home and Nathan parks a few feet behind the truck. When they arrive Ramona and Jason leave their porch where they once sat. Nathan exits the truck to approach Ramona. Their dialogue is very low and short. Ramona approaches the truck to greet Jonathan.

"Good evenin suh."

"Ramona, I am sorry but I am a bit under the weather today. Please excuse my demeanor."

Never Underestimate The Power of A Secret Place

"I'se sorry you feelin low. I got a pot of beans an rice if you hungry."

She looks with sympathy at Jonathan then at the girl.

"You more'n welcomed to join Mista Kennedy an Mista Nathan."

Jonathan looks past Ramona to see Kennedy enter their home followed by Jason. He exits the truck then races inside. Ramona leans in the driver's side door then she waves the girl to come near. She obeys while Ramona carefully inspects the girl. She lifts her upper body so that Ramona can inspect her back. The blanket falls to the seat to reveal her small naked frame. Ramona wraps the blanket around the girl to resemble a dress. Then she eases the girl from the truck until her feet touch the ground. The girl takes Ramona by the hand while she leads her into the house. Their home is similar to the modules at Nathan's Place. It was built to accommodate two adults with a child. Ramona leads the girl into her bathroom while the men chatter in the kitchen area. She runs a basin of water to wash the girl.

"Whats yo name babe?"

"Lana," she says in a low voice.

"Wheres you from?"

Lana shrugs her shoulders.

"Wheres your mama an papa?"

She shrugs her shoulders again.

"You in mighty bad shape babe. But you gonna be alright. They is good mens you with; they can take care of you betta than we can. You do what they say, ya hear me. Be nice to Mista Jonathan, he the white man. Mista Jonathan he gotta chile look just like you. Bout your size an every thang. He been lookin for her a long time. Maybe God sent you to ease his pain. Don't you be no troubles ya hear. Now let me see ya. I be right back let me finds you some decent coverins."

Ramona joins the men while they eat and chatter among themselves.

"How is she," Nathan asks.

"She gone be fine. She been touched like most women just at a early age that's' all. Fixin to wash her up right now."

The men look down at their plates to hide their expression of embarrassment.

"I ain't got no clothes to fit her. I can put her in a shirt for now. Most likely fit her like a dress. I suppose she be fine til she get to yo place Mista Jonathan."

"What about the blood?"

"Oh she too young for a monthly, that comes from when a men touch a women. She goin through the same thang."

Jonathan drops his spoon then falls back into his chair. Kennedy and Nathan pull their napkins from their shirts then place it on the table.

"You like some more? I can cook up anotha pot of beans. We always got plenty of beans."

"Ramona the meal was very fulfilling. I have a few things for you in the truck then we must continue our travels. Will the girl be ready soon?"

"Yes suh, she be ready in just a little while and Mista Jonathan."

"Yes Ramona?"

"Thank you for everythin. The house, food an gettin Jason some work. We expectin a chile this winter. If everythin go well we gonna have a baby in the house."

"Congratulations! I am very happy to hear of your new addition. I will put a reminder in to the truckers to stop by and check on you on their routes."

"Mista Jonathan you knows just what to do. You more than welcomed to stop by anytime. Y'all might as well be stayin the night."

Never Underestimate The Power of A Secret Place

"It looks like it. We may have to stay put until the morning."

"Ain't no troubles, we got enough room for everybody. The girl can sleep with me an you boys know what to do. I go tend to the girl an we gonna turn in soon."

"Goodnight Ramona."

"Good seein you fella's make sho you get some rest."

Ramona gives Jason a light kiss on his forehead before she leaves the room. Nathan and Kennedy rise from the table. They put away their plates in the sink before they walk outside into the midday heat.

"We have a few items for Ramona from the women at the farm. She will be surprised to find the baby items they have packed for her. How is the icebox holding up?"

"Just fine Mista Jon it keeps everythin fresh longa than we expectin. My chicken coop is ready for some chickens. I made sho the foxes cain't get to 'em."

"The chickens will be on their way with the next load which will be in a few days. We have two hens and one rooster to get you started. How is the general store coming along?"

"It ain't gonna be long before we ready for business. Cain't wait for Mista Kennedy to take over. Most of our troubles is gone since they hear we gonna get a sheriff. I just checked on the missus an she doin mighty fine and I suspect she won't have much troubles since Mistah Kennedy be the sheriff."

"That is good to hear. Kennedy will need to train you to drive the truck to make pickups for the store. Pretty soon we will have stores all over the south."

"Yes suh an plenty of work for whoeva wants to work."

"That is our hope. First we will need to unpack Ramona's things before we drive down to the store. There is a large load for the store so we will need some daylight to get it unloaded; let us get started right now."

Nathan leaves the truck to bring Ramona a small bag of items.

"What do you have?"

"I found some old clothes of Angie's in a bag in the truck."

"I intended to give them to a family near the store whom has a small girl," answers Jonathan. "She looks to be about Angie's size."

"I think there may be something here that the girl can wear."

"What about the family I promised the clothes too?"

"We can give the girl something to wear until we get home. The rest we will give to the family."

"I would rather that all the clothes went to the family. We will just have to find something for the girl to wear when we get back."

"What will she wear until then?"

"Whatever Ramona has prepared for her will do."

Jonathan leaves the house to help unload the baby bed that was once Angie Lou's. For a moment he becomes overwhelmed at the sight of the bed.

"Mista Jon, take a look at the chicken coop before we go down to the store," encourages Jason.

Jonathan nods his head while he walks alongside of the house. Behind the house is a large spread of land. The chicken coop rests beside the rear of the house. A barbwire fence circles a small parameter of land where the chickens will be expected to wander. Not far away there is a weeping willow with chairs and a table nestled underneath it. A wash basin sits underneath the table. Beyond the weeping willow is a vegetable garden that spreads north and south. A well pump is nearby where a bucket hangs from the spigot. Scattered modules have been planted throughout the acreage to bring a sense of community to the area. Jonathan peers south of Ramona's house where he is able to see Mr. Kyle. His wife sits next to him underneath an oak tree. Jonathan smiles to himself while he walks back to the truck.

"Are we ready to get down the road to deliver the shelves for the store? We must get on our way while it is daylight," replies

Jonathan. "Remind me to visit Mr. Kyle before we leave in the morning."

The men load up in the truck. The space is small but they have managed before. After a half mile they arrive at the store. The store is bare inside in need of shelves and counters.

"Gather the men we have to get started right away."

Jason lets out a sharp scream that startles the brothers. Kennedy laughs a hearty laugh at their surprise.

"Some things never change, Kennedy teases. Without Jason I could never get everyone together for the store meetings."

Before long men, women and children gather around the truck. Mr. Kyle approaches with a cane to assist him.

"How are you brother Kyle?"

"I neva believe my life to be this happy. I don't want for nothin Mista Jonathan. I cain't let you leave before I tell you how much I love you."

"Mr. Kyle allow me to explain something. Everyone please listen up. None of this is at my hands alone. It is a collective effort of people like you, Mr. Kennedy, Mr. Charles, Mr. Freeman and the many others that I have not mentioned. This is the result of what can happen when people come together who share a commonality despite their differences. Injustice continues to thrive please be not mistaken; but you must never allow fear to overtake you again. Fear not challenged births hatred. If you should ever experience a force greater than yourself that threatens your freedom; pray for God's guidance. If you should ever need shelter come home. Nathan's Place will always be your home."

Nathan pulls Jonathan close to him then holds him tight. Everyone begin to gather around the men. Someone begins to hum a spiritual that lightens the mood in the crowd. The soft gentle hum comes to an end after everyone embraces each other.

"We must unload the truck before nightfall," someone yells from the crowd.

Never Underestimate The Power of A Secret Place

Soon the crowd disperses to begin their duties. Within a few hours the shelves are stationed in the store along the walls. Barrels are rolled out to the center of the floor along with produce tables to create a section for their fresh produce.

"The counter will be delivered in a couple of days to complete the renovation of the store. Thank you for your patience. Now we must decide on a name for the store. What shall it be," Jonathan asks.

"Our store, Mista Jon."

"Are there any more suggestions?"

The crowd becomes quiet.

"Mista Jonathan it only seem right we name it Nathan's Store. That way we ain't gonna forget where we comes from. Every thang come from Nathan's Place anyway. My crate say Nathan's Place. I sit on it every mornin to drink my coffee. Sometimes I carries the clothes from the line in that crate. It reminds me of home; so I say Nathan's Store fits mighty fine," defends Jason.

"Are there any nay sayers?"

Everyone remains quiet.

"Nathan's Store it is!"

Everyone begin to cheer.

"We will have to make a sign for the store," says Kennedy.

"I will get Samson on it right away. He has become an excellent blacksmith," says Jonathan. "How do you feel about it brother?"

"How do I feel about what?"

"How do you feel about the name of the store?"

"It is well with me. My hopes were they would name it Jonathan's Store since this is your inspiration."

"Nonsense, everything Nathan embraces me too. Let us get out of here. We have to get back on the road."

Never Underestimate The Power of A Secret Place

The men return to Jason's home to find the living area arranged to accommodate them for the night. Once nestled onto their pallets they begin to discuss the mystery of women.

"Do you ever wonder why God created woman," asks Jonathan.

"I can think of a mighty good reason," replies Jason.

A smile forms across the faces of the men.

"We need women to procreate that is for certain," replies Kennedy. I am sure it would be terribly lonesome with just the men."

"We must also consider that they are excellent cooks and caregivers," Nathan adds.

"It just does not balance with the strife we must endure to have them in our lives. When I return home I shall set one thing straight. I am the man of the house and they will obey my commands or…"

Jonathan's voice trails off.

"Or what," the other men ask.

"Mista Jon, I ain't too smart but ain't no sense in makin them angry when you gotta live with 'em."

"Oh, what can they possibly do? I enjoy the dog house. It has become my get away now that I think of it. The silent treatment gives me the peace I need. Now that I think about it there is not much more they can do to me," replies Jonathan.

"Mista Jon, I'se knows the most damage a man can do is tell his wife she puttin on too much."

"Why is that Jason?"

"Mista Wayne, he order his wife materials for her weddin dress. When the materials come she ain't ordered enough. She ask Mista Wayne for more money. He says she ain't got enough materials cause she puttin on too much."

"I do not understand. What problem did it cause?"

"Mista Jon, the next mornin Mista Wayne come runnin down the street with grits all over him. His face ain't look the same no mo."

"Kennedy was she jailed?"

"In some fashion yes."

"Whatever does that mean?"

"She has been hired as my deputy. The incident actually occurred long before I was appointed the Sheriff. They are happily married now. I must agree she is a force to be reckoned with."

"Could she possibly be related to Melba?"

"Brother you should consider yourself fortunate. You have tried Melba on many occasions however she has never reacted in that manner."

"There has been times when I do believe she has tried to kill me," Jonathan sighs.

"How long you married Mista Jon?"

"A mere thirteen years I suppose."

"Mista Jon ain't no woman gonna try that long. If she gonna kill you, you be dead a long time ago. But I'se tells you one thang. Sometimes them womens gits tired like they cain't take no more. You liable ta wake up ta find your wife standin over you with a knife."

"Or possibly a gun," Nathan interjects

"Womens don't got no guns Mista Nathan."

"His wife does," Nathan confirms. "She is well trained to handle a rifle."

Jonathan lies on his pallet then he remembers that it was he who taught Melba how to handle a rifle. He raises himself onto his elbows.

"Has something startled you brother?"

"I was just reminded that I taught Melba how to handle a rifle."

"Melba is a very lovely woman. I would never consider her to be a murderer," Kennedy adds. "She has been through a lot lately, however, never have I seen her react irrational."

"Nevertheless she is a woman would you not agree? Very capable to lose control and quite possibly attempt murder," Nathan whispers to Kennedy.

"Melba would not dare…" Jonathan's voice trails off.

"Would not dare what brother? Did you not send her away to your father's? I can imagine how she must feel being torn from her family for such a long period of time. I am grateful it is not I whom has to face her when we return."

"When where you made aware of her return?"

"Mother informed me a few days before our departure. She mentioned that Melba did not feel any need to remain in your father's house. Father begged her to stay but she insisted that she return to her family. It appeared that she made mention of her parent's home but father informed mother that he placed Melba and Cindy on a train to Louisiana. Father also mentioned that Melba was quite unsettled when she left."

"How many days is the journey by train," asks Jonathan.

"It could take at least a few days maybe more. I pray that she does not experience a train heist during her travels. It will only make matters worse," adds Nathan.

"We should arrive at the farm after nightfall if we depart early sunrise. It is possible that her train will arrive some time later. She will be too famished to entangle herself in foolishness," Jonathan convinces himself.

"Whatever shall be shall be," sings Nathan. "We must get our rest. We have a long drive before us. Goodnight brothers."

"Goodnight" the others echo. Jonathan continues to rest upon his elbows. He looks confused by the dialogue that just transpired.

"Mista Jon, I knows Miss Melba cain't wait to see ya. She missin you somethin awful. It be like that when you lonely. Yes suh just wait til the Missus get home."

Nathan glances over to Jonathan with a smirk on his face.

"I agree brother."

"What is it that you agree to?"

"Melba *cain't* wait to see ya!"

"This is not the time brother. Goodnight."

It is early morning sunrise. The men are seated at the kitchen table with warm plates of grits, eggs and bacon placed before them. Fresh coffee brews on the stove. Lana walks into the kitchen but the men do not acknowledge her presence.

"Ain't ya lookin fine in your new dress Lana? Fellas don't she look like a new chile," asks Ramona.

The men nod while they continue to eat their breakfast. Ramona hands a warm plate of food to Lana.

"Go in the front room an eat. This maybe all you gonna get til you get to wheres you goin. Now eat everythang, you hear me?"

"Yes ma'am," Lana answers.

Lana walks away to the front room. She sits on the floor to eat her breakfast. She stuffs everything into her mouth before she takes the plate back to Ramona.

"Girl what you done done with that food I gave ya? I knows you ain't ate everythin."

Ramona walks into the front room to look for any evidence of the food she gave Lana but she does not see a trace anywhere.

"Whens the last time you ate chile? Ima fix you somethin for the road. When you get to Nathan's Place you neva gonna go hungry again. You hear me? You say thank you for everythang you get. Neva be proud. You hear me girl?"

"Yes ma'am."

The men enter the front room of the house.

"We must get on the road. Ramona we are most grateful for the meal," Jonathan adds.

"Thank you, Mista Jonathan. You sho is a good man. The same to you Mista Kennedy an Mista Nathan. God gonna rememba your names."

"That is also our prayers. Please take care of yourself. Kennedy will return to you as the Sheriff in the coming week. I am certain that he will protect the people we place in his care," Jonathan answers.

"Jason we must be on our way. Take care dear brother," says Nathan. "Come here little one. Are you ready to meet your new family?"

Lana takes Nathan by the hand while he escorts her to the truck. She climbs into the truck to take her seat in the middle. Nathan climbs in next to her behind the wheel of the truck. Jonathan circles the truck then disappears for quite some time. Nathan waits patiently for him to arrive. Jonathan reappears while he whistles to himself.

"By any chance are you apprehensive in regards to our return to the farm? You appeared quite restless last night I must say. I have called home to inform them of our intentions. To my surprise Melba has arrived safe to the farm. That should ease your worries brother."

"Did you happen to speak with her?"

"Matter of fact I did."

"Do tell. What was her disposition? Did she inquire of my wellbeing?"

"To put it simply she would rather you never returned."

"Is that so? Who does she think she is? She will not undermine my authority. I have the mind to…"

Nathan interrupts.

"Brother I must interject that the women are also in agreement with Melba's decision to return. You will beyond doubt have a fight on your hands when we return. I suggest you direct their interest to the girl. She will simmer their anger for the time being. That is until you find a way to attract their unwanted attention. You must remember the uproar you caused before our departure. I would not be surprised if they lay in wait to harm you."

"Harm me? That is ridiculous. God created man to rule the home and that is what I shall do. We must stand our ground."

"Brother I have not lost footage in the least. Could it be possible that you have overstepped your boundaries?"

"Nonsense, it is obvious you have become one of them. I am aware that you have begun to enjoy the daily morning gossip with the ladies. Unlike myself, I have always directed my attention to the masculine duties required to operate the farm. I can only imagine what would become of the farm if I did not take charge."

"I often wonder myself brother. Shall we be on our way?"

"We shall however we may consider it reasonable to remain here until the counters have been delivered. We can ensure that we complete renovations of the store before our departure."

"How much longer can you live without the love of your life? My heart aches daily for Betty. I feel that I will not embrace her soon enough. Does not your heart long for Melba?"

"It most definitely does not. I have the rest of my life to long for that woman. I tell you her plans are to kill me if Angie does not return soon. I will find it more and more difficult to face her every waking morning. Who knows when *soon* shall be?"

"Was that your motive to send her away?"

"I sent Melba away to fathers' because I could not imagine my life without her. My desire was to shelter her from the world's injustices. Soon I understood it to be unsound; nevertheless, my intentions were sincere however unconventional they may seem."

Nathan starts the engine then waves Kennedy on. They take possession of the road to begin their journey. Lana leans on Nathan for support. She no longer appears to be frightened.

"Is it just I or do you smell bacon?"

"I have for some time. It is possible the girl has some in her possession."

"Not for long bacon is my favorite morning treat. Tell me little one, what do you have in your sack?"

Lana looks up to Jonathan with a frown.

"Maybe I was not clear. You have what I want. If you share your bacon with me there will be greater days ahead for you."

Lana casts a long stare at Johnathan.

"Perhaps you did not hear me. I can make your life miserable if you do not share your bacon with me."

Jonathan attempts to tickle Lana instead she whimpers which causes Jonathan to draw back.

"I had no idea you have taken to bacon with such gravity. I shall call you Babymouse."

"It ain't my name."

"Nevertheless that is the name in which I shall refer to you, Babymouse."

They continue the drive in silence.

"How much longer?"

"A few more hours if we continue without another bladder break. Now that we are in familiar territory we should arrive late evening. Everyone may have turned in for the night."

"You do say," asks Jonathan. "It sounds like the opportune time to make our appearance."

"Do you suggest that we disturb the others while they rest," asks Nathan.

"Absolutely not, why would we want to bring attention to ourselves? My intentions were to address our overnight accommodations to *avoid* the others. We could possibly seek shelter in one of the available modules."

"If you wish brother but what shall we do with the child?"

"I have forgotten that we have a guest with us. She will keep well in the truck for the night."

"Do you suggest that we secure the child in the truck overnight?"

"Why not? Angie camped in the truck many nights without our knowledge."

"You cannot be serious. Angie did not intentionally camp out in the truck. You left her there during one of your nights of star gazing. You were just afraid to acknowledge that you absentmindedly left the poor child alone in the truck."

"Really brother, is that what you believe? I would never be that careless with any child. I have you know that on many occasions Angie hid in the truck before I left to run errands for the farm. I remember once Angie hid until I reached the Mississippi line. She had awakened troubled to find herself between Samson and I. Samson scolded her so, she never attempted again. She suffered so when I left to deliver goods for the farm. It breaks my heart to think of it."

"Brother that is a sacrifice we all have endured. It is for the best of the greater good that we do."

"I suppose so. I desire with all my power that Angie will return to me soon."

"Until then we have the girl," replies Nathan. "We must make the best of it for us all."

"She will never replace my baby girl."

"I do not expect that she will. But during the time that she is here we must treat her like family. You must remember that she suffers also. Possibly more than we may ever imagine."

"Sometimes I believe God chastises me."

"Why do you question God's love for you?"

"I am sure it was God who revealed to me that Angie was hidden in a jailhouse somewhere. My dream transpired in the exact manner in which the event unfolded the other day."

Never Underestimate The Power of A Secret Place

"Brother may I interject a very important detail that has been overlooked?"

"If you wish."

"What I have extracted from the events that have unfolded is that possibly God chose you to seek out the young girl. Her father for whatever reason did not possess the passion to seek justice for his daughter. Therefore God did not punish you; he just simply used you for his purpose."

"What is his purpose for my Angie?"

"I do not have an answer. I suppose you should prepare yourself for a test of faith."

"What is that?"

"You must continue to pray for her safe return. I am convinced that it was your faith that brought you to her. Perhaps your steadfast faith will bring you to Angie. Amen?"

"Amen."

"I am very thankful to whoever invented the headlights. We should come upon the farm in less than an hour. Shall we plan our invasion?"

"Now there is the brother I once knew. The girl will be our main attraction. I imagine the women will become all warm and fuzzy inside at the sight of her. We must emphasize that it was I that fought for her release although you just simply carried her out of the cell. We must also remind them that we put our lives on the line. Not to mention our freedom. How would the women survive without us?"

"Brother you must never mention that the women would not survive without us," advises Nathan. "They may decide to turn you over to the authorities."

"You must be mad. Melba would never do such a thing."

"Brother this is not the time to test the women's wrath. Especially Melba's she just may follow through."

"What do you suggest," asks Jonathan.

Never Underestimate The Power of A Secret Place

"I will carry the girl in my arms to make it appear to them that she is helpless. They will immediately direct their attention towards her. We will both pretend to feel overwhelmed by her condition then depart to our rooms. It would behoove you to wash up then resign to bed before Melba can take hold of her senses. You will appear to be a hero for a short time. That is until you resort to your foolish antics. Perhaps we should leave the women to care for the child while we search for the girl's home. In doing so, the women will grow fonder of our absence."

"The women will not allow us such freedom. They continue to believe that we are out here wreaking havoc upon this innocent world. How could we possibly get their approval to travel more often?"

"It is very simple brother. We must convince them that we are in search of the girl's family."

"Ahh, you are so brilliant! They will never object."

"So it is planned. No more of your morning antics. Most important we will insist that our travels are to reunite the child with her family. Did I miss anything? We will soon approach the entrance to Nathan's Place in a moment speak now or forever hold your peace," announces Nathan.

"It is a plan. However I will need your protection if you should ever see Melba near a rifle in my presence any time soon. I will never know when she has had enough."

"I am my brother's keeper," smirks Nathan.

After the workers unlock the gates to allow them onto the farm they enter the trail careful to avoid the chickens that wander loose. A few of the chickens flap their wings wildly only to leap a few feet from where they took flight. Sista stands at the edge of the woods in search of Jonathan.

"Mista Jonathan suh."

Nathan slows to a stop.

"It is Sista. She appears to be anxious to say something."

"Mistah Jonathan suh, it is good to see ya. I was wonderin if you saw Ramona on your travels?"

"Yes Sista I did."

"How much time before she has the baby?"

"I have no idea Sista. It was mentioned that she will deliver soon."

"Yes suh. It's gonna be our first babe in the family."

"Is that so? Do you not plan to have any children?"

"No suh. My body cain't hold no chile. No matter how much I tries."

"I am sorry to hear that Sista. I will tell Ramona you send your love."

"Suh, I was hopin I can visit til she has the baby?"

"Of course you can. You are free to come and go as you please. I will make the preparations for the trip. How long do you think you might stay?"

"I was hopin I can stay for eva. I miss her mighty bad."

"Have you discussed this with Ben?"

"He the reason I cain't have no chilluns. He beat every one of them outa me. He a jealous man."

"Does he is still hit you?"

"No suh, he too scared. I figa if I leave here there just might be somebody out there who can love me right."

"Sista there is a home near Ramona's that will suit you fine. I will make contact with Grant to have the house fitted with running water and lights. Are you certain that you want to leave Ben?"

"Yes suh, I wanna new life before mines is ova. That way I won't die with no regrets."

"Goodnight Sista. I will keep in touch with the updates of your move."

"Thank you suh. Goodnight."

"We must be sure that Sista has not married Ben. If so her move may be more complicated than she imagines," Jonathan insists.

"For now we must direct our attention to our current situation. All the women are outside on the front terrace," Nathan reveals. "Who knows their frame of mind at this point?"

"I am a good judge of mother's mood. She appears distraught for some reason. Or it could possibly be indigestion. She has come to that age now. We should park in plain sight of the workers. The women seem to maintain their sense of dignity if they are aware that someone is present beyond you and me. Take the girl in with you. I will follow close behind to avoid any confrontation with Melba."

"I am sure you will."

Nathan carries Lana's limp body into the house while everyone follows. Nathan takes her into the room of the twins then begins to lay her in Angie Lou's bed.

"No not there lay her over there," directs Jonathan.

"What does it matter?"

"It is Angie's new bed where shall she sleep when she returns?"

"Where will Cindy sleep tonight Jon," asks Melba.

"Melba, wife it is such a pleasure to see you. I was so engrossed with the condition of the child that I simply could not bring myself to focus elsewhere. Welcome home love."

"Do you really mean that Jon?"

Nathan nods to guide his answer.

"I have missed you terribly. But I struggle with the thought of losing you if you should return. You do understand? What man would not protect the jewel of his eye?"

"Jon, I thought you would be angry that I returned. Nathan insisted that you wanted Cindy and me to remain with your father."

"Nathan *my* brother said that?"

"Yes, he said that you fretted all night at the thought of us away from your fathers'. I am so relieved that you understand. That is why I have decided to return home. I will support you however I can with the search for Angie."

"Sweetheart let me come close. I have longed to hold you in my arms. My, I am able to reach my arms around you. It has been a long time since I have been able to accomplish that. I am most certain you are not pregnant. Are you dear?"

"No Jon. I have not seen you long enough to get pregnant. The last time..."

Jonathan interrupts.

"Melba! That is privileged information. On that note let us retreat to *our* bedroom."

"Do not think for one minute you will get in the bed with me until you have bathed mister."

"Do not take that tone with me woman!"

"Son, Son!"

"Yes mother."

"Come," Rafael directs him to the living area. "Follow me. I am so happy to see you son. I need you to talk with me for a moment."

Rafael takes his hand into her hands then looks him in the eyes.

"How are you mother?"

"I am happy to see that you have returned unharmed. You must allow your family to remain in their home. They are safe here son. I promise you they will be safe," Rafael reassures him while she presses his hands within hers.

"Now, you must not be angry with Melba. It was I who suggested that she return. I have begun to get lonesome without my dearest daughter and granddaughter. It tears at my heart every summer when we have to send them away. I understand your rationale. I do. But you have wasted years away from your family that you will never get back. I did it for you son. I did it for the girls."

"Mother, I am the man of this house."

"I know son and sometimes even you need direction. You cannot possibly have all the answers son. You must have faith that God will get you through this."

"Get me through what? Nothing is through mother. My baby girl shall return to me. I will not give up until I find her."

"Son have you ever considered that maybe God has answered your prayers?"

"How so mother? She is not here!"

"No son but there is a little girl who needs a family. I believe that God intended for you to save her. Maybe…"

Jonathan pulls away from Rafael. He continues to step backwards until he reaches the door.

"She will never replace my babygirl," he whispers.

Jonathan turns to leave the house and the cool night air greets him. He walks towards a quarter that has been refurbished for visitors. He enters and locks the door behind him; he kneels beside the bed then lies face down on the floor. He feels around underneath the bed in search of his bottle of whiskey. He grasps it and pulls it from underneath the bed; before he stands to his feet he places the bottle on the bed. When he raises himself to sit on the bed there is a knock at the door. It is Melba on the other side of the door. He assumes it is her but refuses to answer.

"Jon, honey I am sorry. I just could not take it any longer. It was either come home or dissolve our marriage. You have become a stranger to Cindy and I and I did not want that to happen. Cindy is advanced in her studies. Your father wishes to send her to college next year to pursue medical school. Cindy asked to spend some time with you before she commits. I will return home to support her during her studies. Please forgive me."

Jonathan listens for a moment then eases down on the bed. The bottle of whiskey rolls to his side. He contemplates to himself.

"She will never replace my daughter. How could you do this to me? You have betrayed me. I thought you were God Almighty. You know very well where she is. This is not right. It is not right God. I ask that you make it right," he whines.

Jonathan opens the bottle then pours the warm liquor into his mouth. It trickles down his cheeks onto his shirt. He leans against the wall next to the bed to prop himself up.

Melba returns to the house unsettled with what has transpired. Rafael opens the door before she can reach the porch.

"Melba, I assure you he will be fine. I will have Nathan see after him before we turn in."

"Mother he will not acknowledge Cindy. He is not the only person affected by Angie's abduction. We cannot allow this to consume our very existence. I love my daughter too. What should I do?"

"Give him time; he is just angry. I agree he is being selfish but we all grieve in different ways. We cannot deny him the opportunity regardless of how he chooses to grieve. I will see after him before I turn in. Come in we must see after the child."

They enter the house with the expectation of confusion. Instead it is dim and calm. Everyone has turned in except for Cindy Lou.

"Mother I will sleep in Todd's room if it is alright with you?"

"How does he feel about it?"

"I sleep there all the time when I am afraid. He keeps me company and I do not know the girl very well. Maybe I should give her some time alone."

"That is thoughtful of you dear. Go on see if Todd is well with your company."

"Melba."

"Yes mother."

"I will bring the girl in with me. She may become startled to find herself in an unfamiliar place."

"That will be good for her. Goodnight mother."

"Wait one minute; I need your assistance with a minor matter."

Rafael enters her bedroom. "Henry, wake up."

"Was I snoring?"

"Not this time but you cannot stay here tonight. Jonathan has made it home."

"Rafy, when are you going to tell him?"

"Henry he thinks you are deceased."

"Why did you tell him that?"

"I did not know where you where for years. You never called nor did you send a word of your whereabouts."

"How could I? I was enlisted without my consent. You could have at least given me a modest farewell; one that could be restored."

"I assumed you had left forever. The circumstance suited you well."

"You were angry. I understand but what are we to do now?"

"I will have to explain to Jonathan the turn of events. He will not be receptive to your plans to return to New York. I promised him that I would stay."

"How long must you stay? He is an adult man with a family. What could he possibly need from you? He has had your attention since he was an infant. When will you realize that you do not owe him anything?"

"Henry I never said that I owed him anything. He is the son every mother could ever dream of. He called every day to see about me before he could read. When he went to summer camp he wrote me every week. When he was old enough he accompanied me on my weekly errands. I received a gift for every birthday and mother's day until this day and he hand delivers them to me himself. When you left me it was Jonathan that went in search for you. He would tell me, mother I will take care of you until he returns. He prayed every night that you would come home and unlike yourself he has never disappointed me. Henry when he graduated with his degree in Medicine he announced to everyone at the ceremony that I saved his life and one day he hopes to become a doctor and save mine. People have come to me to take what they need or what they want from me but this child right here has never, ever asked me for anything. All he asks is that I never leave him and I promised him that I never will. I am going to keep my promise Mr. Henry. If you want to stay it is well with me. If not it is also well with me. What shall it be?"

"I will return to the visitor's quarter until you have spoken to him. Should I keep my distance until then?"

"Not necessarily. If you should happen upon each other we will have to address it then."

Henry gathers his things before he gets dressed. Rafael monitors the hall while Melba monitors the front door.

"Where are you going to take him?"

"He will reside in one of the visitor's modules for now."

"You do realize that Jonathan has taken residence in one himself. It would be more practical if he could room at Charles. He has more than enough room," advises Melba.

"Charles is on the road with a delivery. We can make arrangements with one of the men until then."

"Who do you suggest?"

"The twins, they will enjoy the company. A leveled head will be something they both need."

I will have Nathan to escort him to their home."

Melba climbs the stairs in route to Nathan and Betty's room. The door is partially open. She knocks and the door opens an inch further. Betty sits in a chair reading a book.

"Where is Nate?"

"He is freshening up."

"Mother needs his assistance before he turns in," she smiles.

"I will let him know," Betty winks back at Melba.

Melba crosses the hallway to check on Todd and Cindy Lou. She knocks before she opens the door and peeks in. Cindy Lou is fast asleep in Todd's bed while he sleeps on a pallet on the floor.

"He is such a gentleman," Melba whispers.

"Thank you, I take full responsibility," quips Nathan after he approaches Melba.

"Nathan, mother needs you to assist her for just a moment."

"Why do I feel that it is more than just a mere moment?"

Nathan turns then heads down stairs where he finds Rafael and Henry engaged in a quiet conversation.

"Before you do will you please bring the girl to my room for the night?"

"Yes mother."

Nathan returns to the hall with Lana in his arms and takes her into Rafael's room.

"Is there anything else?"

"I need you to escort Henry to the twins dwelling then see about your brother. He has locked himself in one of the visitor's modules."

"Mother, Henry will not get any rest if I take him to the twin's residence. They are young foolish boys. I will take Henry to the visitor's module behind the house where we keep watch some nights. He can be very helpful stationed there."

"Then so it shall be. Also I have not mentioned Henry's arrival to Jonathan. I do not know how he will react. Could you…"

Nathan interrupts.

"Mother you know very well that Jonathan's instability is critical at this point. We will only add fuel to the fire if he finds out that Henry has returned in your life. We must take every measure to keep them apart. I suggest that Henry should dwell in one of the quarters on Charles's property until brother has gained his senses. You will have to suffer the distance for the time being. I will make contact with Phyllis to make the arrangements in the morning. For now I must get some rest."

"Do what you will. Please by all means get your *rest*!"

"Mother if anyone should know it would be you."

"What should I know son?"

"Oh, do not take that tone with me mother. We all need our rest," smiles Nathan. "Come with me Henry and I will show you to your hiding place."

Nathan grabs the key to the visitor's module from the hall cabinet. Both men slip out the back door into the cool night air. It is a beautiful night among the stars.

"Henry this may be an inconvenience for you this moment but in the end it will be all worth it."

"I have heard that Jonathan is not himself. If you ask me Rafael has coddled him far too long. It is time that he steps up to the plate and become a man."

"Henry, I would advise you to watch your step with Jonathan. He is at a very difficult time in his life where he needs his mother's support. I understand your love for Rafael but I must warn you if you force mother to choose you may not like the results. You are more than welcomed to join the family."

"Rafy and I have made arrangements to spend the rest of our lives together. I have a small place of my own up North. The deed is clean and free. We will never have to worry about a place of our own. My pension is enough for us to get by. I am sure Rafy has some money saved. I think we can make it without anyone making decisions for us."

Both men reach the quarter then stand in silence. Nathan unlocks the door then he turns to leave.

Never Underestimate The Power of A Secret Place

"Henry I hope that you will take the opportunity to become a part of our family. The deed to this property and all the other properties purchased after the conception of Nathan's place are clean and free. We have everything you are looking for; so I encourage you to examine your intentions with care. Our family is here to stay and will remain intact until the end of time. Good night sir."

Nathan walks with measured steps to the big house. Before he enters he looks back at the module to see Henry standing on the porch in the moonlit night. Nathan eases in through the back door with intentions to talk to Rafael. When he enters the main hall he hears voices that trail from the kitchen. He peeks in to find Rafael and the girl. Rafael prepares a meal for the girl while she sits in silence. She turns to face Nathan who glances for a moment at the girl.

"Brother prayed that it was Angie but it was not. It may take him sometime to gather himself. Can you please give him some time before you inform him of Henry's intentions?"

"Henry is aware of Jonathan's state of mind. We both agreed that we will not discuss any future plans until Jonathan is more stable."

"He said..."

Rafael interrupts.

"I do not care what Henry says. I will not consider any fashion of a future with that man until then. If he can not accept my desicion then he must leave. He will NOT add to our misery,"

"Mother you do not have to sacrifice your happiness for ours. Jonathan would want you to live a fulfilled life. Please do not allow us to interfere."

"Son if Henry really loves me, he will sacrifice for me just as I have for him. I waited for him to return for years. Never did I seek another mate for my own selfish needs. Now it is his time to wait. I think I am worth it don't you son?"

"Of course mother you are indeed worth it."

Nathan makes his way to his bedroom where Betty is asleep. Nestled next to her is Todd; his thin frame spread eagle next to his wife. Nathan thinks to himself, *"there is no way my little boy will enlist in the military. He still sleeps with his mother!"* Nathan sits at the foot of the bed to take his shoes off. He then lies across the foot of the bed and falls into a deep sleep.

Morning has made its appearance. Curious Lana makes her way in the direction of the voices. When she enters the kitchen a silence falls amongst them.

Melba greets Lana, "Well hello there. Would you like someting to eat?"

Lana stands in silence for a moment then nods to affirm yes.

"Lana come have a seat," Rafael directs. "I will prepare you a plate in just a moment. Let me check on the biscuits. You do like biscuits do you not?"

"Mother what a ridiculous question; every child loves biscuits especially with jam, Nathan remarks."

"Well you know the rule here no jam for the children it ruins their appetite. You boys never knew jam existed until you both were well in your teens."

"If you say so mother," chides Nathan.

"What do you mean if I say so? That is what I am sure of."

"Yes mother whatever you say."

"Do not mock me son. It is disrespectful to mock your elders."

"Yes mother please forgive me."

"Lana can you do something for me," asks Melba.

"Yes ma'am."

"Come to the window."

Lana stands from her chair and walks toward the window that faces south of the farm.

"Do you see that pitiful man out there?"

"Yes ma'am."

"He is my husband."

Lana looks at Melba in shock.

"I know what you must think but he is a nice man with a big heart. Right now he needs a cup of coffee can you take it to him please?"

"Yes ma'am."

"You don't have to be afraid he has a little girl that looks just like you and before..."

Melba pauses.

"Before."

Nathan chimes in.

"Before you take his coffee to him you must be sure that he knows who is in charge. He is a very cunning character and will ask you to do things against your will. Make sure you look him straight in the eye and tell him no! Another thing do not allow him to call you by any other name than Lana. Now do you have any questions?"

"No suh."

"Are you afraid?"

"Yes suh."

"No need. He is a tall, pale, teddy bear. He will give you anything you want if you pout. Let me see your pouty face."

Lana pokes her bottom lip out and lowers her head.

"I see you are a natural. You will do fine. When you take him the coffee make sure that you give him your pouty face. He loves bacon. Make sure you stop by the oven and take a few slices to him with his coffee every morning and you will become his best friend. Now are you ready?"

"Yes suh."

"Here take this cup of coffee, becareful it is very hot and I shall place the bacon in your pocket. Now do not forget your pouty face. Excellent now go make us proud."

"When you get back I will comb your hair and dress you up real pretty," says Linda.

"The poor child hasn't eaten breakfast. Give her time to settle in before we send her out to that deranged wolf," reminds Rafael.

"Jonathan is not exactly a wolf. He may be somewhat deranged but I would not necessarily consider him a wolf," says Melba.

"I agree he does appear to be a little deranged at times. My hope is that Lana will fill the void that he carries for Angie. She bears so much resemblance and her presence can make all the difference," Nathan implies.

They all approach the window to observe the transaction between the two. Lana approaches Jonathan careful not to spill the coffee. She reaches him without making her appearance known.

"How long do you intend to stand there?"

The cup of coffee falls from Lana's hands before she is aware of it. With one bounce it nestles in the grass. Tiny droplets adorn her legs but Lana does not appear to feel the heat of the coffee. She looks down at the emptied cup until Jonathan reaches for her then she jumps back. He returns to face the pond without a word. Lana continues to stand there until Rafael approaches and pulls her to her side.

"Son I want you to apologize to Lana."

"I would mother if it was warranted, therefore, I feel no reason to apologize."

"Are you certain that is the reply I hoped for?"

"I am sure it is not but to maintain my sense of dignity I must remain steadfast in my decision."

"Lana go inside your breakfast is ready."

"Mother you will not force that child on me. I saved her from her tormentors what more do you want from me?"

"Can you atleast give the child a chance?"

"A chance for what? She is alive. She is in a good safe place. I have gone beyond what is expected of me. WHERE IS MY CHILD?"

Jonathan yells as he pounds his chest with his fist.

"If this is God's answer I do not want it. I will not accept it."

"Son there are many mothers and fathers who have lost their children for some reason or another. Look around you it was once common among the slaves."

"I am not a SLAVE! I am a man and I have rights."

"It sounds like you expect priviledges that the slave mothers and fathers never recieved. You are conditioned to priviledges that are beyond the reach of us SLAVES. You see now that you have been placed in the shoes of a slave father and you expect that your white skin will deliver your colored child home safe. But the fact remains that your child looks colored and nobody cares. Now son I have to tell you as a colored mother to her son. DEAL WITH IT. You do not have to accept it but you will have to deal with it at some point. And just maybe you can deal with it by giving that child the love she needs until she returns home to her family. I expected better from you," Raphael weeps. "You have cared for the freed children in the orphanage and now you behave like this?"

"Mother."

"Do not mother me! I expect better from you."

"I am sorry mother. I promise I will do better."

"Because?"

"Because I know better."

9

A PLACE OF SECOND CHANCES

Raphael turns and walks back to the big house. Jonathan lowers his head then begins to pray.

"Father please forgive me. I do not like the person I have become. Please deter my path to destruction so that I may rejoice in my daughter's return. I pray my strength and wisdom will continue to grow as I search for my Angie . Amen."

"Amen," a voice whispers from behind, it is Cindy Lou. She wraps her arms around him and gives him a tight squeeze.

"I missed you daddy and I hope you are not angry. I wanted to spend a year with you before I am off to college."

"You do say? How old are you now, fourteen, fifteen years old?"

"No daddy, I am sixteen years old. I will be seventeen years old in less than ten months and soon I will be off to college. I want to become a doctor just like you daddy."

"If you follow my lead you will end up with a degree in Medicine and never put it to use. I am pretty sure I disappointed your grandfather. You could be the one to make him proud. God knows I never could."

"Daddy I know granddaddy is proud of you. He tells me that all the time."

"That is what most old people do when they realize death approaches their doorstep. They try mercifully to back paddle into heaven."

"Daddy do you mean to say that granddaddy is going to..."

"It is possible or your granddaddy could scathe by on a broken halo and one wing. I have seen it happen. Now your mother, there is no hope for her. A woman that disobeys her husband is sure to spend some time in the smoker. That vow is right next to the commandment that says have no other Gods before me."

"What about mother Rafy?"

"Now she can do no wrong. She is an angel sent by God and anyone who does or even thinks ill will towards that woman is damned for eternity."

"What about Uncle Nate?"

"He is missing both wings and from what I have witnessed most people like him never even make it out of the pit."

"Daddy did you make this up?"

"Of course not sweetpea; every morning when I come out and sit on this stone I have a talk with the most powerful creator in the world. Did you know that sometimes we go to battle?"

"Who wins daddy?"

"Who do you think?"

"God?"

"Do you have any faith in your old man?"

"But daddy, God knows everthing. I know that he is the only one that knows where Angie is and I believe he will bring her home soon."

"So do I."

"Daddy I would like to go with you to search for Angie."

"You know how your mother feels about that."

"Nobody has to know just you and me daddy."

Jonathan takes a stern look at Cindy Lou.

"Why are you interested to partake in my *shenanigans* with me all of the sudden? Your mother assigned you to spy on me did she?"

"Daddy you can be so paranoid."

"Nonsense! That woman is out to destroy me. She will never forgive me for losing our child."

"Daddy is that what you think? Mommy just wants you to stay home and let the authorities do their job."

"Babygirl it is not that easy. I can not explain it, but I will never let go of my child. I could never let go of you. Even God will leave the masses to search for one lost lamb. I enjoy everybody's company but I have someone that I can not touch right now and until I do I will never stop until I can hold my babygirl again. It is that simple."

"Daddy while I am here I want to go with you to search for Angie. I promise that I will not undermine you. I miss my sister too. Mother cried every night when you sent us away. Will you promise me that everyday you will do something kind for mother?"

"Like what? Everytime I touch her she becomes impregnated."

"Daddy, mother has only been pregnant two times."

"Is that what she told you?"

"Daddy please, just something nice for a change I want to witness it first hand."

"Well that will be awkward. What if I want to plant warm kisses all over her body?"

"Daddy, why do you have to be so disgusting?"

"That is what your mother says. Have you two been talking about our sex life?"

"Daddy you do not have a sex life. If you could concentrate on your hygiene you could have sex life."

"That is exactly what your mother says. I just may reconsider my options. Is there anything else she has divulged to you that may serve as an incentive to be nice to the woman?"

"Daddy do you love mother?"

"I love her with all my heart."

"Then why do you treat her so..."

Cindy Lou pauses.

"So what? I treat her like a queen. She does not want for anything. She is married to love of her life. What more can she want?"

"Daddy you never take her for a drive at night anymore. You both used to sit by the pond almost until the early morning. I can not remember the last time that I have seen you show her any affection."

"Sweetpea love is complicated."

"Uncle Nate and Aunt Betty appear to be very much in love."

"Now there you go! You can not compare them to us. I work tireless to keep this farm in full operation while brother fold clothes and gossip with the ladies. His child is here safe and sound while my babygirl is somewhere out there perhaps being tormented."

"Alright daddy, I understand. I just want us to be a family again before I leave for college."

"I will give it my best."

"Thanks daddy that is all that I can ask for."

"Now your mother will have to do her part too."

"Yes daddy I will make sure of that."

"I hope you will."

"I love you daddy."

"I love you too."

They both continue to sit on the stone until someone approach them from behind. Cindy Lou turns to see who it is then returns her gaze on the pond. Jonathan turns to see Melba.

"Would you like to take a seat?"

"I don't mind if I do."

Jonathan slides closer to Cindy Lou almost sending her to the ground.

"Daddy!"

"Well we have to make room for your mother. Let me help you sweetheart."

"I can manage myself."

"I was just trying to be *kind*," answers Jonathan.

He then winks at Cindy Lou.

"I appreciate it Jon but I can manage for myself."

"Of course you can, what do you need a man for?"

"Is that a question or are you being sarcastic?"

"Sometimes I think you take me too serious. What do you think?"

"If I took you too serious mister you would not be alive today."

"Of course I would."

"Of course you would not."

"I am sure I would sweetheart."

"You would not mister!'

"Mother, daddy I thought you two would try to be kind to each other."

"There is no kindness in that old man. He is just full of foolishness, FULL of foolishness."

"Melba I have tried every way possible to make you happy and it just does not work. What do you want from me woman?"

"I want you to bring my baby home. Everyday you sit on this stone like a crazy frog waiting to catch a miracle."

"I have tried everything I know how to do. I have looked everywhere I can possibly think of. Do you not think that I would have found her by now if I could? Now I have the mind to send you back to my fathers'."

"I am not going anywhere," Melba shakes her head.

Jonathan shakes his head mocking Melba.

"We will see about that."

"We sure will mister."

Jonathan and Melba fold their arms and continue to sit on the stone.

"I guess I can go check on Babymouse," adds Cindy Lou.

"Her name is Lana and that is how you will address her," Melba insists.

"Yes mother."

Cindy Lou rises to leave the two. She looks back at them and for some reason they appear to be happy.

"I hope I never get married," Cindy Lou whispers.

"I heard that," yells Jonathan!

"You are hearing things Jon. It is a sign that you have lost your mind."

"One day Melba you are going to wish you never said that. I am going to prove you wrong and you will have to live the rest of your life in regret. Woman did you know that I pray every day that God will save your pitiful soul."

"MY pitiful soul? Do not waste your time on me mister."

"I can envision it right now. There you are at heaven's gate waiting for St. Peter to usher you in."

"Jon!"

"No now you have to listen. I have planned this methodically through to the end. I have considered it with a precise plan of action. The bible says now quote me if I am wrong. Wives obey your husbands and children obey your parents. It would be wise to assume that in NOT doing so could jeopardize your salvation."

"Jon!"

"I do believe I have the floor sweetheart. Now, if for any reason you should fail the test, because of my love for you I will by all means allow you to enter sinfully; if that is plausible."

"Jon."

"Now Melba how many husbands can you think of that will risk their wings to steal their wife into heaven?"

"I have no idea Jon."

"Now do you actually think I would sit here like a crazy frog and not get anything accomplished? I want to save your pitiful soul at all cost. Now share your conversations of me while you gossip with the women in vain."

"Well Jon, I do not know where to start but here is where I will end. If I were you I would not think of coming to bed tonight. Consider it safe to say that you will retire to the dog house FOREVER."

"But Melba..."

Melba interrupts.

"Do not Melba me mister perfect. I must say you have yourself fooled if you think for one second God would you allow YOU to enter into heaven before me."

Melba lifts herself up from the stone.

"Let me help you dear."

"Do not touch me!"

"If you insist. I just wanted to extend kindness to you dear."

"Jon if I..."

Jonathan interrupts.

"Now, now Melba you are just digging yourself deeper into the pit of hell. If you continue on this path I may never be able to reach you."

"You are crazier than I thought old man."

"If you insist my love."

Melba walks away speechless unable to comprehend what just transpired.

"I heard that," answers Jonathan.

Cindy reappears from a distance.

"Daddy how many girls did you date before mother?"

Never Underestimate The Power of A Secret Place

"I am proud to say your mother is my first love. It was magical. One day on my way to a game of cricket. She was sat at a table poised as if she were taking a picture. Then all of the sudden out of nowhere appears this tall, athletic build gentleman. He irriated her from what I could see. I approached them both and asked if she needed some assistance. Of course she declined my offer. I expected it."

"Why daddy?"

"I imagined she considered me no match for the lad. Well I have always been a bit under weight and clumsy. I experienced a terrible bout with acne and my teeth protruded somewhat at the time. But I must say I was quite the expert when it came to martial arts. Before I knew it your mother asked me to walk her to Frederick College which was a few blocks from the Univeristy I attended. This continued for the rest of our senior year. Of course some other things went on that I will not mention."

"What happened to the guy that annoyed mother?"

"Well it turns out that he was no match for me."

"Are you serious daddy?"

"I had to stake my claim somehow."

"Did you even know anything about mother?"

"Of course I did. She was Betty's best friend. I would often see them together in the flats. Nathan had courted Betty for quite some time."

"Did Uncle Nate introduce you to mother?"

"No, he said I too immature for a woman like Melba. But it never stopped me."

"What did you do?"

"I followed her every chance I could. By the time she knew my name I knew everything about her."

"That sounds illegal Daddy."

"How else would I have gotten to know her?"

"Just walk up to her and ask her out daddy. It is very simple."

"There were alot of obstacles in my way. It was taboo for a white man to ask a colored woman out. I never thought I had a chance until that day. It was in fact the first of many physical altercations I experienced while I defended your mother's honor."

"Are you serious?"

"Your mother is the most beautiful woman I have ever seen. Atleast she is in my eyes. My confidence shot through the roof when I was with her. I was not like your uncle a ladies man. I never wanted to be. Just someone that I could spend my life with was all I ever desired."

"Mother said you gave her the most beautiful wedding a woman could hope for. I wished I could have been there."

"You were."

"I was?"

"Sure you were. Tell me how did your mother describe our wedding?"

"All I remember is that she said that grandfather decorated the courtyard and her gown's trail was six feet long. The maidens' dresses were mint, knee length to show off Betty's legs. She said that you cried while she walked down the isle. More people attended than she expected. Even the cat you fought mother for attended with the girl he took to the ball in the end. Mother said that you looked handsome in your suit. She said it was the happiest day of her life."

"Is that so?"

"Yes daddy but mother never mentioned that I was at the wedding."

"It slipped my mind. You were actually not there at the wedding. Forgive me for the error. Please do not tell your mother. Does your mother ever speak of Eric?"

"Yes daddy we often saw him at the market when we were home."

"How did she react when she saw him?"

"They would often nod at each other while we passed. She never held a coversation with him that I can recall. Mother said that you made a believer out of him."

"Is that so?"

"Mother said that you were known to be lethal with your hands and no one dare challenged you. She said that you often fought Uncle Nate's battles. She knew then that she could trust you. She also said that it wasn't until you began to court her that the ladies begin to take interest in you. You could have any woman you wanted and you chose mother. Not to mention the ridicule you recieved for befriending a colored woman. It was not easy for you was it daddy."

"It was easy for me but not for your mother. We were in and out of the relationship multiple times. She often questioned her value in society. We never attended any of the socials at the University. Most of my friendships grew from the socials I attended at Frederick College. Charles, Kennedy, your uncle and I would ride together to the events and meet up with the girls. It was not fashionable for us to pickup Betty and Melba at their homes, although it was frowned upon if you did not meet the parents before you courted their daughters'. Nathan would make the run to take the women home after the events. I am fortunate that our love endured those times."

"Do you have any regrets?"

"Not one sweetpea. If you should ever meet someone that you can not live without let nothing come between the two of you,"

"What if you do not approve of who I want to marry?"

"Now that is a different story. A father has the final word when it comes to his daughters. A man can sense the character of another man. It is our innate ability. It is the same with women. Always let your parents meet any potential suitors. It can save you a life of misery."

"I will daddy."

Never Underestimate The Power of A Secret Place

"Now I need you to do something for your dear old father. I want you to bring me a can of gasoline and a box of matches."

"Daddy you know how mother feels about the children handling gasoline."

"Who says that she has to know?"

"You want me to disobey mother?"

"How about you obey your father for once? For goodness sakes! I never had this much trouble out of Angie. Now are you going to help me find Angie or not?"

"What has this got to do with finding Angie?"

"I knew it all along. Your mother has sent you to betray me, but I shall not be derailed."

"Daddy, I will see you at dinner."

Cindy Lou braces herself for another argument but silence falls all around them. She leans forward to stand and still not one word from Jonathan.

"Am I having my morning coffee or not?"

"I will get your coffee for you daddy. Do you want anything else?"

"No, just give me a simple cup of coffee."

Cindy Lou turns and darts to the big house.

"Whew! How did Angie deal with daddy every day?"

"I heard that," yells Jonathan.

When Cindy Lou opens the door Lana is in route to bring Jonathan a cup of fresh coffee. Cindy Lou holds the door open for Lana then shakes her head.

"I pray her strength in the Lord."

Slam the door shuts. Jonathan looks behind him to see Lana headed in his direction. He thinks to himself, *She looks durable enough to pull off my next move. I will have to test her loyalty.*

"Mistah Jonathan."

"Yes who is there, he sings."

"It's me. I got some coffee fo ya."

Never Underestimate The Power of A Secret Place

"Is that so?"

"Yes suh."

Lana leans in to hand the coffee to Jonathan.

"My bacon."

"Jus coffee suh."

"I am sure smell I bacon or have I lost my mind?"

"That's what they say suh."

"That is what who say?"

"The missus say you lost yo mind and don't pay no attention to ya."

"You know they just want to turn you against me. I am a rather nice man if you get to know me. If you like I can help you find your family, but it must be our secret. Are you interested?"

"Yes suh, I wanna go back ta my fam'ly."

"Then we have a partnership, but first I need you to do something for me. I need you to go into the house and bring me two match sticks. When you bring me the match sticks I want you to take this cup into that barn over there."

Jonathan points to the barn.

"You will see tin cans on a shelf. Take the smallest tin can and pour its contents into my cup. I do not need very much. Make sure you do not spill any on yourself. That could be disasterous for the both of us; finally make sure no one knows what you are doing. Bring the cup to me and you have earned my trust to begin this partnership. Do you need me to repeat myself?"

"No suh."

Lana trots into the big house to find everyone out back sorting the laundry. She returns to the kitchen and takes two matches from the box on the stove. She places them in her overall long pocket. She returns to the back of the house and counts everyone in her sight.

"Same numba like befo'," she whispers.

Never Underestimate The Power of A Secret Place

Lana turns to walk down the hall to the front door. Before she reaches the door Jonathan has entered the house and hands her the cup. She takes the cup and eases out the front door.

"She is so methodical until it is almost scary," Jonathan says under his breath.

"I heard that," says Lana after she leans inside the house.

Jonathan shoo's her away to continue her assignment.

"There is something familiar about the lass. I have to remind myself to do a little more investigation into the newest member of the family."

Jonathan stands inside the back door of the house and observes the women at their daily chores. He notices that Nathan carries the basket of wet laundry for Betty. Jonathan leans out of the door and calls for Nathan.

"Brother, may I speak with you for a moment?"

Nathan walks at a fast pace in Jonathans' direction. They both began to argue through the screen door.

"Maybe if you did not coddle the women so much we could have some control of the place."

"Brother you can not be serious. It is your nonsense that has the women in discord. Maybe you should try to be more compassionate."

"Compassion you say? I have some compassion for you all."

Lana is now by Jonathan's side and hands him the cup. He extends his hand downward out of Nathan's sight and she hands him the match sticks.

"Excuse me I feel the need to extend some compassion to these wonderful ladies."

Jonathan walks past Nathan who begins to smell the hint of gasoline.

"Lana have you been in the barn?"

Lana does not say a word but follows Jonathan with her eyes. Nathan then follows her gaze while Jonathan walks toward the family's only dog house. Jonathan kicks the dog house to make sure that there are not any animals inside. Jonathan then pours the liquid from the cup and strikes the match. Jonathan turns in Melba's direction before he sets the dog house on fire.

"Look here woman! This is what I think of your dog house."

Jonathan lowers his hand to the dog house and it goes up in flames. He takes a few steps back to gaze at the fire.

"Son what has gotten into you? Have you lost your mind?"

"Maybe I have or maybe I have not. When were you going to inform me that Henry plans to take you away from here? You thought I would never find out did you not? I never thought you would betray me mother!"

The workers began to throw water on the fire while Jonathan continue on with his tirade.

"I expected it from Melba but not from you mother. Now that I have returned expect some changes. It would behoove all of you to seek forgiveness for your sins. I can only imagine the atrocities that were commited in my absence."

Jonathan winks at Lana and heads in the direction of the module where he has slept since his return.

"Mother he has not been home a week and already the foolishness has begun. I do not think I can take another year of this. Please do something; anything he is at the point of no return," Melba exclaims.

"Allow me," offers Nathan. "We will just have to keep him busy mother. Maybe he will be helpful driving some merchandise to one of the stores up north. He seems to be in more control of his wits when it concerns business. Give me some time to make some arrangements with the other men."

"Please do son. I think he has too much on his plate right now. Make sure that he is accompanied by one of the workers. We just can not release him out there in the world. There is no telling what may become of him," Rafael adds.

Never Underestimate The Power of A Secret Place

"Give me a few days to think of something. If I must I will take him with me to search for Lana's family. It may bring some resolve to his troubled soul."

"If you must do something; whatever will appease his distress is fine with me," Rafael offers her support.

"Yes mother my hopes are that this is not the beginning of more sorrows to come."

"Mine too son. Mine too," agrees Rafael.

Everyone continues to stand around the smoldering dog house except Jonathan. He has made his way to the module where he slept the other night. The whiskey bottle lies empty on the bed where he left it; in plain sight where someone would soon know his secret that he has begun to drink again. The awful habit he promised to rid himself of has returned and this time with a vengeance.

Jonathan thinks to himself... *I have to be more careful. It could ruin my chances to find Angie. I need a plan for an escape; alone this time. I can never get anything accomplished with the men questioning my every motive. On my next run I will take the girl with me. She will be my alibi to search for Angie. She has without doubt passed the test and with the greatest of ease I might add. She appears to be quite a natural when it comes to deception. Unlike Cindy who I am sure to be Melba's hand picked spy. Not this time woman! You are outwitted once again."*

The door begins to open and Jonathan nestles the empty bottle behind his back. Jonathan waits for someone to appear but no one appears.

"I wonder if perhaps my aim would render a fatal injury to the intruder on the otherside of that door. Why grapple with it I may as well take my chances."

"Brother it is I not an intruder. Please do not be foolish," cries Nathan.

Never Underestimate The Power of A Secret Place

"A wise man once said; never enter into the abode of an armed man unannounced lest you seek to find an unfortunate end. Now what does this unwelcomed appearance warrant?"

"I am concerned with your well being."

"Really, it sounds more like you were sent to spy on me."

"Brother who knows you better than I. I came to tell you that your wish has been granted."

"Who are you the fairy God mother of some sort?"

"Mother has agreed to allow you to search for the child's family."

"Is that so?"

"Is that not what you wanted?"

"Of course it is but who says that I need the permission of a woman to do a man's job? I am in charge around here and whatever decision I make does not need mother's approval. Is that clear?"

"Yes brother."

"Yes son, I understand."

"Who is there?"

Rafael steps across the threshold of the module.

"It is just I your MOTHER!"

"Mother let me explain."

"Oh you will have plenty of time to explain once you have cleared the mess you made and you will build that poor hound another dog house right this minute."

"Yes mother."

"I do not know what has gotten into you but you better pull yourself together or I will leave on the next train. Did you hear me son?"

"Yes mother. I hear you very well," answers Jonathan.

Jonathan observes Rafaels body language to assess the validity of her statement. She turns her gaze to the bottle nestled behind Jonathan on the bed.

"No mother, it is not what you think."

"I hope not son you are tearing this family apart. In a few days I want you to take Lana back to the place you found her and see if you can find her family. I want you to protect her while she is in your care. Nathan can accompany you on the trip. The others can not seem to handle your rambuctious ongoings. Have I made myself clear?"

"Yes, mother."

"Now what are you going to do?"

"Mother I am not a child anymore."

"Excuse me," replies Rafael.

"Nathan and I will take the girl to find her family."

"Before that!"

"You ask that I pull myself together."

"Before that son!"

"I think she wants you to clean the mess you have made and rebuild the hound a dog house."

"Son, do not rest until it is done. Am I clear?"

"Yes mother," echoes both of the men.

"And another thing, for however long that I am alive and in my right mind you will do what I say."

"Yes mother. But you must allow me to be the man of the house. You simply can not undermine my aurthority."

Rafael takes a few steps closer to Jonathan and he leans back. Nathan steps closer into the corner to give Rafael more room at her disposal. Rafael leans in closer and cups Jonathans face with both hands.

"Son, I will never undermine your authority. But there will be times when I must stop you from making a fool of yourself. Wouldn't you agree?"

Rafael nods yes and Jonathan mirrors her gesture.

"I love you too much to let you fail son. That is all that I strive to do."

"Now get out there and build that poor hound some shelter before the rain comes in. Go on now. I mean this very minute."

Both men leave the quarter headed for the barn. Rafael searches the quarter for more bottles of moon shine and finds one bottle nestled inside a boot that stands in the corner where Nathan once stood. Rafael retrieves the bottle and opens it but it appears to be untouched. Rafael takes the bottle to the sink then considers whether to pour the liquid down the drain. She stands there in deep thought before she screws the top back onto the bottle. She then places the empty bottle in the boot and takes the full bottle and places it in her skirt pocket. She then leaves the module with a wide brim smile on her face.

"Has mother left yet?"

"She has just left and she appears to be happy."

"That can not be. She is never happy when she finds that I have been drinking. Let me see her expression."

Nathan steps aside to allow Jonathan a glance at Rafael.

"What do you think she is up to?"

"I have not a clue. Whatever it is she is quite satisfied with the results."

"Do you think she will really leave here?"

"It is clear that Henry has made an impression on her."

"Should I tell her the truth?"

"Do you want to break her heart?"

"He has already done that. I want her to know the truth so that she can make the best decision for us all."

"What decision would that be?"

Both men turn to see Henry who appears from the background of darkness. He stops to put down the pail of feed.

"How long do you plan to keep Rafy under your thumb? Have you ever thought about her dreams? Have you ever considered that she may want to leave here? You know she is not quite cut out for this country living. Rafy is a city girl by nature.

Never Underestimate The Power of A Secret Place

She loves the finer things in life and here she is your cook and maid. She did not earn a degree in college to be your mammy. Hopefully you have compensated her well for her services."

"You do not have the right to refer to our mother in that manner," argues Nathan. "Now I have told you before, you can join our family or dismiss yourself from our premises."

"Now brother don't be too harsh with the poor lad," Jonathan interjects. "If my memory serves me well I remember on many occasions when I passed you and your wife on my way to grade school. I must thank my father for his interest in photography or else I would not have the slew of pictures of the both of you. Would you like to see them? I have kept them in pristine condition just for this occasion. Now I must warn you that Opio is also aware of your past. We had come to the conclusion that you were completely out of mother's life. But I see I was mistaken. May I warn you it would be in your best interest to tread light during your stay here? However long that may be. But of course, I shall be the judge of that. If you find it fruitful to become a member of the family then by all means do so. Otherwise I suggest you disappear like a vapor in the air rather than challenge me. Have I made myself clear?"

"The bible says that nobody should come between a man and his woman," states Henry.

"I beg to differ dear brother. It is emersed in the context of marriage. I think the correct terminology is husband and wife and you are neither. What shall it be?"

"I have property up north. A fine home and little money set aside. There are plenty of women up north lookin for a good man like me. Rafy knows where to find me. Just let her know I will not wait forever."

"If she is worth the wait you will then... wait," reminds Nathan.

"Would you like me to make travel arrangements for you," asks Jonathan.

"If it would not trouble you to get me to the county line; I can take it from there."

"It would be my pleasure."

"If it pleases you shall we make arrangements for early morning," asks Nathan.

"It suits me just fine," answers Henry. "The sooner I get away from this plantation the better. It is people like you that keep slavery alive. Those slave quarters should have been burned down a long time ago along with the master's house. You do not know what we went through in slavery."

"You are correct Henry. I have no idea what the African's experienced during slavery. But I am sure that I have witnessed for myself the autrocities of hatred. You see slavery was just a system organized by people. The only way such a system can exist is if the majority allows it. It is unfortunate that slavery was able to exist by the hands of only a few people. It was not until the majority became cognizant of this system and its intricate underminings did the majority revolt against it. This tells me that there were more against the concept of slavery than there were in favor of it. When I look at the quarters I imagine the opportunities to receive God's word that he will give us houses that we did not build. I did not envision my hands to commit malicious acts of hatred and either did God. These quarters remain because I have found a use for them despite the original intentions for their existence. You may want to visit the modules that the Africans now inhabit. They are designed by the same builders that renovated the flats. Must I remind you that everyone living in a module owns the deed to their dwelling and the plot of land that it surrounds. That my brother was not my intentions to re-invent slavery."

"It is settled; I will make preparations to leave within the next few days," Henry replies. "I do not want any part in this lifestyle."

"By all means suit yourself. But mother will remain with us," insists Jonathan.

"I will let your mother make that decision."

"That IS her decision," insists Jonathan.

"We shall see."

"You shall see Mr. Henry," answers Nathan.

"If you will excuse me I will gather my things."

"Your things have been gathered for quite some time. We can expedite your departure in a more efficient manner if you will accept the valet services that Nathan shall provide at his leisure."

"Excuse me brother, but I am not at your disposal," Nathan reports.

"I agree. Think of this as a small return on the mercies that mother has extended to us. She is worth the trouble is she not," asks Jonathan.

"Of course mother is well worth the trouble brother."

"You may gather Henry's things from his module then deliver him to the county line. Your truck will be prepared for your journey."

The following morning Nathan has returned from the drive with Henry without Rafael's knowledge. Everyone has begun to gather in the kitchen on this particular morning.

There is a loud knock at the door and Jonathan leaves the kitchen to answer the door.

"Oh, it is you. I am sorry to inform you but visiting hours are over."

Jonathan closes the door then makes his way back to the kitchen where everyone has gathered.

"Who was at the door," asks Melba.

"Not anyone that should concern you."

Minutes later...

"Hello everyone!"

Enters a tall pale skinned male dressed in a black tailored suit. His hair is trimmed into a neat low afro with beard to match.

"Stephen, when did you get here?"

"I just arrived this morning."

"Was that you at the door," asks Melba.

"Yes it was. I must say Jonathan has not changed a bit. He is the same selfish scatterbrain that I left behind."

"If my memory serves me well it was indeed you that left my mother behind while you pursued your selfish desires."

"Boys must you two carry on with this foolishness."

"He is afraid mother; he is afraid that your ONLY biological son has come to take you away. Your time is up Jonathan! Must I remind you it is the prodigal son who the father revered most."

"Is that so? By the way where is your wife?"

"Wife," gasps Rafael. "Stephen I am sure you have not married without my blessing have you?"

"Mother this is the reason why I am here today. I want to clear some things up. Please have a seat mother."

Jonathan pulls out a chair and Stephen does the same.

"Mother please sit down," Stephen asks.

She looks at the both of them while she shakes her head.

"When will the two of you learn? I love you both the same. Nothing can change that."

"Mother you cannot be serious. I am your only biological son."

"I would not pride myself on that if I were you. What son abandons his own mother to elope and marry a woman who is impregnated with another man's child?"

"Why must you be so malicious Jonathan?"

"I must meet you where you live."

"I have had enough of the two of you!"

Never Underestimate The Power of A Secret Place

"Now mother I am in town at a bed and breakfast not too far from here. You are more than welcome to join me so that we can spend some time together before I return to..."

Jonathan interrupts.

"You have just arrived and already you must leave your *biological* mother," Jonathan quips.

"Mother I will not entertain Jonathan's foolishness any longer."

Rafael takes a seat in the chair that Jonathan has provided for her. Jonathan smiles while she leans back in the chair.

"Sit down son."

Jonathan and Stephen attempt to take the seat which Stephen has held out for his mother. Stephen pulls it away before Jonathan can take possession. He lands on the floor with a thump. Rafael shakes her head while she witnesses the event.

"I need some time with Stephen alone to myself," says Rafael.

While Jonathan gathers himself, he looks into Rafael's face with regret.

"Mother."

Jonathan stands to gain Rafael's attention.

"No son, just leave us be. I have not seen Stephen in a very long time."

Stephen takes his seat in front of his mother. He takes her hand and with compassion kisses the center of her palm. Jonathan takes in the gesture before he walks away.

"She is not leaving. She is NOT leaving here," Jonathan yells.

"Son, why are you so angry?"

"Mother, I know what he wants. He wants you to come with him. I need you mother. Please do not leave. I will not make it without you."

"Son, I will always be here for you."

"Mother, promise me."

"Son I can only tell you that I will not leave you now. But some day I will have to leave you and you will be fine son."

"No mother, I cannot survive another loss right now."

"I know son. There is no way I could leave you now. Go wash up breakfast will be ready soon."

"You are jealous aren't you? You have always wanted my mother to yourself."

"YOU..." Jonathan points at Stephen. "You despised your own mother. You were ashamed of her dark complexion. You wanted so very much to pass for white that you even married white. Then you travelled half across the world to disguise your true identity. When were you going to tell mother that you married Natalie? A woman passed around from one man to another."

"How dare you insult my wife."

"Your wife? What about my brother? Did you ever consider that just maybe he may have loved her?"

"When will you let go of the past? Arthur and I have mended our fences. There is no reason to continue this war. Can you not see it tears at my mother's heart?"

"You broke her heart years ago. You were ashamed to introduce her to any of your acquaintances. You practically lived at my childhood home because you wanted so much to be white. Then you portrayed yourself like a friend, to my brother only to elope with his impregnated wife. So tell me now who fathered the child?"

"Mother I have to speak to you alone."

"Is it true son? Are you married to Natalie?"

"Yes mother."

"Why did you keep it a secret?"

"Mother you despised Natalie."

"Honey I despised her ways. She treated me like I was a servant in my own home. I would never allow anyone to disgrace my mother in my presence. Anyone that did would not find their way in my company ever again. What brings you here son?"

"You mother. I have missed you in great depth. Can we please go somewhere to talk in private?"

"Son this is your family, this is the only family we know."

"Mother I am your family. I plan to bring you home with me."

Rafael gazes into his eyes for a minute.

"Mother did you hear me? I want you to come home with me."

"But son, I am home."

Jonathan steps closer to the two of them.

"Did you hear her? She is home and there is nothing you can say that will take her away."

"Get away from me!"

Stephen shoves Jonathan against the kitchen cabinet. The dishes rattle noisily in the sink.

"You must leave before you hurt her again. You should have atleast had the decency to call her to let her know that you were alive. She worried herself sick because of you. Now here you are to drive her to her grave."

"It is ironic that you speak of death. You are very fortunate to be alive this very day Jonathan. Many nights I wanted to smother you in your sleep. You robbed me of my mother. I will no longer stand by and allow it to continue."

Stephen turns to his mother.

"Mother, please just for one day come with me."

Silence surrounds everyone in the kitchen.

"Just for the night mother; you can return in the morning."

Rafael looks at Stephen before she speaks.

"Jonathan."

"Yes mother."

"I will leave for one day but I promise I will return."

"Yes mother."

Jonathan walks out of the kitchen in the direction of the front entrance. He leaves the big house then makes his way to the pond to sit on the stone. He gazes out into the horizon then begins to pray.

"Dear Lord, why am I being chastised? My faith fails me daily. Strengthen me with your wisdom Heavenly Father. I have lost everything that is meaningful to me. This farm means nothing to me without my loved ones. Take it and do with it what you will but please restore my family. It is all that I ask. Amen."

Jonathan hears an engine roar but does not turn towards the sound. A moment later he feels an arm around his shoulders. Rafael places her cheek next to Jonathan's.

She whispers, "Do not fret son. I will return in the morning. I want you to be the man that I raised you to be. Take care of the family while I am away."

She plants a gentle kiss on Jonathan's cheek then stands to leave.

"Mother."

"Yes son."

"I really do love you."

"I know you do son," replies Rafael while she looks in the direction of the car. "I really, really love you too."

Rafael begins her way to Stephen's car. She hears the low sobs of Jonathan's cry. She pauses.

"Go on mother just promise me."

"I promise son."

A few minutes later the automobile enters the trail then navigates its way among the workers who walk along its edge. Jonathan leans back on his elbows to get a better look around the farm. He feels someone behind him then all of the sudden Lana appears out of the corner of his eye. Lana squats to face him but he continues to look forward to avoid any contact.

Never Underestimate The Power of A Secret Place

"When ya gonna take me home," Lana asks.

"Where did you say you lived?"

"I *say* I don't know! You say ya gonna find my home Mista Jon-a-than."

"Believe me I am in persistent search of your home."

"Who that is?"

"Who is who?"

"Per-sista?"

"Why are you not in school Babymouse?"

"My name ain't Babymouse," she shouts.

"You resemble a baby..."

Lana interrupts.

"My name IS Lana."

"From now on I will call you Lana, Babymouse."

"Ya still callin me babymouse," she sighs. "I ain't stealin no more bacon fo *you*."

"Of course you will."

"I ain't."

"You will if you want jam with your biscuit. Must I remind you mother does not allow children to have jam. Being that I am not a child. I am the only adult able to get jam for you."

Lana crosses her arms and begins to frown.

"Do not waste your time. It will not get you anywhere. Besides, I need you and you need me."

"Why I'se need you?"

"First, of all you need me to get back home and second, I need you to help me find my daughter."

"Nobody *knows* where is yo daughter."

"You mean, where my daughter is. Somebody knows where she is; just like somebody knows where your family is. Got it?"

"Got it."

"Now a truck will leave tomorrow morning to deliver some goods to a store in Texas. We will be in that truck."

"No we ain't," argues Lana.

"Can I get you to cooperate with me?"

"Motha say you ain't leavin the farm no mo. You done lost yo mind everytime you leave here."

"Is that what she said?"

Lana shakes her head to confirm.

"What else did they say about me?"

"Miss Melba puttin medicine in yo orange juice."

"You do say?"

"She say you sho full of it."

"Full of what?"

"Sumptin, how's I suppose ta know."

"I thought you knew everything. Oh, I have forgotten you know everything except where you live. Let us go over the plans for this trip. Now, you CANNOT walk into the front of the store with me."

"Why?"

"Because they will think we are together."

"But we is togetha."

"Let me put it another way. Africans can only come in the store through the back door."

"I ain't African. I'se colored," she says with a stern face.

Lana leans forward to stare at Jonathan. Jonathan leans to his side furthest away from Lana.

"Now are we a team or not?"

Lana continues to stare at him. Jonathan leans forward to avoid her glare.

"Now I will enter the store first to look for items to purchase."

"You gonna git me some sweets?"

"Do I always?"

"Not tha last time," she bellows.

"Well, Babymouse you must remember to follow the plan."

"I had ta PEE!"

"The proper word is urinate."

"I HAD to ur-i-nate."

"We will stop along the side of the road before we get into each town from now on. Now where were we?"

"You gonna get me sweets next time."

"I remember, while I distract the store owner I want you to place the picture in the window. Afterwards you come to the counter to ask how much sweets you can get for a nickel."

"He gone say, get out my sto gal."

"Now that is where I take over. You do not say a word. Do you hear me? You must remember if I get arrested then they will take you away. I may never be able to help you find your home. We are going near the town where we found you. I do not want you to get out of sight. There may be a reward for your return."

"What a reward?"

"A reward is money someone will pay to find you. My hopes are they are not in search for you. It has been four years; besides we reported the jail house where we found you so that it can be investigated."

"You ain't gonna shoot nobody this time is ya?"

"Another thing you must never tell the enemy our secrets."

"I ain't gonna get no whippin on yo count."

"Nobody is going to whip you. Although sometimes I have had the mind to put you over my knee and let you have it."

"Miss Melba say you touch me an you gonna sleep with the dogs."

"Can I tell you a secret?"

Lana leans in.

"Sometimes I like to sleep with the dogs. Now get to school. We have a full day of work ahead of us."

The next day…

Never Underestimate The Power of A Secret Place

The sun breaks through the trees while morning approaches. Jonathan turns over to kiss Melba only to find her side of the bed is empty. Jonathan rises but before he can stand to his feet the door opens. Jonathan looks over his shoulder towards the door. Lana appears from behind the door.

"What are you doing here? You know the plan."

"Miss Melba says ta look in on ya."

"Look in on me? Whatever for? I am more than able to care for myself."

"She say you cries in yo sleep."

"Nonsense, I never cry."

"Umm, huh."

"Do not argue with me! I said I never cry!"

"Umm huh," says Lana in a low voice.

"You know there is a particular little girl and I shall not name names. But if she continues to undermine my authority I have no choice but to leave her at the farm on my next delivery," says Jonathan while he squints his eyes in her direction.

Lana looks down to her feet.

"Now after I have cleared the kitchen what will you do?"

"Git ya some bacon from the stove."

"What else?"

"A biscuit fo me."

"What else?"

"Don't get caught."

"Get caught? Nonsense, you will never get caught. You are a natural born thief."

"I wonder whom she may have learned it from?"

A voice from behind Lana bellows. Lana turns to see Nathan then scurries to Jonathan's side.

"I will have to inform mother that you are up to your antics once again."

"Oh, must you be a tattle tale?"

"It is for our good."

"You are just like the others. You all think I have lost my mind."

"I am afraid you are wrong brother. I am certain you have lost your mind. Get along child."

Lana leans into Jonathan.

"Get along now with the other children. School will begin soon."

Lana remains by Jonathan's side.

Jonathan smiles, "Unlike the other children, Babymouse will not be mesmerized by your witty personality."

"In other words, the child has lost her mind as well."

"Of course not we are well balanced human beings."

"If you must say so brother. Now once again little one get on your way to the kitchen for breakfast."

"Babymouse, may I escort you?"

"Yes suh Mista Jonathan."

Jonathan leans down to take Lana by the hand. They maneuver their way around Nathan and out of the bedroom. Jonathan ushers Lana down the staircase then winks at her before they enter the kitchen.

"Good morning everyone."

"Good morning," everyone greets in harmony.

"What an exquisite meal you have prepared for us this morning."

"Son, first of all you will have your bran muffins before you eat any breakfast," replies Linda.

"Mother, I did not see you there. You look stunning today. What is the occasion?"

"Well if you should know son. I got up early this morning to prepare this pan of oat bran muffins just for you."

"You do say! Do not worry yourself on my account."

Jonathan pulls a chair from the table.

"Here please sit down. Allow me to serve you this morning. Have I ever told you..."

Melba interrupts.

"Just eat the muffins so we all can start this morning off on a kind note," interjects Melba.

"Woman, where have you been?"

"I have been here you old rooster."

"Where is here?"

"Not this morning son," Linda shakes her head and extends her finger into the air.

"No mother I must address this now. Each morning I wake up to find you are not in your rightful place in bed with me. Have you become impregnated? Now you will answer me or I will be forced to send you to my FATHERS'!"

"There he goes again. What is the problem," Nathan asks after he enters the kitchen.

"Nathan if you do not level him out I promise I will leave him forever."

"That is my point exactly."

"Son!"

Rafael stands to get his attention.

"Now mother you know very well there has been far too many unexplained pregnancies."

Nathan shakes his head before he leaves the kitchen.

"Oh no, Nathan don't you dare leave or this will be the last time you will see your brother alive."

"Now Melba, you have been aware of his idiosyncrasies' the day you two married."

"I did not imagine that it would take a turn for the worse so soon."

"Well, I am sure the two of you can manage through this minor conflict. You are a strong woman," whispers Nathan.

"What is that," asks Jonathan.

Never Underestimate The Power of A Secret Place

"Son it was nothing."

"No mother he can answer for himself. What did you say to *my* wife?"

"Brother I was simply..."

Jonathan interrupts.

"Stay away from her. It would not surprise me if it is with you that she misbehaves in secret."

"Lana go on to school."

"Is Mistah Jonathan losin his mind agin?"

"So you have begun to fill your venom into Babymouse I see."

"Jon calm down. Have you had your orange juice this morning?"

"Do you mean the poison you have fed me every morning of my adult life?"

"Okay, he is gone."

Nathan attempts to calm her down.

"Melba everything will be alright."

Nathan turns to Jonathan.

"Brother I have you to know that I am happily married. There is no way that I would deceive you. Why would you even consider such an immoral deed?"

"Well look at her, she is the most beautiful creature on the earth. Betty could never match her beauty."

"What did he just say," asks Betty.

"Sweetheart can you not see that he is mad."

"Mad you say? Or maybe I am really on to something. Let me see now, the other day I witnessed with my very own eyes..."

Everyone begin to leave the kitchen.

"Oh, I see. No one wants to bear the truth. Is that WHAT IT IS," he yells. "Of course that is what it is. You are quite a remarkable observer," says Jonathan to himself.

Jonathan looks around the empty kitchen. Then he reaches for a spoon to fill a napkin with jam. He observes the table before he chooses which cup of orange juice to take.

"I shall take mothers." The others may not maintain their dental hygiene to my preference."

He takes a sip.

"Ummm, so mother likes vodka in her orange juice. I must keep that in mind for future arguments."

Jonathan leaves the kitchen to begin his walk down the hallway. He hears the patter of small feet and turns to see Lana sneak into the kitchen.

"Babymouse is a keeper," he says to himself.

Jonathan sits on the stone and leans back on his elbows to wait on his delivery of bacon. Soon Lana sits by his side then she reaches into her trouser pocket to retrieve the fresh warm bacon.

"What did you get yourself?"

Lana pulls from her underneath her overall breast cover a warm fluffy biscuit. She extends her palm to Jonathan and he looks at it.

"Where's my jam?"

"Oh goodness, I knew I forgot something."

Lana begins to push him down to search through his pockets.

"Now now little one, here is the jam."

He places a napkin folded neatly with a red stain in the middle on the stone. With care Lana unfolds the napkin to reveal strawberry jam. Lana places the napkin on her lap then dips the biscuit into the mound of jam. Jonathan watches while she meticulously eats every crumb. She then folds the napkin back into its original form then extends her hand to give it back to Jonathan.

"What am I to do with that?"

"You want me ta get caught with tha evidence?"

"You want to know something Babymouse? You posses a very criminalist mind to be so young."

"I learnt it from you."
"Of course you did not."
"Of course I did too."
"Do not argue with me Babymouse."
"You say give ya the evidence."
"I did say that didn't I?"
"Yes ya did."
"You obey do you not?"
"Yes suh."
"Why is that?   Do you know?"
"No suh."
"You know very well that if I have the evidence the others will chastise me and you Babymouse will get off scot free."

He looks at Lana before she turns her head in the other direction.

"It is not a coincidence that the keys to the delivery truck just magically reappeared inside my overall pants the other day. You were going to steal the delivery truck were you not?"

Jonathan leans into Lana's direction. Lana stands to leave.

"Where do you think you are going?"

"Ta school," she points to the quarters were her class is held.

Jonathan turns to see the other children enter their classrooms.

"Go if you must."

Lana waves to her teacher then begins a slow trot to the quarter. Jonathan turns to watch the workers on their way to their work areas. Charles walks up the trail along with the other workers. He stops to wait on someone at the edge of the woods. Samson appears from the woods and they begin to make their way toward the storage building where the trucks are loaded. Jonathan waves them in his direction.

"Good morning gentlemen."

Jonathan greets them before they all embrace.

"So I hear there is a shipment loaded to leave this morning."

"Yes suh, but Junebug cain't drive this mornin. He say his wife havin the baby any day now."

"This is exciting? We are going to have a baby!"

"Whoa Jonathan! Junebug and Myrtle are having a baby. We are just happy for them," Charles interjects.

"You know my intentions, so what plans have you made to replace Junebug?"

"Well we have considered James but he has work to do on the renovations to his home before his new addition arrives."

"It amazes me how we have grown by leaps and bounds."

"It amazes me also Jonathan. What do you suggest?"

Samson looks at Charles uneasily. Jonathan reads their expressions then takes a minute to respond.

"The two of you can take the shipment scheduled for father's factory. In the meantime I will arrange drivers for the Texas delivery. How does that sound?"

"Are you certain you do not want us to stay behind until you find a driver?"

"No I will manage to find someone. You two can get on the road while you have a full day of daylight. Have a safe trip and by all means please call when you get to the nearest phone. We must know that you both are safe."

"Jon you do not have to worry we will be fine."

"I did not ask for a response just do what I ask. I may not say this often enough but I love the both of you."

Charles and Samson look at each other.

"Suh I love you too."

"Me too," says Charles.

They make their way to the storage building and Charles enters the passenger's door while Sampson climbs behind the wheel. The truck eases out onto the farm to make its way to the trail. Jonathan waves the truck off along the trail onto the main road. The twins make their way to the field after they unlock the entrance gates. Jonathan waits until they approach him.

"Good morning gentlemen."

"Good morning Mista Jonathan," they reply.

"I have need of your services. What does your schedule look like for the next two days?"

"Suh, we just got our normal days work ta get done before the next delivery."

"Is there any way that the two of you could run this farm while I deliver goods today to our Texas stores? I know for certain that I will return early morning if I leave this very minute."

"Suh you want us ta be the boss?"

"I do not see why not. You two know this farm like the back of your hand. I can not think of any other workers on this farm that match your integrity."

"Yes suh an we make you proud suh."

"Without a doubt I know you will. Now I will load up to leave in a few minutes. After I have left I want you to inform Mr. Kyle that I have left the both of you in charge of the farm. He will in turn report it to Opio just for safety measures. I will call Opio after I have driven to the nearest phone and give him directions in my absence. Again do not tell the others of my whereabouts. And another thing if they should ask let them know that I have Babymouse with me. That is ONLY if they happen to notice her absence. Do you understand?"

"Yes suh. Suh?"

"Yes Aaron?"

"Why is you takin Babymouse?"

"I am taking her near the area where I found her in hopes that I will find her family."

"Suh they gonna think somethin ain't right when they see a white man with a colored girl."

"I did not think of that. What do you suppose I should do?"

Never Underestimate The Power of A Secret Place

"Mista Nathan look like her father take him with you."

"Thanks that is what I shall do. Now remember not a word until I have left the property."

"Yes suh," the twins respond.

Jonathan leaves the two before he heads to the classroom where Lana attends school.

An hour later...

"Ahh, this will not be difficult at all. Nathan brother come near."

Jonathan continues to wave at him until he heads his way.

"Brother we have an emergency. We have a delivery with no one to drive the route."

"Why is that?"

"Myrtle is expected to deliver soon therefore Junebug will not be able to drive and that goes for James also. The others have not been cleared to drive. We expected that this would happen at some point; it appears that we will have to take the delivery."

"How much time do we have?"

"If we move out now we can arrive at the store before dusk then we will be able to make our way back to the farm the same day. We should make it back in the midnight hours otherwise we will have to stay overnight and return in the morning."

"How far will we have to travel?"

"Do not worry yourself. Betty will be here when you return."

"I have no worries; if you pay close attention you will notice that my wife loves me."

"What are you implying?"

"Simply that my wife loves me."

"Are you to imply that Melba does not love me?"

"Brother, do not get your wits in a bind. We have a delivery to make."

"Twins please come this way," calls Jonathan.

The Aaron and Moses begin to walk towards both men while they begin to inspect the truck for the delivery.

"Yes suh?"

"Good morning, Nathan and I have to leave the farm for a scheduled delivery. Charles and Samson are also away on a delivery. I ask that the two of you manage the farm in our absence. If you should experience any difficulties please inform Mr. Kyle. Are we clear?"

"Yes suh."

"Please tell our wives that we have taken a delivery route. I am sure that Betty will be unhappy with the changes in our plans," advises Nathan.

"What plans brother?"

"We made plans to get away for a few days to ourselves."

"Brother every evening you two are away in your room for hours on end. What more could you want?"

"It is too complex to explain brother. Maybe one day we can revisit this subject."

The Aaron and Moses smile at each other while they share in the comical secret. Jonathan looks at the two curious to what can be so humorous then he is reminded that he must get on the road soon.

"Well everything appears to be ready for delivery let us get on the road."

Melba appears on the front terrace with her hands placed on her hips.

"Where are you off to woman," yells Jonathan.

Melba turns towards the entrance then opens the door. SLAM the door closes behind her.

"Now that is how you get rid of a woman my brother."

"One day brother; one of these old days," replies Nathan.

"Get in we have to get on the road, no time to waste."

Never Underestimate The Power of A Secret Place

The engine roars when Jonathan turns the ignition. All of the sudden the truck vibrates. The sound of a child's giggle can be heard inside the truck.

"Did you hear that?"

"Of course not, I think you have begun to lose your mind."

Jonathan begins toward the trail while the truck tosses from side to side.

"Owww!"

"Jonathan stop the truck," Nathan advises.

"We have to get there before the sun sets."

"I demand that you stop the truck this very moment!"

"Allow me to time to pull over."

Jonathan continues to drive further down the trail until he reaches the entrance to the main road. Jonathan peers to his left then right, to his left then right again. He enters the road and turns right onto the main road.

"Jonathan when do you think you may have time to pull over?"

Jonathan turns his head to look at Nathan but Lana's head has blocked his view. Jonathan returns his concentration on the road. He continues to drive without giving notice of Lana's presence.

"I can wait brother."

"I shall pull over once I am off the main road."

Jonathan makes another right onto what used to be dead man's road. Jonathan continues to drive along the road before he gives into Nathan's request.

"I imagine this road is wide enough would you agree? I would rather pull over under some shade. It is unfortunate that someone has cut down all the oak trees that lined the road."

"Do you have any idea who that someone may be," asks Nathan.

Never Underestimate The Power of A Secret Place

"I just wanted to bring it to your attention. There I shall pull under that weeping willow. Those trees are a work of God's wonder would you agree?"

"If it pleases you brother."

Jonathan brings the truck to a stop then turns the engine off. He looks around to secure the area. Nathan stares at Jonathan until he acknowledges him.

Jonathan looks down at Lana then asks," How did you get there?"

Lana does not answer but appears to be distracted by the patterns on her shirt.

Nathan sighs, "Brother what are you up to?"

"Do you accuse me without a cause?"

"The twins have already warned me."

"Brother whatever they have told you cannot possibly hold any validity."

"Well let us see. I was told that if I look behind the driver's seat underneath the pile of blankets I will find the young girl that Mr. Jonathan calls Babymouse. They said that he will take her to find her home. I was also told that I was not needed to drive this route. Did you really think no one would actually report you? I watched you scamper to the schoolhouse and carry the girl to the truck. For over an hour that poor child was left in this dreadfully hot truck. Did you ever think of the child's well being for even one second?"

"Of course I did she has a chip of ice wrapped in a handkerchief to cool her. Do not take her too lightly she is a rather rugged lass I have learned."

"Lana have you eaten anything?"

"No suh."

"Did you bring food for the child?"

"Of course we planned well; did we not Babymouse?"

Lana stares at Jonathan until he becomes uncomfortable.

Never Underestimate The Power of A Secret Place

"Well I suppose we can turn back to return the child to the farm. That is what happens when you undermine my authority," Jonahan squints his eyes at Lana.

Lana begins to cry then leans into Jonathan's arm.

"Now, now Babymouse you brought this on yourself. I have told you time and time again you must follow my directions."

The three of them sit for a moment until Jonathan turns the key in the ignition. The truck begins to vibrate and Lana giggles. Jonathan pulls from underneath the weeping willow and continues to head north on what used to be dead man's road.

"I think it was thoughtful of our new Sheriff to allow us to adopt a more acceptable name for this road. Johnson's Road seems more appropriate don't you think brother?"

"Whatever pleases you brother. I take it that we will not return Lana to Nathan's Place?"

"Whatever for the plan is to return the child to her family."

"How do you suggest we do that?"

"We were able to post pictures of my Angie and Babymouse in the windows of many of the businesses near the jailhouse where we retrieved Babymouse."

"You mean to say where we kidnapped her, did you not brother?"

"Of course not! I do not consider myself a criminal. My intentions were to balance the scales of justice."

"Really, is that what you considered to accomplish when you almost shot a man's hand from his wrist?"

"Of course not; my aim was poor I do admit. I had no intentions to shoot him at all."

"I see. So you erred on the side of injustice at that point?"

"If that is what you wish to believe. I am very certain the gentleman will think twice before he mishandles any young child in my presence. Did you ever consider the scars on Babymouse's left cheek?"

"I never paid it any attention."

"Well had anyone taken the time to consider why I took the action that I did it is possible you would have known that he injured the child. He was twice my size what was I to do? Any decent human being should take the offense when a child is being mishandled regardless of what they may have done."

"What did she do?"

"She entered the store through the front entrance."

"Brother the bible suggests that we live in perilous times. The end is nearer than we have ever imagined."

"Quite so but it did not say that we must surrender to evil," Jonathan argues.

"Either did it say arm yourself with a rifle and attempt to kill at your discretion."

"It was in my possession to protect myself and the child."

"How so?"

"Well he had taken Babymouse by the arm then he threw her to the ground outside of the store. While I kneeled over her, he drew back his hand to strike me."

"You were able to retrieve the rifle from the truck to shoot the man is that what you intend to imply?"

"Of course not, the rifle was at my side for safety measures. I simply carried the rifle inside to purchase necessities. I always keep one in the chamber for incidents such as this."

"Why did you not explain the circumstances to the others?"

"Regardless of what I say or do everyone has come to the conclusion that I have lost my senses."

"Do not be silly. You possess the ability to see, smell, taste and those other senses that I have not mentioned. It is your capacity to think rational thoughts that concern most well all of us. It has become a ritual with you. Every morning like clockwork you must put on a performance."

"That is only so that I do not have to eat those dreadful bran muffins."

"Does that work for you," asks Nathan.

"I must say that it does. Did you know that Melba puts a laxative in your orange juice? Does it work for you," asks Jonathan.

"For me? I must remind you that it is Melba who places a laxative in YOUR orange juice not mine."

"Again, I must ask you; how does it work for you?"

"I have no idea what it is that you are implying."

"For days I have taken your cup of orange juice and switched it with mine. So tell me, does it work for you?"

"You cannot be serious. How did you find out?"

Jonathan looks down at Lana.

"I should have known; if she steals bacon for you what else could she be up too."

"Did you ever wonder why mother is so jolly in the mornings?"

"Why do you ask?"

"I happened to take mother's cup of orange juice this morning. It tastes of vodka."

"You don't say!"

They look at each other with grins.

"It explains why she is so calm during my antics. I think maybe we should render the cabinet of spirits to a vacation for a short period."

Jonathan and Nathan begin to laugh to themselves.

"They will think one of the children have taken the key. I say that shall be our first tryst when we return. That is if your comrade does not reveal our devices."

"My hopes are that we will be successful to locate her family on this trip. She was able to recognize some landmarks. Maybe someone has seen the pictures and recognize the child."

"Are you sure there is not a bounty on your head?"

"Nonsense, furthermore my only concern is to find Babymouse's family."

"You will have more to be concerned about if you address this child as a rodent in the presence of her family."

"It is a heartfelt gesture."

"No it ain't, it's our secret word."

"Not anymore. You just gave our secret away," Jonathan says with a frown. "Angie would never give our secrets to the enemy."

"Jonathan I am not your enemy; I am your brother."

"Sometimes I do not know who you are."

Silence falls while Jonathan continues along the country road to Texas. Nathan nods off to sleep while Lana sings to Jonathan. A few hours later they enter the state of TEXAS. The southern border reveals a white sandy beach with crystal blue waters. Nathan awakens from his slumber.

"I think you are about to miss our turn."

"I am sure this is the way."

"Must I say it again? You have missed our turn."

"We can no longer travel that particular road."

"Why not? That is our usual route to Freeman's town."

"Not anymore."

"Why not anymore?"

"That is the road that leads to the store where I..."

Nathan interrupts.

"Where you shot the poor man? So there IS a bounty on your head."

"I ask again. Is there a possibility that you may deter us from our mission?"

"Your mission should be not to get yourself and the child killed and myself must I add."

"Brother must you overreact?"

"Am I really? So where are we off too?"

"Before we drop off the goods we must stop by this small hole in the wall store. Just to see if anyone has heard anything."

"In other words you want to make certain that your picture is not posted in the window along with the others."

"Of course not; it is the girls who are missing."

"That is correct but you could possibly be a wanted man."

Jonathan drives further before he comes to a fork in the road. There alongside the east of the road is an old weathered shack. It appears to have once been a shotgun house with only one window which faces the road and one that faces the field. The dirt road blends with the walk way to the entrance to carry trails of dirt into the store. Outside sits an old colored man in overalls with a plaid weathered shirt. The colors have worn off the shirt so that no one can imagine the original color of the shirt. He nods after Jonathan and Nathan step out of the truck. Lana jumps down like she is familiar with the store.

"Have you been here before," asks Nathan.

She shrugs her shoulders.

"I have some goods I promised the store keeper the last time we visited."

Jonathan climbs onto the bed of the truck soon he eases a large burlap bag to the ground.

"Brother, please take this to the store keeper."

Jonathan leans back into the trucks bed then pulls another large burlap bag filled with items. He eases himself down from the truck then swings the bag over his shoulder. A young colored boy comes from inside of the store to take the bag from Jonathan's hand.

"Did you think I would forget," Jonathan smiles.

"No suh Mistah Jon you neva let us down."

"Where is your beautiful mother?"

"She inside an papa inside too," the young boy chuckles.

"Is he is ready for me?"

"Yes suh, he say he ain't had a good fight in a long time."

"Well we do not want to disappoint him do we?"

Jonathan follows the colored boy into the store while he hides behind him.

"Where is my woman," Jonathan shouts. "Did you miss me sweet Bessie Mae?"

"Who dat," asks the large blind man who sits near the end of the counter. "Bugga git my rifle."

"What difference will it make you cannot see me."

Jonathan wiggles his head.

"Ain't no difference, I jus aim east of that jar of chutney an I bet I git ya right between tha eyes."

Jonathan looks to his right. On a tall shelf is a row of jars that contain chutney.

"You do say now?"

"I think that's what I said. Now who dat calls for my woman?"

The blind man cocks the rifle.

"Clarence have you ever handled a rifle?"

"Ever since I was a chile. Now what ya got ta say?"

"Now Clarence I must warn you I am a master shooter."

"I ain't mind ya bein no masta shootah. What I do mind if ya brung yo rifle in my sto. You musta ain't read that sign befo ya came in my sto. It distinctly say, no rifles allow'd in my sto."

"But you..."

Clarence interrupts.

"Now let me finish."

Clay aims the rifle in Jonathan's direction.

"Except Clay's rifle."

Nathan leans against the counter to witness the tryst between the two.

"You can stop me at any time brother."

Never Underestimate The Power of A Secret Place

"I think you have managed quite nicely, master shooter. Please carry on."

"Brotha, ya mean yo momma had tha nerves ta make anotha one of you? You enough all by yoself."

Nathan laughs out loud.

"Oh, you know him too well."

"My name is Clay."

"It is at pleasure to meet you. My name is Nathan."

"You told me that your name was Clarence."

"Ta you its Clarence ta yo brotha it's Clay."

"When..."

Clarence interrupts Jonathan.

"I let ya know when ya can call me Clay."

Jonathan looks in disbelief.

"Wheres my little girl?"

"Lana runs into the arms of Clarence."

"Has these men been good ta ya?"

Lana shakes her head.

"She says yes," reports Jonathan.

"I ain't heard her say nothin. Did ya hear her say somethin?"

"No suh."

"How she lookin right now?"

"She look good papa."

"Her head combed?"

"Yes suh, must be some woman round."

"Ain't no woman gonna marry ol' Jonnny."

"I am afraid to say he is married," replies Nathan.

"That's what they do when they cain't wait ta leave home; they marry a fool."

"Now I beg to differ. I consider myself to be a superb husband and father."

Never Underestimate The Power of A Secret Place

"You can consider what ya want. Anytime a man come on to anotha man's woman in front of him, you cain't have no common sense."

"Mr. Clarence."

"Just call me Clay."

Jonathan turns to look at Clay then at Nathan.

"Ya see, that's what I mean right there. Around here ya look at somebody like he jus did an they's likely to hand yo behind to ya. If ya know what I mean."

Clay laugh resonates throughout the store. Soon the others join in.

Jonathan continues to look confused at everyone.

"Johnny don't take dis ta heart. Im jus jivin ya man. It has ta be God that sent ya to my sto. I was barely keepin my doors open an feedin my own fam'ly. Then here you come along lookin for yo baby girl. I still cain't believe yo baby girl is colored. I figa ya got ta be a good man helpin me keep my sto open. I prayed I did tha right thang lettin ya leave wit that colored girl. My heart tole me there's sumptin to ya. Bessie Mae come fix these boys a plate."

Bessie Mae appears from the back of the store. She resembles Melba so that Nathan is taken back. Nathan looks at Jonathan.

"It is amazing isn't it?"

Nathan nods.

"What so amazin?"

"She is the spitting image of Melba."

"That is what he say. He say they look jus alike. One day I likin ta meet yo wife Johnny. You neva know we could be some kin. Rememba they tore our families apart when they brought us ova here."

"What ya boys like," asks Bessie Mae.

"Anything you have is fine with me," Nathan answers.

"Take ya seat boys and rest yoself. Bugga take this rifle an watch they truck while they git somethin in they bellies."

The aroma of cornbread drifts from the back.

"Smell like ya gittin tha special tonight boys."

"What is the special?"

"Red beans an rice wit a lil cornbread on tha side. That's good eatin aroun here."

"Is there any meat?"

"Jonathan we are guest," whispers Nathan.

"Johnny I'se givin ya tha best I got right now. Besides we cain't keep tha meat too long befo it go bad."

"I can have ice delivered to your store."

"That ain't tha problem we ain't got nowhere ta keep tha ice ta keep tha meat."

"I am more than capable to get you what you need. Your store is near our routes so we can include you in the deliveries. I will have my workers deliver an ice box in the next few days."

"Johnny, I ain't no proud man now I give thanks fo everythin I can git. But I cain't pay ya back no time soon."

"Clarence the day I came to your store to hide from the men that were after me never did you ask why. You retrieved your rifle then stood beside me shoulder to shoulder to protect Babymouse and myself."

"I knows those fellas a long time Johnny. They neva mean no good. I figa if ya a white man runnin from tha bad white man ya gotta be a good white man. I figa you was protectin tha colored girl tha way she was holdin on ta ya. Ain't no chile gonna hold on ta nobody if they a bad somebody. God musta sent ya this way again cause I think I found that girls kin folk."

"You don't say."

"I keep tellin you that's what I said. Sometime I cain't understand you people."

"What people?"

"You people Johnny," answers Clay.

He becomes cross.

Never Underestimate The Power of A Secret Place

"He merely implies that he cannot believe what you have said when he says, 'You don't say.' It is a comment we often make," explains Nathan.

"I would like to know why you consider me, 'you people'," asks Jonathan.

"It's been said that white people an black people ain't tha same."

"What could possibly make us different?"

"Well now befo I was blind I do rememba that white people look white and black people look black."

"People come in many colors what is your point? I have seen black cows and horses also white cows and horses. No one has mentioned their differences. It is pure ignorance. There are those of us who dwell in God's wisdom then there are those that consider our differences because it allows them to divide and conquer. They can only measure wholeness if it is seen with the physical eye. That is the manner in which they measure a man's worth. But in truth no one possesses the ability but God to know the measure of any man."

Silence falls around them. Bessie Mae begins to serve the meals to the brothers.

"Bugga come on in an fix ya plate. Come on back here wit me so I can fix ya a plate Lana."

Jonathan looks into her eyes and soon he recognizes the fear he saw the day he found her in the jail house.

"I promise I shall not leave you until I find your family. I need you to get warm nourishment for your body before we resume our travels. Also make sure you visit the lavatory before we leave."

"Johnny we ain't got no lavatory."

"Brother I do not think they call it lavatory around here," says Nathan.

"What can it possibly be?"

"We go ta tha can here," replies Clay.

"Make sure you wash up before you eat Babymouse."

Lana walks around the counter, before she passes Clay she looks into his eyes. He turns to avoid her gaze but she continues to stare.

"It is not polite to stare Babymouse," Jonathan admonishes.

"She ain't hurtin nothin. Git on now an eat ya a little sumptin."

Lana eases around Clay before she follows Bessie Mae to the back room. It appears to be a kitchen coupled with a storage area for the store. Jonathan observes the interaction between Bessie Mae and Lana. Before Lana is handed her plate she holds out her hands to Bessie Mae. Bessie Mae wipes them with a cloth that hangs over her shoulder. Lana picks up her plate then takes it to the edge of the sink. She stands there to eat her food like it was a daily ritual.

"How old do you think Babymouse could be now," asks Jonathan.

"She be about twelve years old about now," answers Clay.

"But she is so petite to be that old," Jonathan remarks.

"She was a small chile."

"How can you tell?"

Clay sits silent for a moment.

"I hear somebody lookin fo tha girl a little ways down tha road."

"There are two roads which one do you speak of?"

"One road take ya to tha white side of town an tha otha take ya to tha colored side of town."

"Which one takes me to the person in search of Babymouse?"

"Ya want me ta take em papa?"

Clay shuffles his feet for a moment before he attempts to stand up.

"They don't take kindly ta white folk. I need ta send a word befo I send ya down there."

"Papa they know she comin. They say she can stay til we git paid up."

"HUSH YO MOUTH BOY!"

Everyone looks at Bugga.

"Git back there an fill tha slop jars befo sun down."

"Yes papa."

"Excuse me but may I interrupt?"

"Yo interruptin ain't welcome here," bellows Clarence.

Bugga makes his way to the kitchen.

"Bugga?"

"Yes suh."

"I need you to help me for a moment. Go to the truck; inside you will find a large bag of items for Babymouse."

"I hope ya ain't plannin on leavin her. We got enough troubles on our hands."

"Go on now, do as I say."

Bugga inches past Clay. He is slow to walk towards the entrance of the store. He waits for Clay to command him to come back but he does not.

"Go on, I shall let you know when you may return. Just stand near the truck until I call for you."

Clay's face turns in the direction of the door.

"Ms. Bessie Mae can you please join us for a moment?"

"Anythang you say Mista Jon."

She reaches the counter then wipes the sweat from her face. Jonathan looks down at the counter for a moment.

"Someone kidnapped my baby girl a few years before I found Babymouse. I remember the day when I fell into a deep sleep. The Lord revealed to me a girl or maybe a young lady, however I was not mindful of her age at the time. All that I can recollect is that she was my baby girl and that I had found her. I am reminded of her every day and I pray daily for her safe return. I would give everything I own just so that Babymouse would have been my Angie but she was not. I knew when I found Babymouse that something appeared inhumane and my heart cautioned me not to leave her although my mind considered that it was possible she did something to be in jail. I went with my heart because my heart is God's compass. I will go where ever he tells me to go and do whatever he tells me to do."

"The day I came into your store Clay I knew that you knew Babymouse but I was not sure to what degree. Babymouse ran to you while we sought refuge here and I observed you push her away. I did not question why because I knew that God will reveal the truth eventually. To be honest with you I was not concerned with the condition of your business. I was more concerned with why you would deny your daughter's right to be with her family."

"Now YOU crossed tha line!"

"Jonathan you are clearly out of line," Nathan agrees.

"Am I? Did you ever wonder why I began to call Lana by the name of Babymouse?"

"Brother that is not important you cannot..."

"I CALL HER BABYMOUSE because that is her name. Jonathan stands up to gain his composure. I cannot let you do this. I will no longer pretend that Babymouse is not your daughter. How could you do this to your child? This is a child that God has given to you both to protect."

Ms. Bessie Mae rests her head in the folds of her arms on the counter then begins to weep. Jonathan turns away from the others before he begins to shed tears. Clay leans back against the back of his chair and lets out a sigh while Nathan looks on.

"Johnny I ain't got tha same rights you got, answers Clay. You can walk in a jailhouse an take whateva you want. They kill me right where I stand if I did tha same. You say ya die for yo baby. But tha truth is ya prob'bly won't. I know I'se gonna die.

Never Underestimate The Power of A Secret Place

Ain't no doubt bout it. Everybody in this here sto gonna die if we don't do what tha white man say. Cause they can do it. A cow is worth mo than a colored. Let me say this again, a dog is mo impo'tant than a colored. A colored is tha lowest creature on this here earth accordin to tha white man. But theres one thang I do know. A man cain't know everythang," Clay shakes his head. "Only one man know everythang an that man is God Almighty."

"Maybe I shoulda fight fo my chile; but I figa if I do they kill me, my woman an my boy. All I can do is pray an wait fo God to bring my chile to me. That's all I have is faith in my God. When you come runnin in here wit my baby, I knew you was a good man. So I figa let him take her wit him. That way they cain't come an git her NO MO! Now ain't God good?"

Clay slams his hand on the counter.

"They stole my baby from me an did what they please ova an ova. I say why God? Cause he say he love tha chil'ren. I say if he love tha chil'ren then why mine suffer so? I ain't got no answer for that. I'se so angry I could hear my blood rushin through my veins. One mornin I woke up an I say to Bessie Mae I cain't open my eyes. She say yo eyes is open, then I say I cain't see nothin. I jus cries. I neva feel so low in my life, but when you came into tha sto I knew Babymouse was wit ya. I ain't push her away. I was reachin for her cause I cain't see her no mo. She don't know her papa's cain't see. She think I want her ta go to tha white man so he ain't gonna kill nobody. I allow you ta take her cause I knows ya was a good man. An if she stay they gonna come an takes her agin."

Jonathan wipes the tears from his eyes before he walks over to Clarence. Clarence does not appear to acknowledge his presence. Jonathan leans in then wraps his arms around him. They embrace for a moment while Jonathan motions for Bessie Mae to join them. The three of them embrace. Jonathan leans over to kiss Bessie Mae on her forehead. Clarence breaks the embrace.

"Did ya kiss my woman," Clarence asks.

Jonathan steps back then looks at Clarence to read his body language.

"It was just a natural gesture. I do it all the time."

"Well somebody gotta teach ya not ta mess with anotha man's woman."

Clay reaches for his rifle but he realizes Bugga has it. He reaches behind the counter then pulls out a wooden stick.

He points it at Jonathan then yells, "POW, POW, POW!"

Everyone breaks out into laughter. Bugga rushes into the store to see the commotion before the laughter dies down. The three men observe Babymouse while she stands in the doorway.

"Tell me why do they believe they have the right to take your child at liberty?"

"Ain't nobody round here own nothin, Johnny. We pay tha landowner ta stay on this land ta make a livin."

"Is that so? What has that got to do with Babymouse?"

"They takes my chile when I'se ain't got tha money. They keep Babymouse til I can pay 'em. If they feed her they want mo money. I owes 'em so much money I cain't keep count. The last time they take Babymouse I figa I neva see her agin."

"Why is that so?"

"I neva paid 'em tha money they ask fo befo."

"How much do you owe the landowner?"

Bessie Mae reaches underneath her shirt then pulls out a piece of paper. She unfolds the paper before she hands it to Jonathan He witnesses two signatures. George Rey and it appears to be Clarence's handwriting.

"The note says twenty-four dollars on the first of December. How long have you had this note?"

"Eva since they came an took ha."

"Well it has been at least four years ago since I have taken Babymouse from the jailhouse. Do you think you could recall how long she has been away from your home?"

"No suh, I do rememba they give me ten days ta come up wit tha money."

"Who gave you ten days to come up with the money?"

"Mistah William an tha Sheriff."

"What would happen if you did not have the money?"

"I always has some money. Tha only times they take Babymouse is when it time ta pay. Sometimes I pay two dollars an sometimes I pay fourteen dollars but I neva knows how much to have so most times I ain't got what they ask for."

"When they return Babymouse what condition is she in?"

"Johnny I done tole ya all I wanna rememba."

Jonathan takes in a deep breath then releases it little by little.

"When is the last time you have seen the men who collect the money?"

"I jus seen Mista William the otha day. He havin hard time like the rest of us. I gave him a lot of those potatoes you left me the last time you come. He was mighty grateful. He ain't ask for no mo money. He say I can pay him wit food til he git back on his feet."

"What happened to the sheriff?"

"They say he run outa town. The jail house ain't no mo."

"What do you mean by that?"

"I mean they burns it down, down ta the ground," Clay laughs. "We afraid the white folk might start some trouble with no sheriff aroun but everybody stays in they place, atleast fo right now."

"I am on my way to make a delivery a few miles down the road. How would you like to ride with me to Freeman's town?"

"I hears alot bout that town. They say its a colored town but a few white folk live there too. They say they don't go to tha can down there. They got water an lights in they places. They say they got a sto bigga than mine an a whole lot fancier too," Bessie Mae recalls. " I sho would like to go and..."

Bessie Mae pauses.

"And what Bessie Mae?"

"I cain't leave my family. I mean bugga he gone be a man one day but I don't think he ready jus yet."

"Brother would you be a gentleman and watch over the store along with Clarence's family while I take him to visit the Freemans?"

"It would be my pleasure of course with Mr. Clay's approval."

"To think of it I can also bring Bessie Mae with us."

"Now I jus might considа yo offa."

They all look at each other with smiles.

"We better go Jason will expect his merchandise to arrive soon."

Bessie Mae walks around the counter then reaches her hand out to Clarence. He takes it so that she can lead him to the entrance. Bugga leaps into the chair where Clarence once sat.

"I suppose you are the man in charge Bugga," Jonathan says while he follows the two outside.

"Brother I will be back shortly. Jason has enough hands to expedite the process to unload the truck. Are you armed brother?"

"Yes, I must say I am fully loaded," Nathan smiles.

"We should return before nightfall."

"No need to hurry all is well."

The two embrace and within seconds Babymouse stands at Jonathan's side. He looks down into her gloomy eyes then rubs his chin.

"Not this time Babymouse. You will come with me the next time we leave for good."

Nathan grabs one of Babymouses braids and tugs at it.

"Tag you are it!"

He then hurries to hide between the isles of shelves in the store to disguise his whereabouts. The shelves are bare giving Babymouse the advantage in the game. Nathan pretends that he is invisible although he is aware that Babymouse approaches him. Babymouse stands beside him with her arms folded. Nathan continues to maintain his crouched position.

"Uncle Nate, I found ya!"

Nathan brings his head from between his knees then looks into her face.

"You forgot to tag me. I will have to hide again."

"Ugh,"Babymouse sighs. "Its my turn ta hide."

"I do not think that is the correct manner in which to play the game Lana."

"Uncle Nate I found you now it my turn ta hide," she whines.

"That pitiful expression does not work for me. Alright you win. Just remember you must play the game by the rules."

Nathan rises to his feet while Babymouse giggles to herself.

"What do you find so humorous?"

"You slow like a turtle," she giggles.

"Go on hide before I change my mind."

"You has ta count."

"One he pauses... two pause... three."

Babymouse scurries away before Nathan straightens up. He peeks around with one eye.

"Eight, nine, ten he counts. Ready or not here I come."

Bugga slumps back into his seat.

"Ya shoulda neva let her hide."

"Why not?"

"Ya ain't neva gonna find ha. She probably in ha secret place."

"I have never lost a game of hide and seek. Where do you think she might be?"

"I cain't tell ya."

Never Underestimate The Power of A Secret Place

"Why not?"
"You gotta follow tha rules."
"Of course."

Meanwhile...
"I reckon ya wonda what kinda papa give they chile away?"

"Clay there was a time when I would have never imagined why you did what you did. But I believe if you can come to a place where you can trust God with your circumstances he will deliver you out of them. To be honest with you I wanted so much that it would be my Angie in that jail cell. It angered me so much when I saw Babymouse's face. But I knew that what I must do for Babymouse is what I would want done for my Angie."

"Babymouse attached to Nathan right away. She would not let me touch her during the ride back home. When Nathan left her alone with me she would often cry until he returned. It pained me to think that someone could change the heart of an innocent child to fear someone they never knew. I never imagined that my daughter would return home to a father who resembles the person who had harmed her. I often wondered if she would be able to love me again through her pain."

"I kept my distance from Babymouse when we arrived home. I believed God's promise for my child not someone else's. I was determined she was not going to replace my baby girl. She began to bring me bacon; something that Angie would do every morning for me. Then the day came for the twins fifteenth birthday Everyone prepared to gather together and I just could not bring myself to participate in the festivities. I took to the corn field to bury my sorrows in a bottle of the finest brew I ever tasted. Then all of the sudden I began to fall apart and somehow Babymouse was able to find me. She wrapped her arms around my head then she prayed for me. I will always remember the day. She whispers, 'Hosanna! Hosanna Lord! Thank you Jesus! Thaaaank you Jesus!'

Never Underestimate The Power of A Secret Place

When I looked up at Babymouse she began to wave her hands in the air. I could only watch in amazement. Afterwards tears began to fall from her cheeks onto my head. That went on for some time until she looked into my eyes. She said to me, 'God say he keep his promise wit ya.' She took the bottle from me and poured out my whiskey. She shook the bottle until the earth soaked up the last drop. Babymouse took my face into her hands again and she said to me, 'Let God bring her to ya an dats when ya gonna find her.' "She said that matter of factly," smiles Jonathan.

"Sometimes we think Babymouse is one of God's angels. Sometimes she say things a chile ain't supposed ta know. One night she tole me God gonna take her ta a new home where Mista William cain't find her no mo. She say God got anotha family waitin fo her. I'se scared when she say that. I think she say she goin ta heaven. Johnny when you say ya gonna take her home wit ya I'se know they cain't take her no mo. I knows that's what Babymouse tryin ta say. I'se hopin she stay with ya an have a good life."

"Bessie Mae I pray that everyone on earth have a good life. Babymouse must be with her family. Not only that but she needs a safe place where she can grow up. I hope that I have accomplished that. I have purchased some land in Freeman's town. I have also placed a few modules there for families to call home. The Freeman's own the store in that town also a cafe. I am pretty sure they could use some help to run the cafe. The sheriff there is Mr. Kennedy he is a longtime friend of the family. You will find him to be a very fair and respectful man. My hopes are that you will relocate your family to Freeman's town for a better life. If there are other families who you know may want to relocate feel free to invite them along. We only expect that they are law abiding people who share the same expectations."

Jonathan slows to make a right hand turn then continues until he reaches Nathan's Store.

Never Underestimate The Power of A Secret Place

The following morning the brothers are on their way to return to Nathan's Place. It has been arranged that Clarence and his family will start a new life in Freeman's town.

"I was hoping to say goodbye to Babymouse."

"I have the feeling you will see her again on one of your concocted trips to search for Angie."

"It will become more difficult to convince the others that I must continue the search for Angie now that Babymouse has found her family."

"You will find a way I am sure of it."

"Brother we must not forget that mother has a habit that we must attend to."

"I am glad that we can agree upon this; although it is your mother who has lost her wits. My mother would never do such a thing," implies Nathan.

"Perhaps so but I have also overheard her intentions to court one of the workers."

"Is that so?"

"You must keep watch of her activities. For heaven's sake how will we ever explain another pregnancy in the house?"

"Brother you cannot be serious. Did father have the talk with you?"

"Indeed he has and he confirmed that it is the woman that becomes impregnated. We must be mindful of their activities. With that being said, it may serve as a deterrent to allow the women their daily spirits but now we must entice the others to partake of a glass of spirits?"

"It is not that simple."

"Of course it is we shall implement my mother's deceitful practices. I will continue my normal morning rants which will cause them to leave the kitchen. We will then add a concoction of vodka or bourbon which ever you prefer to their orange juice before they return. Soon we will have them under our control."

"Brother, that does not appear to be a healthy plan may I make a suggestion?"

"If you must I am open to suggestions."

"We will secure the wine cabinet."

"Yo, you was a cool cat back in the day. What happened to the little girl?"

"We will continue this story another time son."

10
A SUSTAINING PLACE

"Pull over behind Nathan's vehicle and let's see what kind of problem he is having."

Shawn pulls off the road onto a grassy field then inches up to Nathan's car before he puts the truck in park. Jonathan steps out of the truck and approaches the passenger door. Cindy rolls her window down so that the two men can converse.

"Brother is everything alright," asks Jonathan.

"I am running low on fuel and decided to pull over to refuel with the emergency fuel we have on hand. There should be a colored service station further down the road and I will top off there."

"It sounds like a plan. I will take over the driving for now and give the poor lad a rest. Something tells me we made a good decision to bring him along. He will be a great addition to our family."

Nathan exits the automobile and both men meet at the trunk. Nathan unlocks the trunk and the hood springs up. Inside attached to the trunks interior is a metal gas can. Nathan loosens the clamps to retrieve the gas can then unscrews the cap. Taped to the side of the metal can is a funnel to transfer the contents of the can into the car's tank. Nathan completes this task then returns the funnel to its rightful place on the side of the can. He hands the can to Jonathan who takes the can and places it inside the bed of the truck. Both men return to their vehicles then continue on the road that leads to the first service station they encounter. Once they reach the nearest service station Nathan pulls alongside the gas pump that faces the station and Jonathan pulls in alongside the gas pump that faces the road. Nathan exits his vehicle and is approached by two attendants.

"Where's you goin boy," asks one of the attendants.

"Excuse me, are you talking to me," Nathan asks.

"Do you speak English boy?"

"I speak English, Kiswahili and French as well," Nathan replies.

Both men surround him to leave no room for Nathan to escape while Cindy exits the car and approach the group of men.

"What do you think you are doing? Leave my uncle alone," she demands.

Jonathan has now approached the group angered by what he just witnessed.

"Now it appears to me that you have incurred a problem," announces Jonathan.

"Who are you," asks one of the attendants.

"I am his brother. My name is Jonathan Johnson."

"Well yo brotha ain't welcomed here. We reserves tha right ta deny our business to yo brotha. Now yo business is welcomed here anytime but yo brotha betta neva show his colored behind here again."

"I understand now if you will assist me I need to refill my emergency supply if it pleases you."

Jonathan hands the empty gas can to one of the attendants who cautiously resign from his position as guard. He continues to eye the group while they disperse from the circle. Nathan and Cindy return to their vehicle while they wait until Jonathan has paid for the gasoline before returning to the truck. Nathan pulls off while he eases out onto the road. He looks for Jonathan in his rearview mirror before picking up speed. Nathan continues another thirty miles down the road before he pulls off the road again. Jonathan pulls over behind him and retrieves the gasoline can from the bed of the truck. He raises the license plate to reveal the opening to the gasoline tank then pours the contents into the mouth of the opening. Jonathan approaches the driver's side door and peers in.

"We should be able to reach another station in a moment and you can top off there. It serves as a reminder to continue the expansion of our stores so that our encounters of ignorance will be reduced; However, I think that we alone will never eradicate it at its very core."

"Have you given up hope?"

"Fortunately ignorance is not innate rather it is taught; therefore if those of us who believe in God's mercy extends to one another the same mercies that God extends to us we will prevail. But we have to also remember that not everyone serves a merciful God."

"Well let us get on our way before night falls. We will need to find someplace to stay for the night."

Jonathan returns to the truck and waits for Nathan to take the road and soon their travels head south for Texas. A few hours pass and Nathan pulls over into a service station a few miles past the Texas County line. Nathan's car begins to show signs that it has consumed the last of the contents from the gasoline can. His car sputters into an unfamiliar station that appears to be abandoned. Nathan remains in his car until Jonathan's truck appears in close proximity. A white male exits the service station's office with a concerned look on his face. He approaches Nathan who now stands at the rear of his car while he waits for Jonathan to park. The two men look at each other for a moment until the service attendant extends his hand.

"How can I assist ya mistah?"

"I need to fill up if you don't mind."

"No siree that is why I am here to serve my customers. What will it be?"

"I would appreciate it if you top off my tank."

"Whateva ya want. Levi, he yells! We got a customa, get ova here son."

A young colored boy appears from the concrete shack with a metal roof. He wears overalls without shirt or shoes. His overalls are weathered and too big for him which causes them to gather around his feet. Dirt accumulates in the folds of the jean material while he continues his routine care for the customers. It appears they have not been washed for days. The young boy approaches the men with a full smile that adorns his face.

"Good aftanoon suh, I git ya filled up in no time."

Jonathan has now approached the men and extends his hand to the colored boy who shakes his hand with passion afterwards Jonathan shakes the hand of the other attendant.

"My name is Jonathan and this is my brother Nathan."

They both look in amazement until Jonathan breaks the silence.

"And who might this young man be?"

"My name Levi suh an this my boss. His name Mistah Gray he own tha place."

"It is good to meet you. How long have you been in business?"

"Oh I reckon about ten years. My boss hand it ova to me and I been workin here eva since. Levi comes around here an helps out to earn a little extra money."

"Is this the only tank you have for your station?"

"Yes suh, this was the first service station around here when they came ta be. You past the new station they built just a few miles up tha road from here; they gits most of tha business around here. I gets most of the colored folks business around here cause they don't serve coloreds up the road."

"The station could use some repairs don't you think," Jonathan eyes Gray.

"We don't bring in enough to repair tha place just enough to feed our families an buy more fuel. Most of tha colored git fuel on credit and pay when they can."

"I would like to invest in businesses like yours that make sacrifices to those less fortunate. Can I interest you in a partnership?"

"This place is all I got. I cain't afford to let somebody come an take it up from unda me."

"That is not my goal. I want you to receive an increase for all the good you do for others. God has blessed me so that I can be a blessing to someone else and that someone else seems to be you. Let me explain my intentions; I can help you restore the physical condition of your business and install another gas pump to meet your demand. I can also add you to our route so that we may deliver daily necessities that your customers may want to purchase; thereby meeting the needs of the people whom you serve."

"It sounds like one of those too good to be true notions if ya ask me. You givin me something an I don't owe ya nothin in return. That sounds fishy to me."

"Me too," Levi adds.

"That is not the idea that I want to convey. What I am trying to say is that I can help you to improve your business then when your business gets off the ground I can help you maintain it by selling you the products you need to increase your clientele. To be honest with you had we not run out of gas we would have never patronized your establishment. I initially thought it was an abandoned building which could be the reason why most of your potential customers do not come here."

"People have told me that before but I don't have the cash to fix this place up."

"I do so what do you say?"

Gray thinks to himself for a moment while everyone looks on.

"Can I talk it over with Levi? He like my sounding board when we have a problem."

"Be my guest."

Gray and Levi leave the men to discuss the matter. Cindy Lou, Angie Lou and Marlon step from their vehicles to stretch. There is a light cool breeze that relieves them from the midday heat. They are surrounded by miles of highway lined with trees and high grass. Cars slow down and appear that they are going to pull into the station but instead increase their speed to continue their journey. Soon both men return to the group.

"Can we put this in writing that way we know what we agrees to."

Jonathan scratches his head.

"Do you happen to know where the nearest motel is around here?"

"I thought we were talkin business?"

"We are but I will need to settle in somewhere for the night then we can work on a contract that we can all agree upon."

"There's a motel down the road behind this station. It's owned by the folks that own the Benford motel up in tha city. They my kin folk even though we all don't see eye to eye sometimes."

"That's with every family. We have patronized the Benford motel and found it to be a wonderful experience. I am sure we will enjoy the accommodations down the road."

"Tell them that Levi sent ya. His momma works the kitchen down there."

"Well now that our living arrangements are settled we will need to pay for your services and get settled in. Nathan and I can return afterwards and draw up the contract. Fortunately I have my typewriter with me in the truck; I will type it up so that it will appear to be a professional document. How much do I owe you for your services?"

"We ain't pumped tha gasoline yet. Are ya filling up both of yo cars?

"Yes that is my plan."

"Levi start pumpin the gas in tha car and if you pull your truck around I can pump your gasoline on tha other side."

Within minutes both vehicles have been filled with gasoline and the attendant is paid for his services to also include a sizeable tip. Nathan pulls off to follow the directions given by Levi. He turns onto a dirt road that follows alongside the service station. Once he approaches a group of trees just to the left of the road a two story house appears. The house appears to be protected by the many trees that surround it. There is a dirt trail that portrays as a drive east of the house and it extends to the rear of the house. The trees pose as a cover to conceal the patrons that visit there. The house is a massive red brick building with windows of various heights and widths. At the rear of the house it appears that another smaller frame house had been attached to the brick home. Once everyone has exited their vehicles they proceed to the rear of the house to find instructions that direct them to the entrance that faces north. When they circle the home to the west they find five round tables covered with plastic decorative tablecloths. The tables and chair are made of iron with various designs and painted with its own color that sets each of the tables and chairs apart from the others. There are steps that lead to a wooden screened door with instructions that directs the group to return to the east of the building and continue north to reach the front entrance. They approach steps that run the width of the porch with only four steps in height. Once onto the porch there is a red brick encasing on each side of the porch that surrounds the porch. Placed strategically on each side of the entrance is a swing that faces the center of the porch. A wooden screen door similar to the one at the rear of the house adorns the front entrance. Jonathan knocks firmly and waits for an answer. Soon an elderly caucasian woman approaches the door. She appears with a white apron wrapped around her waist while her attire is a floral simple dress and brown leather loafers adorn her feet. Her hair reveals years of auburn coloring that has been fashioned into a beehive. Freckles adorn her face to compliment her selection of hair color. She is a petite woman with a soft gentle voice.

"How can I help ya?"

"Good afternoon, my name is Jonathan Johnson and this is my family. I would like to inquire about overnight lodging if available."

"You're more than welcome to step inside. Now the coloreds will have to wait in the back and someone will be there to serve them."

"Excuse me but we are traveling together," Jonathan informs her.

"Makes no difference, coloreds get served at the back."

"Maybe I should explain."

"Ain't no explainin. Coloreds get served at the back and that's the way it is aroun here. You people must be from up north. Like I said befo, tha coloreds gets served in the back."

"Brother it is well with me. Shawn and I will wait in the back," Nathan offers.

"No brother, either we will enter through this door together or we will camp in our vehicles. We will not bow down to oppression."

"Now what will it be? I ain't got all day."

"We will secure our own lodging for the night."

The elderly woman turns and disappears into the background of darkness. Jonathan and the others return to their vehicles while they discuss where they will camp for the night.

"Maybe we can camp near the service station for the night. I just don't consider it safe to be on the road in the middle of the night." Let us meet with Gray or Levi and secure a place to park."

Once on the road that leads back to the service station they pass Levi heading in the direction of the motel. Jonathan pulls closer and rolls down his window.

"Levi I have an offer for you. We are in need of lodging for the night and we would like to secure an area near the service station tonight. Is it possible?"

"Suh, there's rooms at tha motel. My motha she tha cook. She can get ya in tha back door."

"I am sorry Levi but we cannot accept the offer. Can we make an offer for you?"

"Suh tha motel belongs ta Mistah Gray. His motha run tha place. He can make a way ta get ya a room."

Levi turns and begins to walk in the direction of the service station. Jonathan eases up next to him and offers him a ride.

"Get inside you can ride with us."

"My motha ain't gonna let me take rides wit strangers." Go on ahead an I meet ya."

Jonathan continues on at a slow pace so that he does not stir up the dust from the dirt road. It is not long before Levi approaches Gray while he attempts to lock up the station. Their voices are low while they engage in an intense dialogue. Gray hands the chains to Levi who begins to wrestle with attaching the chains to the door. Gray now leans against Jonathan's truck before he exits.

"You have ta excuse my motha she cain't seem to accept that things done changed in this world. She tries to keep tha old ways and I tells her things done changed for tha good. She neva let Levi and his motha come through tha front door and she cooks for tha motel. Tha whites ain't rented in a long time. I tells her to let the coloreds stay in tha front rooms but she won't listen. We never have any trouble out of tha coloreds and they help fix tha place up sometimes. I can get you settled in once I lock up tha place."

"Gray I appreciate your hospitality but if we can pay to camp out here that will be enough for the night."

"Daddy I would rather stay at the motel. I just don't think we will be safe out in the open," Cindy Lou suggests.

"Why do you have to get all girly on me now? There is no way that my brother and daughter is going to receive second class service because of the color of their skin."

"Daddy, what about Shawn?"

"What about him? He hasn't earned his weight to be a Johnson just yet. There are trials and tribulations that he has to endure before he becomes one of us. It is an honor to be a member of this family," Jonathan adds.

"Okay daddy whatever you say."

"Why don't you guys hop into the bed of the truck and we can give it another try," Jonathan offers Gray and Levi.

Gray hops in while Jonathan backs out of the service station with Nathan close behind. Levi begins a slow trot before he is soon running alongside the truck. He takes a leap and successfully lands with one foot on the back fender of the truck. He continues to ride in that fashion until the truck enters the drive to the motel then he jumps off. Once they have parked they exit their vehicles heading in the direction of the front of the entrance with Gray leading the way. Gray climbs the steps to the house to find that his mother stands at the screened door. Her face begins to harden when she realizes his intentions to allow them entrance through the front door.

"Now I don't want no foolishness tonight son. Them coloreds have to go to tha back like tha rest of 'em. Next thing ya know they gonna want ta sleep up front wit tha whites."

"Mama we ain't gonna argue tonight. I done told ya everthang done changed. They money green just like ours. Ain't ya done got tired of hard times? Ya always say God send us business when we need it. We cain't tell God who ta send we just have ta be grateful for whoever he sends."

"You are a very wise young man," Jonathan compliments.

Everyone continues to stand outside except for Gray and Jonathan. They have entered to confront Gray's mother.

"Once again my name is Jonathan, he greets her."

"My name is Mabel and like I said before, coloreds ain't coming through my front door. Things ain't changed around here no matter what my son says."

"Mama when papa finds out you turned away business he gonna move you back to yo mama's. He says long as everybody get along they can stay here. He's gonna be plenty sore when he finds out ya turned business away."

"An who is going to tell him," asks Mabel with her hands on her hips.

"I guess it will be me. These people gonna help me get tha station up an runnin. Then ya ain't gonna have to worry with all them strangers comin in and out of here. Now if ya gonna keep up tha fussin then Ima lock ya in yo room until ya get back to yo senses."

Mabel turns toward the dark long hall and disappears. There is a distant sound that is suggestive of a door closing.

"We take cash up front for payment. You check out with Yvonne she works tha kitchen and cleans up around here. Well she do everything around here ta keep tha motel open. She Levi's mama and they live in tha back. She hopin to save some money to get her own place. I don't blame her; mama can be a handful when papa gone."

"May I ask where is your father?"

"He tendin to the motel in tha city. It brings in a little money to keep the house runnin when we short." Let me take ya upstairs to yo rooms. It's gettin late y'all got a drive ahead of ya."

Mr. Gray leads them upstairs to the second floor. The staircase lands the group onto the center of the house with three rooms lined on each side of the stairwell. The carpet covers the floors in dark blue, green and burgundy colors which reveals years of traffic. Once inside the quaint rooms the wooden floors have been spared and polished with care. The curtains and bedding match with floral tapestry of gold rich colors. There is a large bed with a high wooden headboard that takes up most of the room in the first room. It sits high enough so that luggage can be stored underneath. An oak wooden table with a porcelain bowl stands next to the bed and an oval mirror with gold trim hangs above it. In the corner is a coat rack with many wooden hangers resting on each handle. In the far corner sits an embroidered chair with burgundy and gold designs. It sits next to the only window in the room. The walls are decorated with gold wallpaper and tiny burgundy diamonds scattered strategically. It is cool and inviting with a faint scent of moth balls.

"I guess this will be the girl's room, Jonathan decides."

"I was hopin you fellas would take this room an tha ladies can take tha one next door. We only have two rooms for rentin. The last room is tha ladies room and across tha hall is tha mens. That room belongs to Mistah Luther an tha one next ta it is mine. Mistah Luther cain't see an most times he neva leave his room. Levi an me takes care of him cause he a man an we know what a man needs. He harmless, Gray says nervously. Jus ta let ya know his face ain't like tha rest of ours on account he been in tha army.

Never Underestimate The Power of A Secret Place

We don't talk about it much cause he don't wanna rememba tha past. Let me take ya ta where tha ladies gonna sleep."

Gray leads them a few feet north of the first room and the door is wide open. It reveals a smaller room with the same setup except there is a larger window in the room. The bed is also smaller and the colors are a softer pink and gold like the room was once meant for a girl. Jonathan steps inside and places their luggage on the bed.

"The room is very welcoming. Did it once belong to a girl," asks Cindy Lou.

"Mother was hopin to have a girl but she neva did. She stuck with me fo now. I hope ta get married an give her a granddaughter one day. I guess I let ya get unpacked for tha night. The ladies room is next door. If ya need anything I'm across tha hall," informs Gray while he gazes at Cindy Lou."

Jonathan picks up the luggage and drops it on the floor releasing a loud thump.

"Daddy what did you do that for?"

"I just wanted to clear the air. Now we will leave my baby girls to themselves to get ready for the night. Where did I put my gun?"

"Daddy show them some hospitality. They have opened their home to us and we will return their kindness with kindness."

Cindy Lou shakes her head while she closes the door. Angie Lou begins to unpack while Cindy Lou listens at the door.

"Well goodnight Gray we can meet in the morning to draw up a business proposal."

Both men shake hands while they head to their rooms. So often Jonathan glances in the direction of Gray's room until he enters the room he shares with Nathan and Shawn.

"I think he's got his eye on my Cindy. He's got another thing coming if he thinks he is going to leave my baby girl with another child to raise on her own."

"Brother take it easy; Cindy is a beautiful woman. Besides it takes a real man to step up to a woman with three children. I doubt if he is up for the challenge of raising three bi-racial children in this day and time."

"You know Mistah Jon at first I started to run tha other way when Angie told me tha baby was mine. After I seen her old man I thought he was the daddy but she promised he was mine. I loved her so much I decided to stick with her anyway. My mama said it takes a real man to take care of his own. She said that even after she seen the baby. I said mama you sho cause I ain't neva seen no white baby come from no two black people. She say we all from one race."

"Your mother seems to be a very intelligent lady."

"They say I got it from my mama."

"Who said you got what from your mother?"

"Everybody say I got my intelligence from my mama."

"Oh you have been sadly misguided."

"Brother why would you say that to him? I have heard you say on many occasions," 'no one knows the measure of a man but God,' "and you for certain you are not God."

"I stand corrected. But understand that an intelligent young man like you should not discuss his plans for a father's daughter in his presence. Now if you think *my* daughter is going to have a house full of children you have obviously lost your mind."

"Mistah Jon, tha bible say multiply the earth and that is what I plan to do with the French name."

"You mean the Johnson name."

"No sir, I mean the French name."

"I am certain you have lost your mind. You will fit in fine with the women of the house where you will be outnumbered. Johnson name," Jonathan mumbles.

"French," Shawn whispers.

"Gentlemen we have a long drive tomorrow. Please get your rest," Nathan encourages.

The men settle in for the night. Jonathan has made himself a pallet on the floor while Nathan and Shawn resign to the bed. Jonathan stares straight at the base of the door in wait for any shadow to appear across his threshold. Shawn too has caught on to Jonathan's suspicions. He takes his pillow and joins Jonathan on the floor. Jonathan stares at Shawn in an attempt to persuade him to return to the original sleeping arrangements.

"I thought I keep you company in case my old lady need me."

"Need you for what?"

"Mistah Jon, I'm a man and I know what a man be thinkin when he lay eyes on a fine specimen like Angie. Dude you know what I mean. A man got to protect what is his."

"Right now you don't have anything."

"Sho I do man. Angie my woman and she got my baby. I got a lot."

"She may have your baby but she is my daughter who has my grandbaby. Until you marry her you have NOTHING!"

"Brother! What are you doing down there? Get yourself in this bed Shawn; we have a journey ahead of us."

"I'm just trying to have a man to man talk with my future old man. You know trying ta get to know him betta and get on his good side."

"Can the two of you manage to lower your voices? I am sure these walls are paper thin. We all need our rest!"

"Don't mind him, he is a mama's boy. Let us work on a compromise. You watch the halls for the first four hours then you can watch the halls for the next four hours."

"Mistah Jon that don't sound right it seems like I'm doin all tha work."

"I am helping you."

"I don't see how you helpin me when I'm doin all tha work. Man, it just don't add up."

"You want to get on my good side don't you?"

Shawn thinks to himself for a moment.

"Well don't you?"

"I still don't see how it's gonna help me get on yo good side."

"Well, it's like this. When we return to the farm there is a young lad who took a liking to Angie when they were young. He has turned out to be a rather strapping young fellow if I should say so myself. Of course it would not surprise me if he asked for Angie's hand in marriage then I would be forced to decide who would I give the honors to wed my Angie."

"Yo dude, I am willing to do what it takes even if I have to put my life on the line."

"That won't be necessary; just a few hours of rest is all that is required. Be sure to wake me if anything should surface even a mouse."

"I can do this."

"Of course you can. I have the right man for the job."

Jonathan pulls his blanket around his shoulders to prepare him for a restful night sleep. The spring wind whistles through the crevices of the house and he can hear a light chatter from below.

"Mistah Jon, tell me what happened to Babymouse. Did you eva find the little girl."

"Of course we did, she was never lost."

"Where was she?"

Jonathan turns onto his back and begins to recount his story.

"Clarence I am sorry but Babymouse has been in hiding since your departure. I cannot seem to get her to come out from her hiding place."

"Nathan don't worry yo self; she been hidin eva since she was a babe. She learnt ta hide from tha sheriff when he comes fo his rent. Only time she come out is when he gone or he gonna shoot somebody. She probably done fell asleep somewhere. She come out when she ready."

"Well please let us know when she resurfaces; it is going to drive brother mad that I have lost her."

"Jus tells ol' Johnny she on tha can an he'll understand."

"Will do, please have her call Nathan's Place in a few days so that it will ease our worries. Especially brother's with the loss of his daughter it could lead to more troubles for our family. I hope to see you soon once you have taken residence in your new home."

"Goodbye suh, we hopes ya makes it back to yo family in one piece."

"It is our hopes as well Clarence, goodbye."

It is morning and the brothers are on their way to return to Nathan's Place. It has been arranged that Clarence and his family will start a new life in Freeman's town.

"I was hoping to say goodbye to Babymouse," Jonathan whines.

"I have a feeling that you will see her again on one of your concocted trips to search for Angie."

"It will become more difficult to convince the others that I must continue my search for Angie now that Babymouse has found her family."

"You will find a way I am sure of it."

"Brother we must not forget that mother has a habit that we must attend to."

"You are correct. Mothers' should be well balanced human beings. They are the backbone of the family. We will have to rid mother of her nasty habit. I am glad that we can agree upon this; although it is your mother who has lost her wits. My mother would never do such a thing," implies Nathan.

"Perhaps not but I overheard her intentions to court one of the workers."

"Is that so?"

Never Underestimate The Power of A Secret Place

"You must keep watch of her activities. For heaven's sake how could we ever explain another pregnancy in the house?"

"Brother you cannot be serious. Did father have the talk with you?"

"Indeed he did and he confirmed that it is the woman that becomes impregnated. We must be mindful of their activities. With that being said, it may serve as a deterrent to allow mother her daily morning spirits; except now we must entice the others to partake of a glass of as well."

"It is not that simple."

"Of course it is we shall implement my mother's deceitful practices. I will continue my morning rants which will cause them to leave the kitchen. We will then add a concoction of vodka or bourbon which ever you prefer to their orange juice before they return. Soon we will have them under our control."

"Brother that does not appear to be a healthy plan; may I make a suggestion?"

"If you must I am open to suggestions."

"We will secure the wine cabinet."

"I expected that response from you. You have always coddled the women."

"I do not coddle the women."

"Of course you do. That is the very reason why they behave like they do. The farm would have become a disaster had I not committed myself to its success."

"Is that so brother?"

"You cannot deny the truth."

"So it is the truth that you seek?"

"Always it is the truth that sets us free."

"The truth sets us free from what?"

"It sets us free from ignorance and a life of wretchedness."

"Somewhat like yours would you agree?"

"Of course not, I live a life of truth and integrity."

"I would like to examine your *integrity* beyond words if it pleases you?"

"Please do I have nothing to hide."

"Nothing at all you say?"

"Examine me at your discretion."

"It will be my pleasure. Now, when you took it upon yourself to destroy the hound's only place of residence at liberty I did not consider you an arsonist but merely my scatterbrained brother up to his daily antics. But what I did find rather troubling was the expression on your face when Clay announced that the very jailhouse where we retrieved Lana from was the very jailhouse that was burned to the ground. I could have considered it a mere coincidence or that possibly it was my very own brother who had lost his wits and burned the jailhouse to the ground. Before you offer an explanation please consider that your confession could implicate you regardless of the weight of the punishment."

Jonathan continues to concentrate on the road before he answers.

"Would you care to elaborate on my suspicions? Or could I have possibly shined light on your wretched lifestyle."

"Arson is such a strong accusation my brother."

"How does kidnapping sit with you? They are both crimes punishable by law would you agree?"

"You must be mad I would never attempt such a crime."

"Or would you? Can you explain to me what is underneath that mound of blankets behind your seat?"

"It is just a pile of blankets, now can we continue our conversation?"

Nathan reaches behind him and removes the blankets to reveal Babymouse covered in perspiration. Her eyes are wider than saucers when Jonathan turns to look behind him.

"How did you get there?"

"You says ya need me ta help ya find yo daughter. You done lost yo mind agin Mistah Jonathan."

"I have not lost my mind."

"Uh huh, replies Lana."

"I have the mind to turn this truck around and take you back to your family."

"I think that would be a sensible conclusion brother," answers Nathan.

"How ya suspect you gonna find yo daughter? I'se tha only one who can help ya."

"Nonsense, Cindy would love to join me in search for her sister."

"Well there we have it. You can pull over any time and we shall be on our way to return the girl to her family."

Jonathan continues to drive along and pretends that he has not heard a word that Nathan has uttered.

"Anytime brother, the farther you continue to drive the later it will be when we return to our families."

Jonathan continues to drive in silence.

"I think he done lost his mind agin Mistah Nathan," says Babymouse.

"I thought you were on my side."

"I'se is on yo side but ya got ta tell tha truth. Ya burned down tha jailhouse and ya knows ya did. I sat there an watched ya. Almost killed Mistah William whiles ya at it."

"For the record it is; I am on your side not I'se is on yo side," Jonathan winces. And for the last time whose side are you on!"

Jonathan almost loses control of the wheel and decides to pull onto a grassy patch to continue the conversation.

"I am afraid to ask but I must know who my brother has become because I no longer recognize you anymore. Where is the poor fellow she refers to as William?"

"Him in jail," answers Lana.

"If you are going to speak on my behalf I suggest that you educate yourself on the proper use of grammar."

"That's why I goes ta school; so I can get educated. I gonna be a doctor when I git big."

"Only if God is willing, answers Jonathan."

"My God is willin an able Mistah Jonathan."

"Are you going to continue with this nonsense or is someone going to tell me what happened to William and I want the truth!"

"I guess I'se tell ya tha truth. Mistah Jonathan say he needs ta find his baby girl an he knows where she is. He been drinkin so he cain't see ta drive so he tells me he gonna teach me how ta drive. He been teachin me ta drive fo some time an den one day he say, 'tonight is tha night.' I thinkin he done lost his mind cause he been drinkin but he say it's time I put on my big girl panties an we gonna leave Nathan place afta everybody sleepin. He parks tha truck unda tha tree tha mornin befo' next ta tha trail so we can sneak out an nobody hear us. He puts me behind tha wheel an move tha stick by tha wheel an tha truck start goin an we ain't even turned it on. Mistah Jonathan he runnin next ta tha truck an tells me ta keep straight then Mistah Jonathan he falls down but tha truck keep movin an I'se still in it. I keep thinkin I'se gonna wind up in 'em trees but I hold on ta tha wheel wit all I got. Tha truck comin to tha main road so I'se slide outa tha seat an stand wit both feet on tha pedal an tha truck stops. I'se don't know what ta do next so I jus wait hopin Mistah Jonathan gonna come along. When he come he sweatin an breathin like he runnin from tha sheriff agin. He move tha stick an tha truck don't move no mo. Mistah Jonathan he tells me ta move ova an he drives tha truck ta Johnson's Road. He put a cushion on tha seat an he tells me ta sit on it an take tha wheel an he work tha pedal. He say I drives good fo a girl but I think I drive betta den him. He turn on tha radio an we keep drivin until we git ta Mistah Jason house. We stop cause I has ta ur-i-nate. Miss Ramona say she gonna have tha baby soon.

Never Underestimate The Power of A Secret Place

We back on tha road an we pass my house but we don't stop ta use tha can. An soon we at tha jailhouse where they used ta keep me til my papa pay. By den Mistah Jonathan kinda in his right mind but not all tha way. He goes inside tha jailhouse but I don't go wit him. When he comes out he looks like he done lost his mind agin. He goes ta tha back of tha truck an git tha can then he commenced ta walkin around tha jailhouse like he blessin it but I don't think dat's how ya do it. He goes in one mo time an comes out befo he strike a match den next thing I see tha jailhouse on fire. Mistah Jonathan gits in tha truck an he drives across tha street an we sit unda a tree while he watch the fire git bigga an bigga. A man come walkin out like he blind an Mistah Jonathan say he gonna save him. He helps him ta git in tha back of tha truck an we drives away. He say he gonna take him ta tha Freeman's town ta git him some help. When we gits ta tha Freeman's town he drives to dis place an Mistah Kennedy come out. They gits ta talkin an then go fetch tha man from tha back. They puts him in a bed like the one at tha jailhouse I was at an they tells me ta take a look at him. Mistah Jonathan say can ya rec-o-gnize him an I say yes suh. He ask his name an I say dat is Mistah William from tha jailhouse. Mistah Jonathan say is he a good man or a bad man an I'se say he a bad man cause I remembas what he done ta me. Mistah Jonathan say he neva gonna touch ya agin, he promise. We git back in tha truck an we headin back ta Nathan place an I ask him ain't we gonna find yo daughter? He say, we closer than ya think."

"Do you have anything to say about what the child just reported," asks Nathan.

"Of course I do. When have you begun to call me Mistah Jonathan?"

"Brother this is not the time. Do you confirm the child's account of the events?"

"If you want ta find yo daughter ya got ta tell tha truth."

"Finding my daughter does not rest on whether I tell the truth or not. You continue to fib to all the adults in the house yet I am th one who searched persistently to find your family. Now my dearest brother it serves as deceit however innocent it may be if you take into account that Betty is not aware that you were once engaged to Christine."

"What has that got to do with anything?"

"Deception can unravel even the most devoted relationship. I can only imagine how Betty would feel if she found out that she played second fiddle to Christine."

"That cannot be the furthest from the truth."

"Ahhh! Now we find ourselves with the shoe on the other foot. What shall we do now? Shall we consider a compromise," asks Jonathan.

"If you insist," replies Nathan.

"Little one what shall it be? Would you like for me to visit your trespasses?"

"I'se been good."

"Suit yourself, if my memory serves me well upon awaking one night I happened to notice that one of our delivery trucks had been moved from where it was previously parked. Now it is customary for the drivers to park the truck near the trail in preparation for their early morning delivery. So I did not think twice about it. Since I could not return to a restful sleep I decided to get me a warm cup of milk. It can be soothing to my soul when I am restless sometimes."

"Ya meanin to say a cup of whiskey."

"Babymouse I do believe I have the floor. Furthermore, I no longer drink I have been delivered according to *you*. As I was saying, during my duties of securing the house I found none other than Babymouse not in her rightful place. It appears that at three in the morning is the most suitable time for her to bathe. When I entered the bathroom this horrendous foul smell nearly blinded me.

Never Underestimate The Power of A Secret Place

When I turned on the lights there was Babymouse bathing in the dark. She vehemently denied that she encountered a skunk. I am surprised that anyone wasn't awakened by the odor. It makes me sick to think of it. Nonetheless, I returned to bed for the night. When I awoke I found that truck was still sitting in the same location, so I decided to investigate further. Upon entering the truck I found the same peculiar but horrendous odor in the truck and I thought to myself. What is the meaning of this? After much consideration I finally concluded that someone had the intentions to take the truck but to where? The truck was completely empty so what were the intentions of the driver? More so who was the intended driver? So being of sound mind I finally concluded that Babymouse could drive. There was no reason to train you madam! You knew all along how to drive. If it weren't for the skunk who out smarted you who knows where you would be. I rest my case."

Jonathan looks at Nathan then Nathan looks at Lana who cowers behind the seat.

"There is no sense in hiding. We may want to consider hiring her as a delivery driver," admonishes Nathan

"She has decided that she wants to go to college and become a doctor. It would be in her best interest to return to Nathan's Place to get the proper training before sending her off to college. Of course we will have to discuss it with her parents but I think it will benefit Babymouse to return with us."

"When did the two of you have the time to plan this out?"

"She informed me that Clay was her father while we planned our first trip. I was much surprised myself until she informed me that she was afraid to return because of the 'bad' men. The jail house was still in full operation and I took it upon myself to shut down its very existence. It served no purpose but to continue to mindset of bondage for our African brethren. Babymouse became more vocal revealing intimate details about herself and her family and that is how I came to know her as Babymouse. She began to talk about college and becoming a doctor which troubled me because it appeared to me that she wanted to stay and it would derail my plans to search for Angie. So we decided that she would return with me although her family would be moved to Freeman's town. I discussed it with Clay and Bessie Mae and they were excited that Babymouse will be the first in their family to attend college. Brother I can only ask you to honor our secret for Angie's sake."

"Brother you know I will do anything for my niece. I must say you had me fooled there for a moment."

"We plan well don't we Babymouse?"

"Um huh," Babymouse responds.

The story ends...

Morning has come and Nathan rises from his bed to find the other men no longer in their place. He retreats to the hall to the smell of bacon and eggs lingering in the air. The room that the girls once slept is abandoned with no signs of them or their baggage. Nathan begins his journey down the stairs to the first floor. He encounters a larger entrance that leads to a living area to his left and a dining area to his right. He takes the entrance to the living area and it leads to a very large kitchen with white counters and beige tile flooring. Sitting at an octagon style green porcelain top table with metal edges is everyone from last night. There is a thin build dark African woman at the stove. She turns to acknowledge Nathan with sweat pouring over her face. Nathan nods in her direction then takes a seat at the crowded table. Gray sits at the table across from Cindy Lou eyeing her without taking notice to Jonathan who glares in his direction. Shawn and Angie Lou sits next to each other sharing a plate of breakfast while Levi looks on.

"Whatya havin suh," asks Yvonne.

"A slice of toast and coffee will be fine with me."

"Nathan we have a long road ahead of us. Satisfy your appetite for the journey."

"I'll have two eggs over easy and a slice of ham if it is not too much trouble."

"Neva too much trouble, dis what I do to keep a roof ova our heads. Ain't that right Levi?"

"Yes ma'am," answers Levi.

Mabel enters the kitchen.

"When you gonna get to the Maxwell's? They been waitin fo breakfast much too long. You cain't keep our payin customers waitin. Finish up here and see that they has everything they need."

"Yes ma'am."

"Levi make sho they got fresh towels and gather up the laundry fo your mama. Make sho you be polite to our payin customers. They may leave you a tip."

"Good morning Mrs. Mabel is there anything I can do to assist you?"

"You can put those young ones to good use."

"What do you mean by that?"

"Well they just sittin there doin nothin. They can at least earn their meals."

"Excuse me but they are my children; it is my obligation to feed and care for them."

"Around here the coloreds have ta work for they keeps."

"Fortunately I am not from around here. Where I come from everyone work including myself."

"Well I am the boss and I give the orders and they do what I tells them to do."

"How many workers do you have here?"

"Jus Yvonne and Levi this house been in my family a long time. We rents out the rooms to make ends meet. I runs this place while Gray runs the station down the road and my husband he keeps up the repairs at the Benford motel in the city. The coloreds come here when there ain't no room at the Benford. They complain about everythang. Sometimes I sends them out here with all that fancy talk. Teach 'em a lesson."

"What lesson is that," asks Jonathan.

"Be grateful fo what ya get or go back to where you came from."

"Who owns the station down the road?"

"Gray owns it. Ya thinkin about buyin it? We will sell it to ya for a little bit of nothin."

"I was hoping to make a business deal with Gray and Levi."

"Levi don't own nothin around here!"

"Well I will only offer the proposal to the both of them. It is a package deal."

"We don't want your proposal. How soon you gettin outa here?"

"We've already packed so it wouldn't be much longer. Are you expecting more customers?"

"I know a ruse when I see one. Gray get on to the station and don't take up with the likes of people like him. He don't mean you no good."

"But mama let me see what he offerin; we might can get tha station off our hands. We can pay off this house an that will be more money in our pockets. I can go an help papa at the motel so he won't have ta work so much."

"Now I'm runnin the show here an ya betta do as I say befo' I call yo papa."

"Yes ma'am," Gray replies.

Mrs. Mabel adjourns to check on the visitor's status. Once she is out of ears reach they resume the discussion about the station.

"Didn't you tell me that the station belonged to you?"

"Yes suh but you cain't tell her nothin she thinks she runs the whole show."

"Miss Yvonne can you come here for a moment?"

Never Underestimate The Power of A Secret Place

"Yes suh, let me get this breakfast to our guests an I be right with ya."

Jonathan dismisses the group from the table with the exception of Nathan.

"I think it would be wise to assume that Yvonne is being treated unfairly. She maintains the whole house and she is being compensated with just a small room for her child and herself. I've watched her cook breakfast for everyone in this house and attend to the upkeep of the rooms. When does her day ever end?"

"Brother we cannot interfere with how they operate their business even though we don't agree with it."

"I am going to offer Yvonne a position in the kitchen. Our mothers will be leaving the farm and we need to find someone who can handle a house of our size. I am sure she will be appreciated there; besides Levi could use some guidance himself. I will make her an offer when she returns."

"How do you think Mrs. Mabel will manage without her?"

"I really am not interested at this point. Next time she will be more compassionate towards her employees."

Yvonne enters the kitchen and returns to the stove where she begins to crack an egg into the skillet. Jonathan waits patiently while she prepares another plate filled with ham, eggs and toast. She then places the plate in front of Nathan who looks at it with conviction.

"Ms. Yvonne please sit down."

Jonathan pulls out a seat for her. She hesitates then takes a seat before standing to her feet when she hears the sound of footsteps.

"Ms. Yvonne you are free to take a seat anytime you wish. Let me ask you something; how long have you worked here?"

"Eva since Levi was a babe. My mama said two women can't live in tha same house."

Never Underestimate The Power of A Secret Place

"I have an offer for you. I have a home just like this one in Louisiana in which Nathan's and my mother use to care for. They are elderly now and will be leaving to live with their children. I would love for you to come and work in our kitchen. You will earn your own wages, you can buy a home for Levi and you, and we have close knit family that you will grow to love. Think about it and let me know if you are interested. Here is my card."

Ms Yvonne sits there for a moment and thinks to herself. A smile begins to dance in her eyes. She stands to her feet for a moment then leaves the kitchen.

"What do you think just happened?"

"I do not have the slightest clue. My hopes are that she has been praying for a better life," answers Jonathan.

Ms Yvonne and Levi enter the kitchen with a bundle under each of their arms. Nathan and Jonathan turn to each other in utter disbelief.

"We ready when you ready Mistah Jon," says Ms Yvonne.

"Are you sure you want to leave the only home you know of?"

"We been plannin to run for a long time. Jus didn't know when that day gonna be."

Jonathan, Shawn and Angie Lou lead the convoy onto the highway leading to Louisiana. Nathan, Cindy Lou along with their new family members Ms. Yvonne and Levi follow close. Gray watches as they pull away. It appears that he is cognizant that he has lost his dearest friend. They continue on until they reach familiar territory. When they pull into Freeman's town Bugga approaches the car elated to see someone his age. Everyone piles out of their vehicles and stretch before entering the store. Clay and Bessie Mae stand alongside the counter listening to the radio.

"Well looka here if it ain't ole Johnny. What brings you to my neck of the woods?"

"We need to stretch and fill up before we get back on the road. Where is Babymouse?"

Never Underestimate The Power of A Secret Place

"We expectin ta see her here soon. She mighty proud ta be finishin school in tha fall an hopin ta go ta medical school. I met one of her professa's an he say she has what it takes ta be a docta."

"I believe it; Babymouse has the tenacity to become whatever she wants to be. We've been working on medical school applications and we have narrowed it down to three. Of course it is her choice but I would like her to stay near the family. She is so petite I am afraid someone will take advantage of her. Be sure to let her know that we are planning another celebration. I want her to meet my baby girl. In case you did not hear we found my daughter."

"I sho like ta meet her where she at?"

"She should be coming in soon. She may have stopped for a bathroom break. Bessie Mae what is the special today?"

"We got a full menu wit it being seafood season. I got some shrimp etouffee if ya want ta taste a bowl. What will it be Johnny?"

Angie Lou and the others enter the small diner and take their seats along the counter. The counter extends the length of the diner with only an entrance and exit located in the middle of the counter. Along the cabinets behind the counter are shelves lined with a variety of candies and basic condiments. Further to the end of the counter nestled in the corner sits the telephone and a cash register with note pads and pencils. A stool is stationed there for the person taking phone orders and making cash transactions. All along the four wooden walls are pictures of the Johnson's family with many of the workers. Several round tables located in the center of the diner while a wooden surface incases the surrounding walls with stools nestled underneath. The round tables are covered with red and white checkered cloths. Each table with its own condiment collection nestled in the middle of each table. The diner is dim with the exception of the sunlight casting its glare through the small windows perched close to the ceiling. A few of the townspeople are chattering among those at their table. The group is mostly white customers who have recently moved to the town. Jonathan nods in their direction before taking his seat next to Angie Lou.

"Bessie Mae I want to introduce you to Yvonne she is the newest member of our family. She also has a son about Bugga's age."

Bessie Mae leans across the counter and greets Yvonne. She then takes a couple of steps to her left and greets Levi.

"You gonna like it at Nathan's Place. He got plenty of work and help ya find yo own place. Ya welcome ta come and visit sometimes."

"I be happy ta come an visit. I like it here already. You don't mind if I make myself useful?"

"I could use the company. Come wit me an we can get these hungry mouths fed."

Yvonne and Bessie Mae disappear behind the wall of shelves with goodies in glass containers. Their laughter and the clinking of plates and flatware can be heard throughout the diner. Soon both of the women reappear with bowls filled with steaming hot food ready to dish out to those seated at the counter. Bessie Mae takes one bowl to the customers at the table then returns to fill the cups of the customers at the counter. They continue to chatter among themselves until they are reminded of their scheduled upcoming celebration.

"Well we got to get going so that we can prepare for the reunion. When do you all plan to attend," asks Nathan.

"We will be headed out in tha morning. They say its gonna be the biggest celebration we have ever had."

"I think you are correct our family has grown by leaps and bounds. I agree with brother this will be a massive undertaking. We look forward to your arrival; invite whoever wants to come, the more the merrier."

Never Underestimate The Power of A Secret Place

"We got us some new neighbors in town. Ya don't mind if I bring them along do ya Johnny?"

"Of course not we welcome everyone to the celebration. Well we shall see you soon."

"See ya soon Johnny."

Once again everyone load into their vehicles to continue their journey to Nathan's Place. The mid-day heat makes for an uncomfortable ride. Jonathan directs Shawn while he drives them to the farm. Nathan and Levi start up a conversation about the whereabouts of his father. Yvonne remains silent offering a sigh ever so often.

"Yvonne is there something you would like to say?"

"No suh, I jus hope our life will be betta than what it was before."

"You will love it at Nathan's Place. We all work as a family with everyone working together for a wonderful purpose. You will be cooking for a larger family but I guarantee you there will be others to help with the cooking. You will get to meet Jonathan's wife and my wife as well. You have already met Angie and Cindy so you will be working along with them to meet the family's needs. There are plenty of homes on the property that you can choose from at your liking. Levi can attend school and work on the farm to earn his own money. I believe you will like it at Nathan's Place."

Nathan turns to look into the back seat to find Yvonne quietly asleep. He continues his drive to the farm. When they enter the entrance to the farm the gates are already open. A few of the workers walk along the trail waving as they pass by. Jonathan has made it onto the property and everyone has surrounded them, dancing, humming, and crying. Spirits run high at the sight of Angie. Lizzy embraces her it seems like an eternity then a hush calms the gatherers.

Never Underestimate The Power of A Secret Place

"It seemed like never would ever come but it is here now. My babygirl is now back with her family and we have now multiplied in numbers. Never again will the enemy overtake us. We shall continue to fight to the end until victory comes. It is by the awesome power of our Almighty God that we are conquerors in Christ Jesus! Amen."

"Amen," the crowd confirms.

Everyone begin to disperse to their prospective dwellings. Sleeping arrangements are made for Yvonne, Levi and Shawn. Jonathan takes Shawn to the quarter where Henry once slept. Once they have entered the quarter he takes a seat in the chair stationed next to the window where they sometimes survey the property. There is a bed stationed furthest from the chair with bedding folded neatly at the foot of the bed. A door in the middle of the room stands open revealing a basin to wash up and at toilet next to it. A light bulb protrudes from the ceiling and a thin metal chain extends from the ceiling long enough for a young child to reach. The flooring was renovated with oak wood to match the walls and ceiling; the quarter smells of fresh pine wood. There is a small table in the corner behind the door which is used to eat meals and any note taking that may be needed. There are no pictures on the walls only a branded title above the door: NATHAN'S PLACE.

"Now let us get some understanding. You are somewhat a part of the family but not *really*. You have to earn your place in the family and you will start by not having any contact with my daughter that will perhaps result in another unexplained pregnancy. Now you have been caught with your hand in the cookie jar and because of it you will earn your way into my daughter's good graces as well as mine. I expect you to ask for my daughter's hand in marriage once you have purchased a sizeable ring that meets my wife's approval. Let me inform you that she is very hard to please. I suggest you bath before entering her presence or you will find yourself banned from the family. Sometimes it is not as detrimental as you think. It really could be the most exhilarating time that you can spend with yourself if you plan wisely. You can begin earning your keep by making deliveries to our stores. The distance will help you to appreciate the women because quite naturally there is only so much a man can take. Do you have any questions?

Jonathan turns to look at Shawn who is laid on the bed and finds him fast asleep. He gently slips Shawn's shoes from his feet and winces at the smell released into the air. Jonathan eases out of the door and closes it with care. Once he enters the big house it is calm and dim with not person in sight. He begins his way upstairs to his bedroom then pauses at the door. He sniffs his underarms before entering. Jonathan inches in before seeing Melba with baby Marlon in her arms while she sings a lullaby to him. He waits for the directive to take care of his hygiene but he is not afforded the criticism. Now changed into his night clothes he begins his way to his side of the bed.

"He looks just like you Jon. I am so proud of your faithfulness during Angie's abduction. We may have never found her if you wouldn't have pursued her like you did."

Jonathan eases on the bed cautious to observe Melba for any reaction to his hygiene.

"It is amazing, but for now I must get my rest."

Jonathan leans in and kisses baby Marlon on his head before turning on his side away from Melba. He waits for a response but there is none. Soon he drifts off to sleep. Jonathan is awakened by the sound of a train; when he eases from the bed he witnesses Melba in deep sleep and baby Marlon wide awake cooing to himself. He pulls baby Marlon from the bedding then heads out of the room. When he enters the hall he finds little Nathan standing there with a blank stare on his face.

"What are you doing up so early? Come with me we can get first pick of the breakfast treats."

Never Underestimate The Power of A Secret Place

Slowly they all descend downstairs and the sound of strong winds increase as he walks to the front door. Once outside he witnesses the changes that have occurred in the area. On the surrounding properties many of the houses have been bulldozed including Charle's childhood home. Plans are being made to build a hotel, school and market courtesy of the harvest reaped from the good deeds that have been sown by the dwellers at Nathan's Place. Every plot of land or field has been stripped of its past existence and new promises are being made for those who dwell there now. Jonathan observes his own property and it is then that he remembers his dream. He witnesses an abundance of increase, his cattle has increased, his vegetation has increased, the dwellings has increased, and most of all his family has increased. While he stands on the terrace Nathan approaches him.

"Brother you may want to join us in the study."

Once they enter there is standing room only. Arthur has taken his place at the head of the table with stacks of papers before him. Among them is Miss Mercy who appears to be distraught by information that Arthur is presenting to the group.

"Jonathan, I have before me the slave rolls for the surrounding plantations. What it reveals is something that could be viewed as very disturbing or much esteemed. The previous owner of this property was Mr. Jonathan Johnson who fathered two sons: Jonathan Johnson II and Joseph Johnson. I tracked the activity of Jonathan Johnson II to find that he attended medical school in New York City and became a prominent physician. He never married but did adopt a son by the name of Troy Pennyton. Mr. Jonathan Johnson II then adopted me Arthur Waters as his son. Mr. Jonathan Johnson II went on to father two more sons named: Jonathan Johnson III and Nathan Johnson. I also need to mention Jonathan that your ethnicity at birth read Negro which is why you were able to marry Melba."

"What are you saying? That our lives have been nothing but a lie? When will this madness end?

"Mistah Jon, my name is Mercy an I'se ova a hundred years old. What he sayin to be true. Oldes masta Johnson just like his papa chasin tha women slaves but he had a good heart. He a little of ole masta Johnson an a little of young masta Johnson. I use ta be on the ole masta Johnson plantation an I has my only gal here wit me. Ha name Robin an she my only chile. Oldes masta Johnson he bed ha an she has a baby girl but she dark an nobody say she tha oldes masta Johnson chile. Next thang I know she has anotha baby an we suspectin she the olde masta Johnson's chile cause ha skin not dark like mine. Ole masta Johnson he gets wind of it an say he gonna send my gal away an ha chilluns. Oldes masta Johnson he been up north gettin his education an he comes for Robin an ha gals an takes them up north. I hear later on she dies but my granchilluns stay up north an git they education. Oldes masta Johnson he come ta be a docta an they say he come every now an then an takes some folk up state. I don't hear no mo about my family."

"Miss Mercy can you tell me the names of your grandchildren?"

"They names is Ruth and Naomi like in tha bible."

"And you said that their mother's name is Robin is that correct?"

"Yes suh."

"What she says is true but for some reason the slave rolls only records their birth and shows that there was a division of slaves when Jonathan Johnson II claimed his inheritance to include the following slaves: Scarlet, Leonard, Donald, Doris, Otis, Eric, and Robin all from the Johnson's plantation. Of course there are others but it will require some extensive cross referencing to know who is who."

"Brother it sounds as if we are related to the original owners of the Johnson plantation," replies Nathan.

Never Underestimate The Power of A Secret Place

"If I may interject that not only is the person mentioned by Miss Mercy as the Oldest masta Johnson is indeed who we have known as our beloved grandfather Mr. Jonathan Johnson. According to court records Mr. Jonathan Johnson procured property for family housing in which Robin Johnson and her heirs still maintain ownership to this day. The property mentioned is the mansion in which we lived during our childhood. For this reason I vacated the property according to court orders during my attempt to initiate the probate proceedings. It was then that I obtained the birth records of Ruth and Naomi to reveal their alias as Rafael Johnson and Linda Johnson," Arthur informs.

Everyone gasp as they process the information being delivered. Each looking to one another for understanding until Nathan breaks the silence.

"If what you are saying is true then it means that our mothers are in all actuality our sisters. Is that what you are implying?"

"This is nonsense; explain to me the role of my biological mother whom I have known for all my life," demands Jonathan.

"Veldka is indeed your biological mother and your actual father is none other than Mr. Jonathan Johnson II. It seems that he carried the womanizing trait that your great grandfather has been known for."

"Why did father hide the truth once more? How could he pretend to be our father for so long not to mention his deception of the bonds of holy matrimony? What lengths he went through to seal his very own fate."

"It was Mr. Johnson's request to keep the family together. It was not a secret at all among the others. Rafael and Linda should share in the shame themselves."

"You cannot be serious. Is he telling the truth? Whatever happened to standing on the truth? Something you have taught me since my childhood. How could you have known this and it never convicted your spirit to come forthright?"

Never Underestimate The Power of A Secret Place

"Son it is easy for you to say, you never had to worry about where you would live or where your next meal would come from. Linda and I survived because our father did whatever it took to make sure we survived. He fought for the rights of many slaves since he was a child. I admit he was not perfect but he made sure that everyone around him received equal treatment. He taught those around him that there is one human race and without each other we cannot survive. You have to understand that ignorance reached its peak until we as a people began to educate ourselves with God's purpose for his creation. It took a long time and much suffering for many but today we celebrate a brighter future and because of it we will say Amen," encourages Rafael.

A number of Amen's are released in the air which brings the meeting to a close. A celebration was scheduled for the following days. Baptisms, marriage proposals and reunifications of many of the workers who were made aware of their birth rights. Many of the towns people joined in and once everyone had eaten they began to worship together. The singing, dancing and humming continued well into the night. This celebration marked the day that sins of their forefathers were revisited and forgiven never to return again.

THE END

Made in the USA
Columbia, SC
25 July 2017